LUNAR BLUE

BOOK ONE OF THE LUNAR BLUE SAGA

LUNAR BLUE

BY

LAURINDA D. WILLIAMS

MOTMOT
HOUSE

Copyright © 2020 by Laurinda Williams
http://laurindawilliams.com

Edited by Linda Franklin | Inkwater.com
Cover design by 100covers.com.
Interior design by Masha Shubin | Inkwater.com

Ring of blue fire © Olga Nikonova. Shutterstock.com; Moon courtesy of NASA.

This is a work of fiction. The events described here are imaginary. The settings and characters are fictitious or used in a fictitious manner and do not represent specific places or living or dead people. Any resemblance is entirely coincidental.

Publisher: Motmot House

Hardback   ISBN-13 978-1-7353450-0-0
Paperback   ISBN-13 978-1-7353450-1-7
eBook   ISBN-13 978-1-7353450-2-4

3 5 7 9 10 8 6 4 2

CONTENTS

LIST OF CHARACTERS

Elizabeth: Tyler's love interest, a nurse
Tyler: Elizabeth's love interest
Jason: Elizabeth's coworker, a doctor
Briana: Elizabeth's best friend, a nurse
Elena: Elizabeth's mother
Chogan: Tyler's brother
Ashton: Tyler's cousin
Leanna: Tyler's younger sister, twin to Alianna
Alianna: Tyler's younger sister, twin to Leanna
Messer: Alianna's boyfriend
Blaze: Father of Callie and Emma, husband to Uki
Uki: Mother of Callie and Emma, wife to Blaze, Messer's aunt
Callie and Emma: Four-year-old daughters of Blaze and Uki
Amon: Father of Yutu, husband of Lily
Lily: Mother of Yutu, wife of Amon
Yutu: Son of Amon and Lily
Mama Rain: Tyler's grandmother, Chief's mother
Chief: Tyler's father, Catori's husband
Catori: Tyler's mother, Chief's wife
Angeni: Elizabeth's rival
Audrie: Marcus's pregnant wife
Marcus: Audrie's husband
Mr. Rogers: Jacksonville's chief of police
Cupun, Panuk, Tarkik: Three old brothers/musicians
Bennie, Beamer, and Nova: Elizabeth's pets

CHAPTER ONE

BEFORE THE JOURNEY

Maybe I could have saved her if I had been faster, I thought while peeling my eyes open and reaching for my alarm. It sounded in my ear, jolting my body with each beep. Pressing the stop button, I stretched up toward the ceiling. My aching muscles screamed until my hands returned to the comforter. As I looked around my white bedroom, the morning brought a glow of yellow.

A pile of clean clothes sat upon the red floral-embroidered desk chair. The garments consisted almost entirely of pale green work uniforms, white undershirts, and beige underwear. I strapped my bra on, my favorite one. Once dressed, I glanced at the photo on my dresser. From it, my father's blue eyes beamed into the room. A subtle chill slipped around my bones, making me shiver. Dismissing it, I looked into the mirror and started to brush my thick golden brown hair, but sighed at my brown eyes, wishing them blue – wishing they'd resemble *his* eyes so I could see him without sulking.

Down the stairs, my empty kitchen awaited. It had white counters, white cabinets, white walls – white everything. While starting breakfast, I realized today was Wednesday. My stomach turned as I collected the freshly delivered newspaper from my stoop and peered at the front page. It featured the young girl who had been killed by a black bear yesterday. Her hospital spectacle dripped blood into my thoughts, making my shoulders slump toward the ground.

After brushing my teeth and caring for my animals, I hopped into my little white car.

A quick drive to Medford brought me to the small, three-floor hospital building. Scowling at its dated brick siding and potholed parking lot, I felt my mood further sour. Once inside, I could smell the sterilizer, the stale corridor, even the blood dripping from a boy's nose.

"Good morning, Lizzy," Briana said as she entered the building after me. Her strawberry red hair rested in loose curls around her shoulders.

"Morning, Briana," I grumbled.

"What's wrong? Why the grumpy face?" she asked while clocking in.

I sighed, clocking in after her. "Just moping about the girl we lost on the table yesterday. Damn bears."

She raised an eyebrow. "The girl from the paper? You helped treat her?"

"Unfortunately. I couldn't retrieve and administer the blood bag in time," I said, scowling over the building's deficient, dated layout. Maybe if I had been faster ...

"Liz, blame the bear, not yourself. Cheer up." I watched her lips pull into a smile, a goofy smile resembling a clown ... or maybe the Joker. "Look, I bought these yesterday." She gestured to her shoes. "Do you like them?" Her smile managed to curve up further.

They were hideous pink heels with red bows. Just observing their height made my feet ache. "Oh ... yeah ... I like them."

White teeth appeared behind her creepy smile. "*Sure* you do."

Noting her taunting tone, I rolled my eyes at her. "Oh, shut it. My journey into the deep wilderness starts this Friday," I said, more to myself than to her.

Her face darkened as a crease formed between her eyebrows. I imagined steam seeping from her red face, her hair combusting into a scorching upward blaze.

"I still can't believe you're traveling to the middle of nowhere so you can be dumped into the complete wilderness by yourself. There are bears and wolves all over that place!" she huffed, crossing her arms.

"Shhh, keep it down. Jeez. I have thought this all through and we've been over this. I need to do this for myself. You know ... a little soul searching."

"It's just crazy. I don't understand *why*," she persisted.

"I don't blame you for not understanding."

With a supervisor approaching, I left Briana for my first patient. In the ER, I grabbed a chart and zipped over to Ryan Goodman, pulling back the curtain. He was fifty years old, complaining of chest pain and a cough. He had a history of type two diabetes and coronary artery disease – concerning considering his symptoms. I was glad to see him so soon after his arrival.

"Hello, Mr. Goodman. My name is Nurse Elizabeth. I see in your chart you haven't been feeling yourself lately?" He was heavyset with a balding head and hairy arms.

"You can call me Ryan. I've been feelin' weak and sweaty with a reoccurin' cough ... and some chest pain," he said in a high voice. Ryan then coughed heavily – a dry cough high in his chest.

"I'm sorry to hear that, Ryan. Let's see if we can determine exactly what's going on. Based on your symptoms, I'm worried about your heart. I'll have a doctor in soon, but in the meantime, I'll record your vitals and check your temperature." My eyes rested gently on him.

He said nothing as I checked him over. I noted high blood pressure, scribbling the words on his chart. Goodman's eyes wandered a bit, his expression becoming hazy. My pen slipped from my hand before I could complete the exam, smacking to the vinyl floor. While I was reaching for it, Ryan fell back sharply onto the gurney.

Startled, I turned to lunge for the emergency bedside button and then yelled for the doctor.

Dr. Jason Smoldred and two nurses, Madison and Kyle, rushed over and began to rapidly assess him. I struggled to find his pulse as I fought my fear. My heart dipped – I couldn't lose another patient so soon after yesterday.

"Get the defibrillator!" Jason directed. Madison cut open Ryan's shirt, exposing a chest of thick hair. While Kyle rushed the machine over, Jason connected the man to an EKG. "He's in v-fib," Jason proclaimed.

From the cabinet, I found a bag valve mask to pump air into his lungs while Kyle prepped the machine, then picked up the paddles.

"Clear!" Kyle announced. I pulled the mask back and watched Kyle came down onto Ryan's chest, which jolted with the shock. I replaced the mask and pumped more air into him. We tensed as the EKG remained the same.

"Try again!" Jason sharply commanded.

Kyle nodded. "Clear!"

I jumped back and watched Kyle shock Ryan again, but his heart continued to spasm. "One more time. He has to make it," I demanded while reapplying the mask.

Kyle looked at Jason. "Your call."

"Alright, one more time," Jason encouraged.

We cleared again and Kyle gave him another shock. I sighed, relieved when the EKG beeped a more regular rhythm.

"Liz, give him point five milliliters of atropine," Jason ordered.

Madison handed me the bottle and needle, taking over on the mask. I pulled the dosage and injected it into Ryan's vein.

"Get him outta here. Take him for testing," Jason instructed.

Madison and Kyle rushed his gurney away while I disposed of the needle and put away the EKG. When I tried to hustle after them,

Jason promptly stepped in my way, sporting an obnoxious smile. His blond hair rested within a line of sweat above his forehead.

"Can I help you, Doctor?" I said sharply.

"He made it, eh? Another chunker spared from the pearly white gates ... at least for the time being," he mocked.

My eyes glared. "I'd say it's a victory for his sake. Now if you don't mind, I'm going to follow." I moved to the right and he side-stepped in my way.

"Hold on, wait a second. They got this. Besides, he's Dr. Lindy's patient." His eyes trailed around my face before lowering to my chest. "Mind if I take you out to dinner tonight? Only the fifteenth time I've asked."

My posture turned rigid. "I'm aware. Busy, sorry."

"Always busy. That's our lives, but we must find time to eat. Surely you can make time. ... You know, your biological clock is ticking." He flashed his white teeth, standing over me.

My hands balled. "Step aside, Jason. I'd hate to file a harassment case with the board," I threatened.

He promptly stepped aside. "Not necessary. Carry on, Ms. Allard." He bowed with his hand gesturing toward the door, a smarmy smile on his face.

When my lunch break arrived, I could finally relax my aching arms. As I sat hunched over my food, Briana approached from the corridor, collected a salad from the line, and strolled toward me.

"Hey, how's the grub?" She dropped her salad onto the table. "I just dealt with a crazy mom and her bratty kid." Her eyebrows knitted as she sat down across from me.

"Hey, Bri." I took a bite of my food.

She observed me as I watched her thoughts shift behind her eyes. "Are you sure you need to go on this trip, especially now?"

My muscles tightened. Briana's eyes twitched while her lips

quivered, waiting for me to chew the ham sandwich in my mouth. After swallowing, I replied, "Yes. I *need* to do this."

"But, there's no good reason for it. Your gear could fail, you could get injured, heck - you could lose your way."

My brows narrowed. "You wouldn't understand."

I drove home in a daze. With Friday in my thoughts, my chest rose and dipped like the phases of the moon. The orange sunset glowed on the horizon. The small town of Jacksonville, a few miles west of Medford in Jackson County, Oregon, was my forever home. The views here felt like a peek into heaven itself. The distant mountains behind me were still brown and gray, but would soon be topped with a light layer of morning sun-kissed snow visible on my drive to work. The green tree leaves around me were beginning to reveal different shades - variations of red, orange, and yellow. The beauty was surreal.

As I watched the reddest leaves dance off the foliage, a black blur darted onto the road. I sharply turned the wheel, swerving while simultaneously slamming on the brakes.

"What the hell was that?" I yelled as my car screeched to a halt.

When my eyes focused on the distant creature, I could see the fur of a black animal. A bear? I saw ears that pricked into points, a tail that swayed behind, a slim but massive build - a huge wolf. My mouth dropped as I watched the elusive creature take a roadside deer in his jaws, dragging it into the woods. A sudden horn behind me made me jump, pulling my eyes from the scene.

I arrived home hoping to relax, only to see a white car in my driveway. A moan slipped my lips as my mother waved to me from the porch steps. Gritting my teeth, I pulled my car in next to hers.

"Hi, Elizabeth!"

I got out of the car. "Hi Mom, what are you doing here?" I dared to question.

As I approached, she checked me from head to toe. "You look skinny. Have you been eating enough?"

Unlocking my front door, I let us both inside. "I'm not skinny. I'm in shape."

"Eat more. And I'm here because I want to make sure you're prepared for your trip. You're sure I can't talk you out of it?"

Since my father died, Mom had grown controlling. When I moved out last year, she had an outrageous hissy fit, stomping her feet and crying as I packed my things.

"I have to do this. I need to learn how to love the wilderness again. To discover how to forgive myself and the woods. Call it soul-searching."

She scoffed in my face. "Dear, that's ridiculous. I miss your father terribly, and what happened was the worst thing we've ever been through, but I wouldn't risk my life to *soul search*. Those woods are unforgiving." The harsh tone of her voice was almost as insulting as her words.

"I know they are unforgiving. I don't need anyone to tell me that," I grumbled. "I don't want to discuss this. Are you sure you're okay with watching my animals while I'm gone?"

As I approached their cage, my rats Beamer and Bennie rushed to say hello. I watched them scurry to the door, sticking their noses through the bars. I removed the bungee cord and opened the broken door to greet them, petting their heads.

"Of course. They'll be fine while you're away," Mom said.

Nova, my dwarf rabbit, stared at me from her pen. Her striking blue eyes against her white fur filled me with warmth.

Mom picked up Bennie, his deep blue fur highlighted against her pale skin. "We will all spend some bonding time together while you're gone. I miss having pet rats back at home, but animals were always your thing," she continued. I watched her kiss Bennie's face and in return, he licked her hand.

Once Mom left - I nearly had to kick her out - my thoughts skipped around me while I paced my bedroom, my shoulders sore from the tension. Sorting through my clothes, I found a shirt under the bed. It was black with a high V-neck. When I wore it, the shape curved to my frame. The absorbent fabric texture felt like silk despite being a cotton blend. After adding it to the full dirty laundry basket, I started a load. By the time the beeper on the washing machine signaled its finish, darkness had engulfed my home, yard, and the forest that stretched around and behind the property. Nights on the edge of town were ebony.

After dinner, a warm shower helped relax my shoulders. Stepping out of the steam, I admired my hallway bathroom with its white floors, sunset-orange walls, and white fixtures, the color scheme reminding me of Oregon's views.

In my bedroom, I set my alarm to five-thirty, kicked the towels off, and lay in the queen bed, enjoying the cool cotton sheets against my bare skin. As I envisioned what I demanded from the wilderness - wind through remote trees, wild edible foliage, gray and rusted bedrock exposed past the soil - I slipped into a soothing slumber. It was incongruously peaceful.

The new morning eased my achiness as I felt the lactic acid slip from my fibers. After breakfast, it wasn't long before I made my way back to the place that fed my purpose yet drained my spirit.

As I approached the emergency center, I noticed Briana had a hitch in her step. Every ten paces she'd express the slightest twerk of her legs. After we discussed the nearby construction, she sharply changed the subject.

"Andrew and I are doing well. And guess what? ... It's sorta an issue." Her lips pricked up into that creepy smile.

I raised one eyebrow. "Um ... what is?" I rubbed my arm, further removing the acid.

"He's *huge*. I can barely walk from last night." Although her words were quiet, she started laughing hysterically. I felt the stares of everyone in the vicinity, eyes lingering on our backs from all directions.

I rolled my eyes with a grin. "That's your issue with him?" I chuckled uncomfortably. Andrew Chowdhury, a handsome man from India who had come to America as a young child, was a bit shy but had a charming personality. I pulled my thoughts from envisioning his lower region.

"I'm sore ... but ugh. He's so good in bed," she smirked.

My face flushed. "You'll get used to him," I teased. Like a child, she stuck her tongue out at me. Andrew had been our coworker since I started here. He was a very good nurse and respected peer, but we had never become friends. "Are you prepared to say goodbye to me?"

She sneered at me. "You better not die."

I rolled my eyes with a smile. "I'll miss you, too."

Jason was approaching from the distant hall, making my throat tighten. "Shit, time to go." I rushed down the hall. "See you later!" I called to her, feeling her chuckle as I turned the corner toward the small maternity ward.

On the way out of work, I said farewell to my coworkers. They wished me a safe trip, but I sensed their skepticism.

Once home, I completed a checklist of my gear. I had everything from granola bars to a full-sized sleeping bag. Stiff with anxiety, I walked back downstairs to visit my animals. The rats slept in their hammock, blissfully warm in each other's company. I crossed my arms while observing the broken cage-door, remembering how I had caught myself on it after slipping on my newly polished floors.

Fortunately, my rats had yet to escape from the gap. Seven days after I had ordered the replacement cage-door, it still hadn't arrived.

My eyes turned to Nova, who dropped her foot onto the floor, making several loud thuds. I walked over to her pen and picked her up, feeling her frame tense in my arms. Petting her soft white fur, I relaxed with her.

In my bedroom, I placed the clothing I'd be wearing for the entire trip on my desk. A pair of breathable camouflage pants sat on top of the pile. They had two upper pockets with some lower side compartments. The pants were water resistant, yet warm and comfortable. My originally chosen shirt was a slim-fitting black round-neck T-shirt, but the one I had found under my bed was laid out instead. My lightweight jacket was suitable to tie around my waist. It was black and had two pockets.

While putting away some laundry, I let my thoughts wander. Father used to make a soup of wild dandelion, crisp onion, and bitterroot when out on camping trips. The flavor was untamed, like the forest itself. Mom hated those soups and gagged on them. In honor of my mother's disgust, Dad named her most hated recipe "momster" as a joke. He would laugh at her repulsion whenever she was tempted to try his wild cooking. But my taste buds longed for the wild I remembered before the hell I had subsequently endured.

I smiled at the bittersweet memories. The light of his existence lived within them.

Ten years ago, I had begged my parents to take me camping since summer was ending and school was soon to begin. My father agreed, but Mom would not join us. On the seventh night, I remember looking at the stars and soaking in the wilderness. Dad told me stories of the forest legends as the night's wildlife lurked in the darkness. The melodious song of the elusive wolf had danced into my ears, relaxing my soul around the peace of the trees.

Tears overcame me as an agonizing memory unraveled, a film of blood forever enveloping the forest I used to relish.

CHAPTER TWO

DEPARTING

I was in the dream realm, but this wasn't a dream.

I was running - running faster than my legs thought capable. Running as my heart hammered against my ribcage. My lungs burned as the sticks snapped under my stride. The thunderous roar snarled behind our panic.

"Faster! Move faster!" he cried.

But I couldn't run faster - I could barely match his pace. My hamstrings screamed as the scorching blaze chased our movement through the tall trees, crispening everything in her path. The dried thick brush allowed her to grab at our ankles. Deer bolted past us; birds flew into the open sky while squirrels charred against the bark. The heat curled my hair, drying it out under the strain.

"Faster, Elizabeth, hurry!" he cried in desperation. Squinting at him, I saw the acute terror in his eyes. Smoke choked our burning lungs, but he would not let me stop running. He would not let me perish in the flames, but she was impossible to outrun. The blaze's thunderous roar echoed behind as she strove to claim our lives along with the animals.

Approaching a hill, Dad didn't break stride as he grabbed my arm and plunged us down the rocky dirt terrain, our backs grazed by the flame. Tumbling, we felt the sharp sticks, rocks, and brush cut our flailing bodies – slicing our limbs open. During the fall, dirt had entered my mouth while a throbbing pain enveloped my arm. Halted at the bottom, as I tried to spit, I felt blood seeping into my eyes, prompting me to wipe it from my vision. I then looked back at the hilltop where the blaze was beginning to creep down. Through the fire's roars, the sound of torment filled my ears. Turning my neck sent stabbing pains down my spine, but I had to look toward that sound – his cries of agony.

My eyes opened the same way they closed – full of tears. *That damn memory* – plaguing me, tormenting me. Its torment was why I needed this journey; I couldn't run from my memory any longer.

I glanced at my phone, its screen blinding me as I read five o'clock. My body shivered and I moaned at the chronic invasion of my dream world. The stubborn memory within my vivid nightmare had my stomach in knots and my veins flooded with adrenaline.

I used the extra time to take a long hot shower, warming my bones and soaking in the steam. Afterwards, I put on my clothing and blow-dried my hair, allowing the heat to encircle me.

My lightweight black boots glided me down the stairs to where my backpack rested on the floor by the front door. Shaking away the adrenaline, I skipped coffee and retrieved orange juice from the refrigerator. The tangy-sweet liquid calmed my veins and brought life to my pale face. Turning on the television, I rechecked the weather. The forecast promised clear skies with a midday high of seventy degrees. The following days would be cooler.

It should be dry. My chest tightened.

After watching the news, I walked over to my animals. Beamer's nose stuck out through the bars as he greeted me, but where was Bennie? My heart sank when I realized he was not in the cage. "Bennie!" I called for him as I looked under the cage and throughout the room, but he was nowhere to be found. Tears welled. Unable to locate him, I placed some food and water on the floor; all the while, Beamer's lonely eyes never left me. I hoped Mom would find Bennie while I was away. Unwilling to call her, I put a note on the kitchen counter before leaving - my heart low in my chest.

The dark-green helicopter's hum flooded my hollow ears as we buzzed over the terrain. Through the headset, the pilot's voice emerged. "Five minutes until landing. Are you doing alright back there? It will be a rough ride down so be sure to expect that," she instructed.

I nodded at her with my jaw clamped shut. Her copilot, Phil, looked back at me and stretched his smile, revealing his hidden lip scar and missing teeth.

The chopper dipped and rocked as the pilot lowered us to an open brush field, contacting the soil - a remote location fifteen miles from town. As the blades slowed, Phil gestured for me to remove my headgear and restraints, but the chopper's seatbelt stubbornly resisted my shaking fingers. A feeling of child-like helplessness came over me as the copilot helped remove my restraints. I grabbed my bag as the door opened and jumped down to the untouched soil.

"Good luck!" Phil encouraged while climbing back into his seat.

The blades picked up speed. From inside, he gestured for me to move away and I quickly stepped back. The takeoff kicked up a whirlwind of eye-slicing dirt. I closed my eyes and put my arm over my face until the natural winds regained control.

With the chopper at a distance, my lungs could capture the crisp air, recharging my damaged soul. I could see the early morning dew collecting on nearby foliage while I listened to distant insects resume their disrupted chorus. My shoulders lightened, but my stomach tensed as the memory of the fire's devastation lingered.

I felt something on my body move. What was that? It moved again. Taking my bag off my back and placing it on the ground, I unlatched the top and opened the cover. Something deep inside my bag shifted, causing the hairs on my neck to stand up. What on earth was in my bag? Looking deeper, I could see a small blue animal. Oh my God, it was Bennie! Scooping him up into my hands, I cuddled him fondly while he held the remains of a granola bar in his mouth.

"How did you get in my bag, Bennie?" He seemed unfazed by the ordeal and continued to happily munch on the food he claimed his own. I should tell my mother I had him and ask for her advice. Taking out my satellite cell phone, I called her number. She picked up immediately with a worried tone.

"Lizzy? Is everything okay?"

"Ye – yeah Mom, I just have a bit of a problem. I found Bennie in my bag shortly after the chopper left. I am not sure what to do with him."

She was quiet for a moment before laughing at my dilemma. "Well, you can bring him along with you. It would be too much of an ordeal to bring him back now, but having him out there is risky. You'll need to be careful. Why don't you bring him back and just cancel the trip? That would be best for you both."

My eyebrows lowered. I wasn't canceling. If I returned Bennie to the house, my trip that had taken ages of anticipation and planning would be in shambles. "I will bring him along. I'm sure he will be fine with me." I sighed at my words.

Saying goodbye, I hung up, eager to start my hike. I placed Bennie on my shoulder and then fished out the compass. With a deep breath, I tossed my bag onto my back and started my trek south into the tree line. With each step, I watched spiders scurry around their webs in the bushes while chipmunks scampered between rotting branches along the ground. Mule deer galloped from my steps, weaving through the trees in a dance-like motion. The foliage stood proudly all around me - massive pines and colorful maples that reached high into the blue sky above. Bennie had no trouble keeping himself balanced on my shoulder, using his nails to grip my shirt. Sticks cracked under my boots, creating tension in my core. Despite myself, memories crept in and my stomach turned. Visions of fire edged behind my back, laying its hand upon my tensing shoulder. Stop this! You are strong, I told myself. I paused, shaking my frame and wiping the sweat from my forehead.

My silver compass led me down along the bedrock until I approached the base of a small cliff. Trees aggressively stretched their thick roots and branches along the boulders, pushing themselves into any unclaimed sunlight. Looking in both directions, I saw the cliff extend for miles, effectively trapping me in a difficult position. I had to keep Bennie in my bag while I focused on myself. Opening my canister, I took a sip of water while mapping out my climb. When I stretched out an arm to grip the first ledge, I felt the cold stone rip the warmth from my fingers. My bag pulled me down as I struggled to keep hold. My hands continued up the rock until my left foot slipped, causing my heart to strike against my chest. Rocks fell to the ground, smacking to the stone many feet below. Regaining my foot's position, I steadied my breath and resolutely climbed higher.

I was relieved when I reached the top, allowing my nerves to steady. At the top of the climb, I could see smoother hiking southeast via an easier track. With every step, my pants took the abuse of sharp foliage while my boots eased through the terrain. A coyote in the nearby brush set her eyes on me. I jumped at her and she hurried away, her bushy tail waving behind her. The encounter led me to look down at my revolver, which rested on my hip, the sun sparkling against its silver shine.

By the reading on my GPS device, I knew water was available six miles further south. In one hour of brisk, relatively level hiking, I had covered four miles, putting me close to the first camping point. The snippy breeze refreshed my heated body while I paused, resting on a mossy boulder. When I opened my bag, Bennie was happy to come back out into the open air. I noticed my gluttonous rodent had claimed all my remaining granola bars. After helping myself to the canister water, I provided Bennie with the cap cover filled for his use. He quickly licked up as much as he could fit in his full belly. I sighed, regretting not giving him water sooner. He was so quiet and well behaved that it was easy to forget he was with me. I continued with him back on my shoulder, where he seemed more comfortable with the view. I smiled as he sniffed into my ear, brushing his whiskers against my skin.

The remote wilderness chorused with sounds, their sources hidden in the foliage. My shoulder tension diminished as my soul soaked in the hum of wild bees, the force of the breeze, the shift of the trees' leaves – their green veins licked with new color. By the afternoon, I reached the river, which harbored more life than the previous sites I had explored. The crystal water teemed with active fish, splashing their tails against the water's surface. The crickets cried their eerie song while the frogs jumped and bellowed. The untouched river rocks rested under the calm water current, a shade of beautiful gray-blue.

Smacking away a swarm of mosquitoes, I gratefully set up the small pop-up tent I had carried on the front of my pack. Inside the tent, I removed the sleeping bag from my pack. Bennie had gnawed a few small holes in the bag's liner. I narrowed my eyes at him as I fluffed up the material.

I spent the afternoon making fishing gear out of sharp branches, a bit of string, a metal hook, and a worm. I tried my luck in the shallow pools where a small fish species I didn't recognize proved prolific. With my hook dipped in the calmest water, I slapped away the insects until I managed to catch some fish. After slicing away their scales with my fixed-blade knife, I feasted on raw fish in the tent, sharing it with Bennie.

The nocturnal sounds rattled my nerves, nearby coyotes crying in their social bickers. Bennie crawled into my sleeping bag and settled himself in the cradle of my arm. With him by my side, my tension eased and my heart relaxed. We fell asleep together under a night sky studded with thousands of stars.

CHAPTER THREE

CHICORY

R unning - running faster than I thought possible. Running only to jump down a hill and crash-land in the ground cover below. The blood filled my eyes - I wiped it away before searching the direction of my father's screams as the fire roared. My body shrieked at me while I fought to stand. The hill held back the blaze as it slowed, allowing me to search for his location.

"Dad," I called out, but I could barely hear myself. The blaze grew impatient as she crept down the slope using the few trees and staggered brush to continue her chase. The smoke quickly thickened around me. With the pulsating pain in my arm, I looked down to see the twisted bone.

"Elizabeth!" he called for me before changing his screams to a quiet cry. My eyes watered when I spotted him twenty feet away. Scrambling to reach him, I tripped over the brush that grabbed my legs. Kicking free, I crawled over the rocks, agonizingly stretching my arm ahead. Once I was by his side, he placed his hand on my face. My eyes traveled down his leg - it was sideways, snapped in half, blood pouring from the open wound where his bone had ripped through the skin and flesh. My tears flowed when I realized his fate, but he tried to be strong for me.

"Elizabeth. You must keep going. You must survive."

Prompted by gentle licks, my eyes gradually opened. As my gaze greeted him, Bennie proceeded to lap up the tears that had leaked down the side of my face. Despite my sorrow, I smiled at him and kissed his face. Checking my wristwatch for the time, I saw it was seven o'clock. I packed everything up and made my way to the river's edge. The fish were still plentiful. Even after last night's dinner, sushi would be a welcome breakfast. Using the same tools, I managed to catch a large trout. I briefly admired the animal's glossy purple shine before using a rock to take its life. I then made easy work of opening the fish with my hunting knife. My father had taught me how to slice the meat with the blade in the correct cuts. He had also taught me the risk of eating raw fish – especially wild-caught. Treating myself for parasites when I returned home would be a necessary precaution.

Bennie grabbed the proffered fish enthusiastically. The cool meat was delicious despite its decidedly mild flavor. I relaxed with my contentment, embracing my full stomach, then chose to catch a few more fish to bring with me on my route. Once they were packed away, I took one more look at the crystal water while washing my hands and then brushing my teeth.

With Saturday's morning sun, I was pleased with my progress so far. I trekked upstream, seeing a few black bears along the way whose view I tried to escape by camouflaging myself within the trees. A large male noticed my presence despite my efforts, but he didn't bother to investigate me. He tossed his head up, busy within a bee's nest up on a spruce. Bennie relaxed, blissfully unaware of the danger.

A half-mile from the first camping point, I stumbled on a few bungleweeds. Making quick work of gathering several plants, I snapped off their roots to keep for future use. I then veered off south of the river, happy to be away from the mud. My dirtied boots scraped against the ground cover as I hiked.

Although my legs were feeling sore, I persisted despite the pressing skeletal aches. Pausing for a moment, I noticed some chicory plants at my feet. Bennie's nails gripped my shoulder while I squatted to collect the plants that happily sat in the sun within a break in the trees. The beautiful blue flowers were almost unmistakable. Ripping the three-foot plants from the soil, I thought about chicory's multiple uses. I grinned at my find while wrapping them into the same plastic bag that held the bungleweed root.

Within another half mile, I approached a rocky bed that created a small opening within the vast span of trees. My stride made fair work of the terrain, rocks crunching under my steps. A bald eagle's piercing cry made me jump. When I looked up, the bird's impressive size blocked the sun as she soared above. Maybe her keen eyes spotted Bennie on my shoulder. Perhaps realizing he would make a delectable meal for such a predator, he did his best to hide within my hair.

In my distraction, I misplaced a step, causing the unsteady rock under my foot to slide inward. My boot did its best to protect my ankle, but I gasped with pain while falling onto my backside. Bennie nearly slipped off my shoulder from the sudden movement. My curses filled the peaceful air as I realized my predicament, but despite my frustration, I soon elected to vent internally. Making loud, dying-animal sounds in a location full of large predators could easily attract unwelcome individuals. My wristwatch read midday, and I fumed as the sun beat down upon my face.

After several moments of rest, I did my best to work through the nagging pain. Struggling upright, I took several careful steps, but the discomfort shooting into my ankle's core forced a longer rest. Calling it a day, I chose to set up camp again. While hobbling around, I unrolled my sleeping bag and spent the remainder of the early afternoon watching Bennie and messing with the plants I gathered. The leaves and blue flowers on the chicory wilted in the crisp air, and I placed the plant in the sun to dry out. During the afternoon, the eagle circled back around. I listened to the wind rustling the loose leaves in a spiritual rhythm, the sound relaxing me, allowing my sore muscles to ease.

By four o'clock, my ankle felt well enough for me to try making a fire. A fire - although I dreaded meeting her again. Leaving Bennie in the sleeping bag, I limped around the woods, gathering dry branches and sticks. As my flint's click ignited the bits of wood and brush, the fire grew eagerly. My body tensed at the flame's burn, but what it promised encouraged me. Still, watching it flicker and grow generated flashbacks that zapped behind my eyes until my heart raced. My lungs tightened while my stomach turned and my breath shortened. I looked away from the fire's licks, hearing the wood crackling as it started dying from my lack of care. My vision darkened until I felt something jump into my lap. I shot my eyes at it, my heart skipping until I saw Bennie resting on my thigh, looking up at me. His bright eyes dug into mine as I worked to calm down. By this time the fire was out. I caught my breath and relaxed my heart - frustrated with myself. I could do this.

With fresh materials and Bennie by my side, I restarted the fire and watched it catch to a licking orange blaze. Although my breath shortened again, I managed to keep myself calmer by narrowing my attention to Bennie's company. I refocused my thoughts. You're okay. Fire is good. Fire is good. Repeating those words countless times, I envisioned being with my father around the camp's bonfire, listening to the crackling when it meant something beautiful.

Bennie stayed by my side while I coped with past trauma. When a loud pop of moisture from the fire sparked new flashes of hell, I picked Bennie up and cuddled him in my arms. I thought I could do this alone - that I had to do this alone - but at that moment, I realized that a friend by my side, no matter how small, was what I truly needed.

The hours dragged as I dealt with my turmoil. I thought words of positivity in the presence of the fire, struggling to make peace with her. When it was time for dinner, I took out the pot that was hanging on my bag. With the water from my canister, I put the pot on the fire to boil. When the water was ready, I added the chicory plant, and after a while, put in the trout, which cooked nicely on the fire's low flame. My stomach growled as the smell reached me. Once the meal was fully prepared, we feasted quickly, the chicory imparting a delicious earthy-meaty flavor to the trout. Listening to Bennie's teeth happily chattering allowed me to fully relax, the fire's torment slipping off my shoulders.

As the sun had set, the nightlife emerged, frogs and cicadas loudly announcing their presence. I settled into my sleeping bag. The trees claimed most of the sky, but without the light pollution from cities and towns, you could see so much more of the galaxy beyond. I stared through the branches into the stars, ignoring the fire's crackling until my eyes forced themselves shut and fatigue finally claimed me.

Startled awake, my eyes opened to darkness and the sense that something sinister had approached – there was a presence nearby. With my fire died down, I scrambled to add more wood from the nearby pile I had gathered. While I blew on the cinders, I could hear the breathing of a large and powerful creature, sticks quietly cracking under its weight. Rocks shifted as the dark mass circled my position. My heart raced and I quickly pulled my gun from my case. The stars barely lit the creature's size. A bear? Two howls sounded in the distance. A wolf.

The rocks and sticks of the forest floor rustled into the distance under its stride as the cinders caught, sparking a new fire and lighting the darkness around me. I grabbed my flashlight and darted it around the trees, lighting the bark and branches of the foliage with my gun pointing - but only the trees remained. I checked my watch in the fire's light. It was several minutes after midnight. My head was spinning. Bennie nestled deep within my sleeping bag, fully awake. I went to hold him, but he jumped away from my grasp with a loud squeak.

"Bennie?" I tried picking him up again but he gasped another squeak. Recognizing that he was unwilling to join my arms, I left him alone. The haunting sound of a nearby owl's hoot crept into my eardrums as I struggled to slow my heart rate.

CHAPTER FOUR

STRANGER

A s I stretched in the new morning, the core of my ankle ached. It was a mild ache, one I could overcome. After stomping out the cinders excessively with my good leg, I felt proud to have slept next to my old enemy. I felt more at peace with her, but the fundamental hatred remained. My shoe buried her out of existence.

I was sorry to have nothing other than dried root for breakfast. Bennie wouldn't eat the bitter, earthy pieces I offered, dropping them shortly after tasting, then looking up at me as if I had offered him poison. I chuckled at his expression while packing up camp.

Starting my hike, I limped along – slinking through the trees. Bennie resumed riding on my shoulder, sniffing his nose into the air. On my GPS, I could see the small lake I needed to reach. I passed around a small ledge, working my way farther south – taking in the beauty of each pine tree I passed. I listened to the sticks snapping under my feet, no longer made uneasy by the sound. My heart was confident, my spirit high. I could feel it in my bones – forgiveness – for the forest if not for myself.

When I reached the lake, I dropped my pack and stretched out my arms into the air. The water was neither clear nor murky. Small fish fry hid among the plants near the water's edge. I placed Bennie into my pack after retrieving the large water canister and fishing supplies. Peering into the water's movement, I saw the swirls of liquid shifted only by the wind. My eyes narrowed for anything more than a dragonfly's kiss upon the surface.

Using my knife, a long stick, some of my string, and an unlucky worm – I set my cast. Nearly an hour passed with no bites. I sighed while watching Bennie groom himself. He rubbed his arms over his head and then rolled his hands around his whiskers. Looking into the distance, I counted sixty thin trees along the lake's span. After reeling in my short cast, I turned my focus to edible plants. Not far from my bag, plentiful hard-stemmed cattails grew in the water, the stalks sprouting with frankfurter-shaped flowers. Cattail had many uses, making it one of my favorites. I was able to harvest them without having to wet my boots and then focus again on the water. With the encouragement of a fishtail splashing the water's surface, I was determined to try again. I retrieved a fresh worm, one that wiggled more than its predecessor. After twenty minutes, my line got a bite, and I rushed to pull the fish to land. It was a trout, somewhat small, and I smiled at its glossy scales.

Unwilling to start another fire after yesterday's stress, I offered a raw piece to Bennie, who happily devoured it. I ate the rest for lunch along with some bitter cattail shoots. The crunch of their stalks against my teeth felt like eating celery covered in raw potato peel. After gathering water, I turned away from the lake.

Bennie resided in my bag as I continued my hike south, a few hours passing as I trekked. While admiring the huge pine trees that exploded from the soil into the sky, I heard a peculiar sound that pulled me in its direction. It bounced against the tree bark, wiggling along with the fallen leaves. Its familiarity nagged at my core, turning my stomach. As I gained ground toward the source, the sound grew distinguishable, scraping across my eardrums and rattling my soul. Flashes of my broken father zipped into my memory, buckling my legs. I collapsed into the pine needles, tears welling in my eyes like the blood once did as I listened to the familiar agony. With a jab in my neck, I looked up toward the direction of the screams. My legs tensed, frozen in place until the screams subsided and the sounds of wildlife reclaimed the surroundings. I managed to kneel while crossing my trembling arms. The tears poured from my eyes; a sob slipped my lips. I fought to regain my composure. Snap out of it, Elizabeth. I focused my thoughts, willing my pounding heart to soothe itself.

Feeling determined, I struggled to stand and walk on my shaking legs, moving toward the direction of the subsided cries. I trudged for a couple hundred feet before approaching a massive Oregon white oak. I observed the bark reaching up its trunk, withered by age. The tree's aggressive roots stretched down a small hill beside it. Walking to the left, I came around and down the hill that the tree sat atop.

When I reached the bottom, I felt a presence behind me. A dark gap below the base of the tree drew my gaze. There was a large hole in the earth and, to my shock, an injured man lying close to the opening. Hairs rose on my neck as I observed the trail of blood droplets along the forest floor leading to his lifeless body. He wore no shoes or socks, and blood stained through his torn white shirt and ripped jean shorts. My fingers numbed as I forced my legs forward. I walked up to him and kneeled next to his side, my throat tightened by the sight of his broken left tibia, evident by an abnormal bulge in his shin. Multiple lacerations in his upper leg dripped blood, and a small cut lay next to his right eye. He was young with perfect night-black hair several inches long, fair skin with a faint olive undertone, and a well-groomed short beard around his jaw and mouth. He looked nothing like my father, but the familiarity of the situation caused my vision to spot.

His injuries appeared to be animal inflicted. When I placed my fingers upon his cheek, he felt ice-cold, but he was breathing. Rushing into my bag, I pulled the satellite phone from the bottom. Almost fumbling it out of my grasp, I raced to dial for help.

The phone answered. "Jackson County Sheriff's Office. What's your emergency?"

"Yes, hi. My name is Elizabeth Allard. I'm in a unique predicament." My shaky voice managed to briefly explain the situation.

"Okay, what are your coordinates, Ms. Allard?"

I fumbled for my GPS, but before I could state them, the line cut. What the hell? I pulled the phone down from my ear. It was dead. How could that be? "Dammit," I said, sighing loudly.

I glanced at the dark burrow under the tree base just twelve feet from where he lay. I shuddered at the thought of what wild beast might be lurking within, but no sounds came from its depths. Electing to investigate the cavity with my flashlight, I discovered the cave was empty and spanned ten feet deep, its sides formed from bedrock with huge thick roots ripping throughout the surrounding soil.

Building a fire was my next task. A fire – how I hated her, but with the man's temperature feeling dangerously low, I had to endure her again. After gathering nearby wood, I started the fire as quickly as I could manage, but the flame was being stubborn. I felt my stomach turn when she sparked to life. Despite my hatred, I welcomed her orange glow and heat.

Questions raced through my consciousness. So many questions. My head started to spin as I thought for far too long.

I went to check his pockets for a wallet with the hope of identifying him, but no luck. My thoughts switched to the possibility of brain trauma. With shaking hands, I gently opened his right eye and used my flashlight to check for a response. His striking blue iris peered into the light as his pupil contracted normally. My heart skipped. Blue eyes.

I then checked his heart. Despite the blood loss and shallow breathing, his pulse was strong. He needed to be stitched in various places and his leg had to be set. The wound on his thigh, still bleeding, was most worrisome. Putting my bag down, I started digging for the first aid kit. Bennie tried climbing my arm shortly after I opened my bag. With the emergency, I had forgotten about him. I placed him on the nearby ground, where he stayed next to my things. I unzipped the kit to find my hand sanitizer and gloves. His wound needed staples, but regular sutures were all I had. Using my medical scissors, I cut some of his shorts fabric away from the wound to perform the minimal stitch job. My hands were trembling too much for me to accomplish the task.

Seeing this man lying in a familiar forest revived painful memories. Flashes of my father the moment before his death blurred my eyes and accelerated my heartbeat. I couldn't get myself together, my vision was fading in and out. Hours passed like this, but while I was helplessly watching him bleed, thin clotting finally stopped the slow drip. He was still breathing. I sighed, furious with myself.

My hands continued to shake throughout the afternoon. Unable to help him any further, I decided to cover him with my sleeping bag with the hope that he would stay warmer. I started thinking about my trip and how this gorgeous injured man had changed everything. I could go no farther on my journey, but I didn't care.

I placed Bennie on my shoulder while collecting more wood to burn. The afternoon brought out a lovely orange sun peeking through the trees. My stomach growled, and I arrived back to find the stranger just as I had left him. With my cooking pot and some water from my canister, I started to make my dinner. Ignoring the pit in my heart as I faced my old enemy, I boiled the rest of my chicory plant. Once finished, it made a suitable meal with the cattail seeds; Bennie was hungry enough to eat the seeds I offered to him.

After my meal, I checked the stranger's temperature. He was

warmer, with his pulse even stronger. As night fell, I set up my tent and did my best to fall asleep within. I felt bad leaving the man outside, but with no way to safely move him, it was best to leave him be.

That night proved to be a rough one, punctuated by wolves howling in the distant shadows. The moonlight beamed down on us as I fed the fire after sleep failed me for too long. The stranger lay as still as before. Lying down once more, I felt fatigue set in and my eyes closed for the night.

The next morning, I first noticed that my eyes weighed down heavily. I could hear birds singing above me as I rolled to my back, their songs stabbing my ears. I jumped up when I remembered the stranger. Unzipping my tent and peeking out, I saw he was lying exactly where I had left him. I crawled out of the tent and rushed to his side, checking his pulse and breathing, and relieved to discover he was still alive. Sighing, I left him to answer nature's call in the woods. Upon my return, I fetched Bennie from my bag, where he had slept for the night. He stretched and yawned in the open air. The stranger shifted, making me jump. A groan flowed from his lips as his consciousness returned and his beautiful eyes opened to greet the morning light. He looked up at the birds and trees above, then turned his head toward me, seemingly unfazed by my presence. His expression showed only pain.

I stared at him until I finally broke the silence. "My name is Elizabeth, but you can call me Lizzy or Liz. You were injured in an animal attack."

He studied my face but chose to say nothing.

"You don't need to speak. It's okay," I assured him.

He stared at me for several moments more before shifting his frame. With every movement, he winced, gasped, and groaned in agony. I wanted to help him, but I wasn't sure what he was trying to do. Pulling himself backward and away from me, he used his arms and one leg to slowly shift his position so that he was lying propped against the raised ground behind him.

Bennie walked over to him, and the stranger turned his eyes to my curious rodent. The man raised one eyebrow.

"That's Bennie, my pet rat."

His expression remained the same as he observed the friendly rodent beside him.

"Did you get attacked from something in there?" I asked, pointing toward the cave. He slowly shook his head side to side. I watched as his eyes watered and he wiped his nose. My heart sank, feeling intense sympathy for him. "What's your name?"

He lowered his eyes to the ground before answering. "Tyler."

I smiled at his husky voice. It suited him, as did his name. "Okay, Tyler. It's a bit late for it, but we should close these wounds. They've clotted but the clot probably won't hold. I also need to set your leg." He shook his head no. I could see the worry in his eyes; my heart remained full of pity. "You don't want my help?"

His eyes moved down to his injuries. "No, I don't."

"Well, you need it," I said firmly. His face remained unsure, his eyes silent. "So, how did you get out here?" He lowered his head, ignoring my question. I sighed as the minutes of silence passed. With his failure to reply, I shifted my attention to his upper leg. The clotted puncture wounds and torn skin were at greatest risk of infection. The punctures looked big enough to be from a bear. "What attacked you?" My fingers tapped on my thigh.

He looked up at me and sighed. "A wolf ..."

I raised an eyebrow. Wolf attacks were rare and the size and spacing of the punctures in his skin were rather large for wolf bites. The broken tibia was equally perplexing. First, I needed to give him an antibiotic shot near his worst puncture, but would he try to stop me? He required stitches for the lacerations and a hand-made splint for his tibia. I moved to my pack and removed my first aid kit again.

My hands started to tremble, but this time I managed to calm my nerves with careful thoughts and breathing. I pulled the air into my lungs with steady breaths. Talking to him had helped me feel less freaked out. I took out a sterile needle syringe and a bottle of antibiotics. Forgetting his condition, he shifted away from the needle in my hand, gasping at the pain caused by his movement. Blood spat from the leg wounds as the thin clot caved. Dammit, I was afraid that would happen. He gritted his teeth, raising his arm to me in a defensive stance.

"No ... please no. Please," he begged.

I knew he needed it; if he died, I would have blamed myself forever as I had for my father's death. Tyler had become my responsibility. I proceeded to draw the antibiotic liquid from its bottle. Despite his plea, I moved to put the needle to his thigh.

"No, stop! Please, I don't want it!" he begged. His weak hands shifted to his thigh, where he saw my needle reaching.

My heart sank once more, crumbling under his pleas. I pushed his weak hands away, placed my hand on his thigh, and injected the needle centimeters from the worst puncture wound.

"Ouch, dammit!" he gasped. His eyes watered as his teeth ground together.

Pulling the needle out, I gave him some time to calm and collect himself. His head turned toward the cave while his eyes closed – breathing heavily through the pain. How am I going to treat his wounds like this? I thought. If only I had been strong enough to have helped him yesterday.

As he settled himself, the blood from his thigh continued its steady drip while the sun quickly disappeared – a thick cover of cloud had encased the day's skies, dropping the temperature.

"I'm sorry. I don't take it lightly to do something against someone's will," I said, wishing I had cloth to apply some pressure to aid in clotting the worst wound.

He was mostly quiet while he waited for the pain to abate to a bearable level. His dark brows remained low and tensed over his tightened eyes. He began to shiver, but I knew the small tent would not fit us both. I was grateful for the cave behind us, but moving him would be difficult.

"Tyler, you need to move into the cave. I can keep you warmer if you're out of the wind chill – and a fire would trap the heat inside. Are you able to move?"

He assessed my request before concluding what I already knew. "I'm ... I'm too weak."

"Can you sit up for me?"

He managed to do so, allowing me to get awkwardly behind him. I put my arms under his shoulders and began to turn him to the cave. As I slowly dragged him, he gasped several times. With each loud complaint, I stopped and gave him a moment. When he was inside the cave resting on the ground, I collected the sleeping bag and placed it on top of him, eager for a new clot to form.

I walked over to the old dying fire and put it out with my boot before leaving him to find materials. Farther south, I looked for straight branches and ivy vines to create a splint. The dense cover of Douglas fir, pine, and spruce trees made easy work of finding what I needed. Ivy stretched itself around the trunk of a Douglas fir just fifty feet from the cave. With the removal of its leaves, ivy would make the perfect securer for the splint without having to use my actual rope. Using my knife, I gathered what I needed and brought it back to the stranger.

I set the materials down inside the cave across from him. Removing the sleeping bag from over Tyler to check his wounds, I was pleased to observe that his leg had created a thin clot again.

While I worked on making the fire right outside the cave's entrance, Ty was resting his eyes. As the fire caught, I noticed my reaction to her was no longer so strong. She licked upward, crackling on the branches and dried pine needles.

My next task was splinting. "I'm going to set your leg now. This will hurt."

He opened his eyes and turned his head toward me while I readied myself on his side. My jacket would do the job. I placed the two straight branches on each side of his lower left leg without touching him and readied the vine ties.

"It's okay," he assured me.

Was I the one being comforted?

He winced, eyes tightly shut as I gently placed my jacket around his shin and calf. I then put the two branches right against him before proceeding to place the vine around the top and bottom, fitting the wrap into the wedges I created within the wood to hold it in place. He handled it well until it was time to shift the bulging bone into the correct position.

"Agggh! Dammit!" he screamed.

I carefully pushed the bone down into place and wrapped the pressure around it. I noticed his right leg pull up and rise - the perfect stance to kick me across the wilderness. His bare dirtied foot now more noticeable, I made sure he couldn't reach me easily from the side until he lowered his leg. If I was in his position, I'd want to kick me, too. We were both relieved when the brace was complete and the vines were set. By this point it was noon and my stomach growled, but this treatment had to come first.

Although his wounds had clotted again, with the struggling to secure his brace, they had reopened, spitting fresh blood. I had no choice. They had to be closed.

From my medical kit, I removed the needle driver, needle, suture, scissors, and gloves. When he spotted the needle, his eyes widened.

"You're not touching me with that! Stay over there!" he commanded.

"You don't have a choice. Those wounds are too wide to heal on their own. The clot won't hold and you're still losing blood."

He tried to sit up, but the maneuver proved too painful. Lying along the cave floor, he stared at me. I needed a way to restrain his arms to prevent his interference. It wouldn't be hard to overpower him. I noticed all around the cave walls the thick, heavy, and secure roots that reached close to his head. They would make the perfect restraints for tying his wrists. As I tested the roots' strength, his eyes widened. This solution to his stubbornness, although admittedly a bit cruel, would work well to restrain him.

"Don't ... you ... dare," he warned. I was glad I hadn't used my rope for his leg. Retrieving it from my bag, I wrapped it around the root above his head, then went for his wrists. He began to panic. "I'm serious! Stop! You're mad!" he cried while flailing his arms away. Despite his efforts, I grabbed his weak wrists and fought his remaining strength, tying his wrists to the heavy root.

My heart sank at his struggles against the restraints. I knew that for a fully conscious patient, sticking needles into painful wounds without painkillers was simply torture, but he needed it. As I contemplated my handling of him, he breathed rapidly. When he stopped struggling, I removed the gloves from their packaging and put them on. His entire body was tense in anticipation, yet he remained quiet. He watched me prepare my tools. I started by further removing some of his shorts material from around the injury. In some places the fabric had become glued to his skin with blood, while other areas still dripped.

"Aagh!" he suddenly cried when I pulled a piece from a deep wound.

"Sorry, I'm trying to cause as little pain as I can."

"I'll try to manage," he gasped.

Once the wound was cleared, I readied my equipment. If only I had staples instead. He closed his eyes and turned his head away toward the cave wall to be brave. His body tensed harder. The lighting in the cave was lousy, but the injuries couldn't wait any longer.

"Try to relax," I said, but he remained tense, his body trembling.

Starting with the worst laceration, I inserted the needle through his skin with the first suture. He cried out while his arms pulled on the restraint. I worried he would hurt his wrists. Working as quickly as I could, I closed the first wound with minimal stitching, hoping it would hold. Throughout the suturing, he screamed and cursed – almost forgetting to breathe at its worst moments. My eardrums ached from the worst of it.

The location of the damage kept oozing fresh blood, enlarging the stain on his jean-shorts. I started on the next thigh wound. His screams resembled those of my father, making my heart race as I worked to multitask – fighting my memories and fighting to close his skin.

His complaints grew quieter and his muscles started to relax as he began to lose consciousness. When he fell silent, I could see his reddened face resting, tilted toward me. Fresh tears rested on his lower left temple next to his eyes. I checked his breathing, shallow but steady. Relief swathed my tired hands. I continued with him at ease, my eardrums still ringing. After I finished working on his leg, I moved to his chest injuries. Using my scissors, I cut a square out of his shirt. Only the worst laceration needed to be closed, the rest already on their way to scabbing over. I made easy work of closing the wound while he rested. Since he seemed to heal quickly, I decided to leave all the wounds uncovered by bandages so exposure to the fresh air could help the scabbing process. Once finished, I placed the tools back into the medical kit after a quick rinse and put my bloodied gloves in a small plastic bag.

I then removed the restraints from his wrists and placed his limp arms along the sides of his body. The red marks on his skin generated vigorous guilt within me. In the hope of making him more comfortable, I emptied my pack and used it as a pillow for him. When I lifted his head, he remained unresponsive to my touch. After handling him, I ran my fingers through his irresistibly soft hair, admiring his perfect face. The outline of his jaw complemented his cheekbones. Where did you come from? Questions about this mysterious man cornered my thoughts. I had no answers other than a first name. He could have been a serial killer – I shivered at the thought before dismissing it.

My stomach interrupted me with a growl. I had to gather enough food to feed the three of us. Wait, where was Bennie? I had nearly forgotten about him again with all the activity. He was cowering against my pile of loose supplies.

"Bennie, come here, sweetheart." He looked at me with uncertainty until I reached my hand toward him. Moving toward me, he welcomed my grasp. I cuddled him before setting him onto my shoulder. He had to be hungry, too. I needed my compass, knife, water canister, snares, fishing supplies, and my gun while hunting. I gathered my supplies and fed the fire before leaving.

CHAPTER FIVE

HUNTING & GATHERING

My ankle felt healed – the ache missing from its core – and my steps were firm. I worked my way back north toward the body of water I had visited before finding Ty. It was a few hours until I found the lake again. After gathering edible plants of clover, bitterroot, Indian pipe, northern goldenrod, ground ivy, dandelion, knotweed, and more, I placed them down near Bennie. Removing my clothing and boots, I stepped into the frigid water. The hair on my neck rose while bumps formed on my arms. I dipped my clothing in, shuffling it under the water and, to my annoyance, disturbing a cloud of dirt and muck. I stepped in deeper, feeling the chill shoot up my spine. The water rose over my knees as I felt the slimy bottom between my toes. Twitching my nose, I dipped my clothing again.

Exiting to place my wet clothes on a low branch, I returned to the water to rinse my armpits and wet my hair. As I entered deeper, I cleaned my lower region. Shocks from the frigid water zipped up and down my spine until I finished bathing and waded out of the lake.

While my clothing dried, I put my revolver around my hip.

Drops of water sparkled on my bare body. I left the lake to walk through the damp woods, covered by a harsh new fog. Finding small passageways in the brush that trailed with small-animal tracks, I set my snares – hoping a critter would slip through. The thick cover of wild ferns and assorted foliage felt hard on my feet as I traveled through the dense fir and pine trees. Sharp vines intermittently scratched my bare skin. Despite the sense of fulfilling someone's fetish, nudity in the woods felt natural, like the wilderness itself. The wind caressed my curves, drifting through my drying hair.

Returning to the lake, I greeted my little rodent. I realized any water I would bring back would be needed for Ty and cooking. Filling the canister, I gorged myself on the water – stuffing my stomach to what it would comfortably hold. While I watched Bennie through my sips, a mass of reddish-brown caught my attention in the trees across the lake. It was a coyote. She seemed to be predominantly cautious of us, yet her stare fixed on Bennie, who groomed his face and coat entirely oblivious to the danger. Grateful she hadn't come by when I left him to set snares, I realized how careless I had been with him. I shouldn't have been so quick to forget the many hidden dangers the forest contained for us both. Her gaze momentarily left us as she took a quick drink. I could see her winter coat was starting to replace the old one. She soon left in a hurry, illusive between the tall trees.

The sun returned to the sky, beaming down on my clothes. I fished the lake while I waited, with only a few small fish as reward in the passing hours. Tyler could have been awake by now; I had no way of knowing. My socks and underwear were dry before the rest, but I couldn't wait any longer. When my damp clothes were on, I gathered Bennie and the plant bundle, filling my oversized canister before heading off to check the snares. I had no trouble finding the first snare, which was placed under a log, and was ecstatic to find an oversized squirrel within it, already dead from the struggle. The four other snares proved empty. The one lucky catch elicited my smile as I trekked back to camp.

Upon reaching the tree that clutched the cave below, I raised my eyes up to its mostly green leaves, then looked down to its entrance to discover him exactly as he had been this morning - peacefully sleeping. I placed more snares around our camp before I joined him in the cave. His temperature felt cold again, but his pulse was strong.

The fire was low. I worked to restore its life - adding fresh dry branches and sticks. Bennie snuggled into my hair while I worked, nearly slipping off my shoulder when I leaned over to gut the squirrel. My knife made the unpleasant event quick. I threw the innards into the fire and then worked to remove the pelt. A sharp stick through the squirrel with an angled placement over the flame made the perfect meat roaster. I then rinsed my hands and worked on boiling some water to prepare the plants. As the water came to a boil, I heard a low moan next to me, signaling that Tyler was regaining consciousness. His pained face apparent, I moved over to him. Using my bare hand, I wiped the sweat off his forehead and waited patiently for his eyes to open. I fully expected him to be angry with me, but when those beautiful eyes finally greeted mine, his expression softened. He wasn't mad?

"How are you feeling?" I asked.

He stared into my eyes, hiding some pain within his lightly watered irises, but he was too weak to hold that fixation long. He closed them and sighed his lungs empty in a heavy exhale. Maybe he *was* mad. Despite the victory created by his improved condition, I felt guilty. I moved to get the water canister. Holding his head up, I fed him the water. He drank a considerable amount of the remaining gallon. The water brought some strength to him.

"I'm cooking some food for us. How do you feel about boiled momster soup?"

He looked at me bemused. "Momster?"

"It's an old family recipe."

"Is it meat?"

"No, but I have a squirrel cooking."

He perked up with bright eyes. "That's preferred."

"I'll let you have the whole squirrel then. You need it more than me."

I was delighted to see his first smile. It was a light smile full of hidden pain, yet it made my heart spark. While I adjusted the food, I felt his gaze on me. Blue peered in from the corner of my vision, unfortunately reminding me of the way Dr. Smoldred would obsess over me back at the hospital. My posture grew rigid.

"So, what is your full name?"

He chuckled at the question and removed his eyes from me.

"What?" I asked.

He coughed and gasped at the sharp new pain before answering past the groans. "My full name is Tyler Bardon." Anguish darkened his face as he waited for the pain to settle.

"I'm Elizabeth River Allard, but I prefer Lizzy or Liz."

"Yeah, you've said that."

My eyes narrowed. "Indeed, I did."

I played with his full name, twirling it around my tongue. When the food was finished, I offered him the stick of squirrel meat. Steam slipped from the crisped flesh. He gathered his strength to hold the meat, taking it from me. Before it was cool enough, he tore his teeth into it. My eyes widened at his sudden ravenousness. While remaining on his back with his head still propped slightly by my bag, he consumed every edible piece of flesh the animal provided. I had only eaten half of my soup when he was finished.

"Do you want some of the soup?" I offered.

"No. Thank you though. That was delicious."

"You're welcome," I said. My lips formed a smile, but I could tell something was bothering him as he struggled not to fidget. "You okay?"

"I have to pee," he said after a moment.

I raised an eyebrow. "Uh ... if you're okay with it, I can help you."

He thought for a moment. "Can you get my shorts and boxers down without looking?" His face flushed with a subtle red hue.

"Yeah, I'll try." As I unzipped his shorts, his frame tensed. "Try to shift your weight to the good leg and lift yourself slightly."

He did his best to comply despite his discomfort. With my help, we were able to get them to come down. I almost forgot to look away, finally shifting my eyes to the cave wall. I handed him the small empty canister and let him do as needed.

"Here," he offered me the canister when he finished.

I placed it aside to dispose of later, careful not to look down. His face was flushed. I expected more difficulty pulling up his shorts and boxers, but he found the strength to assist. He was relieved when the ordeal was over.

I watched him pick at his fingers and glance at his wounds, then yawn - showing off his bright white teeth. His eyes were growing heavy. With them closing, he soon met the comfort of sleep. I placed the sleeping bag back over him and left to dispose of the canister contents before checking the snares. Another fat squirrel was caught in one under some bushes. The rich forest made for easy pickings.

Darkness consumed the forest shortly after I returned with my catch and some more wood. Bennie fell asleep in the corner of the cave until I gutted and skinned the catch within the fire's light. He lifted his nose, smelling the air. I wondered if he was bothered by us killing and eating his distant cousins. I suspected not. I watched him walk over to me and place his little hands on my thigh; he seemed to want a taste. I placed the meat over the fire. Bennie curled himself on my lap. When there was nothing left to do, I looked at the man, listening to his light breathing. My heart fluttered while watching his soft eyes rest peacefully in the fire's flickering light. I smiled at his twitching fingers. Something grew in my chest that I hadn't ever felt before. It was a pull. A spark? Whatever it was, I knew it wasn't welcome. I only knew his name. In my perception, he was still a stranger, but the pull building toward him – it was something different. Something about Tyler was different. My eyes trailed along his face while I longed to lie beside him.

The temperature of the night was dropping quickly. With the wind chill, it felt about sixty degrees. I shivered in the light breeze. Looking at my jacket around his leg, I wished I was wearing it. The fire helped, but my arms were riddled with goosebumps. A faint howl in the distance drew my attention – bouncing off the trees and creeping toward the cave. A few more hours passed with me staring into the fire as I fed her. How this old enemy served me now; she had become a welcome demon.

I wondered what my father would have thought of Tyler Bardon. His name rolled around my tongue. Using a stick to play with the fire cinders, I sensed a presence that made the hairs on my arms and neck stand up. Looking out from the cave, I heard sticks crack under the quiet gait of a large creature. I scrambled for my flashlight and pulled my revolver from its holster. At first, my light reached nothing but trees, brush, and ferns ... until I saw him. The distant beam met a huge gray wolf forty feet from our position – peeking through the trees. He was impossibly large. My gun pointed toward the beast. His eyes reflected the light as he peered back at me. He snarled just loud enough for me to hear the low, haunting grumble. Hackles rose on his shoulders, pointing toward the crested moon. My heart pounded and my breath shortened. Another howl sounded in the distance, causing him to look away. He turned his eyes to me again before running off. I dropped my gun and light, confused by this creature.

Despite the now empty woods around us, I couldn't sleep knowing we could be attacked. After meeting such a powerful animal undoubtedly enticed by the smell of blood, I didn't want to risk another animal encounter while asleep. I had to stay awake. My eyes sagged as Tyler rested. Jealousy arose in my fatigued brain, but I couldn't hold it against him.

To occupy my tired mind, I pondered questions about Tyler. I needed answers. How did he break his leg? Was that gray wolf the one that attacked Tyler? How did he get all the way out here? And where were his shoes? So many questions. Tomorrow I'd get him to talk.

I staked the cooked squirrel in the cave as the night grew colder while the hours passed. By three o'clock in the morning, I couldn't hold myself up any longer. I lay next to him, doing my best to stay awake, but I soon lost the battle. I dreamed of meadow flowers and tall grass – the first pleasant dream I had had in a while – until the morning arrived.

My heavy eyes peeled open and blue was the first color I saw – Ty's eyes watching me. He was propped up on his left arm with his torso turned to me. I sprung up.

"Oh! You're awake. How are you feeling?" I yawned modestly.

"I'm feeling better today," he replied.

His husky voice pulled at me. I noticed he looked much stronger this morning. His color was further improved, his eyes were brighter, and most apparent was his ability to hold himself up.

I grabbed my hairbrush, feeling disheveled. Since when did I care about how I looked around a man?

"Good. That's good." The dirt scraping along my scalp felt awful. I frowned.

"Something wrong?" he questioned.

"Not really. I just have dirt in my hair and barely got any sleep. I stayed awake until three in the morning to guard the cave." He seemed confused by this. "There was a huge gray wolf that stalked us in the night after you fell asleep. Likely attracted by the blood."

His eyes widened. He looked away and frowned. "Oh, I see."

"Is that the wolf that attacked you?" I sounded a little too excited.

He nodded. "Probably. Maybe wanted to finish me off."

"Well. I wouldn't let that happen. He would be shot dead if he tried." I thought that statement would have made him feel more at ease, but he remained tense. "Are you hungry?"

"Very."

"I have some soup. Here." I offered him the pot.

He wrinkled his nose, raising an eyebrow at me. "No thank you. Do you have any meat?"

"Oh! I forgot I had this." Perhaps he had seen it before asking, but the squirrel remained staked on a stick near the dying fire. I handed it to him, and he eagerly dug in. Setting more snares was on today's list. "Do you like fish? I can go fishing today." He nodded as he chewed. "Alright, I will try the nearby lake while I gather the water. You seem much stronger today."

He smiled at me through his meal. I ate the soup and offered some to Bennie. When Ty was done eating, he handed me the stick and remains.

Once I finished my meal, I wanted to check him. "I'm going to look at your wounds, okay?"

He nodded. I peeked under the jacket, careful not to hurt him. The color of his leg looked good and the bone was still in place. I was pleased, but I nonetheless needed answers from him. I started with the most pressing one.

"How did you get all the way out here?"

He was somewhat hesitant when he answered. "I was hiking. Traveling like you."

"You have to give me more than that," I said while feeding the fire.

He frowned. "I wanted to explore the wilderness. I wanted to be outdoors and leave civilization for a while. What about you ... why are you out here?"

"Soul-searching. I am a nurse on break from the stress of my job ... and dreams."

"Not much of a break considering." He looked down at his body.

I giggled, shifting my position. "No, I suppose not. What do you do for a living?"

He hesitated again. "I am a woodworker. I carve sculptures with a chainsaw and tools."

"Oh, that's pretty neat!"

"You think so? Doesn't really compare to your profession."

"Nonsense. I wish I had a creative artistic side. I've envied people who can draw and sculpt works of art."

He smiled at me. "Well, you sculpt skin together," he teased. "How old are you?"

"I'm twenty-six. You?"

"Twenty-three. Turned twenty-three a few months back. Do you live in Oregon?"

"Been living here since I was little. How did you break your leg and get mixed up with the wolves ... and where's all your gear?" I questioned, pointing to his leg.

He tensed, sitting himself up while leaning against his arms. "I was hiking when one attacked me. I lost my shoes in the struggle. I was pretty near this cave when I was mauled. I crawled for a bit before passing out from the pain. I dunno what caused him to stop. Maybe he sensed you nearby. If so, I owe you my life."

I pondered his explanation until I noticed a detail missing. "But how did you end up with a broken leg?"

"When I was fighting him off, my leg slipped into a narrow animal burrow."

That made sense. I felt at that point I had enough answers to ponder. I was ready to get going when he asked me something a little random.

"So, why a pet rat?"

I chuckled as he stared down at my little rodent. "Rats make awesome pets. They are intelligent and social. They love people."

"I honestly don't see the appeal."

"Well then, I will leave him with you for some time to get to know each other. Who knows, he may just change your mind." I smirked at him as I got up to gather my things. Taking my pack from where it lay behind him, I filled it with snares, my large canister, and everything else I might have needed. "You'll be okay while I'm out?"

He nodded in reply.

"Good. It will be at least a few hours before I return," I said, placing the small designated urine canister next to him. "I assume you'll need this soon. You seem strong enough to handle it now."

He glared at me as I left.

CHAPTER SIX

SHADES OF BLUE

Without Bennie on my shoulder, I was able to move faster. It was already Tuesday. I wasn't going to get Tyler back to the drop-off point by Friday. He wouldn't be able to make the rough hike and there wasn't a way for me to alert the chopper company to delay the pickup. Maybe a rescue team was searching for us, surely alerted by my brief emergency call.

Following my tree marks back to the lake, it wasn't long before I found it again, along with some fresh animal tracks in the dirt along its edges. I set new snares in the brush and prepared my gun for a coyote. If one traveled near again, this time it would be dinner. If only a deer would come close. A squirrel here and there was not enough protein for us three; they barely had enough meat for one.

I drank my primary water intake for the day. When the canister was filled, I worked on fishing while waiting for some luck on bigger game. The bites were slow to none. I sighed, picking at my fingers as the day dragged. I wanted to hunt something quickly, so I could get back to him sooner. What if that wolf returned? That was only part of my eagerness. I wanted to get to know him. As the time passed,

I managed to catch five small fish, all hardly worth keeping. They were silver with a black row of scales stretching along their length. The motionless water sparkled in the sun, but the water's spirit was absent. I thought about how my dad used to take me to the local lake when I was a child. He told me not to splash in puddles or I might fall through them, but I'd splash in them anyway. Bittersweet memories reminded me of the joy that should surround the thought of him instead of the pain.

My thoughts shifted to the gray wolf. He was unbelievably large. I didn't know they could grow to such an impressive size. I thought about his eyes and how my light reflected against them. These woods had secrets to share.

I then thought about what Ty had said. The more I pondered his explanation, the more holes I found. With his gear somewhere in these woods, why didn't he send me looking for it? Surely he must have had at least some valuable or useful possessions. His shoes and socks were missing. It made no sense as to why they weren't on him or around where I found him. His feet were dirty and rough like he'd been walking miles without footwear. So much I didn't understand. To my dismay, his mysteriousness only added to his appeal. I frowned at myself.

Frogs chirped and croaked around the water's edge. Maybe Ty liked frog legs. They were small frogs, slimy-looking, and seemed difficult to catch. I decided against chasing them. By past midday, I started heading back. Checking all my snares, I found none had any catches. Ty would have to work with fish and my vegetation soup. Maybe he'd be up for a fish stew.

As I reached the camp, my body felt stiff, like something urged me in another direction. Coming down to the cave entrance, my heart jolted when I saw it was empty. Both Ty and Bennie were nowhere around. Panic started to set in. How could he have wandered off? Did something grab them both? My heart raced in my chest.

"Tyler! Bennie!" I called out, fearing the worst. "Tyler!" I tried to calm myself. Breathing deeply in and out, I shifted to tracking. Surely there would be a trail leading to where Ty went.

Before I could start to figure out the marks in the soil, I heard a voice.

"I'm over here!"

I ran toward his voice to find him sitting against a pine tree only thirty feet away.

"What are you doing? How did you get all the way over here?" I crossed my arms.

He shifted toward me. "I was trying to catch your rodent. He ran off. And then I had to go to the bathroom, so I struggled with that."

"Wait, Bennie is gone?" My eyes darted around the foliage. He could have been anywhere. "We have to find him! He is defenseless." My hands scraped through my hair, pulling on my roots.

"I'm sorry, I tried to catch him. He was too fast," he said while looking up at me, his eyes apologetic.

I deeply regretted leaving Bennie with Ty, but it wasn't Ty's fault. It was entirely mine. I shouldn't have left him. He was too bonded to me.

My eyes watered. "I will look for him. First, we must get you back to the cave. You're in no condition to travel yet."

He nodded and moved to pull himself up. He struggled upright, using my strength and the trees to stand. He was tall; I labored to help him balance himself. Unwelcome butterflies kicked around in my stomach as I held him, my fingers pressing into his strong arms. Ty winced and complained, holding his broken leg up. The exposed healing skin was lit up in the open air. Ty didn't move and I took the moment to examine the wound. It was healing well.

We struggled to move back to the cave. Upon reaching it, I saw Bennie in the cave's entrance, waiting for us. I nearly made Ty fall.

"Oh my gosh, Bennie! He's there!" Ty didn't say anything as he focused on moving. Once back into the cave, he lay down with a heavy sigh of relief before turning to look at my mischievous rodent. I scooped Bennie up and held him fondly, petting his head and back.

"So, the little rodent is fine after all. How wonderful." Ty rolled his eyes at my happiness.

"What's your problem?" I felt my skin heat as my eyes narrowed on his face.

"Nothing. I'm just hungry, that's all."

"I'll make you something."

"Do you have any meat?"

What was with this guy and meat? "Not much. Just some fish and plants."

"I'm okay with fish."

"You won't eat any plants, will you?"

He didn't reply – just frowned at me, waiting for me to decide what to offer him. His face looked sad and vulnerable. After restarting the fire, I offered him every fish I caught. He gratefully and greedily ate them all. I ate some raw plants from Monday's gatherings. A lot of them were wilted and bitter. Bennie picked the fish bones clean, unwilling to touch the plants I offered him.

"I can set more snares around here, but if I don't catch anything, I won't have any meat for your dinner."

He contemplated before answering. "It's okay. I'll be fine."

"I guess you'll have to be," I said, still annoyed with him. My tone was harsher than intended.

He stared at me before finally responding, "I'm sorry if I offended you. I never had a pet before. I wouldn't understand that kind of bond."

His words softened me. I felt my annoyance releasing. "I suppose not then." My brain explored the various questions I still had for him. "You never had a pet ... maybe I can explain the bond in another way. Are you married, or do you have a girlfriend?"

"No. I don't have either ... never had either."

My eyes widened ever so slightly. He's never had a girlfriend. He's never had a relationship? How? Maybe he wasn't straight. The thought worried me.

"Oh, well, never mind then. Do you have any brothers?"

"Yes, I have a younger brother."

"Okay, well a pet bond is sorta like a brotherly bond. Pets are a part of your family. They fill your heart."

He shrugged his shoulders. "I don't really have that kind of bond with my brother. We don't get along."

"Oh, I'm sorry to hear. May I ask why?"

"Umm," he hesitated. "A power struggle, you could say. A bit of jealousy and anger involved. We still fight a lot despite being older now."

"How old is he?" I questioned.

"He's twenty." Ty seemed pained by the topic. He held his head a little low, and his eyes focused on the dirt.

"Oh, so a young adult now. Give him more time. He's your brother. I'm sure he'll come around."

"Do you have any siblings?" he questioned.

"No, I wish I did." I could sense a *then you wouldn't understand* comment coming, but he didn't say anything. Instead, he messed with his fingers, picking at his nails. "I get the vibe you're more of a loner at heart," I said. The thought saddened me.

"Why do you say that?"

"You have never been in a relationship. Your profession is artistry. You went off into the woods to be even more alone –"

He cut me off. "Well, so did you."

"Yeah, but I have been in a few relationships. I work as a nurse, which is very people oriented. Do you have any friends?"

"I am more outgoing than it seems. With my lifestyle I just don't meet many new people."

I could tell he was talking more to himself than to me. My next question escaped my mouth without thinking. "Are you straight or gay?" His jaw dropped ever so slightly before he laughed, likely at my horrified expression. I couldn't believe I asked that. "You don't have to answer that." My face flushed.

"It's okay. I'm straight. And you?" His gorgeous smile was overwhelming.

"Same." I chuckled at his composure. It pleased me to see him so full of life. At least I gained something from that uncalled-for question. I could allow myself the hope of getting emotionally closer to him. Perhaps that was psychologically dangerous. He may not have wanted a relationship and I may not have fit his preferred type, assuming he had one. "Sorry, that question was uncalled for."

"It's fine. I don't mind." The smile remained on his handsome face, his light beard still oddly just as perfect as when I first found him. I contemplated my earlier thoughts, wondering again about the holes in his story.

"Ty, where's your gear? Maybe I can locate it. Do you have a satellite phone?"

His smile disappeared. "Uh ... I'm not sure."

I felt he was lying. "You don't recall where you dropped everything?"

"I was running for a while, trying to escape the wolf. I dropped everything so I could run faster."

That did make sense. "Oh, okay. I was hoping I could look for your things and maybe use your gear to call for help." Realizing I had yet to set new snares, I ended the conversation there. "I'm going to gather more firewood and set more snares nearby. I'll be back shortly."

When I offered him the canister of water, he took it without another word. As I got up, Bennie rushed over to my feet, eager not to be left behind again. I scooped him up and gathered my snares before leaving Ty.

As I set the snares in the brush, my thoughts raced repetitively through our recent conversation. From the information about his relationships – or lack thereof – to the topic of his sexuality, I felt oddly pleased with the new intel.

A hawk flew overhead while I collected dry wood, circling us until she landed in a nearby tree. Bennie seemed to have sensed the predator and burrowed into my hair. So many wild animals had been noticing him, but despite the dangers, he was a smart rat with good instincts. I heard him sneeze several times while I worked.

Appearing tired from the day, Ty greeted me when I returned to the cave. My wristwatch read four in the afternoon. Time had raced away.

"Hey," he said, welcoming me.

"Are you feeling okay? You look tired."

"Yeah, I'm getting drowsy." He yawned, stretching his good leg and spreading his toes.

When the wood was set down, I wanted to check his leg again. I searched his leg brace, peeking under my wrapped jacket. The circulation of his leg looked good and the bone was setting well considering the circumstances. Even with rapid healing, it would be at least another seven days before he'd be able to stand. A selfish feeling swept me. I didn't want him to heal *too* fast. What would happen when we return to the reality of the world? I might never see him again. No, we'd probably keep in touch. The thought brought my next question to mind. "Do you own a cell phone?"

He looked at my face. "No. Not much use for one. Lack of relations and all."

I was a bit bummed, feeling my heart sink. Why did I feel anxious to stay with him? It was unrealistic and premature. "Was just wondering how nomadic you really are." I managed a playful smile.

His face returned a smile, allowing my heart to rise back up. I felt my stomach flutter. These butterflies were getting annoying. I wondered if he also felt the igniting chemistry. I had never experienced it before.

"What is it like, being a nurse and all?"

I was pleased he asked. "Well, it's a hard job. You often feel overworked and undervalued. You're not a doctor, but you feel responsible for the people you help. The coworker drama is a bit of entertainment. Always who is fooling around with who, and who had an affair with who. Your business never stays your business. The doctors can also be very arrogant. Sometimes, I wish I entered a different field, but helping people makes it all worth it. My job gives me a purpose greater than myself." I studied his face, watching him process what I said. "What about you? Why wood carving?"

"I just like it. I make decent pay and it's enough to live well. I like my simple lifestyle. I sell the carvings in our family shop. My father taught me how to woodwork with the chainsaw."

"That's really nice. I'm wondering ... have you completed any schooling?"

"Yeah, I graduated high school. I never tried college. I knew it wasn't for me."

"Maybe you had the right idea. I'm still dealing with student loans," I sighed with a coy smile.

"That's one of the reasons I decided against it," he said.

"Understandable."

He yawned, moving his hand to cover his mouth. The forest was draining our energy – the surrounding evergreens made me feel like a minuscule needle in a massive green, autumn-licked haystack. The chill of the wilderness and the bug bites on my arms scarcely distracted me from the looming wait for help. Getting him to safety was all that mattered when it came down to it. Not me or my feelings, not keeping him with me.

"Do you regret it? The journey out here. Do you regret it?" he asked.

"No. How could I?"

He looked down at the dirt as he propped himself on his arm and leaned toward me. I watched his frown deepen. "You could die out here because of me."

Such a sudden dark thought. "Why do you say that? I think we are doing well. I made this trip knowing the dangers. ... When I found you, before you awoke, I managed to call for help with my satellite phone. They know we are out here." His expression remained the same. "Ty, why do you feel so worried?"

He breathed in deeply and exhaled an unsteady breath. "I just worry about the wild animals. That wolf has me on edge after what happened. I would hate to have something happen to you because of me."

I smiled softly at him. "I'll be fine. We will get out of here. I promise." It was a promise I was determined to keep. I would have been distraught all over again if I failed to save him. He depended on me. I had left my father to die in these woods and I'd rather die than leave Ty behind.

"Part of me wishes I never left home, but then I wouldn't have met you," he said.

My heart skipped a few beats. Was he flirting? I couldn't quite tell. Maybe he was just being nice. My brain twisted. I wanted to say something in reply, but my mouth wouldn't open. My heart moved up and down in my chest with the inner struggle of back-and-forth thought. He was flirting. No, just being nice! Say something back.

"Uh, yeah I feel the same." Oh jeez. "I just mean, it's nice that we crossed paths despite the circumstances." I smiled with a twitch in my lip.

He returned a soft smile, but I could sense the stress in his posture. "What's your favorite color?" he asked.

"The color question, really?" I grinned, wrapping my arms around his curiosity. It was such a simple question. For some reason, knowing someone's favorite color is a part of just *knowing* someone. His patient blue eyes reminded me to answer. "It's blue. Not a pale blue like the sky, a deeper blue, like your eyes. Certain shades of blue appeal to me more. Royal blue is one of my favorites. What's yours?" I expected him to say a common color like red or green.

"That rhymed. It's golden-light brown, like polished butternut wood ... or your hair."

My heart fluttered. I felt my cheeks blush. "That's very specific."

"I suppose. Working with wood, you learn to appreciate the colors. I enjoy seeing them elsewhere."

"I can't say the same about my profession. Blood, disinfectant, and fecal matter are hardly worth appreciating."

He laughed loudly, shaking his head at the visual.

"Shhh, you'll scare the wildlife away from the traps." I was serious, but my playful laughter made me hard to take seriously. He had a nice laugh - one I could get used to.

"Sorry, that was pretty funny." He ran his free hand through his hair.

"I suspect you are a movie person. What's your favorite film?" I asked him.

His smile dropped. "Uh, I don't really have one. I don't have the time or keep the tech for films."

I raised, then narrowed, my eyebrows. "You live under a rock."

"Sounds like me." The playfulness in his tone had disappeared and his eyes lowered.

I might have offended him. "It's not a bad thing. It's just ... you're so different from other people I know. You're independent. You make your own path. You distance yourself from society. It's a really unencumbered lifestyle."

"I guess so. But I *am* close with most of my family and family friends. It's how I was raised."

"Oh. Well that's good. Do your parents live around here?"

"Yeah, they live near me. What about your family?" he questioned.

"My mother is in my life. She can be a bit overbearing, but I couldn't imagine life without her. She's my only family."

"What's her name?"

"Elena. She's a nice person. Just stay off her bad side."

He smirked. "I intend to." I watched his left eye wink.

My eyes widened. I'm sure he noticed. Did he intend on meeting my mother? "You want to meet her?" The surprise in my voice was obvious.

"Yeah, I will likely meet her. After all this, I expect we'll stay in touch."

My heart skipped. If he thinks he'd ever meet her, maybe he is also hoping for a relationship with me. To meet her, he'd need to be around me a lot.

"Do you want to stay in touch?" he asked when I failed to comment.

"Yes, I'd like that." I softly smiled. I could feel the blush on my face.

"Good. I'm glad." He then shifted his leg. "Ouch! ... Crap." His face tensed under the pain.

"You okay?" I moved closer to his side to check the brace.

"Yeah, still some pain when I move."

"It's early yet. You have a lot of healing left to do, but your body is recovering well, faster than I expected. Try not to move."

He nodded and sighed heavily. With his sigh, I watched his chest rise and retract. "I hate not being able to move around."

"I know how that feels. I'm gonna go check the snares and feed the fire. It's getting late. Are you hungry yet?"

"Yes, very."

No surprise there. Lunch was light for us both. "I'll be right back." I got up and gathered my gun, then added some wood to the fire before leaving him. Bennie balanced on my shoulder for the walk. The woods felt cold. Not physically, but cold in spirit, like I was being watched by the wind. One of my snares had a squirrel, but the third had a large American mink. I was overjoyed to see it caught for the taking. With these two catches, Ty and I would eat well tonight. In probably less than half an hour, I had returned to the cave.

Ty's eyes fixated on the catch. "Oh wow, is that a mink?"

"Yeah, I'm excited to have it. It will be delicious." I set Bennie down and took my knife from next to him. Slicing the mink down its belly, I threw its organs in the fire. I next removed the pelts and placed the mink over the fire first.

"Where did you learn how to do all of this?" he asked.

"All of what ... hunt and stuff?"

"Yeah."

My head and eyes lowered, and I could feel the frown on my face. "My father taught me everything I know."

"He did a good job teaching you," he said with a soft voice.

I offered him a light smile, but the pain behind it was evident. "Thanks."

"So, is Bennie your only pet?"

"No, I have others. Another rat and a Netherland Dwarf rabbit."

"Why did you bring Bennie with you?"

"It was an accident. The cage door is broken, and this little bugger managed to sneak into my bag. He was after my granola bars. I didn't notice him in there until after the chopper left me."

"Oh, I thought you brought him on purpose."

"No. I wouldn't have purposely brought him along. Although I've loved having his company, this trip has been dangerous for him."

We both fell silent for a long while. Night had descended over the woods. By the time the mink was cooked through by the low flame, my wristwatch read eight o'clock. Ty was mid-yawn when I offered him some meat. We shared the food equally, but he ate much faster than me. My eyes bounced on and off him until he was finished. He tossed the remains in the fire and lay back down into the soil. Bennie also ate quickly, occasionally sneezing during his dining. Full and tired, I finished up with my meal and rinsed my hands in the canister water before grabbing the sleeping bag and joining him on the ground. I purposely lay close to him, stretching the opened sleeping bag over us both like a blanket. Bennie curled up in my bag. The fire kept the cave warm enough for us three to drift into a peaceful sleep.

CHAPTER SEVEN

DESIRES

I had faced the fire, but the vivid memory still invasively unfolded in my dreams.

I was running again. Running faster and faster, falling into a pit of agonizing pain and crippling heartbreak. He needed me to leave, to leave him for the fire to claim. To say goodbye forever.

"Elizabeth, you must keep going. You must survive. You must make it back to Mom. You can't leave her alone."

"Dad, I can't. I can't leave you." Tears poured down my broken face. My heart was in my throat.

"You have to, Elizabeth!" Tears welled in his eyes, but none would fall. His tone shifted sternly. "You cannot die here with me. Your mother needs you."

His battered face blurred through my heavy tears. "Mom needs you too. I need you. I can help you."

"You're not physically strong enough. It's okay. We're running out of time." The blaze was making her way down the sides of the rocky cliff, rushing to take him from me. "You're mentally the strongest person I know. You can and will keep running. You will survive."

I was beside myself, sobbing heavy tears that blurred his face. The physical pain of my broken arm and fractured skull felt numb compared to the pain in my heart.

He lifted my lowered chin with his bloodied hand, smiled at my sobs, and moved forward to kiss my red forehead. "I love you, Elizabeth. Keep going for me. I will always be with you."

I could barely speak through my anguish. "I ... love you too ... Dad." His hand dropped from under my chin as his eyes closed, and he fell limp. "Dad! Dad, please!" I shook him. Desperation set in. "Dad, please wake up!" I could barely breathe through my sobs. I had to leave him to die. My arms wrapped around him for a final hug goodbye when I noticed the silver necklace and locket around his neck. It was the one my mother bought him for their recent anniversary – the one with a photo of us three inside. I struggled trying to unclip it, but my shaking hands and blurred vision wouldn't allow me to take it. As I saw the blaze creeping closer, it took everything left in me to turn away and leave him forever. I forced myself not to look back as I continued to race from the fire.

I awoke to Ty's finger brushing down the side of my face. My back was against his chest, and he was leaning over me, propped on his right arm. Embarrassed, I sat up and wiped the tears from my eyes and cheeks.

"You were crying in your sleep." His expression was soft, the concern evident in his eyebrows.

"I'm fine ... just reliving the worst day of my life in my nightmares." I sighed heavily – both from frustration and the heaviness in my chest.

"You can talk about it ... with me."

He wanted to know about what happened. I wanted to tell him, but I didn't know if I could. "I'll try."

"It's okay if you can't or don't want to."

"No, I want to tell you. Just give me a minute." I did my best to collect myself. Aside from my mom and the police, I had never told anyone about what happened. I was so ashamed of it, knowing it was my fault. He was out in those woods because of me, and I had lived with that knowledge for ten long years.

I took a deep breath. "I was sixteen when I asked my parents to go with me on one last camping trip close to this time of year. My father agreed to go. A powerful forest fire swept us one week into our trip. It chased us to a cliff, and we were forced to jump or be torched alive." I paused, trying not to cry. I took another deep, shaky breath and exhaled. "At the bottom, we landed maybe twenty feet apart. I had a fractured skull, a broken arm, and many lacerations. I was still able to walk, but when I found him, his leg was snapped and he was bleeding out. The fire was making its way down the cliff when I was forced to say goodbye to him."

I started to cry in front of Ty. Tears flowed despite every attempt I made to collect myself. He sat up and moved in to hug me, and I accepted his embrace. "It's my fault he's gone. I will never be able to forgive myself."

"I'm sure you've been told this before, but it's not your fault. You had no way of knowing what would happen."

Even though his words changed nothing, hearing them from him made me feel a bit better, helping lift the heavy blame, even slightly, I carried on my shoulders. I cried in his arms for a while longer before finally letting his embrace go. He pulled away in response and leaned back, placing his arms behind him. I was able to gather myself, wiping my eyes as I steadied my breath.

"That's the reason I went on this journey. It was a memorial for what happened to my father almost exactly this time of year, ten years ago. I needed to soul-search, to face the nightmares I still live with, and to forgive the fire and the forest, if not myself. The team that helped save me explained it was the first fire in those woods in a long time. A volunteer team tried to locate his remains but came up empty. He's still out here. ... I was hospitalized for months to treat my physical and mental injuries. I've suffered with PTSD for a long time, and I've only recently been able to tolerate being around fire, but its presence still stresses me." I managed to stop crying, but my sinking chest kept the tears pooling in my eyes.

"Although I haven't met too many people in my life, you're the strongest of them all." He gave me a soft smile full of sympathy.

"That means more to me than you could know," I returned with a pained smile.

My watch read ten minutes past six. The eastern sky was lightening, the sun soon to emerge, and the rough wind made the changing leaves and loose pine needles dance off the trees. I felt cold, which meant Ty probably did, too. After adding more wood to the fire, I left the cave to stretch my legs. Without looking back at Tyler, I ventured off for a long walk through the nearly untouched wilderness. I needed time to clear my head. I had been walking south for twenty minutes before I realized I had forgotten my gun, although I had a small knife in my lower pants pocket.

I ventured to a huge pine and sat at its base, feeling dizzy, my brain spinning and my eyes blurring. Putting my head between my knees helped, but the painful memories still swirled. Tyler was very understanding, but he couldn't stop my pain. It would always be there.

As my head began to clear and my thoughts refocus, I heard sticks and brush rustle in the near distance. My head snapped up in its direction. My eyes blurred, unsure of what they were seeing. I managed to focus on a large black bear that stalked me through the trees. I could see she had large scars on her face, looked underweight for the time of year, and walked with a heavy limp.

Scrambling to my only weapon, I pulled my knife, simultaneously thinking of ways to kill her, but my pitiful blade felt smaller than I remembered. I kept my eyes on hers, feeling her body language and expression. I heard her growls, deep in her throat. Her soul felt hungry and desperate. To my horror, she charged toward me. The passing seconds slowed as my adrenaline forced my brain into survival mode, the same mode that pulled me from my father's side. I sprung up and rushed to climb the large tree behind me. My heart pounded into my rib cage while I scaled the branches. When my body allowed me a look down, she stood at the tree's base staring up at me. My eyes met hers. She lifted her nose, sniffing the air. I watched her stretch her frame up and then weave her way up the dense branches, grunting as she moved. My hands grabbed each limb firmly, rushing farther up as fast as I could scramble.

If she killed me, Ty would surely die.

I climbed as high as I could with the bear following close behind – her breath heavy as she heaved upward. The branches became so thin and underdeveloped that I could hear the wood's core cracking from the pressure of my weight. She vocalized her frustration as I remained just out of her reach. I eyed a nearby tree, questioning whether I could make the jump. She reached her paw to me and swiped her claws into my shin.

"Ouch, shit!"

I kicked at her face, throwing my boots carefully around her huge skull. Sap glued to my fingers as I intensely grasped the branches. How could I get out of this alive? Before I could figure out what to do, the limb holding most of her weight snapped. She growled and roared, struggling to catch herself with her malnourished limbs as she fell through the branches. After her body snapped through most and smashed against others, she landed with a deafening thud on the ground – a thud that radiated up the tree and echoed into my fingers. I held my breath waiting for her to move, but she lay lifeless. Shock riddled my veins and I began to feel dizzy again. The tree was shifting through my daze. I struggled to cling on, working to calm myself with careful breathing, in through my nose and out through my mouth.

When the dizziness subsided, I started to climb down. The damaged and missing branches made it far more difficult. I jumped down next to her still body, feeling the pain in my shin. I looked at her dull pelt, her scrapes and scars. She was starving to death from what seemed like an old injury. I couldn't help but feel sorry for her despite her attack. Without looking at my leg, I rushed back toward the cave, my stride proving wobbly under my exhaustion and emotion.

Ty was twenty feet out of the cave when I approached, still running. "Ty!" I took him off guard. Balancing on his good leg, he lost his footing and fell onto his backside.

"Ouch! Shit. Elizabeth. You scared me half to death," he hissed.

"Sorry. What ... are you doing?" I said, walking up to him while catching my breath.

"I left for a bathroom break and was going back." He then noticed my disheveled appearance: hair full of pine needles, hands covered in sap, torn pants. "What happened to you?"

"A black bear attacked me. She chased me up a tree."

His eyes widened. "Are you okay?" He struggled to stand, using the tree next to him to pull himself upward. I watched in mild amusement as he struggled.

"Yes, I think so. Just my shin is hurt. Before I look at it, let me help you back."

"But -"

"Ty, hush."

Once in the cave again, I started by rinsing my hands using some of the canister water. I ignored my stomach as it finally rumbled for breakfast. Bennie slept nearby as Ty started to pull the four-inch needles from my hair. He was tenderly gentle, taking his time to remove them. I waited patiently for him to get them out.

"Did you kill it?" he questioned.

"Sorta. In the tree, the branch snapped, and she fell to her death."

"The longer we're out here, the longer I keep you in danger. You should just leave me." His words were laced with guilt, and I could hear the lump in his throat.

I turned myself around to face him. "Don't be ridiculous. I couldn't live with myself if I left you here. I can barely live with myself after leaving my father to die. This time, I have a choice. Besides, I *chose* to be out here in the first place. Please don't push me away." My head lowered.

He placed his finger under my chin and lifted my eyes to his. "Then don't put yourself in unnecessary danger." With a light smile on his face, his hand moved to tuck my hair behind my left ear. I blushed as he leaned in closer. The sparks in my heart and the butterflies in my stomach danced as I leaned toward him. His breath within my own, my lips were inches from his when a buzzing noise hit the cave. We both broke toward it, confusion sweeping the lust from us.

"What is that?" I asked. We continued to listen as the buzzing turned into a chopping sound, the unmistakable sound of a helicopter. "It's a chopper!"

I rushed out of the cave toward direction of the sound. Ignoring the sting of the brush smacking my injured shin, I ran as fast as I could. High ground, I needed high ground. Panic set in when I started to see the red chopper's paint through the treetops. It was close, and I was swallowed by the forest. In desperation, I screamed over the engine's roar.

"I'm over here! We are down here!" I jumped in the air repeatedly - arms waving as hard as I could swing them overhead and down - so hard I felt they might detach from my shoulders. "Over here! Please! We are here!"

But the chopper flew by without breaking its pace.

I stopped moving while my watering eyes watched help vanish from sight. Anger, pure frustration, consumed me until I couldn't bear it. At the top of my lungs, I screamed my favorite profanity until I fell to my knees in defeat.

"Elizabeth!" Ty shouted my name several times before I got up, sulking my way back to him.

When I approached the cave, Bennie was standing at the edge near the fire and Ty was staring out at me. My leg throbbed as I joined them both.

"Let's have a look at that leg." He moved closer and then pulled my ripped pants up to below my knee. I winced, afraid to look down. "It doesn't look too bad. Mostly bruised with some shallow cuts."

When I looked, I could see that his description was accurate. It could have been much worse. I grabbed the first aid kit, but he took it from me. "My turn to help you."

His wide smile transformed his perfect face as he opened the kit and used the hand sanitizer. He then took the antibiotic spray and used it on my wound. I pretended not to feel the intense sting, but I sensed he could see past my lame poker face. "I'll let that air dry before wrapping it."

"Thank you."

"You're welcome. So, how big was this bear?" His smile remained.

I sensed he was trying to distract me from my failure to flag down the chopper.

"She was an older adult with an old injury, starving, based on her body condition."

"That's probably why she attacked. Black bears normally wouldn't mess with a human unless cubs are involved."

"I feel sorry for her."

"Yeah, that's pretty sad. I wonder how she was injured," he replied.

I raised an eyebrow, surprised by his agreement.

Ty's distraction worked. The loss of the chopper was slipping to the back of my mind. A sudden growl in my stomach pulled my attention. "Are you hungry?" I looked down at my watch.

"Yes, I didn't want to eat the squirrel without your permission," he said.

I had forgotten we had that. It was staked inside the cave. "Oh, you can have it. You don't need to ask."

I was no stranger to hunger. When I left my father to die in the woods, I wandered lost through the wilderness for ten days without eating. I was so sick to my stomach over what happened, I couldn't keep anything but water down despite finding plenty of edible plants. Shortly after I was rescued, my mother called me a bag of broken bones. I nearly threw a book at her head.

"We can share. I can hear your stomach. But first, let me finish bandaging you." The spray had dried. He took the gauze and wrapped my wound. Using medical tape, he affixed the gauze to my leg. When he was finished, he pulled my pants leg down over it and placed the kit to the side.

"Bennie, come here." He was wrapped in a ball beside the fire. I grew concerned when he didn't respond. "Bennie?" I shifted over to him, placing my hand on his fur, and he jolted awake. "Hey, boy. Are you okay?" He looked up at me, the light in his eyes dull, the color in his paws pale. He shivered and crackled out a cough and sneeze, the unmistakable symptoms of a respiratory infection. "Oh God, no." I picked him up and kept him close to the fire. He was cold and weak. My eyes watered. How could I have let this happen?

"Is he okay?" Ty questioned.

"No, he's sick. It's too cold out here for him." Ty watched me ponder how I could help Bennie, but my mind drew a blank. I had no more antibiotics, no way to treat his illness. "Ty, hand me the squirrel." He reached for the staked carcass and handed me the meat. With my knife, I cut a piece and offered it to Bennie. My stomach sank when he rejected the food. If he wouldn't eat, he couldn't make it out of these woods. Taking the sleeping bag, I placed it close to the fire and wrapped him within the material. He welcomed the new resting place. With no other ways to help him, I shifted my attention to feeding myself. Dividing the meat equally, I offered Ty his share. I sensed his reluctance when he took it. "Something wrong?"

"No," he replied with his deep voice.

I started to eat. The rough morning had left me famished. When I looked back at him, he quickly removed his eyes from me while he finished eating. "I need to get more water and food. You'll watch over him, right?"

He nodded. "Of course. Be careful out there."

"I'll try." With that, I gathered my things and stood outside the cave. My joints felt out of place, angry at the bare ground. I stretched my arms and spine, reaching for the sky's cloudless blue.

"Wait," Ty commanded. I turned around to look at him. "Can you wash my shirt?"

It was obvious why he wanted me to. The sweat stains and dried blood that encrusted what remained of the battered fabric couldn't have been comfortable.

"Yeah, sure." It didn't immediately dawn on me that for me to wash it, he'd be removing it. *Duh.* I watched him carefully lift his shirt over his head. My eyes widened ever so slightly. He had perfect pecs and well-defined ab muscles. The scars forming from his stitched wounds created trails of dried blood that flowed down his side and chest. Old faint scars marked him in a few areas.

I gawked a little but quickly felt sorry for him. With no way to bathe, he looked pitifully bloodied and battered. I'm sure he felt as dirty as he looked. I had to re-enter the cave to clean him up. Using his shirt, I emptied what remained in the water canister onto the dingy white fabric. When I sat next to him, he looked down at my hand as I placed it on his lower chest. I rubbed the shirt over his body, trailing his muscles. A more tantalizing butterfly fluttered within, low and heavy, as I wiped the blood away from his chest, his side, and around his healing wounds. His breathing deepened, particularly when I looked up at him. Those intense blue eyes met mine. He then looked down at my lips. I could feel the burn grow low inside me, a burn that had started with a spark shortly after we met. With his breath tangled in mine, I looked at his mouth as I moved closer. My stomach turned to knots when our lips met, the burn now a fire. I led his lips around mine as our breathing shortened. My arms wrapped around his head, my fingers into his deep black hair. I couldn't believe this was happening. My passion for him was something I had never felt with anyone before. It was likely infatuation and therefore terrifying, but irretrievably my reality. How could something this amazing between two people ever end? With that passing thought, he pulled away from me. My arms retreated as he steadied his breath.

"Sorry." I wasn't sure why I felt the need to apologize. Did I go too far? I rubbed my arm.

"It's okay. I just ..."

"I overwhelmed you, didn't I?" It was a rhetorical question, but the intense lace of self-doubt under my words could have choked a llama.

"It was my first kiss, that's all."

My jaw dropped. His first kiss? Seriously? "You're joking. You never kissed anyone?"

"Not like that. Never met anyone I liked enough before," he said.

My heart skipped a beat. He really did like me. "Well ... you're a natural." I watched him brush his thumb and index finger over his bottom lip. I picked up the damp shirt from his thigh and continued to clean his chest. Doing my best to control my desires, I wiped him as clean as possible. "Lift your arm." He complied. One at a time, I wiped the dried sweat from his underarms. His light smile expressed unspoken gratitude. "I'll wash this when I reach the lake. Watch over Bennie." I checked him within the sleeping bag. He remained as he was, lifting his weak head to look at me. I sighed in my worry.

CHAPTER EIGHT

WOODED SORROWS

The woods were eerily quiet. I followed my trail back to the lake while I set snares. Only the forest wind spoke to me, the heavy breeze whipping my hair around its invisible strength. The pine needles and freshly fallen leaves crunched under my boots while the sun tried to warm me, but I wasn't easily reached from the shadows.

The lake seemed smaller today. After drinking my water intake, I washed Ty's shirt in the water, doing my best not to stir up dirt. Blood stubbornly seeped from the sad fabric. With it lying on a low branch to dry, I filled the canister before trying my luck at fishing again. I let my thoughts wander around the past few days. The chopper had yet to circle back. Even if it did, it would still be impossible to flag down. The bear was a bit traumatizing, but I came out relatively unscathed. Bennie was sick. It was an uncomfortable fact, but I held onto hope. With any luck, Ty would be able to walk on that leg in a few weeks. I could help him make the hike back to town. It's already Wednesday, too soon to move him in the attempt of catching Friday's return helicopter. We'd never make it there in time. It was depressing to think about, so my thoughts shifted to a more enjoyable recent memory.

That kiss was incredible. I believed his claim of being inexperienced; I could tell when I led him in the movements, but to be his first – that was hard to believe. He was twenty-three but had never kissed anyone. How could anyone that beautiful go through life for so long without at least kissing another person?

A bite on my line pulled me from my contemplation. It was a strong jerk, but with a few pulls, I quickly brought it to land. The flapping ten-inch fish was a species I didn't recognize, with a silver body covered in vivid scales and featuring devil-red eyes. I found a rock nearby and hit its head, producing an unpleasant crunch that made me wince. I wrapped the dead fish in my bag and set my line again.

At the water's edge, the sun was keeping me warm, but the breeze soon brought in clouds that swallowed the rays. I began to shiver, my shirt too thin to hold enough heat. I endured it, knowing I'd be warm next to Ty soon. My wristwatch read just past three in the afternoon.

A large spider balanced herself on a cattail leaf just above the water's edge. She had webbing throughout the plant and seemed to feed herself well with the remaining insects. With the frost approaching soon, she'd be gone by next month. As her sparkling black body captivated my attention, a piercing howl erupted from the forest. I jumped from my skin. The source of this howl was extremely close. Now standing at the water's edge, my eyes darted through the woods. The hairs on my neck rose as my body tensed with the thought of how close he was. I gathered up my things and Ty's half-dried shirt, then ran back through the trail. With my stride, I reached the first snare quickly. It was empty. I gathered it before running off. Memories of how I raced through the woods being chased by an engulfing fire burned my vision. The fire was everywhere, swallowing trees, animals, and air. An elixir of blood consumed the wilderness. *No!* I couldn't breathe. Before I could reach the second snare, I fell to my knees with my palms in the dirt. Dizziness twisted my brain, spinning the trees around me.

In my vulnerability, I felt my heart thudding against my chest as my eyes observed the dirt my hands rested upon. Breathing in and out, I took control of my evasive thoughts, shifting them to the wolf – an animal with massive size, raised hackles, and aggressive eyes. He could attack, yet I was helplessly planted in the dirt. A heat of anger swarmed through me. Knock it off! I screamed internally. In my temper, I pulled myself from the ground and started running again, quickly reaching the second empty trap. When I reached the third, I found another large mink had been snared, and I scrambled to get its lifeless body in my bag. With the snare stuck around some branches, I yanked it free, tumbling backward.

When I reached the cave, I was in a panic.

"Ty! Tyler!" I didn't see him as I came around, stumbling down to the entrance. Focusing my vision, I saw him sitting at the very back of the cave with a knife in hand.

"Liz, I'm okay," he said with nervous eyes.

Dropping my things, I joined him within the cave, explained my flight, and handed Ty his shirt. I then pulled my gun from my hip, holding it to my side as I scanned the trees.

"I doubt he'll attack now. He's alone and we'll see him coming," Ty explained.

"How do you know he's alone?" I asked while pulling Bennie's bag deeper into the cave.

"No howls answered him."

Ty put on his shirt. My throat felt narrow, my mouth dry. I checked Bennie while we sat in silence. He remained as he was, snuggled in the fabric. He had since chewed some new holes in the liner, giving me more hope. As the hours passed, darkness started to claim the landscape. Before dark, I had to get more wood, but I was afraid. Despite my discomfort, we needed the heat, and the fire would also provide crucial lighting.

"I have to get more wood."

"Okay, please be careful," he said.

I nodded to him and then exited, starting my search. The shadows of the trees had me on edge, but to carry wood, my gun needed to remain on my hip. I pushed myself through the brush, finding mostly large sticks – some of which scratched my skin. The larger pieces I found had started rotting and were full of insects under the bark, which crawled onto my arms, making my skin tickle. Trying not to drop my gatherings, my teeth gritted as a centipede crept onto my wrist, wriggling up my limb. I felt the tickle of its assault while struggling to shake it off. *Blah!*

Back at the cave, Ty was holding Bennie. I dropped the wood and entered.

"He doesn't look so good," Ty said as I moved over to them.

"Oh, no."

Bennie was weak in Ty's hands. My heart dropped, witnessing his labored breaths. The light in his eyes was leaving. I felt so help-less, so useless – I couldn't stop myself from crying. Even the color of his fur looked bleak in the light of the dying fire. I took him into my hands, knowing he was running out of time. I had to say goodbye. My heart throbbed up and down, aching my core.

I barely noticed Ty's struggle to add wood to the fire and despite his discomfort with the task, he remained quiet as I mourned.

While the fire crackled and the sounds of night echoed, I watched my beloved companion take his last breath in my arms – a final gasp that ended his fight. Bennie had fallen into his peaceful forever-sleep. I sobbed over his lifeless body, petting his beautiful blue fur. I felt so sorry, so sorry for letting this happen, for not being more responsible. The guilt was overwhelming.

"It's not your fault," Ty said.

But it *was* my fault. I failed to keep my pet safe. Watching the embers glow through my tears, I reflected on Bennie's short life. I thought about burying him, knowing I couldn't bring myself to cre-mate him in the fire. Just outside the cave I placed his body down and started to dig a hole with my hands. Ty watched my tears fall into the growing cavity. With my slow movement, by the time I had made enough progress, Ty had fallen asleep. I kissed Bennie goodbye before placing him into the earth with my dirty fingers.

"I'm sorry," I whispered as I filled in the hole over him. Tears fell even harder, but I did my best to keep quiet.

The night was soft and brisk, and I used some of the canister water to wash my hands. Midnight approached while I fed the fire and watched Ty sleep. He was so peaceful. Watching his soft face resting in a deep sleep helped me come to terms with the loss of my furry companion. Tyler was a welcome distraction. His fingers twitched occasionally, and he seemed warm despite being farther from the fire. The insects were quieter, and even the wind made no appearance. It was as if the world had stopped for me. Losing pets to age had always been difficult, but to lose one in an accident, or accidental carelessness - if there was such a thing - was worse. I hated feeling guilty; I was all too familiar with it.

I realized we had both skipped dinner despite having food available. With my catches hardened and my failure to gut them, the meat had become inedible.

I startled when Ty turned over. He shifted awake from the pain in his leg, those blue eyes still startling in the dim fire's light. "You're still up?" he questioned.

"I doubt I'd be able to sleep."

"Come lie with me," he said. Ty had a way with distraction. My heavy eyes and cold frame couldn't resist his invitation, so I crawled over to him, turning my back to his chest. Lying beside him with my head on his arm, I could feel his breath on me. A faint smell of blood still emanated from his jean-shorts. He wrapped his right arm around my waist and held me close, his embrace calming my pained heart, letting me feel secure. I was nearly asleep when Ty spoke. "Have you ever felt burdened, like with a certain obligation expected of you?"

My groggy brain struggled to process the question. Why did he bring this up now? "Sorta. I was pushed to go to college and get perfect grades. It was expected of me. But that's all ... why do you ask?"

"Just wondering."

"Something on your mind?"

"Yes, but don't worry about it. It's complicated family stuff," he replied.

"You're sure you don't want to talk about it? I'm a good listener."

He pressed his lips to the back of my head. "I don't doubt that for a second. It's just a lot to explain. It's a part of my life that gets pretty crazy. My family and our culture are unique compared to the average American ... I will tell you all about it soon. Get some sleep."

Fighting my heavy eyes was difficult, so I said nothing more. His body was comforting, like the sun's warmth. I fell fast asleep.

CHAPTER NINE

EXPECTING WEATHER

Wolves danced around my eyes in a forest of white birch, but the white was neither stripped trees nor snow, it was the ashes of a burnt forest filled with the corpses of charred animals and trees. A large gray male was running through the cinders, chasing down something fleeing. The creature he chased – panicked in a hopeless fight for life – ran through the white birch, kicking up the dust of the dead as the sun fell and dark of night arrived. But before he caught his prey, the heavens poured down a thick saliva-like rain that swallowed up the ashes of the departed. He reached the hindquarters of the galloping animal, only to snap his jaws on her ankle – for she was not a deer, but a fleeing being of terror. She was trapped in his mouth, a set of teeth sharper than razors. She was *me* in an endless forest of endeavor. A howl of frustration seared the damaged landscape with his vengeance.

My eyes opened slowly. The dream had me twisted inside. Despite it, I felt rested. Ty slept with his arm still around my waist. His position caused him to snore ever so slightly. Perhaps that triggered my odd dream, or more likely yesterday's events were messing with me. When I tried to shift his arm off me, he awoke. Wincing from pain, he stretched his arms and flexed before bringing his hand to his neck.

"Ow," he said as he rubbed himself, propped into his favorite position.

"What's wrong?" I sat next to him with my legs in a pretzel.

"Slept in a bad position. My neck is sore and stiff." He continued to rub himself.

"Do you want me to massage you?"

"Yeah, that'd be great." He smiled at me – a smile I quickly returned. Moving behind him, I positioned my hands on his trap muscles at the base of his neck. As I rubbed upward in a circular motion, he moaned deep in his throat with appreciation. "That ... feels ... amazing."

"Glad you think so." A light laugh escaped me. Feeling his muscles sent unwelcome urges to my groin. I had the uncomfortable urge to bite his beautiful neck.

"Where'd you learn to rub muscles like this?" he asked.

"Self-taught." After twenty minutes my hands ached, and our stomachs complained. It had been a while since we last ate. The spoiled meat of my last catch would attract predators, and I needed to dispose of it soon.

Looking outside, the forest was a cloudy shade of gray. Fog filled the tree line and the sky looked displeased. Ty thanked me when I had finished rubbing his neck. Looking down at my wristwatch, I read one in the morning. That couldn't be right. I looked closer and could see the minute hand wasn't moving. Damn! The battery must have died. Although it wasn't a real problem, it was inconvenient. I did my best not to look at the disturbed soil near the cave's entrance where Bennie's body rested. My heart ached like my stomach and sore hands. To distract myself, I checked Ty's wounds. His leg looked great and his cuts were healing incredibly fast. Mesmerized, I stared at the stitching he no longer needed.

"Are those ready to come out?" Ty asked.

"Yes, overdue even. I'm surprised at how quick they healed."

"I heal fast. My whole family does."

I nodded in fascination. With quick work, I used my scissors to remove them. Scars were already forming. With nothing for breakfast, we drank a lot of canister water. I then worked to salvage what was left of our dying fire. It took a while to restart. Ty dragged himself nearby to watch me work it back into a low burn. I'd need to gather more wood today. My back ached from the cold ground, causing me to crave my soft warm bed. I missed my pets, friends, and mom. I could have killed for a warm cup of coffee. It had to be around fifty degrees this morning. Without a jacket, it was brisk, but I still functioned through movement, the fire nearby, or Ty's warm arms. My thoughts deepened. Perhaps all the above.

Looking out of the cave, I could see that the sky indicated bad weather soon. While avoiding thoughts of Bennie, I tossed the bad mink into the fire.

"I'm heading out. Do you need anything?" I asked.

"No. Just food if you can find any more meat."

"Are plants out of the question? They are easier to catch." I smirked at him.

"I can't stomach forest veggies," he said.

"Not sure how lucky I'll be today with catches."

"The wind shifted. The weather is turning."

"I noticed, but I can't tell when it will arrive," I said. I looked up at the sky again.

"I'll bet tomorrow by the smell," he guessed.

"I'll move quickly. See you later." I gave him a half-smile before gathering up my things and leaving for the day.

I brought my bag along with me this time as the odor of fish in the fabric had become intense. Despite traveling the path to the lake various times before, I found my previous trail difficult to identify. There were other marks in the trees surrounding those I'd made, fresh marks I had not noticed before. Perhaps a bear had smelled my presence around the trees and made some scent marks of his own, but the marks were horizontal. I strategically placed my snares as I moved. When I reached the lake, it looked even more pathetic than yesterday. At the water's edge, I found myself looking back through the trees toward where the wolf had howled so close to me. My body shivered, not from the cold or even the fog-saturated brush, but from the animal's eerie song that had started to disturb my already plagued dreams.

I opted out of fishing today, instead searching for edible plants near the lake. With my water canister full again, I began scoping the area as I trekked. While walking around to the other side of the lake – the side I had yet to explore – I spotted some sweet flag plants. I wasn't entirely sure they would be suitable for consumption, but my hunger convinced me to collect them. From what I understood, the roots were edible raw but were best cooked. Using the water to wash the roots, I removed them from the stalks and placed them in my bag. The cold water and lack of sun made me lose enough body heat to shiver, a painful tremor I couldn't throw. My entire body trembled lightly in the hope of warming itself. I had to move faster not only for the sake of time but for the sake of my health.

Moving away from the water, I used my compass to head farther away from Ty. Along the way, I found miner's lettuce and speedwell, both of which had edible vitamin-rich leaves and stems. They'd make a suitable ingredient in the meaty soup I hoped to prepare. Soup with greens and water stretched any valuable protein caught. I remained wary while I moved, careful to listen for the sounds around me. My gun was in my bag – not the best way to carry it. I discovered silverweed and wild ginger next; the leaves of silverweed

LUNAR BLUE

could be eaten raw, but the roots were great for soup cooking. I gathered the entire plant – with a struggle to pull it from the dry, tough soil – nearly falling backward.

While I continued my search, the ache in my heart festered. I found myself visualizing Bennie running through the brush and feeling his weight on my shoulder. Silent tears trailed my cheeks before I realized their presence. I was glad to be away from Ty. I could mourn to the extent I needed with only the forest to hear my sobs. My walk slowed through the trees while I let myself go. This emotional breakdown wasn't just from losing Bennie. I was finally homesick and felt emotionally exhausted. Maybe that made me weak. I didn't care.

I took the time to prop myself against a tree. My growling stomach couldn't have been helping my emotions. The speedwell plant leaves were my meal, the crisp crunch of the stalks and slight peppered taste feeling incredible going down. When you were this hungry, everything tasted delicious. My emotions settled while I watched for birds flying overhead, but there wasn't a single bird around, which felt strange. None could be heard, neither their wings nor song. My father used to say that the first sign of trouble could be found with the birds.

My throat felt tight. I pulled my gun from my bag and wrapped the holster around my waist. I hoped the birds were simply missing because of the impending weather. The clouds were now an intense angry gray. With the stormy sky overhead, I had to hurry about for more food. My stride nearly a jog, I darted around for whatever I could recognize and gather. By the mid-afternoon, I had gathered enough plants for the rest of today and tomorrow, but I still needed meat. I wasn't sure how far I had traveled from the lake. I had been so busy gathering that I failed to properly mark my trail. Only my compass guided me.

While moving, I spotted my own shoeprints, a comforting

indicator I was going the right way. Between the days shortening and the impending storm, it was dark by late afternoon. I reached the lake in good time. Moving past it, I reached my traps soon after, one by one. A strange small mammal was still alive in one of the snares. It had a dark brown coat with black overcast, a narrow face with a small head, large claws, and flaring teeth – clearly a predator species. My thought was a wolverine, but they were normally farther north and usually larger. This animal was only around fifteen pounds. It snarled, snapped, and growled. Only its back right leg was caught in the trap, a fortunate grab ... for me. Pulling my gun from the holster, I steadied my hold, waiting for it to stay still enough for a clean close-range headshot. After a few moments, it settled to sniff the air, allowing me to take the kill. After gutting it, I carried it by the tail.

The rest of my snares were empty. Upon reaching the cave, my feet were aching, my mind and body exhausted. Nonetheless, I needed to gather wood and make dinner. The weak fire was still going. Ty must have brought some branches while dragging himself out for a break. Inside the cave, in the dim light, he was messing with his leg brace.

"Hey, I'm back."

"Welcome back. I heard the gunshot. I was worried."

"Found this in one of my snares. Had to shoot it. Should make a nice dinner. I'll go gather some wood. Be back shortly." I left him to rejoin the chill of the forest. My shivering continued; I wondered if he noticed my shakes. I was looking forward to spending the rest of the night and tomorrow with him. With the likelihood of rain, we wouldn't have anything to do besides talk. After several silent trips, I had stockpiled enough wood to last a while. Inside the dry cave, it would serve well, but the fire needed to be shifted inside if it was to be safe from the weather. With my last armful of wood, I joined him in the cave for the night. Ty said nothing as I got to work shifting the fire's dying embers with one of the branches. Using nearby rocks, I lined the fire's perimeter to ensure it remained contained – especially important with it closer. Dry smaller branches caught by the embers; it took a while, but I got it back to a nice size for cooking. With my small pot and the canister water, I started boiling the roots and plants. Cutting the meat proved difficult. It was tough and gamy – not the best meat for boiling into a soup stew – but with no other options, I made the best of it. It was easier to cut up once the pelt was fully removed. Blood had stained my hands.

"That looks great."

"I'm sure you're starving," I replied. I half expected him to pretend that going without any food this long didn't bother him. Instead, he nodded in agreement with his light smile. He was not one to lie or pretend. I was used to obnoxious men. "Good. I have plenty here. I'm surprised how easy it is to trap in this forest, especially without bait. Maybe we've just been lucky."

"Lucky," he scoffed.

"You don't think so?"

"In some ways we are. I just wish we could get out of here. The woods are dangerous. I stress every time you leave. I'm wondering if the chopper is still looking for us."

"The issue is, they have no idea where to look. Nobody knew my route. Without coordinates, finding us in the vast and dense wilderness is near impossible. In hindsight, I should have told someone my complete route ... I've been foolish ... all we can do is hold out until you're healed enough to travel," I said while rinsing my hands. I took a drink before handing him the water. He took it without comment and drank his share. "My chopper is supposed to pick me up tomorrow. I'm supposed to be back at work Saturday morning. If work and my mother don't yet know I need help, they will soon. Maybe the police have contacted Mom." I adjusted my position, shifting closer to him.

He watched me intently. "Do you think they are worried?"

"They were worried before I left town. What about your family? I'm sure your folks are worried."

"My parents are likely wondering what I'm doing. My brother is probably hoping I don't come home."

I raised an eyebrow, not sure what he meant by that. "Surely they miss you, Ty."

He nodded with a frown. "I must admit to you, it's nice being away from them."

It was clear there were things going on with his family I didn't understand. "What are the names of your parents?"

"My mom is Catori. I'm named after my father."

"I love your mother's name."

"Both sides of my family have some distant Native American heritage. My grandparents felt the name was fitting when she was born. It means spirit."

"I love it. It's unique. What's your brother's name?"

His smile vanished. "It was agreed since I was the firstborn, I'd be named after my father, but I never cared for my name. My mother chose my brother's name. She picked Chogan."

"I like that, too. What does it mean?"

"Blackbird. It sorta fits him with his black heart." Ty drew circles and animal shapes in the dirt of the cave.

I watched him draw for a few minutes. "Have you ever thought of skipping town? You know, getting away from them for a while?"

He let out a low sigh. "Yeah, I thought about it. That's sorta how I ended up out here."

I thought about traveling with him and showing him the rest of the country. My parents had spoiled me with vacations when I was a child. I could tell Ty hadn't been away from town much. Sightseeing was a great way to spend time with someone, but Ty was still very new to me. Such thoughts were premature, and I had a career to focus on. Hopefully, my boss wouldn't get too annoyed with my unexpected extended trip. A painful growl reminded me of the food. It was now cooked enough to eat. I picked the pot up and offered it to Ty along with the stirring spoon. "Here. You eat first."

"Thank you," he said. I watched him pick out half of the meat, leaving the rest.

"You can take all of the meat. You need it and I ate something earlier." It didn't do much, but it was something.

"I can hear your stomach. You need it. You're expending a lot more energy." He continued to hold the pot to me, intent on giving me the remainder. I gave up and took the pot from him. The soup was delectable, a blend of earthy flavors achieved in no other meal. Maybe my famished body made it taste more delicious, but it didn't matter.

Like Ty, I had finished the meal within five minutes. Placing the pot to the side, I felt satisfied and comfortable. The cave was warmer than previous nights, and I emotionally kicked myself for not setting up the fire in its current position initially. Maybe it would have prevented Bennie from getting sick. Maybe not. I couldn't let myself ponder those what-ifs.

The soup had a powerful soporific effect on us. I yawned heavily while covering my mouth. Shortly following, he yawned, too. I chuckled at him, those enchanting blue eyes heavy with sleep – he smiled at me, waiting for our conversation to pick up again.

"I'm wondering if you'd leave with me ... if I were to skip town," he said.

I was surprised by such a proposition. We barely knew each other. On a fast note, I'd go anywhere with him by foolish judgment – a mysterious dark-haired, blue eyed wild-like partial stranger – but my life was here in Oregon. Leaving was not something I'd undertake lightly, especially for a new relationship – if that was what we even were. "I'm honestly not sure," I said.

He kept his expression stolid, but he was hiding disappointment, evident by the slightest new slouch of his shoulders. Perhaps he also felt prematurely involved with me. This was one intense spark between us, or the forest had distorted our sensibilities.

"Not sure of leaving or not sure of me?" he replied.

A bold and straightforward question. I had to be upfront with him. "Honestly ... both. I'm assuming you feel that spark, too. It's quite intense for me, but what we are forming is very new. Leaving town is a huge deal. Not a decision I'd take lightly."

"Yes, I feel it. It's like nothing I've felt before. But I understand."

I was thrilled to hear he felt the same, but there was a lace of desperation behind his urge to leave. It made my heart jump and then sink. Whatever was going on with his brother, it must have been serious. I regretted putting that idea in his head. Leaving town wasn't a smart topic to bring up, especially when I wanted more than friendship with him.

Despite the current mood, I had an internal happy dance over what he said – we both felt the same about one another. We both felt that ridiculously captivating spark, a magnetic pull of lust.

I brushed my teeth with toothpaste and spit the residue out of the cave. Offering the toothpaste to him, he did the same, using his finger as a brush. With my eyes growing heavier by the minute, I opted to lie on my side facing the fire. As expected, Ty carefully shifted himself behind me, wrapping his left arm around my waist. "I hope you don't leave," I said.

I could feel a light smile behind his breath. "I'm not going anywhere."

I watched the fire and listened to the crackling wood. Outside the cave, absolute darkness blanketed the forest, no moon or stars there to light the blackness. It was romantic but baleful, perhaps symbolic. The only light was the one that surrounded *us*. The strain of our predicament, the pain of losing my father, the stress of losing Bennie – all nearly melted away when I was in his warm arms.

Remembering his neck issue from last night, I thought it ideal to provide him with a pillow. Carefully grabbing for my bag, I pulled it over to us. "Here, rest your head on this." Half-empty, its thick fabric was the perfect height to support him.

"That's a great idea. Thank you." He shifted it under his neck and adjusted himself.

I used his right arm as a pillow again. While my eyes rested awaiting sleep, a light rain started. I could hear its unmistakable pattering against the forest floor and surrounding trees.

CHAPTER TEN

GAME OF QUESTIONS

I awoke to the same pattering I fell asleep to, sensing Ty was not yet awake. No longer tired, I let my thoughts take me wherever they dared. I had quickly noticed the distinct light pressure to my lower backside, which sent my mind straight into the gutter. I visualized exploring his body within the comforts of my bedroom. My hand riding down his chest and abs to his belt, only to remove it and travel a little lower.

Ty shifted, interrupting my inappropriate fantasy. I could tell he was now awake. When he noticed himself, he shifted his waist from my backside. I pretended to be asleep for several more minutes before shifting and sitting up. With my broken wristwatch, there was no way to know the exact time, but it didn't matter. I visualized my pickup chopper arriving at the grounds to wait for an itinerant woman who'd never show. I sighed heavily.

Ty sat up. "Something wrong?"

"Just thinking about my chopper. It's Friday. Unless they were alerted, they'd be arriving at the location for my return home."

"Ah, that's right," he said.

My attention moved to breakfast. I had some meat left. I offered it to him, along with some edible foliage. For myself, I chewed on wilting plants.

"Thanks, Liz, but are you sure you don't want this?" Referring to the meat, he looked at it and then at me.

"No, I'm fine. I'm happy with the plants." I moved what remained of my bundle into the rain to help prevent further wilting.

We sat in silence, watching the rainfall in the new day. It was coming down a little harder, making puddles and splashing in front of the cave's entrance. With the fire burnt out, I worked on restarting it once my meal was finished. From the heat accompanying the rush of inappropriate thoughts this morning, I hadn't noticed how cold I was. I shivered in the nip of the morning, while Ty had goosebumps on his forearms but otherwise seemed fine. The humidity made restarting the fire difficult. I looked around for dry material in the cave and found some detached roots that would work to rub in a new fire. Only thanks to the warm embers was I able to light it. "Yes!" I said as it crackled to life.

"Nice work."

"Thanks." I smiled at him, proud of my patience. With the stored wood in the cave, I adjusted the fire to the desired size. Soon, I had to pee and I'm sure he did too. The rain had lightened up a little. "Restroom break. I go left, you go right, and we meet back at the cave after." I jumped up and promptly left the cave. The droplets hit my head, moving along my scalp. I welcomed them, yearning for a warm bath at home. Aside from the rain, my footsteps, and my breathing, I could perceive no other sounds. An eerie dim day – I felt I should be watching over my shoulder. Conceivably, my uneasiness was from my lack of weapons.

I wasn't surprised to be back before Ty, with him hopping on one leg and using the trees as crutches. I was much quicker on my two feet. Back inside the cave, I adjusted my hair and used my brush to remove the knots. Our lack of hygiene was getting embarrassing.

Maybe I could get us both to the lake in a few more days. Ty's leg looked great; although it would take the entire day to get there and back with him, he would at least be cleaner, and it would give us an idea of how long we'd need to delay before attempting the long trip back to town.

While waiting for Ty, I used my knife to clean under my nails. I was getting worried. About thirty minutes had passed since I returned to the cave, and he couldn't have gone that far. Maybe he got hurt or maybe he fell or knocked himself unconscious. My heart started to race, so to distract myself I tidied up the cave, rinsing the dinner pot and moving my bag to the cave's edge. Most of my items were stored within it, aside from my gun, which I propped against the cave's wall within easy reach if needed. Ty then appeared next to a tree not far outside the cave. Tired from the ordeal and completely drenched, he resembled a wet poodle. I rushed out to help him. Using my body as a crutch again, he made it back inside.

"Thanks," he said, completely exhausted. His breathing was heavy, and his body shivered. His wet clothing ripped the warmth from him.

"Take your shirt off. It's pulling too much heat."

"Okay." He removed it and handed it to me. I draped it over the woodpile to dry, ignoring his beautiful exposed body. He got close to the fire, desperate to warm up.

"Don't get too close," I said.

He chuckled through his shivers. "I'm not."

"Chilled to the bone, I see."

"Ye – yeah," he replied.

"What took so long to get back? You had me worried."

"I went too far and got lost for a bit."

"Oh, why didn't you call my name?"

"I did. You didn't hear me."

"Really? Maybe the rain blocked it out," I pondered.

"Probably. I don't know why I got lost so easily. This rain must be messing with my senses."

I was tempted to hold him to help heat his body, but I didn't want to seem coddling. Instead, I added more wood to the fire. Even if I did hold him, I doubted it would help. It was probably in the mid-fifties this morning. Not too cold, but with a core chill - it's enough to shake most. Only the fire and a dry shirt would help him.

While he warmed himself, I eyeballed his chest injuries. They were already fully scarred over with barely any scabbing left. Impressive immune system and healing responses. Good genes. Ty noticed my gaze.

"Still looking at that?" he questioned.

I nodded. "It looks great. If you heal that quickly overall, I'm wondering if we can push your leg to leave sooner. A trip to the lake could be the test."

"Might be worth a shot. I haven't attempted any weight yet. Not getting far with hopping."

I shifted closer. "Can I see your leg wounds? I should remove the stitches, providing they are ready to be taken out." I had been meaning to ask for his upper leg.

"Yeah, sure."

He adjusted his position so that both of his legs were stretched out, with his upper body weight leaning back on his arms. I carefully shifted the fabric. The wounds looked good with no sign of infection, and the stitches were overdue for removal. I moved over to my bag to fish the scissors out. Ty seemed to trust me more. Maybe it's because he knew I had no reason to cause him pain. Maybe it's because he was dependent on me and had no choice. Whatever the reason for his ease, it was a simple procedure.

"There, done."

"Thanks again." He smiled with appreciation.

My heartstrings were pulled by his gratitude. "You're most welcome."

He then shifted himself to the fire's heat. I could tell his leg was less sensitive. The bone was fusing and therefore no longer causing discomfort, but the process was in a very delicate state. In my nursing career, I had seen broken tibias several times. Depending on some factors, it took anywhere from three weeks to six months for complete healing. The younger and more fit the patient, the faster healing typically goes for any injury. I wondered if I could make him some crutches for the trip back. It would take forever at that pace and we no longer know what the weather will be.

With my shoulders pulled back in a satisfying stretch, I thought about my need to know him better. "I'm bored. Know of any games?"

Ty shrugged. "I'd say *I-spy*, but the answer would always be tree."

I chuckled. "No, that wouldn't work. How about the game of twenty questions? We could get to know each other better by it."

"That works." His eyes lit up. "Simple questions, simple answers. I'll go first. What is your favorite food?"

"Um ... can you be more specific?"

"Favorite fruit?" he asked.

"Raspberries."

"Good one. Mine is red apples ... just for the color."

"I didn't ask what your favorite fruit is," I teased.

"Oh, right. Okay, what's your question?"

"Let me think," I pondered. "Do you own a car?"

"Nope." He lightly shook his head side to side. "Have you ever skinny-dipped?"

"Well, that took an interesting turn," I chuckled. "Technically yes, when I was bathing at the lake earlier in the week."

He smiled at me with those perfectly white teeth. "Okay, your turn to ask," he replied.

"Has anyone ever seen you naked?" I smirked at him. This was a fun game.

"Well at some point, you are eventually seen by someone."

"Not much of an answer." My eyes narrowed. "But fine. Your turn."

"Have you ever been intimate with another person?" he asked.

"Yes. Several times. If I ask that same question, the answer would be no from you?"

"Are you actually asking or just assuming?" he taunted.

My eyes narrowed again. "Asking."

"Then you'd be correct."

My eyes widened. I wanted to ask him how that was possible at his age – especially considering how handsome he was – but the game was too interesting to stop there. "Your turn again."

"Have you ever been intimate with a woman?" he asked.

"Oh no. I don't look at women that way. My mom does though. A long while after my father died, she dated a woman." I watched him rub the back of his neck. "My turn." I pondered for a bit. "Have you ever had an interest in men?"

"No. Not at all. I told you, I'm straight."

"Okay, fair enough. Your turn."

"Have you ever watched porn?" he questioned.

At this point, the uncomfortable questions had become less awkward. "Yes."

"How many times?"

"Hey, no – it's my turn!"

"Okay, go."

His question prompted my next one. "Are you circumcised?" I asked.

"No, thankfully not."

"I assume you want me to answer your earlier question?"

"Yup."

"I have watched it several times, but never liked it. I'll leave it at that," I stated.

"Fair enough. What's your next question?"

"Same question you asked," I proposed.

"The porn question? No, I don't watch it. ... Have you any regrets?"

I sighed, lowering my eyes to the dirt. "Just my father's death. And now Bennie's death."

I scraped through random questions regarding foods, animals, and life experiences. "Were you homeschooled?"

"Yes, I was. Never saw a public school. ... What's the best day you've had to date?"

That question required thought. I stopped to think about my life experiences, the happy moments I had enjoyed before the long streak of sadness. The happiest days of my distant past were with my parents – all of us together as a family, but within the last decade, happiness was difficult to determine.

"Ever or within the last ten years?" I asked.

"The last ten years I guess."

"I'm not sure. This past week has blurred everything. It sounds silly, but probably today."

He lowered his eyes to pick at his fingers. "... I actually feel the same, well minus the injury component, but I've really enjoyed your company. You lifted me in ways you might never understand," he said without looking at me.

I must have looked like a complete goof, my smile stretching ear to ear. At least it matched his. "I'm glad you feel the same. It's my turn. Let me see ... what's your favorite animal?"

"Dogs. Always wanted one. Never had one. What about you?"

"I like most small animals. For non-domesticated, lions and wolves – although the wolf I've met on this journey is making me dislike them now," I snickered.

"I don't blame you there."

"Why don't you get a dog?"

"Um. I guess I'm afraid I wouldn't be a good pet owner. Growing up without pets has made me feel like I'd be an unsuitable caregiver. I also feel dogs just don't like me."

"I fail to see why any animal wouldn't like you." Then I remembered the wolf. "Well, aside from wolves."

He chuckled, continuing to pick at the dry skin on his finger. "Yeah, I either repel canine species or unintentionally piss them off."

At this point, we dropped the game and conversed freely. "Seems that way," I said lightheartedly. I started to wonder about his home and what it looked like. I was under the impression he lived in his own secluded place not far from his family, but away from town. "What is your home like?"

"... I have a cabin."

"That sounds nice. How far from Jacksonville is it?"

"Uh, not far."

That was vague. "So, it's out of town, but not far?"

"Yes." He shifted his position before changing the subject. "I'm wondering how long it will rain."

My eyes watched his expression. It was clear the previous topic was no longer welcome. "No idea. It doesn't seem to be lightening up - getting worse if anything. Friday was supposed to be nice. It makes me wonder if my chopper can even fly into where I'm supposed to get picked up."

"That's a good point. Maybe it's not as bad in that area," he said as the wind whipped the rain around the pines.

The roots of the tree above, which entwined the cave's walls and ceiling, practically sang from the strain of keeping hold. It made me uneasy - as if it would collapse and kill us both. A crack of thunder and flash of lightning startled two of us.

"That made me jump," he complained.

I said nothing while I watched the storm. Another flash of lightning and roar of thunder caught our senses. I added more wood to the fire. Since the cave was slightly tilted upward from the entrance, the ground we rested upon stayed relatively dry. I looked at Bennie's grave. Now drenched in water, his resting place looked like my heart had felt – flooded with emotion. I could feel it weigh down my chest, the yearning to have him back.

My thoughts shifted to why Ty didn't want to talk about his home. Maybe he was embarrassed or perhaps his home was rugged and rundown. Maybe he was a hunter and it was full of animal skins or maybe he's a pig, living in a pile of mess filled with empty pizza boxes and crumpled beer cans. Or perhaps he had human bodies in his freezer, chopped up into little pieces. By the look of him, it all seemed unlikely. I decided to re-spark the questioning game as the storm roiled above, but before I could speak, he broke the silence.

"What are you thinking?" Ty asked while reaching for his nearly dried shirt. I watched him put it on.

I gave him a light, reassuring smile. "Just wondering if you hunt, like me."

His shoulders relaxed. "Yes, I do. Deer is my favorite. The meat is clean and tender."

"What gun do you prefer?"

"Um." He looked down at his healing leg. "I guess I don't have a favorite."

I followed his gaze. "Is that splint bothering you?"

"A little. I might be okay without it now."

"You still need it. It's been a very short amount of time. You can't possibly be healed. The leg needs the protection."

"I heal fast, remember?" His right eyebrow rose and he grinned at me.

"Not that fast. You need at least another week with the splint, but you may be able to put pressure on it soon."

"No, really. I snapped my arm in half as a teenager when playing with my brother. I was out of the cast and fine in a week."

"I find that extremely hard to believe," I responded.

"Just take it off. Worst case, you need to put it back on."

"Fine. But I think you're crazy." Muttering *idiot* under my breath, I knew there was no way he had healed enough in less than a week. I thought earlier that he could heavily limp on it with the splint and maybe hand-built crutches, but even that was unlikely. Ty seemed tense as I adjusted myself next to his leg. Carefully removing the vines, I then took off the supportive branches and unwrapped my jacket. My eyes focused on his exposed skin and searched the shin for any sign of the break or bruising, but it looked completely normal externally – as if he had never been injured.

"Huh ..."

"Told you. At least I have that uncomfortable splint off." He lay back into the dirt, clearly feeling relieved to have it off.

"Unbelievable. Your healing response is impressive. Maybe we will be out of here sooner than I thought." My heart lit up. I longed for the comfort of my warm dry bed and a hot shower; I was tired of being cold. Being out here really made me appreciate domestic luxuries. I missed everyone, and Briana was probably freaking out. If they didn't know I was missing before, they did now.

"I told you, I heal fast."

"For our sake, I hope that's true. We need to get you checked out at the hospital." I frowned at our predicament. Despite things looking up, we were still stuck here for the time being.

"What's wrong?" he questioned.

"It's like this forest hates me. Maybe it remembers how I escaped. Maybe it wants to claim what it failed to have before." My brain raced around everything I had been through within the forest. The race for my life, the loss of my father, the injured ankle, losing Bennie, Ty getting hurt. If not for meeting Ty, I'd curse this place.

I wanted to forgive the woods, but I only felt angry about how difficult that was proving. I could have taken a torch to it, but that would put me back into the very mess that started everything. While I was glad that I had met Ty, I wished it could have been in a different way.

"You love the forest despite the trauma you had, but the forest can't hate you."

"Feels like it does ..."

"That's how I feel about that wolf who kept coming back. He hasn't been around in a while though. I think he gave up." Ty crossed his arms under his head as he lay in the dirt, looking at me and then at the cave's ceiling. I watched his eyes peer at something above. He was tracing the maze of roots. A labyrinth of brown shades intertwined with one another, fighting for any available dirt against the rocky surface. The textures of the root varied from butter-smooth to crusty-coarse. I decided to distract myself with it as he did. I lay next to him, mimicking his position, staring up at those explosive roots. In the darkness alone, with nothing but the moonlight, these comforting roots would seem to be an insidious blanket of infinite horror. Instead, in the glow of the fire, they were a welcome distraction from our predicament.

"It's beautiful."

He smiled without moving his gaze. We enjoyed the lengthy tangle in silence while the rain poured down. As the fire lowered, the deeper crevices became less visible. The storm had made the sky nearly dark as night. I sat up and moved over to the woodpile to feed the dwindled flame. My jacket sat on the soil nearby, dirtied and defeated. I worked to straighten up the dwelling, moving some things to a neat pile and putting other items in my bag. The cave was starting to feel like a home away from home. Tired of seeing it lie in the dirt, I fastened my holstered gun around my hip. Ty seemed too lost in thought to pay me any attention. I wondered what this mysterious man thought about. From getting hurt to meeting me as a result – I liked to imagine he felt the same as I did, but despite his claims, I couldn't be sure.

My next thought was to put my jacket out in the rain for a quick rain wash. I peered out for a place I could rest it. A horizontal branch twenty feet from the cave would make a perfect spot for a rain wash.

"I'll be right back. I'm going to put this out in the rain." I prepared myself for a jog through the cold sky water. Ty sat up to watch me. Jacket in hand, I rushed through the chill. The rain turned my hair into a wet mess while I rushed to place the jacket. The crack of thunder had more intensity outside the cave. I practically slapped it onto the tree branch, only minimally adjusting it before running back. Despite my quick trip, I was near drenched. "Ugh," I complained, "maybe that was a bad idea." He chuckled, causing me to scowl at him. "It's not funny."

"Sorry. You're right. It's not."

I moved closer to the fire and added more wood. My hands felt like ice. Most certainly a bad idea. My stomach started to growl. It was around noon. Ty was probably getting hungry again, too. He had finished up the meat, but my plant bundle was plentiful.

"Are you hungry yet?" I asked.

"Not really."

I wasn't going to wait for him to want lunch, so I pulled my plant bundle inside and removed some of the less appealing items. They were very bitter and hard to swallow, but thankfully less wilted. Ty was lying on his back again, enjoying the cave's natural beauty. I admired his attention to detail. Likely a skill he had developed with wood carving.

"You seem to really like those roots," I observed.

He shifted his arms to better support his head. "The way they've grown out of the soil ... around the bedrock, burying each other – it's interesting."

I said nothing, casting my eyes outside the cave. I gradually became uneasy, an angst filling my core. My eyes narrowed while I peered out into the heavy rain. Something felt off like we were being watched, but I may have been inexplicably on edge. At least that's what I hoped. Ty didn't seem bothered by anything. When I looked back at him, he had his eyes closed. His face muscles relaxed and his breathing grew shallow; he had fallen asleep. I wanted to join him for a nap, but the angst persisted. A half-hour passed before the feeling finally subsided. The rain still dropped in buckets while Ty remained peacefully asleep. As he rested, I quietly placed the canister of water in the rain.

My thoughts didn't want me to rest. I pondered my still unanswered questions. Where were Ty's shoes and socks? He still didn't care to have me search for his gear. How did his injuries manage to heal so fast? My mediocre patch job couldn't have been that adequate. To my annoyance, his mysteriousness only continued to pull me closer.

After an hour, Ty awoke. He sat up dazed. "I fell asleep?"

I smiled at him. "Yes."

"How long was I out?"

"Not long. The rain is making me feel drained as well, but something had me feeling uneasy."

"You didn't see anything out there, did you?"

"No," I replied.

He sighed and looked out of the cave. "This is a bad storm."

I nodded. "Are you thirsty?"

"Yes."

"Here." I took the canister from just outside the cave and handed it to him. He took a sip and handed it back.

"Thanks." Placing his arms behind him, he leaned back on their support. "When I was a kid, storms like this meant a day of rain tag. Back when my brother actually liked me, we would bond over racing through the mud and puddles." He expressed a pained smile. "It's one of my better memories."

"That sounds really fun. I used to wish for a younger sibling, but my parents wanted to spoil an only child. I remember extravagant birthday parties every year until I was sixteen. Dad loved to spoil me, but I always remained very grateful," I reminisced.

"At least a sibling can't hurt you when you don't have one."

"What do you mean?" I questioned.

He lowered his head and turned his gaze away. "I told you before, how Chogan became hateful toward me. Well, by the time I hit my late teens we would get into a lot of fights. Violent fights that would terrify my mother. Dad had to stop them. It was always Chogan who started them and most of my scars were his doing. He'd do things to harm or upset me like damage something of mine or slap me. For someone younger, he's been very ..."

"Cruel. A bully."

"Yes, exactly."

"Did he grow bigger than you?"

"No. He matured shorter and weighs less. He's been better in recent years, but lately, he's been acting out again – of course taking out his life frustrations on me. I could kick his ass if I wanted to, but I try to play damage control. Fighting fire with fire isn't ideal."

"Family struggles like that are emotionally draining." While I couldn't relate, I still sympathized with him. "I'm sorry. I wish I could help."

He gave me a light smile. "Talking about this with someone outside of family, especially you, has helped a lot already."

I was glad we were talking about this. "Do you think I'd ever meet him?"

"Chogan? Absolutely not. I wouldn't want you anywhere near that animal," he huffed. I watched his eyebrows narrow and lower with that statement.

"Okay, fair enough. What about the rest of your family?"

"I don't know. I would love for you to meet everyone, but with Chogan typically lurking around, I'd have to wait for him to be in town before I could bring you home."

Bring you home. Those words danced in my skull, banging within the walls of my cranium. I tried to hide my inner glow. "I hope I get to meet them."

"Me too."

The rain was lightening up. I looked out of the cave and watched the downpour turn into a reasonable rain shower in a matter of minutes. "Storm looks to be finishing."

"Yeah, it may stop soon."

Watching my jacket sitting in the rain, I thought it might be worth retrieving now so I could dry it. I could have waited for the rain to stop completely, but then it could easily get worse again – even within minutes. "I'm going to get my jacket, so I can dry it by the fire." Heeding the anxiety I felt before, I kept my gun and holster on my waist, then made my way out. This time, I didn't rush. I allowed myself to enjoy the wildlife around me despite my recent anger. Anger ... such a strong emotion that poisoned me. For that reason, I could no longer be angry at the inhospitable nature of the forest. I needed to let go. To completely forgive the forest and myself. After all, that was what this journey was about.

When I reached the jacket, I inspected it before picking it up. Turning back toward the cave, I slipped on the mud, landing on my backside. "Dammit."

"You okay?" Ty called out.

"Yeah, fine." I turned over, feeling defeated. When I looked up, I noticed the mass of a gray wolf racing toward me, the sound masked by the rain. The quiet rhythm of his stride raced forward with impossible speed through the distant trees. My eyes could barely process what rapidly approached, closing the gap to kill me.

CHAPTER ELEVEN

SURVIVAL

I rapidly flashed over my ending future – with Ty, my career, my friends, and my mother. It wasn't my past life that flashed, but an acute end of everything I had yet to experience. Children, wealth, eternal happiness, a true romance – seeming to only now just blossom.

My body jolted with a shock of panic. In my desperation, I grabbed the only thing near my hand in the few seconds – a thick branch lying on the ground beside me. Before I could properly grasp it, the beast pounced, throwing his weight onto mine, pinning me backward into the mud. I pushed the branch up into the animal's throat while his jaws tried to reach my face. The monstrous animal snarled and snapped at me, his massive teeth inches from my eyes.

I could hear Ty yell to me, "Elizabeth!!" In the corner of my vision, my overdriven senses perceived the horror on his face. "Leave her alone!" he screamed at the wolf.

The wolf's brown eyes full of anger, his attention shifted to Ty, allowing me the split-second I needed. Using both of my legs, I shifted them under the animal and kicked up as hard as I could with all my energy. The wolf's frame sprung up and he tumbled over my head, face planting into the ground between myself and the cave. While the animal snorted muddied water from his nostrils, I turned over and could see Ty trying to reach us. He limped toward me, completely defenseless. I knew he couldn't help – only get himself killed. "TYLER! DON'T MOVE!" I screamed at him.

He stopped in his tracks as the wolf stood up facing him. I fumbled my gun from its holster with an unspoken prayer. The beast stared at Ty, snarling while I readied my aim. My thoughts feared the worst-case scenario. In a split second, which seemed to have slowed into milliseconds, I thought about how if I missed the wolf, Ty would be struck by my bullet. The wolf then lunged forward to where Ty stood frozen, and I pulled the trigger.

To my relief and simultaneous horror, the bullet shot from my gun. Milliseconds slowed to microseconds as I witnessed the sound of the shot and its inevitable result. Several things happened nearly at once: I could hear Ty yell, the animal tumbled onto the ground directly in front of him, and I dropped the gun in shock.

"NO!" Ty cried. The wolf lay still at Ty's feet.

Sitting back into the mud, I fought to catch my breath and straighten my head, but my blood was so full of adrenaline and my body so exhausted from the struggle, I could manage only to remain conscious – not to move or even blink. With the rain pouring down again, I started to cry from the shock. I cried until I felt Ty's hand on my shoulder. The adrenaline slowly subsiding, I shivered in the cold.

"Elizabeth, here. Get up ... let's get back to the cave."

I nodded twice, too stressed and emotionally drained to say anything. Despite his leg, he was able to help me up, but his heavy limp had me helping him back more than he helped me. We stepped around the wolf's body. I noticed the pool of blood trailing with rainwater from the back of its head. Once back inside, we collapsed in exhaustion. I found myself kneeling with my arms supporting my upper body and my face toward the ground. We rested in silence, still in disbelief over what had happened. I tried to steady my breathing. With a quick glance, I saw he was staring into the dirt.

After several minutes I could feel his eyes on me. "Are you hurt?" he questioned.

With my body shaking, my trembling voice managed to reply. "N - no." The event unfolded in my head over and over, like a skipping film. I thought about the flash of massive white teeth snapping at me, the shot of my gun, my heart skipping six beats. I realized that if I hadn't slipped in the mud, the wolf would have run up from behind, undetected. He would have had me in his jaws and dead before I knew what grabbed me - and then he'd have finished what he started. Tyler would have died too. I looked out at the animal's body, lying in a pool of red water. I realized Ty might have hurt himself in the panic. "How is your leg?"

"I think I'm okay. It aches, but I don't think I damaged anything."

Soaked with mud, I added more wood to the fire while I thought about the mass of gray fur lying nearby. Where was its pack? With that thought, I heard a chorus of howls erupt through the thin air. Ty tensed before pulling his legs to his stomach and hugging his knees. He was just as shaken. I tried to see it through his eyes, how the event felt and looked. Terrifying, still. I decided to lie next to the fire, not caring that I was covered with mud. Goosebumps remained on my arms. After a few minutes, I heard him shifting over to behind me, grasping me in his arms.

Ty hugged me tightly, his chest against my back - like we had known each other for years - and then reached to kiss my cheek. His affection calmed my jitters and helped me feel a bit warmer. We lay like this for what felt like an hour when he broke the silence, "I thought you were going to die."

I quietly sighed, finally feeling safe again. "So did I." The rain had ultimately stopped, and our nerves had steadied. I needed a bathroom break and some more water. In the back of my mind, I realized my jacket still rested in the mud where I had been attacked. My gun had sunken into the mud near it. "I need a rest break. I won't go far."

"I do, too," he replied.

"Keep within fifty feet. I'll go right, you left."

I used what energy remained to pick myself up and struggle out. With the storm gone, the lowering sun peeked through scattered clouds. It started to set, shining a golden beam of light behind and over the wolf's saturated pelt. Morbidly beautiful.

My inner hunter pondered skinning the beast, but despite its death, I was still afraid of it. Although I would never go out of my way to kill a wolf, it was a shame letting the creature's remains go to waste.

I walked through the trees, choosing not to look back. Despite the risk of its pack coming for revenge, I felt oddly safe as I made my way, alone and tired. The subsided rush of adrenaline caused my muscles to ache. I was proud of my body for its resilience and strength. I never could have prepared physically for the struggle I endured, but considering the result, how could I not be proud? I had saved not only myself but Ty as well.

While I took my break, I wondered why the wolf attacked when it did. Surely we had been more vulnerable at other moments. Why did it attack today? Why that moment? There must have been a reason. I thought about the cave and wondered if it had belonged to the wolf. Did he want it back? I'd never know, but at least we were safe again. I did my best to brush off the drying mud from my clothing and hair.

I returned to find Ty already back in the cave. Without a word, I lay down next to the fire and we resumed the previous position - my back to him with his arm around my waist. This time, I curled closer to the flame. Sandwiched between the two, I finally felt warm. While my clothes were drying in the late evening, exhaustion relaxed me. We watched the fire in silence, waiting for hunger to evoke dinner as the sun retreated behind the horizon. The bright orange embers glowed in the darkening cave. The near-death experience I had endured made me feel appreciative of the small things – like Ty's embrace, the dry cave, the edible forest foods, drinkable water, the clean forest air, the warmth of the fire, and the beautiful colors it expressed. It made me feel a little more at peace with the forest and maybe even with the flame that had destroyed my happiness for so many years.

My stomach growled, loud enough that Ty surely heard it. I sat up and moved to pull the plant bundle closer. Most of the remaining foods were wilted and soggy. I fished out the firmest stalks and offered them to Ty. "Here."

He raised an eyebrow. "I'm not *that* hungry."

My eyes narrowed. "Take it." I handed him the plant. He sniffed it before taking a small bite. The face he made was so comical, I erupted into laughter as he spat it out. It was a few minutes before I was able to collect myself. "Oh, come on!" I giggled. "It's not that bad!"

"I'd rather eat week-old beaver meat than this." He offered it back to me. I took it, knowing he probably wouldn't budge.

"I don't have anything else." I looked at the nearby wolf carcass. "Unless you're open to wolf meat." I watched Ty's eyes widen before lowering. "What's wrong?"

"Nothing," he said, clearing his throat. "Just hungry."

As I ate my dinner, I thought about the small animals I could hunt tomorrow now that the rain subsided. He could use several fat squirrels. My thoughts then shifted to his leg and how I should have probably checked it over again. "Can I see your leg?" I asked when I finished eating.

"Yeah, sure."

Shifting over, I placed my hands around his shin and calf, feeling the bone for anything out of place, but nothing felt amiss.

Although still weak, he should be able to limp the journey back to town soon. An incredible reality considering it should've taken far longer to heal with *proper* treatment. The thought of home in reach lifted my spirits – a rush of enthusiasm. "It seems good. We may be able to leave as early as tomorrow. Much sooner than I initially expected. Do you think you can handle it?" I wanted to get home, but I didn't want to push him past his physical ability. He could easily re-injure himself.

"Yeah, probably. It would take a long while to get back to town, but we really need to get out of here." He frowned, glancing at the animal's hide.

I nodded. The wolf's death could bring company and I wouldn't be able to drag the body far enough from here. Dead animals attract scavengers. I also thought about his pack coming for us. Never did I imagine wolves would be the biggest danger on this journey. My thoughts shifted to Briana again, who had warned me of the forest predators. She was undoubtedly miserable, wishing she had stopped me from leaving in the first place. Knowing her and my mother, they had probably gathered a team to search for me, but these woods were too vast.

Ty remained quiet, likely falling asleep. My thoughts continued to drift around the events we endured. At least with *this* near-death experience, I was powerful in my reaction and outcome. If the situation had to happen, it couldn't have gone better than it did. We came out unscathed. I kept repeating the word, whispering it in my lips. Unscathed. Ty's gentle snores vented behind me. With night upon us and exhaustion in control, I succumbed to the sleep that had already claimed Tyler.

That night, I dreamed of our rescue. I dreamed of my warm bed and cotton pillows. I dreamed of Ty's touch within my sheets and his warmth within me. The feeling of our groins within one another – his body's movement on top of mine, pushing into me with powerful bursts of pleasure. The erotica of the dream felt so real, I awoke with a pleasurable twist against him. But it wasn't my body's movement that awakened me. It was Ty's gasp when I pushed my backside against his groin. Startled by his gasp, I sprang up and quickly realized what had occurred. Ty was almost as flustered as I, feeling the heat in my cheeks.

"I ... am ... so sorry." I blushed heavily. "Please tell me you weren't awake long."

Leaning on his elbow, he ran his fingers through his hair with a coy expression. "Uh, no. Just woke up," he lied.

I could have died of embarrassment if I hadn't been distracted by a harrowing realization. Something was missing in the corner of my eye, something that should've been there. Only when I looked up did I realize what was gone. The wolf's body had vanished. My jaw dropped, and I gasped. No. He had to be dead. All that remained was a faint stain of blood in the mud. I jumped up and raced out to investigate. There were no tracks in the mud, no drag marks – nothing.

"Ty! Where did it go?" I scanned the woods around us in panic and looked back at Ty in dismay.

Ty looked unimpressed with the animal's missing hide. "A bear probably dragged the body off," he said.

The birds had returned since the storm's passing. A stunning day for such a shocking occurrence. I estimated it was around seven o'clock. The mud was quickly drying in the warm day and all the trees sparkled with a blanket of dew. I glanced at my jacket and gun, caked into the mud where the nearby branch remained. I left the cave, walking over to the branch. Animal fur was stuck within the jagged grain. My arms ached with intense soreness. When I reached for my gun, the pain of my movement persisted. I pulled it from the dirt and mud. It wouldn't fire with drying mud clogging the barrel. I took my jacket from the earth nearly covering it and walked back to Tyler, musing through my memory.

Ty looked back out of the cave and took a deep breath. "My family sees wolves as sacred spirits of the forest. It's said that when they die, they vanish with the rising moon to join their dead." His eyes watered with sadness.

I wasn't sure what to say. "I need to go to the bathroom. I'll be back in a bit."

"Okay," he replied while shifting himself to follow me out of the cave.

I walked off without looking back, envisioning him standing up and limping off to correspond with the sounds he made behind me – his tough and dirtied bare feet meeting the ground cover. I never considered Ty's native roots as a wolf-worshiping culture. Maybe that was why he chose to run from the animal instead of fighting it, but I had to kill it. There must have been a logical explanation as to how the animal's remains disappeared. Bear? It seemed unlikely, but surely the wolf didn't rise to the heavens in the moonlight. I ridiculed his cultural explanation in my thoughts to assuage my new guilt, but after some time, it only made me feel worse.

My stomach growled. I gathered some edible plants while I walked about. Using the time to myself, my thoughts blew around like the wind within the swaying branches above. I paused at that moment to meditate. Meditation was something I rarely did, but the moment felt perfect for it. I sat in a pretzel facing the breeze that glided through my dirty hair. With breathing exercises, I focused on the sound of a nearby cricket chirping in the brush. Its song lifted my saddened soul. Inhale, exhale. I matched my pace to half its wing speed. The stress in my heart released and my shoulders lifted. "Much better," I said to myself. Standing up, I made my way back to the cave.

Ty was waiting outside it, leaning on his good leg. "You okay?" he questioned.

"Yes. I was just taking a moment to myself. After everything, I needed a moment."

He nodded and watched me begin to gather my things into my pack. It was time to get out of here.

Ty's leg healed unbelievably fast and these woods, although peaceful again, had not been enjoyable. I needed a shower, clean clothes, and my bed. A professional massage would also be welcome. "Ready to go?" I asked when everything was gathered.

"Yeah. I think so," he said with a sad smile.

I smiled back at him. He seemed strong but emotionally tired as I did. Ty started to limp to the first tree. Before I joined him, I shifted my attention to say my final goodbye to the one creature who almost never left my side – the one true friend I'd never forget. I leaned down next to Bennie's grave beside the cave that had sheltered the three of us through his final days. A nearby stone made the perfect grave marker. With my knife, I carved his name and placed the rock above his resting place. I imagined we'd meet again someday. As I stood up and followed Ty, the light brush beneath my stride was watered. Ty pretended not to notice my tears while he focused on remaining upright, using the trees to help him move along. Patience was of utmost importance today. He needed to rest frequently and progress was slow, especially when we reached obstacles such as rough terrain or dense brush. Ty's legs were scratched heavily from the foliage that grabbed at him. I felt sorry for his body, but he didn't seem bothered by it.

By what felt like the early afternoon, Ty paused to rest beside a tree, sitting with his back against its broad trunk. I sat down next to him and offered some water. We were nearly out despite conserving. He sipped a small amount and held it in his mouth before swallowing. My compass was all that guided me after noticing my GPS was glitching. Without it, Ty navigated the wilderness ahead for most of our trek, occasionally looking back at me for directional assurance. Watching him struggle was difficult, but I couldn't help him. My arms were intensely sore, and he was heavy.

"I don't know if I can go on any longer – at least for today," he said.

I thought about our location and whether I could build a fast shelter in case of rain or wind chill. Looking around, I noticed a nearby nook in a cluster of trees that would allow a quick structure to shelter us.

"That's okay. We can camp here," I said without taking my eye off the spot. With low water, if we reached the lake tomorrow, we would be okay. I stood up and walked over to the spot that we'd rest in. It would take me a few hours to build the shelter and fire – just enough time to get it done before dark. I might even have some time to set a few snares, but I'd risk getting lost from him. Considering that possibility, I scratched the idea. The plants I'd collected as we traveled would have to do us well for dinner. Hopefully, Ty would eat them. "I'm going to build us a quick shelter here. A fire, too."

"Sounds good," he said as he rubbed his leg.

"How does it feel?"

"It aches badly."

I went back over to him for a quick check. I had checked his leg ten times since we left the cave. He seemed okay externally each time. He still looked fine, with the bone staying in place. I offered him some of the edible foliage I had collected. "Here," I said with a smile.

He glared at the greens. "I can't eat that. I'm sorry."

A frown quickly took my smile. "Yes, you can. Eat."

He shook his head in protest. "No. I really can't stomach it. It's okay. I'll manage."

I didn't have any energy to argue further. "Fine, but I won't give in so easily next time. You won't make it back to town without eating."

He said nothing, just stared at me with those beautiful eyes. It was hard to pull away and focus on the shelter and fire. It didn't take much effort to find fallen branches sturdy enough to support the weight of the structure, but I was unable to find nearby vine for tying it all together. I decided to change my design. A slanted ground shelter would require more branches, but no vine. The forest was littered with usable wood, allowing me to complete the slant rather quickly. Once completed, I built the fire and Ty moved in.

He smiled at my efforts. "I'm impressed."

"Thanks." I was proud of my work. The cave was warmer, but caves weren't easy to come by. We were at a high spot in this location, allowing us to glance at the distant mountains through the thick trees. They were the same mountains I saw every day on my way to and from work. I thought about the black wolf I nearly hit with my car on that favorite tree-lined street. With wolves on my mind again, I continued to ponder the missing gray wolf I killed. I realized its pack had not howled since. With their voices traveling many miles, I knew they had since been silent.

The temperature was dropping. I shifted close to the fire after finishing my dinner – a young chicory plant. Ty still wouldn't eat. It saddened me to watch him go hungry, especially when he didn't need to. Despite his growling stomach, he watched in acrimony as I munched on the plant and roots. His demeanor felt almost resentful. Perhaps it was just his aching leg making him seem grouchy. I shifted my eyes toward the fire's orange glow.

"If you could have let him live, would you have?"

I was confused by his sudden question. "What do you mean?"

"The wolf. If you didn't have to shoot, would you have let it live?"

"Of course. Wolves are one of my favorite animals. I only take a life for two reasons. The first reason is food. The second is defense."

He looked at the fire in thought. I wasn't sure what brought that question on. Surely, he didn't think I would have killed that animal in any other situation. "You think I wanted to kill it?"

"No. I just feel bad he had to die."

I nodded. "We were in his woods. He had the right to his space." I wasn't talking to Ty. My words were directed to myself. Ty was still upset over the death of a creature his family and culture valued. It made me worried that his view of me had shifted into a negative light. Maybe he no longer looked at me in the romantic light I saw and felt toward him. "Are you mad at me?"

He looked at me. "Not at all, Elizabeth. Just sad for the animal. That's all. It's not your fault. I only blame myself. You were in the position because of me."

I couldn't quite understand what he felt or meant. I was just relieved to hear he still cared for me the same as before – if he was being honest. He seemed to be going through an inner struggle he needed to work through on his own. I remained quiet, giving him mental space. Hours had passed with the falling night, and the wind calmed, allowing us to keep warm.

"Who are you missing, now that you've been gone for this long?" I asked.

He thought for a moment before answering. "I just miss my bed."

I chuckled. "Me too."

"What about you?"

"I miss my best friend. You'd love her. Briana is a hoot."

"How did you two meet?"

"Work. At first, I thought she was too loud and bold for my liking, but I quickly grew to love her quirks. She'd love to know all about my journey and especially about you. I'm sure she's currently just praying I'm still alive." I frowned.

"You sound pretty close."

"Yeah, we've grown to be. She's helped keep my head up despite ..." I trailed off.

"Despite what?"

"She doesn't know about what happened to me ... what happened to my father."

"Oh. I'm surprised you never told her."

It surprised me, too. I had been good friends with Briana for some years now, and despite knowing Tyler for less than a week, he knew my darkest secret. I stared into the fire. A rush of anxiety clawed through my body, but I thought I hid it well.

"Are you okay?"

"Yeah, why?" I replied.

"I can sense you're tensing up."

"You're good at reading people."

He smiled. "Just you." Those eyes of his lit up in the glow of the fire.

"I guess so." His smile relaxed me. "You better stick around after all of this. I'd hate for you to vanish on me."

His eyes playfully narrowed with a smile. "I'll be around as long as you want me to be."

"Better get used to Netflix and sleeping over then," I taunted.

He chuckled and sighed. "Sounds like a date, but what is Netflix?"

I giggled at his question and curled into his arms. My face snuggled into his chest where the shirt exposed his scars. He held me close while I felt the beat of his heart. So much had happened since the day I stitched him together. The question was: how long would this last? It no longer mattered if what we felt was premature. Instead, it only mattered how long I'd get to enjoy him. He had already nearly been taken from me. Despite being stuck in the wilderness, for the time being, I savored every moment like this one. I was different with Tyler. I had been with other men before, but never did I feel such a connection. Could it be how we met? The vast forest that claimed my father also brought me my new joy. The bond we had formed in such little time was overwhelming. I could only hope he *truly* did feel the same – a spark of internal flame for one another.

That reminiscence of spark brought me back to the darker thoughts I previously enjoyed. The thought of me wrapped around him in my bedsheets kindled desire within me again. I couldn't help myself. I worked to entwine my leg between his slowly, hoping he would invite the advance. My heart skipped when he lifted his thigh. I carefully placed my groin against his and rubbed myself into him. He gasped lightly; his breath deepened. I took his hand and placed it onto my groin so that he cradled my crotch. He didn't resist – instead, his breath grew shaky. I could sense he was unsure of his hand's placement. I rubbed his fingers into me through my pants. It wasn't long before I noticed his groin bulge. Although he felt aroused, I could sense his nerves. It was written in his breath ... he was afraid. Was it of sex? Perhaps of me? He could be the *no sex before marriage* type or maybe he wasn't as interested in me as he previously claimed. I brought his hand back to my waist.

CHAPTER TWELVE

WOLF CRY

Ty was already awake when my eyes opened, my face nuzzled in his chest. When I looked up and his eyes met mine, a mutual smile spanned our faces.

"Good morning," he greeted.

I rolled to my back and stretched my arms over where the fire pit smoked, its dying heat greeting my cold fingers. Despite my having fed it in the middle of the night, it was ready to burn out. I yawned with a sigh, grateful for the new day and my lack of dreams. I blushed at my behavior last night. I couldn't be sure what had gotten into me. "Morning. Sleep well?"

"Very," he replied.

"Good, I'm glad. We should get moving."

"Wait. Elizabeth." He placed his hand onto my arm. "About last night."

"You did nothing wrong."

"But I did. I froze. Forgive me for my lack of response. I –"

"I was confused by your reaction," I said cutting him off, "but I don't want to make you feel pressured into anything. I'm the one who should be apologizing. I'm sorry. Please, let's not discuss it further. We have a long trip back."

I didn't want to think of last night with the new day ahead. Breakfast and more water needed to be our focus. Ty was slow to get up. His body ached from the travel of yesterday, and his cold and callused feet were sore. When he was up, I kicked dirt on the dying heat of our campfire, and we started back on the hike. Despite Ty's complaints, he seemed strong. He stepped with a much less noticeable limp and no longer needed the trees to help him along. I had never seen someone heal with such speed and strength. Part of me wanted to lock him in a lab and run tests on him.

I snacked on plants and roots while Ty turned up his nose at everything offered as we moved miles along. I felt more hopeful about getting home with this new pace. As we carefully made our way around a thick patch of pines, a faint sound caught my attention. We had reached the lake, and our response was to gorge on water.

"I'm gonna clean myself up." I splashed the water over my arms and washed my jacket before using it as a wipe. While I cleaned, Ty rushed into the water from beside me with loud steps splashing as he submerged. "What are you doing?" I said, startled.

"Having a bath."

I watched him swim out to the center. "That must be freezing," I said to myself.

"Yup!" he playfully confessed.

Wow, he heard that?

I tried my luck and managed to catch a few fish away from where he disturbed the water. Ty ate them raw after finishing his bath. We didn't stay more than an hour, occasionally talking about topics like favorite pastimes, childhood experiences, and my past pets. Ty put his shirt back on but was undoubtedly cold.

In a few more miles north, we had reached something new, a small stream that poured from the tree roots above into a ditch of pooled water roughly five feet across. The recent storm must have created it.

"Wow, it's oddly beautiful," I said.

"I bet it tastes crisp in minerals."

I cupped my hand into the water and took a sip. He was right – the rich natural minerals were heavenly. Tyler sat down and leaned back to rest his weight on his arms. His head fell back, and he sighed. It was then that I noticed his foot was bleeding.

"You're hurt? Why didn't you tell me?"

He sat up and followed my eyes to a few cuts on the bottom of his right foot. "I didn't even know. My feet are so cold, I can't feel them that well."

My heart sank. We really needed to get out of these woods. Today must have been about fifty-five degrees. With no shoes, I had no way to protect his skin. A bandage wouldn't hold. "Come on. We need to keep moving." I put my bag on my back and headed off. He was slow to follow. I estimated it to be around ten in the morning based on the position of the sun, but sun location and directional or time correspondence was never something I had studied. I tried not to rush forward with Ty's continued lag. It was frustrating, but it could've been worse ... much worse.

After several more hours, I noticed Ty's steps stop behind me. When I turned around, he was staring at the woods behind us.

"What's wrong?" I questioned.

He stared for a few moments longer before turning back to me. "Nothing. I thought I heard something." I could see the raised hair on his arms. He started to walk toward me when a figure slipped through the trees behind him.

"What the hell was that?" I said. Ty rushed to my side before turning around. A wolf's cry then filled our ears – its song sad and low. The animal was very close.

"Stand behind me," he commanded. "Don't take your gun out."

I didn't have time to question him, but his voice was so sharp and confident I could only trust his judgment. The wolf then revealed herself. She stood next to a large pine twenty feet away, her brown eyes glaring at us. She bowed her head and let out a low growl. Despite my fear, I had to admire her stunning snow-white fur and impressive size. "Back off!" Ty demanded.

The animal raised her head to the sky and let out another howl, louder and sharper than before. Moments later, we found ourselves surrounded by massive wolves approaching from every direction. A red wolf approached from the left while a few grays came in from the right. A gray and white male then rushed in from behind. My eyes snapped around to all of them as my heart started racing. Most of them snarled, baring their massive teeth, until a gray female advanced next to the white one. Her eyes were sad and filled with pain. She kept her head low to the ground while she stared at us. My breath shortened. I was certain we were about to die.

"Get lost. I won't warn again!" Ty's voice was laced with anger. The wolves had stopped growling until I reached for my gun. "Don't, Elizabeth," he said, without looking at me.

A huge black wolf with a graying muzzle, bigger than all the others, of a near impossible size, raced up behind the sad female and came within five feet of Ty. His head was level with Ty's chest. My jaw dropped as he approached, but Ty didn't flinch.

"Back off," he repeated. His eyebrows narrowed at the animal. The wolf snarled at him and then turned his attention to me. "She's not to blame."

What did Ty mean? The white female came up to us and stood beside the black male – he dwarfed her in comparison, but she was still impressive. She whimpered and sat back as if trying to beg for something. The black male looked back at the weeping gray female. Her head was still lowered; her eyes still watered. Sweat pooled from my underarms. When were they going to maul us? What were they waiting for? The black male suddenly rushed the distance, throwing his huge head into Ty's chest, tossing us both backward to the ground. Ty landed partially on me, gasping in shock with the hit. I tried to pull my gun, but Ty's body weight prevented my fingers from retrieving it. I felt helpless while I awaited the pain of their mauling. My eyes closed in anticipation. Waiting. Waiting some more – but the only thing that happened was Ty's removed weight. He stood up. "Are you okay?"

I opened my eyes and he was holding his hand out to me. I looked around, but the wolves were gone – gone with the breeze itself. "What? Where did they all go? Why didn't they ki – kill us?" My voice cracked.

"Probably our lack of aggression. Wolves are not as savage as people think."

"But the gray wolf who attacked us, attacked you..."

"He had to be acting alone."

My nerves were so shaken, the event became blurred. I felt I was going into shock. My breathing was all over, and my arms trembled.

"Hey, calm down. We are okay," he said. Ty sat down next to me and took me in his arms.

To calm myself, I listened to the rhythm of his heart – working to focus on the beat and nothing else. When I was relaxed enough, I began to process everything. "How did you know they wouldn't attack?" I questioned while pulling away from him.

"I didn't. But with living in the woods not far from here, I have met this pack before. I've even fed 'em from time to time."

I decided it didn't matter. We were losing daylight and needed to keep moving.

CHAPTER THIRTEEN

DEFEATED

It must have been Wednesday again. The days were blurred, the unforgiving forest laughing at us while we suffered. Ty hadn't eaten anything since we left the lake, and it had been days since our encounter with the wolves – which was the last time I had my compass, dropping it during the encounter. Since then, a blanket of heavy fog and clouds swallowed our surroundings and hazed our senses. It was so thick in some areas, it engulfed the brush and distorted the trees, causing us to circle in a large loop, crossing over the same log twice. The stubborn fog refused to leave, determined to keep us disoriented, while the lingering clouds declined to budge. I kept smacking the GPS, but the screen continued to glitch.

Ty's feet were so bloodied, bruised, and cold he could barely carry on. Frigid temperatures and the cry of animals were intense every night. I didn't know how much longer we could continue. I paused to rest at the base of a pine, and he joined me – grateful for the pause.

"What do you think our funerals will look like?" he was only half joking.

"Probably full of roses and weeping friends. They'll say she was the fool who practically followed in her father's footsteps – death by the wilderness." My tone was light.

"My family would be distraught, but my cousins would happily snatch up my house. I'd get buried next to some big ol' tree in the middle of the family cemetery."

"Wait, your family has their own cemetery. Like, private cemetery?"

"Yup. Many generations buried there," he said.

"Maybe I'll get lucky and your family will find and bury us both. That way, my mother doesn't have to see my corpse and cough *I told you so* over me."

"She deserves closure, too." He frowned at the visual.

"I suppose." I could occasionally hear Ty's stomach growling. I was tired of commanding him to eat what I found while we walked. Every day, he grew weaker. "Why won't you eat?"

"I told you a million times ... I can't eat the forest plants. My stomach is too sensitive."

"Eating them despite your repulsion is still better than starving."

Under the fog, I found some new edible plants as we continued toward what I believed to be north. They looked like chicory, one of my favorites – but something was different about them. Contemplating my hunger, against my better judgment, I decided to try them, crunching on the flowers and leaves.

"Are you okay?"

"Something's wrong ... that wasn't chicory." I fell to the ground, swallowed by the fog while the world spun.

"Elizabeth? ... Oh God. What do I do?"

I remained conscious, but unable to move. Ty picked me up, leaving my bag behind, and carried me for miles. I wanted to protest, to tell him to stop. His leg couldn't handle my weight with his own.

He managed a long while before finally dropping me, tumbling us both to the ground. We lay in the torment of our bodies until I was able to move. Dehydrated and disoriented, I dragged myself to him.

"Tyyyluuer?" I slurred, struggling to his side.

He gave me a defeated glance. "... I just need some time."

His face no longer had the glow I'd come to know. His tired eyes and low spirit told me what words had failed to. Tyler wasn't going to make it - we both weren't. Dehydration wouldn't allow tears to well. My muddled brain contemplated leaving him to save myself, knowing I might fail to make it out anyway. I pondered turning my back on him like I did to my dying father. Tyler finally noticed my distress when I tearlessly sobbed, but he said nothing. He knew the reality of our situation before I did. Giving up, I lay beside him.

In my drifting consciousness, I remembered my mother's embrace. It wasn't just any embrace, but the moment when she finally saw me awaken after unconsciously battling smoke inhalation. It was the moment of hope that I would be okay. The embrace felt both sharp and sweet to me. I had felt her nails dig into my arms while she wrapped herself around me on the hospital bed, too tight for comfort - the same hospital I now worked at - or at least used to. I held Ty this very way now, lying on the floor of the forest that took everything from me. I wanted to hold onto hope with this final embrace.

Darkness took me again until I awoke from the snarl of a wolf, but I knew this wolf was in my head and not truly with us. A product of severe dehydration and a poisonous plant. So badly I wished him to appear and kill us both, as he would have done before the bullet. How much easier it would have been to die in the jaws of a powerful animal. The taste of death - the taste of blood on my lips as I contemplated welcoming death's embrace for us both. I had bit my lip too hard thinking about how my mother and Briana were right. The forest, the very wilderness that once shattered my life in the past had far more hell to offer - and I was not prepared for it. Never did I expect to become lost in a pool of blue before ending up in the fight of my short life. I opened my eyes and sat up beside him to look into the pool of blue one last time, but the eyes I so irrationally fell into were forever shut. His shallow breathing and battered body were all that remained.

In my disorientation, I pulled out the gun and held its dirty handle in my calloused grasp. The color, the scratches on the barrel, the dirt in its maltreated crannies – all looking marvelously beautiful through my impaired eyes. I briefly looked around, trying to determine how much time had passed since Ty dropped. It felt like forever. How was he still fighting? How was I? I couldn't let him fight anymore. We were meant to die here. I cocked the gun and aimed it at his forehead.

I'm so sorry, Ty. I failed us both. This horrid, cursed forest finally got us. I studied his face, losing myself in the contour of his perfect jaw line and lightly resting eyes. With a deep breath I pulled the trigger.

My weak heart skipped, but there was nothing. Just the pitiful click of the mud-jammed bullet – my aim to the ground beside him. My heavy arm fell to the dirt that I kneeled upon, dropping the metal. So many emotions flooded. Relief, anger, sadness, happiness – even if it fired, I couldn't manage to aim the damn gun at him. With my last bit of energy, I picked up the gun and threw it as hard as I could behind Ty before lying with him again, holding him within the cascade of fog. Not even the birds could see us now.

CHAPTER FOURTEEN

RESCUED

I could hear music. My body felt oddly comfortable. Where was the pain and cold? My eyes wouldn't open. Open, dammit! Why wouldn't they open! I must be dead.

"Do you think she'll make it?" my mother's fearful voice said – a voice that flowed around me.

Mom! I wanted to call out to her, but my body wouldn't respond. Why is heaven so stuffy? Wait, Mom shouldn't be here.

"She's suffered severe dehydration, has some kind of poisoning, and she's underweight, but I think she'll be okay," a man said.

That's Dr. Jason Smoldred! I can't be dead.

"Why hasn't she woken up?" Mom asked with that painfully worried voice I normally loathed, but her voice never sounded sweeter to me.

"We are bringing her back slowly. She will awaken soon. Elizabeth attacked some EMTs when hallucinating on the chopper ride here. Screaming something about a missing man, but we only found her. It must have been the effects of the dehydration and plant she ingested.

Missing? Oh my God, where is Tyler?

"Good heavens. Do you think someone attacked her in the woods?" Mom questioned.

"I thought about that too. She was found with no injuries and her clothing was intact. I wanted to check her for genital trauma. It seems your daughter simply lost her way. She's extremely lucky the search team located her, especially considering that heavy fog."

I could hear Mom sigh. My heart rate started to increase when my foggy consciousness realized Tyler had vanished. There was a chance he was still alive, no matter how slim.

"She's almost awake," Jason said.

Finally, my eyes lightened and opened for me. Uncomfortable lights, beeping machinery I was all too familiar with, and my mother's beaming smile greeted me. Jason looked as creepy as ever. The room overflowed with flowers, candles, and cheap teddy bears.

"Hi sweetie."

"H - hi Mom." I quickly noticed my chapped, dehydrated lips and the IV in my hand.

"Oh, Elizabeth. What happened, dear?"

I took a breath. "Where is Tyler? He is tall, black hair, blue eyes. The last thing I knew, I was lying on his chest waiting to die with him." Mom didn't know how to respond. She seemed a bit stunned and looked back at Jason for commentary. "Well?"

"Nobody was with you when you were found. Just you. Your gear was missing. They recovered your gun ten feet from where you were found," Jason informed me.

"That's impossible." My EKG machine beeped faster. "He had to be there!" My hands formed fists. I needed to see him.

"Lizzy, sweetie. Please relax. We can look for him later. He might have run for help."

"No, Mom. He couldn't walk, let alone carry on." It made no sense. Where could he have gone when he was moments from death?

The room door opened. A squeal resembling a baby pig made me nearly jump from my skin. "LIZZY!" Briana cried, "I'VE MISSED YOU SO MUCH, YOU BABOON." She practically jumped on the bed and proceeded to give me the largest bear hug ever. Weakly, I did my best to reciprocate the freakishly tight hug. Jason hustled out of the room. "You scared the beeswax out of me! I thought you were dead or worse!"

"Wait, what's worse than death?"

"Double death. Death by two unique reasons simultaneously of course! Silly. Now, tell me everything!" I managed to get my mom to leave and after a few hours of explaining the insanity I endured for almost two weeks, Briana wanted to see my tall, dark, handsome missing man almost as much as I did. "I can't believe a bear chased you up a tree and nearly ate you! And the wolves, oh my gosh. I knew the forest was nuts, but this is all crazy."

She was right. It did sound *really* crazy when I said it all out loud to her. With Ty's vanishment and hearing my own story, I had begun to question my sanity. Could I have hallucinated everything? Was I eating that strange plant the entire time and brain-fabricated everything?

"I really hope he survived 'cause I have never seen you so into someone before. Overall, you look like shit, but the look in your eyes is a glow all new to you. It's ... wow," she continued.

"I need to find him."

"Lizzy, what you went through is something I can barely imagine despite you literally just explaining every detail. Shooting that wolf ... you're so brave."

I chuckled. "Yeah, well ... I don't feel very brave." My eyes wandered. I didn't notice my staring into the bed sheets, but somehow Briana knew what I was thinking.

"You're not going after him ... are you?" she questioned. "I don't mean to sound harsh, but if he really was nearly dead when they found you, he is likely dead for sure by now."

Tears welled. "No, you're right."

"Oh, Liz. I'm so sorry." She hugged me. The emotions overwhelmed me when I realized he must be dead. I allowed myself to cry in her arms.

My hospital stay as a patient was brief. Once hydration and nourishment were achieved, I had no reason to stay and was discharged. My mother drove me home, driving in silence for a short while.

"I had your car towed home from the helicopter station."

I forgot my car would have still been there waiting for me. "Oh, thanks." My eyes never left the trees zooming by. Maybe I'd see him standing there at the forest's edge, healthy and smiling, those blue eyes gazing back at me – the eyes I longed for. Maybe I would see his frail cold body instead. Tears nearly overwhelmed my eyes, but I dared not let them fall in front of my mother.

"Are you going to be working tomorrow?" Mom questioned.

"I don't think I'm well enough yet." I had used most of my vacation days, but my sick days were still available. I couldn't go back while feeling this crushed.

"I understand, sweetie."

When we pulled into the driveway of my home, the first thing I noticed was that the grass had overgrown to near jungle length. For some reason, this made me smile if only for a moment. My frown was back faster than it had left. I got out of the car and rushed to get inside my home before I started to sob. Mom let me leave without another word. I nearly slammed the door behind me before sliding to the floor and caving into my emotions. Tyler was dead.

CHAPTER FIFTEEN

EMOTIONS

My failure to save Ty's life weighed heavily on me, nearly as much as losing my father. I didn't know Tyler for long, but he touched my heart in a way I had never experienced before. Part of me wanted to hold onto the extremely unlikely chance he somehow survived, but I was a realist who knew it was near impossible. Looking at what remained of my pets, I could see Beamer was depressed from his loneliness – he apparently sensed Bennie would not return. Watching him pace the cage in search of his missing sibling broke my heart all over again.

There was no food in the house, so I ordered pizza and decided to put on Netflix. While I waited for my dinner to arrive, I sat down on the couch with Beamer and searched for anything action packed and nonromantic. I settled for the first Jurassic Park movie. This film would normally have immersed me in its before-its-time graphics, but my thoughts betrayed me. I sighed heavily at the deeply depressing knowledge of Ty's permanent absence. My heart was in my stomach.

Thirty minutes passed when I heard a knock at the front door. I wished for Ty to be behind it.

"That'll be twenty-one forty-nine," said the thinly built young man when I opened the door.

I handed him thirty dollars. "Thanks." Then I slammed the door in his face and brought my pie to the kitchen. My appetite was near nonexistent but imagining Ty's disapproval if I starved myself over his loss prompted me to eat. If he made it and I didn't, I'd want him to live his life and move on. Besides, pizza was hard to ignore no matter how terrible you felt. I walked back over to the couch with my slice and sat down, offering a piece to Beamer.

After dinner I took a much-needed shower and then changed into pajamas. I was already exhausted at nine o'clock. My bed was just how I left it and never looked warmer. After sleeping in the dirt for almost two weeks – which felt like months – I slithered under the sheets as if they were the skirts of a heavenly cumulus cloud. It wasn't long before I was fast asleep.

I awoke to being soaking wet. No, I was in a pool. A crisp pool of bluish-red water, water that darkened redder with every passing second until it was a thick soup of warm blood. I was swimming in blood, struggling to get to the side of the pool, but something was pulling me back. Something had my right ankle! I turned back to look and with a kick upward I saw it was a hand that wouldn't let go. It held onto me and begun pulling me under. I screamed for help. Someone save me! I thrashed harder and harder, trying desperately to pull away when the bloodied water caught fire. The blue fire swept around me, forming a ring when I finally kicked free of the hand's grasp, but it was too late. I was surrounded by a smokeless flame. It shot high into the sky allowing nothing but a fiery wall to be seen. That's when I felt something hit my forehead and splash into the water in front of me. When I looked down to see what hit me, something was looking back. Four eyeballs with blue irises rolled in the soupy pool of blood.

"NO!" I screamed, jolting up. My breathing was ragged. It was a dream. A horrible, disgusting dream. I felt for my cell phone from the nightstand. When I found it, I turned on the screen, blinding my eyes. It was only three in the morning. I sighed in relief. I was okay.

That's when I heard something in the corner of the room shift. The hairs on the back of my neck pricked up. There was something in the room. My thoughts raced for any possible explanation for the movement I heard, or thought I heard, but in my near panic nothing really made sense. Maybe it was the heat expanding the walls, maybe I wasn't fully awake, maybe I really was going crazy. I reached for the nightstand lamp and turned the switch. It clicked and quickly filled the room with light. My heart still pounded despite nothing being there. Aside from myself, the room was empty. The window remained cracked slightly open just as I had left it. It must have been the wind blowing the curtain. I got up to close it, taking the moment to calm myself. I turned around and looked at my disheveled bed. I must have been tossing all night. While fixing the blankets, my thoughts betrayed me again. I thought about how Ty would never belong to my bed as I had wanted so badly. I'd never get to hold him again or feel him within me. Tears welled. I crawled back into bed and cried until I was asleep again.

The next thing I could comprehend was being in my backyard. It was overwhelmingly cold with a wicked blizzard snapping through the surrounding pines. I was wearing my night robe and purple rain boots. I must have been dreaming again, because the night turned to daytime in the blink of an eye. I tried to move my feet, but they were frozen in the thick blanket of snow. Birds were singing all around me – black birds with yellow wing tips flapped around the trees. One abruptly shot down and flapped within inches of my face. Then they were all doing it, grabbing my hair and scratching me. I flung my arms around trying to scare them off. *AH! GO AWAY!* I screamed out, but no sound was produced. It was then nighttime again. I could hear a sharp howl pierce the lonely trees; it was a cry laced with intense sorrow. A black wolf appeared. It pricked its ears toward me, standing only twenty feet away in the calmed weather. I could barely make out its shape. That's when a sharp pain hit the back of my head. *OUCH!*

The nightmares were getting to be too much – vivid, intense, hard to forget. I awoke minutes before my alarm. I now had to decide whether to go to work or take a sick day. I took a moment to evaluate my physical and mental state. Between the harsh dreams, lack of proper sleep, and continuing depression, I determined it was still best to take the day off. While work would help distract me, I was in no condition to perform my job properly. A mistake in some areas of my profession could kill or injure someone. I called in sick for work before leaving my bed. It took me forever to get dressed. My arms felt like two limp weights on each side of my body. I really hadn't looked at myself since I was rescued. The mirror wasn't nice to me in reflection. I had baggy eyes with discolored skin; my complexion reminded me of zombie movies. When I vigorously brushed my hair, a lot of it fell out. I moaned in annoyance.

While I was making a quick breakfast of instant maple oatmeal, Briana had texted me: *Hey, how are you feeling? I'm off today. Do you wanna hang out?*

Company would be a great way to distract myself, but Briana might want to play therapist to help me deal with everything.

Wanna go for a run? My suggestion surprised myself. After everything, I wanted to run through the woods.

Hell yeah.

Odd. Why didn't she try to argue I wasn't fully back to my old self and therefore shouldn't attempt such exertion? If I was honest with myself, my physical condition was still weak. I knew why I wanted to jog. I wanted to scan the remote forest for him. It would be like looking for a speck of gold in a mountain of dirt, but I was so mentally lost from Ty's disappearance, my very soul needed to find any evidence he really existed.

I texted back. *Great. Meet me at my place in twenty mins.*

I had just finished prepping myself for the cool weather run when Briana pulled up in my driveway. I rushed out to meet her, fully prepared to defend my choice of activity, but she didn't challenge me – not even when we left the driveway. Instead, she turned on the radio and started to gently bob her head like a pop-fan-teen. I found myself scanning the woods while we sped along. As expected, Briana took us to our usual jogging trail – which I had learned to be comfortable in. An ache hit the pit of my stomach as she pulled up her Ford truck to the trailhead. The trail stretched four miles, but we never traveled more than two miles deep into the woods. My consciousness wallowed in the foliage. The woods still felt like an old frenemy.

Briana patiently waited for me to shake my nerves away. "Take your time, Liz. There's no rush."

I understood Bri was trying to be understanding, but I already missed her normal brusque vocabulary. In frustration, I opened the truck, climbed out, and slammed the door back at the oversized, gas-guzzling, pink-pig of a vehicle in an effort to get a reaction out of her. She knew how much I hated her truck. As she walked around to the passenger side, I could see her biting her lip ever so slightly. I was both impressed and disappointed by her restraint. I thought I'd want her to be quiet about everything, but I realized I wanted her to dish out the topic that continued to consume me.

"You ready?" she questioned.

"As I'll ever be." My frown deepened when I watched her put her earbuds in. We jogged along in silence. My earbuds in, I overplayed the rock songs and even threw in a screamo for good measure. My sadness over everything I had been through turned to anger. If Ty was somehow alive, perhaps he left me to die alone. But that wasn't why I was angry: it was the powerful emotions I felt toward someone I had known for so little time - if at all - and here I was intensely searching the forest. I darted my vision around every off-trail tree, stone, stick, and leaf. This wasn't normal behavior. Briana must have been pretending not to notice my obsessive scans of our surroundings. She hummed to the words of her pop songs. At the two-mile mark, she stopped to turn around, but I couldn't - I had to keep going. At first, Briana tried to object. She grabbed my arm, unable to make me hear her through my music. All I had to do was glare back at her and she let go. I didn't care if she turned back and left me to continue alone, but she soon caught back up with me.

The cool wind bit my face while I tried to overcome what was happening to me. I was beginning to scare myself. Focusing on my breathing, I slowed to a speed walk and tried to let go of everything I'd been through. Taking some seconds to close my eyes within the strides, I reopened them and was startled to see a figure creeping out behind a distant tree. I stopped dead in my tracks. I could feel the blood draining from my face as I pulled out my earbuds.

"Liz? Liz! Hey? What's wrong?" She rushed back to where I stopped and waved her hand in my face. When I pushed her hand away, the figure was gone. It had to be Ty!

"It's Tyler! Ty! Wait!" I ran as fast as I could to where I saw him. I met the large tree he was behind only to find empty brush. My eyes darted so fast around, I thought they'd roll out.

"What the hell are you doing?"

"I saw him!"

"There's nobody here. I didn't see anything."

"No, I know I saw him. I know it!" I searched the trees, soil, and leaves for any clue of his presence.

"You're scaring me. Let's go home. Maybe we can get some hot chocolate."

"NO. HE'S OUT HERE!" I was shouting at the top of my lungs. "TYLER!" Briana had seen enough. When I tried to run deeper off the trail, she grabbed my arm and twisted hard. I buckled to the ground. "Ouch, what the hell?"

"That's enough," she scolded. "No more!" Her face was painted with anger, but fear was also visible. "You're going crazy. I'm taking you back to the hospital to be checked again."

But I saw him. I saw someone ... didn't I? Maybe she was right. I was going insane. I stood back up and brushed my backside off. Tears welled until they flowed, and my surroundings blurred.

Briana wasn't surprised when I didn't let her take me to the hospital. I might have been losing it, but the hospital would have only made me worse. She dropped me off at home. I sharply thanked her and rushed inside. I realized I wouldn't be winning any *friend of the year* awards.

CHAPTER SIXTEEN

VISITOR

A month had passed since my woodland episode with Briana. An entire month I fought with myself. Tyler was not real. Tyler was not real. I saw nothing. I repeated it over and over. True or not, it helped me move on. I was almost ready to fully accept that Tyler was a mental fabrication and never existed. I forced Briana not to mention anything related to my mental breakdown or the reason for it. I threw myself into my work more than I ever previously allowed. Everything became about work. For the month, I had pushed away everyone – even Briana. She gave me some space but would occasionally ask me if I was alright – which I didn't mind. I was glad she cared. The past few days, I was reaching out to her more.

"Mom is calling me almost every night at around eight," I said while eating a salad in the hospital cafeteria.

"Avoiding her?"

"Somewhat. I gave her my rabbit and rat for the time being and she's not too sure about it."

"Maybe she just wants to talk?"

"I'm sure she does." I took another mouthful. I had an empty house – completely pet-less. It felt strange, but through my depression I could not care for them properly.

"She's just going to drive to your house if you don't answer soon. I'm surprised she hasn't yet."

Briana was probably right. I'd answer the phone tonight.

"How are you ladies doing today?" Jason butted in.

"Good! You?" Briana replied. He stared at me waiting for a response that never came. "Umm, so Lizzy was just telling me she wanted to get her nails done with me tonight. Care to join us? Because who doesn't need a *manicure*?" Briana's challenge of Jason's masculinity made me smile.

"I'm good. You ladies have fun, alright?" He smiled at me and then walked over to the desserts.

I giggled with her. "I'm not getting my nails done. He knows I am not into that kind of stuff," I joked.

"It *would* be fun if you gave it a try. And who cares what Jason thinks? I didn't want to bring it up, but I've noticed his eye for you has been even stronger since your *supposed to be solo* journey."

I glared at her. "Oh, I've noticed." Ever since my return at work, Jason had been more annoying and aggressive than ever before. He kept asking me on dates, once with a post-it note he folded and left in a patient's room addressed with my full name. Inside it read "*date night, please*" with a question mark and wink face below. My theory was that he was jealous to see me with feelings and interest for someone else. "Do you think his aggressiveness is jealousy?"

Briana knew exactly what I meant. "Yes, I think so," she replied, and then put another forkful of salad into her mouth.

"So do I. I remember hearing him say to my mother that he wanted to do a genital check on me. Please tell me he didn't ..."

Briana gasped. "Ugh, NO! ... There was NO WAY I was going to let *him* do that. He suggested it with Dr. Lindy, but we both shot that down *really* fast."

I flushed with embarrassment. "Thank goodness."

After work, I drove home slowly, listening to the hum of my

car. An old man tailgated behind, blowing his horn as I dragged along. Despite the one lane, I watched him speed around me with his finger raised high. I was soon on my favorite street, where oaks and maples dominated. The leaves no longer filled their canopies with the colors of fall, but instead bore stripped branches ready for the harsh winter nearly here. I heard a rumor there was some snow on the weather forecast for tonight – the first snow of the season. I loved snow for its beauty, but it made traveling a nightmare. I was glad not to have work tomorrow.

Dinner was seasoned chicken and potatoes. I ate while watching the weather forecast. "Tonight, we will have six inches of snow in the lower elevations, up to eighteen inches in the mountains, with five mile an hour winds over most of Jackson County," stated the weatherman. Glancing out the glass back door as I chewed, I saw there were already two inches of crystal snow blanketing the dark yard. The mystic nature of snow had captivated me since childhood. I stared into the dancing flakes with awe, their company helping me momentarily forget about all I had faced in the past few months. My surroundings dropped from reality when something moved in the yard, just barely noticeable. I got up and walked over to the back door for a closer look. The snowfall was picking up, making it harder to see into the forest behind my property, but I sensed something shifting in the darkness. The sudden sharp house phone ring made me jump from my skin. *Dammit.* I grabbed my heart before walking over and answering.

Before Mom could say hello, I knew who had called. "Hey darling, thank you for answering. I've missed you so much ... your animals do too."

"Hi Mom. Thank you again for taking them."

"Yes, about that, sweetie. Are you sure you don't want them back? I love them, but I'm worried about you being all alone in that house with nobody to cuddle up with. Do you want us to come over? We could have a movie night together."

Mom worried about my mental health. I didn't blame her considering how crazy I'd been acting after being rescued. "No, it's fine. Time alone is actually helping me collect myself. Thank you though," I replied.

"Okay. Just know you can always call or visit. I'm here for you." Before I could respond, something outside caught my eye again. I stepped to the light switch and darkened the room. Something was there – or was I imagining things again? My heart started to race. "Honey, you there?" she asked.

I couldn't respond.

The figure moved closer to the house. It was large and wide, black in color. I dropped the house phone; it was caught by the cord and smacked back against the wall. I could hear my mother's muttered panic on the other side, but I was frozen. The figure stopped moving when it reached the tree line of my open yard. I could make out fur. A bear? Curiosity urged me to move closer to the glass door. I managed to slowly walk up to it, never taking my eyes off the creature. My heart pounded in my chest and my breath shortened.

The walls of the house creaked against the building weight of the snow.

When I reached the glass, the creature moved forward again – slowly and cautiously. It stared back within the darkness, its face never shifting into focus. I contemplated running upstairs to get my gun, but a voice inside my head told me not to move. This voice then told me in all its craziness to open the door. I almost listened, reaching for the door's handle before snapping myself back. What am I thinking? Maybe my mom had more reason to worry than I thought.

The creature moved forward again. My heart jumped when I realized what it was. A huge black wolf. In the dim moonlight, he stood tall within the mounting snow. With my irrationality present,

I involuntarily opened the door and stepped outside. The freezing shock of snow against my bare feet was scarcely noticeable. The animal walked closer again, slowly, until he stood just ten feet away. And that's when I noticed the pools of blue.

Those pools of blue I longed for – the wolf's eyes were unmistakably familiar. I was drawn to him – a familiar magnetic pull I had only felt once before. I'd never seen him before, but I knew this animal – how was that possible? He bowed his head down without breaking eye contact, his breath filling the air around him with sharp clouds of fog. I didn't know how it was possible, I didn't know if I was truly insane, but this animal was *Tyler*.

CHAPTER SEVENTEEN

LONG DAYS

"HELLO?" Briana yelled.

I jumped, startled. "I'm up. I'm up." I peeled myself from the cafeteria table.

"You're lucky it's a slow day. Are you okay? I've never seen you so ... tired."

"Yes, I'll manage. Give me a few minutes." I held my head in my hands, staring into the table. It had been two days since that encounter in my backyard. I hadn't been able to sleep since. Tossing and turning all night long or pacing around the house while staring into the backyard was all I could accomplish.

"I'll get you some coffee." She got up and left me to my thoughts.

Was I officially nuts? Had I lost it? What I saw - or what I thought I saw - was impossible. Moments after my impossible realization that night, the animal tossed his head toward the falling snowflakes and sang the most beautiful howl I'd ever heard. He gave me one final glance before turning around and darting back into the darkness of the trees.

This was madness. I couldn't tell anyone. I would have been sent to a mental institution. Maybe I should've been in one. I didn't feel crazy, but people who are crazy often can't tell they are. It was okay to not have all my marbles, but maybe I should see a therapist.

"Here ya go. Exactly how you like it. Dark like your soul," Briana mocked.

"Ha ha. Very funny ... thanks." I pulled the cup to hold in my cold hands. There was still snow on the ground. The temperature had been dropping ever since.

"How are you feeling ... emotionally?"

"I've been blue." If only she knew the double meaning behind those words. "Mom is mad at me. I accidentally gave her a scare."

"How?"

"Thought I saw something outside and dropped the phone mid conversation."

"Ah. What did you see?"

"... It was nothing. Something caught in the trees." I had been a poor liar from the time I started talking and Briana's face told me she knew I wasn't being honest. I wanted to kiss her when she dropped it.

"Jason asked me what you like yesterday. He asked me for courting tips."

My eyes nearly rolled out of my head. "That man is a thorn in my ass."

"I know. It's sorta sexual harassment," Briana said while frowning. "I told him to give it up."

"Good. I swear, he will never leave me alone." I sipped my coffee.

"He's not used to rejection."

"Boo-hoo. I'm tired of that being an excuse for a man refusing to piss off," I hissed.

When our break was over, Briana headed off to the ICU while I was called for a delivery. When I entered the room, the mother was in distress. To my anguish, Jason arrived to assist with the birth. When the screaming newborn made her entrance, Jason handed me the cord clamp while he stitched the mother's tear. "Aren't you going to cut the cord?" he questioned when I waited.

"Not yet. Delayed cord clamping, remember?"

"Oh ... right."

When we finished up with the birth, Nurse Andrew took over the newborn's tests. Jason followed me out of the room and gently closed the door behind him before turning to me. "I just wanted to say thank you for the reminder."

I was slightly taken back by his gratitude. Jason was normally a very selfish and self-absorbed man, too proud to thank anyone for helping when he fell short. "Just doing my job." I gave him a soft smile.

"Listen. I know you've been ignoring and avoiding me. I'm sorry for nagging. I realized it's unwelcome and unappreciated."

My jaw dropped. "Uh ... um. Just please respect my space from now on."

"I will." He smiled, but the smile was not innocent. I saw something behind it, like this was a new tactic he was hoping would work.

"I have to go meet Briana," I lied. Turning away, I hustled toward the elevator. I was grateful when the doors opened only moments from hitting the down button, but before the doors could close behind me, Jason had stopped them and stepped in. I sighed and he noticed.

"Something wrong?" he questioned.

"No, just tired." I wanted to say I was tired of him. He didn't reply, just stood uncomfortably close to me. The doors opened for the floor below. We made space for an older woman in a wheelchair and her escort, Nurse Madison Brown, who immediately lit up when she saw Jason.

"Good afternoon, Doctor," she purred while completely ignoring me. Madison was jealous of Jason's lust for me. I had heard through the grapevine that she had commented on how I was foolish not to date him – she'd jump at the chance … again. I almost rolled my eyes at the thought alone.

"Hello, Nurse Brown," he replied with a smile. I tapped my foot, wishing the elevator wasn't snail slow. When the doors opened again, we were on the first floor. Nurse Madison pushed the patient's wheelchair into the lobby and I quickly headed toward the ICU, hopeful Briana was still there. To my annoyance, Jason was following me.

I decided to be bold. I stopped short and turned around. It took him by surprise and he nearly walked into me. "Dr. Smoldred, is there something you need from the ICU?" I sharply asked.

"Uh. Um, I was informed I should direct my services to the ICU patients."

"Hmmm. How convenient." My eyes narrowed.

He raised his hands. "Easy, Tigress. It's a slow day and I could be of more use in the ICU."

I didn't buy it. Working with Jason made me feel like I had a monkey on my back. A huge blond monkey. "I see. Carry on then." I gestured for him to advance past me. He chuckled and moved along. Before he could look back, I rushed away to the restroom. Inside, I bumped into a woman, knocking her purse from her hand. "I'm so sorry, I'm a clumsy fool." I quickly collected her bag from the floor before meeting her eyes. She was about sixty-five, medium height, tired eyes, and most apparent – her head was bald.

"It's okay. Honest accident," she responded while I handed her the purse. Her eyes lit up. "You're avoiding someone, aren't you?"

"That obvious?"

"As obvious as my bald head." She chuckled. "I'm a cancer patient here. About to get another awful treatment."

"Shouldn't you be wearing a face mask?" I questioned.

"Nah, I'm on my way out of this world. Might as well be from a cold. This cancer is winning … and I can't let it get me in the end."

She gave me a huge smile. I suddenly felt my problems were extremely manageable. "So, who are you avoiding?" she continued.

"Oh, just my coworker, Jason."

"Ah, and he's not the one. No. There's someone who has your heart. I can tell." I blushed at her statement. "You see, it's in your face. I had someone that special to me once. He was killed in a motorcycle accident when we were both thirty-five. Left me with two beautiful children. I'm excited to see him again soon."

My heart sank. "I'm ... I'm so sorry."

"Don't be. We had a great life together while it lasted. The spark I felt for him was like nothing I've experienced before or since. Such lust and love ... so precious and rare." She winked at me with another smile. "Well, I'd best be on my way. Happy hiding."

She opened the door and left me alone with my racing thoughts. I turned to the sink and placed my hands under the faucet, the sensor activating the cool water. I washed my hands and then patted my face. In the mirror, my eyes were heavy and sad, my skin discolored, and my hair disheveled. I looked terrible. Was this the face that woman recognized?

The sudden ring of my phone made me jump. I took it from my pocket. It was Briana. "Hey, what's up?" I answered.

"Wondering where you are. I could use some help with a patient."

"Sure, I'll be there in a minute."

The rest of the day was a blur. Blood, vomit, medical equipment, and the equally tired faces of my coworkers followed the day into a late night before my fourteen-hour shift finally ended.

I could barely make it home. The lines of the road were shifting in ways I thought only alcohol could produce. Pulling into my driveway, I dragged myself out of the car – ignoring the odd feeling of eyes on my back – and all but crawled into my frigid house. It was cold in both temperature and atmosphere. Empty never felt so lonely. Locking the door behind me, I resembled a sloth on my climb up the stairs. Only out of necessity did I shower and change into pajamas before retiring for the night.

I awoke with a shiver. It was freezing in the house. Looking at my phone, it was almost noon. I slept that late?! Jumping out of bed, I rushed to locate my work schedule only to realize I was off from work. Huge relief. I put on a heavy sweater. Was my thermostat not working or did I forget to pay a bill? Maybe out of oil? As I walked downstairs, it quickly got colder - so cold, it was nipping my face. At the bottom of the stairs I felt a draft and then realized my back door was open.

"What the hell!" I rushed over to shut and lock it. Worried someone was inside my home, I hurried into the kitchen and grabbed a knife. I saw no signs of a break-in, no signs of robbery. Everything looked completely untouched. In my exhaustion, had I opened the back door?

Looking outside the sliding glass door I could see fresh human footprint tracks in the snow. A knot was building in my throat. Should I call the police? Should I tell my mom? Could this be a sick prank? I tried to come up with a rational explanation. A thief wouldn't break in and take nothing, and the door wasn't damaged. A murderer wouldn't leave me unharmed. The tracks led into the woods behind my property line. A sudden, unwelcome, and somewhat crazy thought came to mind. Could this have been Tyler? No. That was a ridiculous thought. The only logical explanation my emotionally drained state could reasonably accept was that my frail consciousness took me out of bed during the night. I must have strolled into the woods until I found my way back. Sleep walking. The snow must have kept my feet clean. Yes. This was logical if not sane. Still horrified by the event, I struggled to eat breakfast while watching the news. Nothing major had been occurring. I managed to smirk at a reporter's over-accentuated tone, especially regarding the story featuring boring winter events. This reporter was young, maybe early thirties, and with each mediocre story he covered, he featured the classic news reporter speech style my family had mocked over the years. His brown hair, square jaw, and pleasant voice calmed me with my cup of warm coffee. The couch cradled my tired, cold frame while I curled into a throw blanket. It was a pleasant moment, if not brief.

Abruptly, I heard a massive crashing sound followed by a wave of glass flying in front of the couch from the direction of my back door. I sprung up and lunged myself off the back of the couch toward the kitchen, away from whatever had just exploded into my living room. Before I looked to see what caused the destruction, I grabbed the knife from the kitchen island. Jaws snapping, snarls, and loud yelping – I heard something crash around my room while the weatherman was still reporting on the TV. I hid behind the island, clutching the knife with all my strength. My heart raced against the noise. The animal had to be massive and rabid, smashing all around in the bed of glass. It sounded like it was fighting something. I peeked from behind the island. It was huge and there were two of them – a black wolf and a gray and white wolf were trying to kill each other in my living room. I watched them tear into each other's flesh and vocalize screams I never heard an animal make. Their eyes wide with aggression, the gray wolf pulled away and raced out back through the broken glass doors. I tried not to breathe while I prayed the other massive animal would do the same, but it only stood there – staring out the back door while breathing heavily. I could hear the warm blood from the animal dripping onto the floor. Maybe it would be dead soon. As I stared, it glanced toward me and that's when I saw them – those striking blue eyes.

It stared at me for what felt like an eternity. Those all-too-familiar eyes belonged to a substantial creature that did not kill me in my time of emotional weakness – yet here it stood, dying inside my home. Blood was dripping down its black coat from the shoulder.

Before I was able to catch my thoughts, the animal collapsed with a thud in front of my couch. Did he die? I couldn't see him past the back of the couch.

My heart was racing. I grasped the knife firmly and slowly stood up. I wished it would vanish like the gray wolf I killed. My shaking legs slowly moved toward the couch. Every step was daunting. When I walked around the couch, my eyes were confused by what they saw – the bloodied back of a naked man. I gasped.

CHAPTER EIGHTEEN

SHOCK OF A LIFETIME

It took me a minute to regain composure while Tyler bled onto the floor, cradled naked in a sea of glass and black fur - a lot of which rested on his back. *Hurry!* There was no time to process. I rushed upstairs and ransacked the storage closet and bathroom for every towel and medical instrument I had. I acknowledged that if I called for help to take him to the hospital, Tyler's secret could be exposed. I tried not to think about how this entire time, Ty really wasn't dead - or a product of my imagination. What I had witnessed, despite its impossibility, *must* have been real.

Gathering everything into a basket, I ran downstairs. At his side, I brushed as much loose fur off him as I could and then pulled the large couch throw-blanket over his backside. Most of the damage was dangerously close to the back of his neck, but primarily centralized between his shoulders. With no way to move him, I let him remain on the patch of bloody glass. I worked to put the skin of his back in place and then applied pressure. I needed help. I couldn't do this alone. When the bleeding slowed, I rushed to the kitchen phone and dialed.

"Hi Lizzy. Wha -" Briana answered.

"I need your help! It's urgent! You're working today?"

"What? What's wrong? I'm at work, yeah."

"Thank goodness. Rush to my house as fast as possible! Bring everything you can for an animal attack victim, but DO NOT tell anyone. Do you understand?" I yelled to her.

"Liz, what is –"

"DO YOU UNDERSTAND?" I repeated.

"Yes. I'll be right over," she said sternly.

I hung up. Rushing to my front door, I unlocked it and raced back to his side. Briana was my most trusted friend. I knew she would come through for us.

"Tyler, stay with me!" I heard him moan, seemingly conscious. "Can you move?" I held the pressure on his back despite the glass. His arms were above his head on the floor.

While I was trying to figure out how we'd move him, he pulled his arms down to move them to his sides as if to lift himself. I anxiously waited to see if he would try getting up, but he only held them there – making no further effort. His face was to the side, his eyes were closed, and his expression was blank. I thought he had lost consciousness until he shifted his left leg. I released the pressure from his back and carefully lifted his head to put a towel between his face and the glass. "Tyler, you need to get up." I tried to lift him, but his dead weight made it impossible.

Waiting for Briana's help was agonizing. Ty occasionally moaned in pain. My heart was in both my throat and stomach. It was painfully quiet. I barely noticed how freezing cold the house was. Ty was shaking, but maybe it was shock. I nearly cried when I saw Briana open my front door.

"Lizzy? Liz! What the hell!" Her expression was a combination of utter disbelief and shock. She collected her jaw from the floor and, with a large medical kit, rushed to us.

"Thank God, Briana. I can't thank you enough. It's just you, right? Did you bring everything?" Tears welled in my eyes.

"Is this Tyler?" She stood over him gawking in confusion.

"Briana, focus! Did you bring everything?" I snapped.

"Yes. I managed to sneak blood, but I couldn't get medication. They're too strict."

I sighed in both relief and minor annoyance, but I wasn't surprised. Drugs were heavily regulated. "Help me carry him upstairs."

"Upstairs?" Her left eyebrow rose.

"Yes, we need to get him on my bed."

I struggled to lift one side of his pelvis and then the other to wrap the blanket around him. "His back is torn up from an animal attack. He needs staples. Ready yourself to lift him. He's lying on glass."

"Why is there so much fur? And why is he naked? And what happened to the back door?" she asked.

"No questions!" Ty then lifted his body slowly so that he was on his hands and knees. His arms quivered under his weight. "Tyler, here." I held the blanket around his waist as Briana and I took his arms around our necks. He was weak but managed to carry most of his weight up the stairs. He collapsed next to my bed. "Shit. We need him on the bed." Blood dripped everywhere. "Come on, get up!" I commanded.

Briana looked at me with judgment. Ty was lying on the floor, exhausted and in pain. Those beautiful eyes opened to meet me while he breathed in distress – now holding the blanket around himself.

"I ... I can't," he said quietly between his fight for each breath. He was very pale and needed an IV.

"Yes, you can," I said now on my knees with my hand holding his face. "Come on."

I pulled back the comforter and with Briana's help, struggled to help him into the bed. Red quickly soaked the sheets. His chest, hands, feet, and forearms were full of glass pieces, but his back bore the worst of the trauma. When I prepared the needle, Ty was too weak to notice what we were doing. He laid his head back into the pillow. When the blood bag was set up, I pulled his right hand closer and inserted the needle into his largest vein. Tape held it in place and soon, blood was entering his body. "Help me turn him to his side. We need to staple up his back. Briana aided without a word until she focused on the damage. She gawked at his flesh wounds.

"This needs a hospital. Why aren't we taking him to the hospital?"

"Trust me, dammit." The expression on my face was the same expression I had when she had stolen a kiss from my ex. I had punched her in the arm and ignored her for a month for that betrayal. This look was all it took to keep her from further questioning.

"Okay, but without morphine, we're stapling his back while he's awake - feeling everything." She winced at the thought of what we were about to do to him.

"We don't have a choice." We prepped for stapling him, putting on gloves, picking fur from the dripping wounds, and readying ourselves. Ty laid on his side facing away, quiet with his shallow breathing. I began to pull his skin together for the staples and understandably, Ty cried in pain - shifting his back away from me. I felt Briana's wince. "I know it hurts. Try to stay still for me. Deep breath and hold it." He did his best to listen, taking in a large amount of air. I quickly pulled his skin together again and stapled. He gasped and then growled deep in his throat - more animal than human. It scared me, but I had to trust he wouldn't hurt us. Without warning him, I completed the second staple. This time, he screamed.

"This is madness. He's suffering!"

"Briana." I almost growled at her. "You NEED to trust me. He cannot be brought to the hospital." I turned back to Ty, proceeding to pinch another section of his torn skin. From there on, the click of the stapler never failed to make him cry out or gasp. Halfway through, Briana had taken over while I sat on the bed next to him holding his hand, doing my best to soothe him through the pain. His eyes leaked with the torment. After a half hour and over thirty staples, his cries dwindled. There was one staple to finish when Tyler passed out. "Briana, he's lost consciousness." I placed my fingers on his neck. His pulse was strong.

The stapler clicked again. "I'm finished," Briana said. I got up and walked around to see Briana's finished work. His back looked like a horror movie prop. Tears started to fall now that I was able to truly process everything. Briana got up and hugged me despite her bloodied gloves. "He will be okay," she comforted.

I sniffled. "He needs to be." She released her embrace and looked me in the eyes. "I don't know what's going on, but you're my best friend and I will always have your back."

"... Well, technically you had *his* back today."

Briana giggled. "I guess that's true. Let's remove that glass from his skin before he wakes up."

I looked at my phone for the time. It had been a while since she arrived. "You need to get back to the hospital. You're going to be in enough trouble as it is with the amount of time you went missing. I can handle it from here."

"You're sure?" she questioned.

"I'm sure. Thank you so much for coming to the rescue. I don't know what I would have done if you didn't."

"You owe me. But really, an explanation would be enough."

"Just don't mention this to anyone ... ever."

She gave me another hug. "I won't. Take care of him. He's going to need some TLC." She winked at me and then left the bedroom. "Oh - my hell, it's freezing down here!" I heard her jokingly yell when she got to the bottom of the stairs.

I shifted my attention to Ty. He needed to be wrapped around his chest and back, but first the glass needed removal. Despite my strength, I struggled to turn him to his back. When he was in position, I was able to focus on the extent of the glass. All the pieces were small and on the surface. I put on fresh gloves and started to remove them using tweezers.

Ty was unresponsive. I felt the same relief as when I stitched him in the forest. The thought reminded me of how he left me for dead. Or did he? Each bloodied piece was set aside in a collection pile. I counted as the pile added up. Twenty-four larger shards and nineteen smaller shards – all smaller than a quarter inch. Ty began to awaken when I was finishing up with the removal. I could hear subtle moans in his throat. I paused and waited. Soon, he opened his eyes halfway and looked at me. I smiled. "Hi Tyler. Are you okay?"

He breathed in with a sigh. "Never better," he joked.

"I'm surprised you'd crack a joke considering." My eyes melted within his. Even in his condition, he was beautiful beyond words. "Can you sit up? I need to wrap your back and chest." He took a deep breath and held it in until he was upright. I didn't say anything while I started to wrap him. When I was done, he looked like an unfinished mummy. "You can lie down now but try to move to the clean side." Looking at the blood on the sheets made me feel oddly guilty as if this was all somehow my fault. I couldn't make sense of why I felt this way. He had settled on his stomach when the doorbell rang. Who could that have been? Tyler didn't seem to notice, with his heavy eyes fixated on the IV in his hand – he had taken most of the blood bag. I got up and looked myself over while taking off the gloves. There was a bit of blood on my clothes, but it wasn't noticeable. I made my way downstairs to the front door. Wind whipped into my home, reaching around the furniture. I opened the door a crack only to see my very concerned neighbor standing on the steps.

"Hi, Elizabeth. I'm so sorry to bother you. Is everything okay? I heard a lot of strange commotion over the past hour."

"Everything is fine, Zach. Um. I was watching a movie with a new surround system. Sorry about that." Great ...

"Really? Wow, that must be some great system. What movie was it?"

"Um. I don't recall. It's something I found on Netflix." Zach gave me an idea. "Hey, do you mind if I borrow a pair of gym shorts and a large T-shirt?" Zach was about the same build and height as Tyler.

Zach raised his eyebrows and tilted his head as if I had asked to borrow the left shoe off his foot. "Suuure. May I ask why?"

"... I have a friend over who spilled soda on his clothes. He'd really appreciate it." It wasn't long before Zach returned with black gym shorts and a plain white T-shirt. I thanked him profusely. Back upstairs, I knocked before entering the bedroom. Ty was still lying off the bloody section. "I have clothes for you," I said while gently smiling at him. My arm stretched to offer them.

He took the clothes and inspected them. "Thank you. Where did you ... ?"

"My neighbor is a kind man ... and your size." I said while taking down the blood bag. "Give me your hand." He complied, and I removed the needle before he could blink. "I'll leave you to dress." I left the room to collect fresh bed sheets while he struggled to put on the clothes.

CHAPTER NINETEEN

ANSWERS

I walked past the mess of my living room and opened the kitchen refrigerator, then the freezer. I managed to concoct a quick meal of chicken thighs - remembering he was a meat lover.

I hurried upstairs and into my bedroom. Ty had his eyes closed but smelled the food and looked to see what I had. "I hope you like chicken," I said a bit dryly.

He gratefully took the plate and started eating, nearly dropping some food on the bed. "Thank you," he said through his speed chews, but my jaw dropped when he started eating the bone.

"What are you doing?" I demanded to know, the shock in my voice obvious. He only continued - the crunch of the bone in his mouth nauseating me.

He didn't answer until every piece had been consumed. "Sorry, I should have warned you. My guard is down with you now that you know my secret." He lightly smiled at me and then looked down at the plate as if he wished for more. "I appreciate you not saying anything to your friend. I know that must have been difficult."

I sighed. "No, not at all. There's nothing difficult about keeping a secret that involves two gigantic fighting wolves smashing into my glass back door only for one of them to collapse into a man." His eyes snapped to me as I let the sharp sarcasm flow. "But it's not just any man. He's the man who mysteriously left me in the woods to die despite being in worse condition than me. Yet, I survived and now everyone except *maybe* Briana thinks I'm batshit nuts." My eyes trailed off to my desk. I glanced at a cherished photo. "What happened? What are you? You need to explain before I lose my mind completely."

"You're not crazy." His face was apologetic. "I didn't want you caught up in all this. My world can be dangerous for regular, *normal* people. When you found me in those woods, you walked into a heap of trouble."

He stopped there. I stayed quiet hoping he'd continue, but after a few minutes it was clear he needed to be encouraged. "It's okay. Unless you have a way to erase me from ever meeting you, I'm already too entwined within your world. I need to know more, or it will haunt me forever. ... For better or worse, I've been brought into your world and it's best for me to know everything and be prepared for things like what happened in my home." I held out my arm and gestured toward downstairs.

He nodded in acknowledgment of my compelling argument, seeming to agree that at this point with everything we'd been through, sharing the missing information was necessary. "I suppose you're right. By now, it's more dangerous for you not to know." He sighed and tried to get comfortable. "All I ask is that you don't interrupt. Save questions for the end."

"Fine." I was not entirely sure what to expect. The missing puzzle pieces were vast. I lay on the fresh bed sheets beside him.

"I must warn you ... this is going to be a lot." He rubbed his face. "My species behave a bit like regular wolves do. Each family or clan occupies a specific territory. We run, hunt, and live in our territory, which typically borders other dense woodlands occupied by fellow families. Our species population was estimated at roughly a few thousand spread all over the West Coast. ... As far as we know, nobody has migrated east, but some have moved to Alaska. It's hard to track since a lot of us are very difficult to keep in touch with. The woods you entered are occupied by my family. You saw them when they surrounded us in the woods."

My jaw nearly hit the bed.

"No. Don't say anything. Please wait," he pleaded.

I nodded. My head felt dizzy and my skin paled.

"The red wolf is a family friend who joined our clan, the Varg clan, five years ago. He earned the love of my father and was proposed as a partner to one of my twin sisters – who are both gray like my mother, Catori. The black wolf with the graying muzzle is my father. The gray and white male is my cousin, Ashton. I was fighting with him in your house because he wants to kill you."

"What? Why?" I was in shock.

"You killed my brother, Chogan, and Ashton was close to him."

I couldn't breathe when I realized what Ty was saying. The gray wolf I killed in the woods – this couldn't be. I felt my throat knot and my belly twist. Flying off the bed, I raced to the bathroom toilet and heaved until I vomited.

"Elizabeth?" Ty called to me, concerned. "It's okay. I don't blame you. He gave you no choice."

Surely he heard me being sick, but I was too horrified to care. I *killed Tyler's brother.* It was an hour before I could settle my stomach from the realization of what I had done. I cried heavily for a long time. Tyler knew I had to come to terms with what had occurred. He gave me time to swallow the fact. I brushed my teeth and returned to the bedroom. My legs and hands trembled. Nearly tripping over myself, I made it to the bed and lay beside him, but I couldn't face him.

"Continue," I commanded.

"I don't think I should."

"Continue," I said again louder and sharper.

"Fine. Okay." He pondered where to continue. "The reason you found me in those woods was because my brother tried to kill me. I knew he wanted me out of the picture. I stupidly let my guard down after a wolf run. I just wanted to be human, alone in the woods – like you ... with you. I stumbled across you in the night while in animal form. You were sleeping under the stars with your rat, but I woke you. Something about you pulled at me. ... I felt drawn to you. I wasn't sure how I'd introduce myself being so far out in the woods with no gear or shoes. I don't know what I was thinking. When I returned to human form, Chogan used the opportunity to attack me in the remoteness, but he stopped. I don't understand why he didn't finish me off. Maybe he changed his mind in the moment as I begged him and screamed. Maybe he was worried my cries would be heard by the family. More likely, he figured I'd die out there alone, but I guess he later attacked you when he realized we were surviving together. I assumed you found me right after he first ran off."

That was why Ty wasn't surprised to see me when we first officially met. As answers came, so did questions. "Why did Chogan want you dead?"

Tyler's expression shifted. He was visibly uncomfortable. "I said no questions."

"Don't hold back now. I need to know everything," I hissed.

"Ugggghhh ... fine. There's one more wolf. She's the white one. Do you remember her?"

I flashed the memory. She was the first one to approach us before the group swarmed. "Yes, I do."

"Her name is Angeni. She's promised as my wife. Our pairing is supposed to unite her family, the Shadow clan, whose territory borders ours, with the Varg clan after years of territorial conflict."

My heart sank and I turned over to face him. "I see. And you won't have her?"

"No. I feel nothing for her. But my brother was obsessed with her. Even though I said he could have her, Angeni was not promised to him. The pairing was arranged with the hope of what offspring would be produced by myself and Angeni. Black and white wolf pairings are considered a sacred match - a perfect pair. Angeni is younger than me. Ten years ago I was promised to Angeni, but the alliance had to wait until she was eighteen and ready to marry. When she turned eighteen this year, my father worked to arrange the marriage ceremony. I guess my brother grew desperate."

I processed this information, plugging it into what I experienced and what I already knew. I didn't want to feel jealous of the match, but I couldn't help it. I wanted to be with Tyler even after everything. "So, what happens now?" I asked.

"My family is mourning Chogan's death. They took his body that night and buried him in the family cemetery."

I felt sick again. He surely would have killed us had I not killed him first, but it didn't make me feel much better acknowledging that. At least now I knew what happened to the body that seemingly disappeared. Tyler noticed my green hue.

"It's not your fault. You got caught up in a horrible family feud."

I thought about what happened that day. Chogan must have known I would shoot and kill him. Why would he attack? I suspected that maybe he wanted me to kill him if he failed to finish off Tyler. If he loved Angeni enough, he might have felt it was do or die trying - it wasn't worth living if Angeni was by Ty's side. But it didn't make sense. Chogan attacked me before Tyler. His massive jaws vividly snapped in my memories. Nothing justified his attack, but maybe Tyler's species behaved differently from regular people. More questions popped. "What do you call your species?"

"We call ourselves three different names ... depending on who you ask. Amarok for the legend, or Amaguq after the Inuit wolf goddess - a blue wolf - but Amarok is more commonly used. It's easier to pronounce. There's also Amaruq, which is Inuit for wolf ... or we call ourselves any Native American word that means wolf. Despite the Native blood, the first shifters were of the Inuit people."

"Where did your species come from? Are there any other kinds of animal shifting communities?"

"As far as we know, we're the only shapeshifters and the only true creatures of human myth or folklore. There are two legends – one ancestral story said we were born through human-to-animal bond. It's called the Legend of Amarok. An old weird story of a man who fell in love with a wild wolf who was white as snow like Angeni. Through their bond they united, and he transformed into a black wolf. Their offspring were the first wolf shapeshifters who crossed with regular humans and regular wolves for a while. It's just a story at heart. No one actually knows how we came about," he explained.

"And the other legend?" I questioned.

"The goddess Amaguq, the only blue wolf, created us. This is the story more commonly shared as truth."

"I see. Does the government know about you?"

"No, and I pray they never discover us." His expression shifted to match his concerning thought.

"Oh. Well, I'll definitely keep your secret. I promise." I smiled lightly at him.

"I know you will. Now my only concern is protecting you."

"What do you mean?"

"Ashton came here to hurt you for revenge. We tore each other up pretty bad. My family is surely furious even though the only thing I did *wrong* was protect you and delay marrying Angeni. I have to go back and continue to plead with them."

"Delay?" I repeated the word involuntarily.

He lay on his side facing me, allowing his face to sink into the pillow. We now matched positions. "I am not marrying her."

"What about the arrangement and uniting your families?"

"It's my life. ... My father is just trying to make peace with the tension between the clans. The black and white coat color combo was his way of convincing her clan of the match. ... I don't care if he kills me over this ... I'm not marrying her."

"He dare not harm you." My thoughts raced. "Do you think he would?"

"No. I'm now his only son." He chuckled harshly.

My eyes widened and then narrowed. "Wait. He won't kill you not because you're his son, but because you're now his *only* son?"

"I don't think he'd harm me either way, but he's pretty upset with me and recent events," Ty said with a sigh.

I pondered everything I had learned at that point. There were minor questions still, but so many of the pieces I was missing had been supplied. There were still some things I didn't understand. "Why did you never date other people or move away from this craziness?"

"I wanted to leave many times because of Chogan's hostility toward me. But I'm tied to my family by more than bond. As for dating, our matches are often arranged. Plus, no one has ever caught my attention like you have." His soft eyes peered into me.

My face must have flushed. I could feel myself warm with his words. My heart raced while I processed. "You really feel that drawn to me?" I sat up.

"Yes, I do. It started when I saw you that night sleeping under the stars, but I first took interest in you when you nearly ran me over with your car."

I gasped. "What! Wow, that was you?"

He laughed hard. "Yes. It was my fault. I was hunting near town to avoid my brother. Typically, we never let people see us in wolf form. When you were in the woods under the stars, I caught your scent while running."

"Wow." I smiled at the memories. Both were scary, particularly when it was night and I couldn't see what stalked me. It felt like I was being hunted for fresh meat. The thought reminded me how Ty never ate anything other than meat for all I've known him. "Wait, so do you only eat meat?"

"Cooked or raw, but I prefer raw. Very few of us can handle eating anything not heavily meat based."

"Wow. I mean ... wow ... hmmm ... I guess I'll stock up the freezer."

He chuckled. "I have to say you're handling my world extremely well. I really thought you would have run for the hills by now."

I gritted my teeth. "The only things that bothered me were learning I killed a man, especially a man that's your brother, learning your family wants you to be with someone else, and the target your cousin put on my back." I sighed with my sinking heart.

He nodded. "You seemed rather relaxed with most of it."

"I am ... what about the carpet of black fur that was left after you changed back?"

"Oh, when we turn back, we shed all the fur. It grows to form a coat when we shift to a wolf, but it doesn't reabsorb during the change back to human. It's kinda gross ... sorry."

"Don't worry about it. I figured as much." His eyes were visibly heavy. "I'm going to let you get some sleep while I clean downstairs and online shop for a new back door. I'm thinking metal instead of glass this time."

He smiled and then yawned. "Good idea. Just ... please be careful. Ashton could return."

CHAPTER TWENTY

REFLECTION

I pulled the covers higher for him and then left, closing the bedroom door behind me. Down the stairs, I felt far more vigilant after learning Ty's secrets and acknowledging his warning. Ashton had put a few dents in Ty, but Tyler ripped him up pretty well also.

I put on my jacket and began sweeping up the fur and glass. The blood had dried so I next used diluted bleach to scrub the floors and walls. Cleaning took forever, but I was too caught up in my thoughts to notice. I felt Ty's expressed feelings boded well for the future I wanted with him, despite it all.

By the time I had finished bagging bloody fur and scrubbing, it was seven at night. The eerie backyard air crept into the room and around through the kitchen. My arm hairs stood up while my eyes kept darting to the yard twice a minute.

I made use of my laptop to search for a company that could put in a new door with much more strength. I found a company that had the model I liked and could install it tomorrow. It was perfect except for the price. Ashton had cost me over two thousand dollars, but at least he didn't cost me my life - all thanks to Ty.

I briefly had awakened Tyler for dinner. He was groggy and uncomfortable with any pressure on his back, and he quickly went back to sleep after eating. As bedtime arrived, I realized I needed to sleep somewhere. Should I sleep next to him? ... Maybe I should go to the guest bedroom. I didn't want to be alone, never mind away from him.

I decided to take a quick shower. Grabbing a towel, I headed for the hall bathroom. The hot water felt amazing. I let it flow over my face as I tried not to think about Ty or his family and how they all must wish me dead, but my thoughts failed me. I pulled my gaze to the ceiling, so my skull touched my back. The steam circled around until it landed in pools of cooling mist on the tiles above. As I thought about Ty being my lover, concupiscent urges poked around my core. The only things between us were his family and whether his secret would be manageable for me. It was almost poetic – something you'd read in Shakespeare. How could I win over his family after what happened? It felt hopeless, but Ty didn't seem discouraged.

Out of the shower, I wrapped myself in the towel. My eyes widened at a thought. Shit. My clothes. I cracked open my bedroom door. It was dark and I couldn't see much. Opening it further, I saw Ty lying how I left him – resting with his back facing the ceiling. I crept over to the dresser and pulled out a pair of pajamas before going back to the bathroom to get dressed. Back in the bedroom, I closed the door and then locked it. My cell phone's light helped me find the spot next to him. I realized Briana had sent me twenty texts since she left, but I was too tired to read them. That night, drifting into a deep sleep proved strangely easy.

After a dreamless sleep, I woke to a bright room and pools of blue. Ty's gorgeous eyes were watching me. I flushed.

"Good morning," he greeted.

I sat up and stretched. "Morning." I felt amazing – undoubtedly the best sleep I had in a long time. Ty was a hot mess. Even with a mummy-wrapped chest under a thin white T-shirt, he was beautiful. I looked at the small wounds on his arms and hands. They were healing quickly. I was pleased to see how well he looked. "I suppose werewolves heal faster than the average person?"

My eyes stayed on his arms, but I could feel his smile. "Correct, but medical assistance helps us heal faster and properly. Infection can get us, too."

"I see. Will all of this scar?"

"Probably not since the worst is stapled. We heal really well."

"Definitely faster than average." My eyes tightened on the bandaging visible through his T-shirt. Breaking my observation, he got out of the bed.

"Where is the bathroom?"

"Oh, uh ... there's the master bath but I typically use the one in the hall. You can use either."

"Thanks." He walked into the master bathroom, leaving me on the bed. I watched him close the door.

I hopped up to retrieve my clothes from my dresser and then fetched my neglected cell phone. While getting dressed in the hall bathroom, I kept reading through the messages Briana had left. She was blathering on about getting in trouble at work and how she made sure they didn't expect me to come in today. Thank goodness. Work was the last thing on my mind – I even forgot about it. Her earlier messages were concerns for Ty and what she saw yesterday.

I quickly texted her: *All is fine. Ty is recovering well. It was a bizarre animal attk, but please dnt tell anyone. Thnks for the work cover.*

Once dressed, I crept past the bedroom. He was still in the master bathroom and I could hear him using the sink.

I decided to go downstairs after bundling up. In the bright morning light, I could see areas of the living room that needed more attention – some blood stains and a lot of scratches in the floor. Part of the wall had damage where it looked as if it had been hit with a mild shock of lightning. It wasn't long before I heard Ty stepping down the stairs. I saw him quickly glance at what remained of the room. He met me in the kitchen, moving slowly with a distinct stiffness to his form. His face was light and bright despite the clear pain he was experiencing. That gorgeous hair was now a bit longer than when we met in the woods – his perfect beard never altered.

"I'm truly sorry about the mess."

I gulped my saliva. "It's okay. It really was a close call for the both of us." I quickly matched his frown.

"We shouldn't dwell. Are eggs on the menu?" he questioned.

"I only have oatmeal. I'll order some groceries and have them delivered. I could make the rest of the chicken if you like?"

"Sounds good," he said while I offered him a tall glass of water. His frequent smiles were already returning.

The day was peaceful. Ty spent most of his time in my bedroom, where it was warmer. I showed him how to use the small desk TV. He commented how he had only used a television one other time in his life. Watching his enthusiasm as he flipped the channels was like watching a teen play an amazing new video game. He settled down to watch Animal Planet.

I warned him not to try helping when the groceries arrived. He could've pulled out the staples. "Just stay in bed for a while," I directed.

After the groceries arrived and were put away, the door installers showed up.

On my steps, a tall man around thirty-five years old with brown hair and a light voice greeted me. "Good afternoon, ma'am. We are here with the door ya ordered. We're sorry for the delay." He had a distinct effeminate tone in his voice.

"Yes, come on in with it. It's for the back door."

Ty had the TV off or lowered and seemed to be listening to their installation. I watched them carefully remove the old door frame and fit the new one in place.

The man who first greeted me took interest in the damage and grew too curious. "What happened to yer back door if you don't mind I assk?" He stretched the last word.

"Rabid buck." I smiled.

"Ah."

His confusion amused me.

The installation went flawlessly, and I was pleased with their work, tipping them for their service and accepting the bill for the job. We thanked each other and they were out by two in the afternoon. The heat was back on, cranked high.

Past lunch time, I whipped up a batch of chicken legs and beef stir fry. Meat-only meals were alien to me. At least I wasn't a vegetarian. Ty smelled the food cooking and came down from the bedroom. I smiled at him when he joined me. When I looked back at the food, he placed his arms on my waist from behind and then moved his hands around to my stomach. I froze, the unexpected and somewhat sexual affection taking me completely off guard – yet it felt welcome.

He whispered in my ear, "I'd prefer natural ... raw."

Goosebumps on the back of my neck emerged while an internal electric pulse shot down my spine and into my groin. I felt the double meaning to his statement, one being less innocent.

I stayed still other than continuing to stir. "I'll keep that in mind." My breathing shortened.

"Are you sure you can handle me?" he taunted.

"I sense a double meaning to that question." I turned around to push him toward the island until his backside hit the edge. Looking up at him, I found it painful to resist kissing him. Despite the distance, his lips felt magnetic.

"It's more than double." His expression was welcoming but his body language turned guarded.

I decided to pull back. "What do you mean?" I turned toward the food and shut the stove off.

"Can you handle what makes me different ... can you handle a struggle with my folks? Can you handle becoming like me?"

I nearly dropped the pan while putting the food onto two plates. "Becoming like you?" I questioned, turning my eyes toward him.

I watched him swallow. "I just meant becoming a part of my life."

"Oh. Yes, I'm certain at this time."

He nodded with a shy smile. "Good."

I handed him the plate. "Here. You'll get raw next time, but don't be offended if I don't watch you eat."

He laughed. "It's alright. Thank you."

While we ate, I wondered how long it would take for us to kiss or advance further to more *exerting* activities. Keeping my hormones in check, I'd be patient with him – letting him lead. The small progress we had made was enough ... for now.

When Tyler was nearly finished with his plate, he snapped his head toward the back of the house. His body tensed and the hairs on his arm rose.

"What's wrong?" He was reacting to something. Watching him made my throat tighten.

He didn't answer at first. Ty's lips were pressed in a hard line when he turned his attention back to me. "I have to leave. I'm being called back." Before I could protest, he placed the plate on the island and kissed my cheek abruptly, then rushed to the newly installed back door.

"Whoa, wait!"

He ignored me to run off into the back woods until I saw nothing of him. I felt safe with him here, but his sudden tense exit had shaken me. My legs quivered under an immediate spike of fear.

I locked the door and prayed Ashton stayed at bay.

CHAPTER TWENTY-ONE

RAINSTORM

Watching the large hospital cafeteria windows - the way the rain trailed down in various patterns along the less than clean glass - I acknowledged our luck in having a warmer storm rather than icy rain and terrible road conditions. I had no appetite while observing the brewing storm bathe the bare bushes and dead leaves.

Aside from a letter in the mail, it had been a long while since I had heard from Tyler. Shortly after he left me in my kitchen, I received a letter in the mailbox with no stamp or return address.

> Sorry for not coming by. I am trying to smooth things over with family. Ashton has been really difficult. My family still wants me to marry Angeni and I've been having a really rough time getting them to move on with the fact that she and I will never happen. I miss you so much. I will return when the time is right.
>
> Yours truly - Ty

Not seeing him for so long was a little disheartening, especially when I thought things were starting to progress between us. I knew

Ty's world would require patience and understanding for things I could barely comprehend, but I expected him to at least show his face. It was his family keeping him away, and I resented them for it.

While watching the rainwater stream, I could see Briana approaching in the glass reflection. I felt her concern as she stood next to me, momentarily studying my sorry head resting against the glass. She sat down across from me. Despite everything Briana knew and didn't know about Ty, she didn't press. She must have understood how delicate I was and assumed things hadn't gone as I had hoped. Regardless of her lack of knowing, she was extremely understanding. I didn't deserve such an amazing friend – one who only gave me her unconditional support.

"Christmas Eve is tomorrow," she finally said after watching the rain with me.

Our hospital coworkers were full of festivities and my mom expected I'd soon join her for a quaint gathering at her place. She had been calling me often after I rejected some more visits. I couldn't have her see my house when there were still signs of the trauma.

"I am joining my mother for Christmas," I said without moving. My voice was dry.

"Cheer up, Liz. There are other –"

"No. No, no. Do NOT say there are other *fish* in the sea," I begged.

"I was *going* to say there are other people out there. Even some uncharted territories."

"What. Like Jason?" I rolled my eyes and finally looked at her. Jason had been with just about every attractive employee. Even Briana had her go with him once upon a time. I had been the only one he had failed to sway, and he was trying hard to have what he could not.

She chuckled. "No, that was not where I was going."

I turned back to the rain with my break almost over. It had been an unusually quiet day of work. "Thank goodness."

Briana could sense I needed space. "I'll leave you be. I think this gloomy weather is affecting all of us, but you mostly. Cheer up, okay? I'll be in the ICU." She got up and hurried off, her beautiful red hair bouncing behind her.

Maybe Tyler lost interest. Maybe he couldn't convince his family that he wouldn't marry Angeni. Perhaps he had been married off already, never to return to me as mine. I rested my head on the cafeteria table and folded my arms around my gloomy headache.

I drove home late that night after a long shift. The passing car lights glared on my dashboard. It was still raining with a light hail, but I didn't care. My eyes fogged as the wipers beat back and forth in a steady rhythm - a lullaby in their motion. I tried to focus on the passing cars while the hail tapped on the glass.

I reached the road that had become overly familiar. After Ty left me, I had spent my time on it hoping I'd see him against the forest edge or racing in front of my car again - scanning everything except the road. I searched with hope each time, but he was never there, and I had run out of hope. With Ty's marriage to another likely, I had begun to realize my probable loss. I would no longer be a part of Ty's world - a dangerous yet exhilarating world I had only scarcely tasted. Maybe such thoughts were premature, but it was how my heart felt.

The road was painfully dark. I had to drive slowly to see anything through the rain. A familiar dark blur darted in front and I brought my car to a gravity-intense halt while pulling over to the shoulder.

Tyler?!?

Could it really be him? It had to be! I shot my eyes around the surroundings outside. To my right, I noticed movement through the dark tree line. In the swishing pine trees and blackness, I could feel a large presence. I stared, waiting to see the familiar eyes and coat. The rainwater trailed along the glass, blurring everything. I rolled down the window halfway. Lightning lit up the surroundings, illuminating a gray and white coat and brown eyes, not more than fifteen feet away.

"Ashton!" I cried in horror while racing the window back up. Lightning flashed, the crack of thunder hiding his snarls as he eliminated the gap in one massive leap. I closed my eyes against the impact only to feel his jaw smack the raised glass. Looking back up, I saw that the window had cracked but stayed intact. He circled the car in front of my headlights. Rage enveloped his eyes while his bottom jaw dripped fresh blood. He continued around to the back of my car. In panic, my shaking hands shifted the car into drive. Gunning the accelerator, I felt my car lunge forward and Ashton hit the back before I sped off. Engine roaring, I raced in the rain. I could barely see the road until the lightning lit the pavement.

My heart pounding, I clipped my mailbox as I turned into the driveway, doing twice my normal speed. Turning off the car, I fumbled with my house keys, thinking I was not safe here. Visions of Ashton and Ty falling through a wall of glass clouded me. I then remembered the new door. With my keys readied, I bolted out of the car into the rain for the front door. As I closed the gap, it seemed to shift further away – like in a nightmare. My panicked adrenaline worked against me. I slipped on the slushy rainwater and landed hard on my side at the bottom of the steps, gasping for breath as I hurried to pull myself up and inside. Each step felt higher than the previous until I finally reached the door. My key slipped to a slow turn of the knob until the door swung open. Speed-crawling inside, I kicked it shut and stretched for the lock.

Was I safe? Looking around my dark house, I was too petrified to move my back from the front door. Aside from the storm shifting outside, I heard nothing. While my heart started to calm, I pulled myself up and limped to the light switch. Halfway expecting Ashton to be sitting in the center of the room, I flicked the lights on. The house was empty.

My back against the wall, I slunk down and started to shake. Not only was Ty gone, but Ashton was still trying to kill me.

I called in sick on Christmas Eve morning. Lying in bed, I looked over at the window and watched the snowflakes fall. Each one was so pure and promising for a white Christmas.

Ashton's attack scared me to the core. I was triggered by every thunder rumble, every wall creak, and every wind howl that plagued last night. A shower didn't help and neither did playing music. I was traumatized.

Having to pee in the new morning, I reluctantly pulled the covers back. I crept to the master bath to avoid leaving the room, only to wish I hadn't. Since Ty left me, I hadn't been in this room. Ty had left signs of his presence inside it. My heart sank. Working to soothe myself, I heard my cell phone chime. I limped to the nightstand and picked up my phone.

Briana had texted me. *Hey. I heard you called in sick. You okay??*

No. I really wasn't. I couldn't tell Briana even a quarter of it.

No, not feeling well. Sorry I cnt be there. Thnx for checking in with me. With a sour expression on my face, I sent her the text. I badly wished I could tell her – or anyone. When I had Tyler to talk to, it was easy to keep the secret.

Okay, but the board is gettin annoyed with you. Be careful.

I had a leg gash and a bruised hip from my fall, although it was nothing in comparison to what I had avoided. I wished I could have talked to Ashton face to face – preferably with him chained to a huge tree. Surely Ty had told Ashton what Chogan did to us. How could he not understand?

He needed to understand.

CHAPTER TWENTY-TWO

HOLIDAYS

"Hello darling!" Mom answered the door while I admired the yellowing cream-colored trim of the frame - the paint untouched for almost two decades.

I hugged and greeted her, hiding my limp as I entered out of the snow blanket. Christmas day remained just the two of us. We gave this time to no one else because today, no one else mattered.

Despite our small numbers, Mom spiffed up the house as if a herd of less-than-comfortable relatives would be joining. Every surface was perfectly dusted and polished: not a speck of fabric on the couch out of place, not a pebble of dirt on the floor. She was mistress of her domain and queen of her fortress. Being retired, cooking and cleaning had become a way of passing time for her instead of an energy-sucking chore.

It was hard to believe any animals resided within. My animals. Beamer, now chubby from the frequent treats, had found a home in my mother's kitchen. When he saw me, he filled with excitement - so much I'd thought he might've popped. I pulled him from the cage and gave him a hug.

"Aww. He missed you. Are you planning to take them both home?"

I missed my pets but knowing I couldn't give Beamer enough attention in my depressed state, being with my mother was best for him. I thought about how I could probably manage just Nova. Without Ty and my pets, life had been empty.

"I want you to keep Beamer. I might take Nova back in time. I miss having a pet."

"I was hoping Beamer could stay. I've grown so found of him."

"I'm glad. Just try to find him a new rat friend. He'll be happier."

For Christmas dinner we enjoyed roasted ham, cheesy potatoes, string bean casserole, mashed sweet potatoes topped with toasted mini marshmallows, and canned cranberry sauce – enough food for a week.

While eating, we talked about my work. Mom even snuck in some boy questions, but I didn't reveal another word about Ty. She explained how she wanted to try dating again – how she wasn't getting any younger and missed putting herself out there. Sitting on the table, Beamer happily munched on the various foods. His boggling eyes made me swoon with fondness.

After pulling out the apple-blueberry pie, Mom began slicing an uncomfortably large piece for us to share as her conversation shifted.

"So, I keep seeing a wolf in my backyard. At first I –"

"What color?" I spoke far louder than intended, my thoughts racing and my heart in my throat. *Ashton!*

"Elizabeth. Why are you shouting? Is something wrong?"

I couldn't breathe.

"It was a gray color, maybe gray and white," she said when I didn't answer.

"When? When did you see him?" My eyes stared her down. I stood in her face, bodily begging to know.

"Uhh ... uh ... yesterday and last night."

"I have to leave. Thank you for Christmas." I kissed her cheek and began to put my jacket on.

"Wait! What's going on? Why the hurry?"

"Nothing. I just think I left the lights on at home. I will call you soon. Please be careful. That wolf is dangerous." The words lingered on my lips.

I found myself rushing. Why was I rushing? And to where? The road dragged through the trees with considerably more traffic than usual.

Ashton was hunting my mother. How did he know who my mother was? It had to be him. It was a threat. Tyler never mentioned anything about his kind murdering innocent people. Despite the threat, it felt empty. Ashton was trying to scare me into his jaws.

I was too smart for it.

My mailbox remained sprawled in the dirt. My eyes darted around for his presence in the shadows of the moonlight along the trees and brush. With my mind cleared, I readied for the door – another dash for home.

I made it inside without another spill. Locking the door, I rushed for the lights. I expected the house to be empty. It was always empty. Perhaps the smell of faint musk in the stale air should have warned me. With the lights turned on, Ty was standing beside me. I screamed.

Ty jumped back.

I felt my heart in my throat. "You could have killed me with that scare! What the hell are you doing ... how the hell did you get in my house!" It wasn't a question; it was an accusation.

"Oops!" he chuckled. "I didn't mean to scare you. Your second-floor window was unlocked."

I pictured him creeping around my house, then climbing around until he found my home's only weakness. "I see. I'm glad to see you, but you cannot barge into my house like this, especially when I'm not home."

"Sorry, I was cold while waiting for you. But I understand ... happy Christmas." A goofy smile spread across his face.

I scowled. "Where have you been?" The question was almost rhetorical.

"Did you get my letter? I have been working on family issues."

"Yes ... I did. That was a long while ago." My voice fell low. "I thought you moved on."

"No. I have been dying to see you. The family makes it hard to slip away. They seem to be dealing with the arranged marriage failing, but they've kept a sharp eye on me – especially my father. My mother stopped caring about my decision, but he won't let it go. With the holiday, I was able to slip away. Dad has been drinking."

"How long can you stay?" I was no longer angry. How could I be? He was mine again.

"Not long. But I promise ... things will get better. He can't fight me forever," Ty said.

I sensed uncertainty in his words, but I hoped he was right. There was so much to tell him. I didn't know where to begin. "Come upstairs." I snatched his wrist and led him up the steps. Within my bedroom, I locked the door and then shut all the bedroom blinds. Ty stared at the bed. It was a place of healing and a place of the unknown. I sat on the far side and gestured for him to sit across from me. "Ashton has been trying to kill me."

I started with how he attacked me in my car, revealing every detail: his snout dripping blood after smacking the glass; his circling the car. I was surprised Ty *wasn't* surprised. His expression remained calm, serious, and attentive even with the additional news of Ashton's threat on my mother. He said nothing – only listened.

"What do we do about him?" It was the first question I asked, and the first time Ty spoke since I started explaining.

"Nothing. He isn't trying to kill you."

"What? How do you gather that? Were you listening?" My voice sharpened.

"I know what he's doing. He's trying to scare you. He's trying to chase you out of our world. His goal was to scare you into running away from me. That's what this has been from the start. I should have known when he apparently raced off to *kill* you the day we ended up in your house. I didn't know what he was planning so I chased him down and we tumbled into your door as I grabbed his flank. Ashton was angry, but he had never made himself an aggressor before Chogan died. Still, I was too scared he'd hurt you to risk the chance. But back at home, he never made it seem like he was still taunting you." Ty's lips pressed into a hard line.

"But ... even if that's true, he damaged my car. He tried to break the glass. I know he would have ripped me apart if it had broken."

"He must have wanted you to think that. You'd be dead if he truly wanted you to be."

A knot formed in my throat. I should have been relieved, but was it really that easy for Ashton all this time? "How do you figure?"

"... It doesn't matter."

CHAPTER TWENTY-THREE

A BREATH

S he was a breath. Not a normal breath – she was a breath of crisp air. Her aura crystalized around her. Her white coat flickered with the beam of lemon-yellow sun. Her brown eyes were perfectly still.

Earlier that day, I went to the gym for the first time in a long while. Briana was too eager to join in her excitement of our normalcy returning. It was just like old times.

We started with a twenty-minute treadmill jog before moving around the gym, exercising every area of the body. My muscles loved it; my heart loved it. We felt the admiring eyes on our figures, but it was mostly women who stared with the *I-want-to-look-like-that* glare. Briana's gorgeous hair bounced around the space.

She chatted with me about her Christmas family drama while I half listened. With healthy adrenaline, the gym was a place of stress relief.

During a quick food shopping run after the gym, she followed me around the store – a trail of bouncing red and peppiness. This time, the men stared, and I blushed when eyes landed on me. I enjoyed wearing comfort fit leggings, but they attracted more male attention. I avoided eye contact.

When we reached the meat department, I peered at the freshly wrapped meat. Briana didn't bat an eye until I placed the third tray in my cart. She raised an eyebrow at me that seemed to rise higher and higher as I continued until the cart held ten meat trays. It looked as though I were about to throw a huge barbecue.

"Starting a high-protein diet?" she questioned.

"You could say that," I said with a smirk. I didn't know when Ty would return, but the freezer would be stocked for when he did.

"Suit yourself, but that's a lot of protein."

Briana brought me and my army of groceries home. I started to wonder if I'd be able to fit everything in the freezer. While helping me move everything inside, she stared around the living room and then looked momentarily at the back door. Despite her obvious thoughts, she said nothing.

With the groceries jammed away and Briana gone, I was left to my own thoughts.

Ty had spent some time with me the two nights before. As a last-minute gift, I took a picture of us using my instant print camera and gave him the photo. He loved it. Soon after, he left in another hurry. Ty heard something acute – likely a call from a great distance which my average human ears couldn't detect. But that happened after our more intimate connection.

In my memory, I could still see the faint red hue in his cheeks. He was looking down at my lips. I shifted closer, a growl deep inside that wouldn't tame without him.

Goosebumps formed on his arms. We felt the burn of our tension far more strongly than before. He leaned in and I mimicked his motion until our lips met. My hands automatically cradled his head as my eyes closed to dance with his kiss. He tasted amazing, like the tang of honeydew melon. I felt his hand explore under my clothing, feeling my curves.

I pulled away to remove my shirt and he did the same before

admiring me. We reconnected – his skin against mine, his bulge to my lower belly as we embraced.

I pulled him down to the bed so that we lay next to one another. My deep inner craving of excitement peaked as I started to unzip his jeans. With the bulge of his eagerness under the zipper keeping my attention, I hardly noticed his discomfort with my advance. Before I finished unzipping, he shifted away and jumped from the bed.

Faint scars stretched his back as he faced away from me, reaching for his shirt on the floor. I felt dreadfully disappointed by the rush of unsatisfied hormones. What a massive tease. "What's wrong?"

"… I'm not ready. I'm sorry." His eyes reconnected with my own to show an apologetic glow.

That's when I saw him freeze up. It was as if something gave him a mild shock. His eyes widened and he made a swift exit down the stairs, calling back to me that he'd be back as soon as he could. I was left alone with my hormones.

But that was two nights ago.

The news played on the TV: "It's a sunny winter morning in Jackson County. A small snowstorm is expected to pass over southern parts by the late afternoon. Expect between two and three inches at lower elevations, up to a foot in the mountains."

Unlike most people, I loved the snowstorms here. The cold never bothered me. Briana, however, grew up in southern California and never cared much for winter.

While mindlessly dusting the kitchen as the snow fell, I saw a large white movement in the sunset-lit yard. Through the window's frame, a stunning white wolf appeared. I was not afraid of her. I chose not to be when I opened my back door. We acknowledged each other until she turned back toward the trees, her coat allowing her to vanish.

I thought she had left until a woman appeared from the brush wearing a thin damp T-shirt and a small pair of gym shorts. Her bare feet pressed in the snow as she approached, her golden-brown hair bouncing behind her. Big brown eyes almost too big for her face met mine. Her fair skin had an olive undertone like Ty's.

She was beautiful – painfully beautiful – but obviously young. As she approached, her steps grew shorter. She said nothing until she paused ten feet away.

"We need to talk." Her voice was the only thing average about her.

"Come inside." I gestured indoors. I wanted to befriend her, although it felt unlikely. What did she want?

I watched her gawk around the room, inspecting every detail of the space. Was she looking for something? She might have been looking at the room for the remaining signs of struggle. Maybe the smell of what happened? "Would you like some coffee or tea?" Her eyes narrowed as she refocused herself to what truly lay on her mind. "I'm sure this is about Ty," I said with a sigh.

"That's what you call him?" Angeni's body language further shifted as she crossed her arms. The lightness in her face darkened and I no longer felt her welcome. "He's not meant for you. You know this, right?"

It had been years since high school, but I suddenly felt thrown back in. "That's for Ty to decide," I said.

"*Tyler* doesn't get to decide. He's been promised to me and now that I'm finally of age, I'm not about to lose him to some human who has no business in our world."

"Maybe you're right about one thing. Perhaps I don't belong in your world. I never intended to meet Ty, but I did. ... I think you should go."

"You won't win. I'll make sure of it." She turned to leave, fumbling with the door momentarily before running off.

It was New Year's Eve night when Tyler appeared again. Watching a soap opera, I heard a tap on the back door and my body tensed. Cautiously opening the door, I was greeted by his bright smile. He wore gray sweatpants and a black T-shirt, with bits of loose fur stuck to his clothing.

"You scared me, ugh." I jumped up and wrapped my arms around his neck, breathing in his delicious musky scent. His perfectly groomed light beard brushed my temple. I had a powerful urge to bite his neck. He walked inside from the cold.

"Sorry ... I have a fix for that," he said, smiling. Seeing him, it was as if he had never left. "I have a gift for you. Sorta." Out of his pocket, he pulled a small, cheap cell phone.

"Umm." I raised one eyebrow.

"It's my new cell phone. I want you to be able to call me, so I got one."

"Oh, that's great!" My heart lit up as we exchanged numbers. I then remembered my meat stash. "Are you hungry?"

"Famished." A low warm growl built in his throat. I barely had a moment to process it when his lips locked with mine. The growl and kiss sent shock waves to my pelvis and back up my spine. He pushed me to the couch.

We kissed timelessly, a large bulge from his sweatpants pushing into my thigh as I lay under his frame. My hand reached for his groin, fully expecting he might pull away from the advance – but as my hand felt him, he only continued to kiss me. I rubbed him harder. "Having fun with that?" he asked between kisses.

Keeping my right hand on him, I pushed his chest upward. Looking down at his groin and feeling him around, he was undoubtedly impressive. Would he let me go further? I enjoyed myself a bit longer before trying my luck. Placing both of my hands on his pants waist, I attempted to pull them down, but he grabbed me. I sighed heavily, but I had expected his reaction.

He shifted over, expressing a brilliant smile. "I could use some food now," he said.

"You're such a tease, you know?"

His smile widened. "I see no reason to rush us."

Pondering his reluctance, I thought about his culture and why he wouldn't go further. "There has to be more reason than that."

"You're right. There is. In my world, mates are carefully chosen. When we lock physically, we lock for life until death do us part. Meaning, we stick loyally to one partner, so we have to be completely sure of one another."

I was surprised. "Is that a species rule or a culture rule?"

"Both. It's hard for us to be libido-interested in others after pairing physically with someone. It stems from our blood. A wolf pair typically mate for life and build their pack with their offspring."

It all made sense, explaining the true reason why Ty remained virtuous. I thought about Angeni's threat – she was worried I'd bed him. It was somewhat stinging to realize that Ty wasn't sure about us yet, but deep down I had already known this.

"I'll wait for you to decide, then."

He smiled. "Wait," he repeated. "You'll wait for me?"

My hand reached over to his face and caressed the side of his facial hair. "Of course."

CHAPTER TWENTY-FOUR

SPRING TO TRAUMA

Migrating birds rushed to greet the spring community while neighborhood dogs jumped through puddles of mud. Dandelions sprouted and bulbs erupted to reach the warming sun. April rained her showers to restore the foliage. The trees budded; the brush greened – just as every year.

Winter had been filled with long nights cuddled in Ty's bare chest, falling asleep together on the couch or bed – his warmth against mine. I discovered my favorite pastime was watching Tyler's gorgeous face sleeping peacefully, every muscle in his body at absolute rest and comfort. He was a deep sleeper. I loved to gently kiss his sleeping body – especially his soft eyes and the corner of his mouth. It made my heart wrap within itself. I'd caress down his arms, around his bare chest if exposed – watch his nipples harden as I trailed my fingers around them.

When I wasn't working, he was often with me, helping me do chores and simply spending time with me.

At the gym, Ty made every other visitor jealous with his

ridiculous strength and stamina. Briana verbally expressed how impressed she was by him every time.

"He's crazy strong," she said while we jogged on the treadmill, watching him on the bench press. I simply smiled and nodded.

Briana was happy for me; she was happy for us. And she could keep a secret – she never spilled the beans about it to our coworkers. I decided to let no one else know of our relationship aside from my mother. The only con to this was dealing with Jason's continued advances. *I'm not interested* just wasn't a reason he could accept.

Throughout the winter, especially as January barreled into February, Jason had become borderline unbearable. A harassment claim was beyond justifiable, but I was afraid to file one. To do so would be social suicide from coworkers. No one would dare file such a claim against perfect Dr. Jason, yet his egotism had me overwhelmed. He'd chase me around the hospital when he wasn't busy, asking other workers where I was last seen. Over time, he had tried to give me flowers, ridiculously expensive jewelry, chocolates, and tickets to events, and had asked me to take drives with him, but most infuriating were his attempts at finding me alone.

Tyler knew about Jason's harassment and encouraged me to stand up to him, to really tell him off and report his behavior. "He needs to take a hike and get lost," he'd state in irritation while we talked on the phone. I learned not to discuss Jason because Tyler's happy mood turned sour when he was mentioned. Jason was *my* problem.

Ty managed to fight his family to the point of limiting their reluctance, yet, as Tyler admitted, they planned to never accept me. It was something I could live with even though it bothered me.

Angeni hadn't shown her face since that first visit. When I told Ty about her stopping by and her threats, he chuckled and told me not to worry about her. It made me feel better about any lasting insecurities she had caused me.

Things were mostly peaceful until I attempted to bring Nova

home from my mother's house. When Ty came by after her arrival, he ran out of the house demanding to know why I had food jumping around. Apparently, rabbit was a favorite on his menu. As he faced the street trying to calm his prey-triggered growl, it became clear Nova wasn't safe around him. The next day, I brought her back to Mom's house. I told her that Nova felt ill-fated with me. Mom didn't question it and was happy to have Nova back.

When Mom met Tyler, it was a bit comical. He was inspected all around before she smiled and said to me, "Wow, he's very handsome!" Ty was rendered her victim as she made him wash dishes while working to get information about his personal life and past. He gave her as much information as he could manage.

April proved most beautiful. Jason finally let up on the harassment. Ty and I were powerfully bonded, and nothing felt amiss.

While we rested on the couch watching a werewolf movie one night, I lay upon his chest and listened to his heart. The rhythm of his beat was better than a glass of wine. He kissed my head as the movie reached its end.

"Can I tell you something?" he asked.

I raised my eyes to him. "Of course. What is it?"

"I ... I love you," he said, his breath a bit shaky. My heart skipped a beat while the words danced around us.

"I love you too, Ty." I reached up to kiss him passionately, running my fingers through his hair.

Ty said he loved me, and he said it first. We felt strongly for one another. There was no better word for it. *Love.* I was in a land of bliss with those three words wrapped around me as intensely as he was.

Everything was perfect.

It was May when events began to plunge us into the next stressful hell.

Tyler and I were walking around the neighborhood after a jog. He never left my side despite his ability to leave me in the dust. We chatted about different plants and how there were some with medicinal uses. Others could be confused with dangerous species, as I learned so personally in those woods with him. I had already disclosed how I thought about shooting him in the head while under the influence of whatever I had ingested, and Ty had previously explained how his family came to his rescue - leaving me for dead. He also explained that when they had removed Chogan's body from in front of the cave, he had refused to go with them while I was sleeping.

"It's interesting. We have a lot of medicinal plant tonics we make, but I never cared to learn them," he commented.

"I am by no means a botanist, but my father was a good teacher and learned from my grandfather. I'd love to learn more." Our walk slowed. We were a few blocks from home when I decided to hold his hand. He reached down to kiss me. Our lips pecked when a familiar car drove by, slower than normal. The windows were tinted, but the car was watching us.

Back at home, Ty showered and changed into fresh clothes he had previously brought over after I cleared a dresser drawer for him. In the kitchen, I had defrosted chicken and rabbit. With the smell of meat, his ravenous bounce down my staircase had me smiling - a smile he quickly returned.

"Looks delicious," he said, picking up the plate and sniffing the raw flesh.

I was getting used to watching him bite into raw meat, but part of me might never be fully comfortable with it. His teeth must have been sharp since he never struggled.

After I made him brush his teeth, we spent the rest of our night watching TV while I lay by his side, my head resting on his chest as I typically did. I hardly noticed the movie while listening to Ty's soothing heartbeat. The perfect rhythm filled my eardrum until I drifted into a peaceful sleep.

Dreams of warmth and safety with Ty's arms around me: I

dreamed of our untouchable happiness that gods could be jealous of. I dreamed of our future with rings on our fingers and children in our arms. Children – something I hadn't previously considered – but Ty made me dream of ours, envisioning their black or brown hair and blue eyes, their dimples and giggles.

It was one of the few mornings I awakened with Ty still there. At first, it startled me to feel him under my weight, still on the couch. I sat up to watch him; he lay motionless in complete rest. I kissed his forehead and gently ran my fingers through his thick hair over and over.

Ages could have passed before I checked my phone for the time. It was only five in the morning and the day's shift started at eight. I spent the early morning watching him sleep, his gray shirt snug against his pecs, his perfect beard that never grew. I tried to picture him without facial hair, but the short clean beard along his jaw, cheeks, and mouth was so a part of his look, I found it difficult to imagine him without it.

Today's shift was the last before some days off. Quietly, I strode upstairs to dress. It was getting warmer out, so I put my hair in a ponytail. Ty was still sleeping when I locked up the house and started my commute to work. The drive was quiet. I wondered how Tyler would respond to awakening in my home – the first time he was left there alone. It was a bit thrilling to know he would be there without me, but I wished I could have stayed there to enjoy him.

Once at work, I was bummed to realize Briana had the day off. If Jason was bothering me, joining her typically chased him away. Her bold personality worked to distract Jason from me. She'd even pull him away from my direction from time to time. He visibly found her annoying and both of us drew satisfaction from his irritation. It was nice she could sometimes return the favor for me.

It was a busy day due to a late morning pile-up on I-5, swamping our building with bloodied patients crying in pain. Andrew was among the nurses who assisted me with urgent care. We rushed to set up IVs, check medical records, and provide pain relief while doctors worked to stabilize the more seriously wounded.

A late lunch was a well-needed respite from the day's bustle. I found an abandoned newspaper resting on an empty cafeteria table and made it my new friend in Briana's absence. The Medford *Mail Tribune* was fairly thin; mostly national stories and some Oregon news filled its pages, with not a lot happening locally. Jackson County was usually quiet. I ate my chicken and sweet potato while I flipped the pages of advertisements.

As the day drifted into night, I took a moment for myself. Back in my favorite hospital restroom, I stared at my pale face in the mirror after washing my hands. The two-stall room smelled of cheap soap and chlorinated water. A light film of caked dry soap covered the floor tiles under the sinks, with the occasional long black hair lying around. Overall, the room was unpleasant – but that made it perfect to utilize. Fewer people entered here than the newer restrooms. It was the best place for temporary escape.

The mirror reflected a less familiar face.

My eyes were full of light. Pulling out the ponytail allowed my thick hair to fall past my shoulders. It had a beautiful shine to it and felt glossy to the touch. My cheeks were full and brightly highlighted with a slight rose color. I felt happy with my appearance.

While fussing with my hair's placement, I noticed a shadow under the door before it began to creep open. The sound grew increasingly loud and drawn out as the movement slowed to enhance its obnoxious sound, only to reveal a person who shouldn't have been opening it to begin with. Jason stepped inside the women's-only restroom and peered at me.

"This is a women's restroom, Dr. Smoldred," I hissed.

"Oh, I'm aware. I see you hide here often." He stepped toward the stalls and peered into them. "What are you doing in here by yourself?" His breathing was shaky.

"Fixing my hair. But I don't see how it's any of your concern," I challenged. My arms crossed as I turned to face him.

"No. I suppose it's no longer my concern given your attention is elsewhere."

I paused. "What do you mean?"

"You know. The one girl I find most interesting, most promising. The woman who is most difficult to get and therefore most rewarding ... she's the only one I've been unable to win over despite ages of trying. Have I not earned your affection? Do I not deserve you?" He stepped closer with his eyes narrowed.

"I don't owe anyone anything." The atmosphere around him seemed dangerous. He no longer felt like the typical annoyance I was used to - instead I felt cornered by a venomous snake. He blocked the door, leaving me to back up another step toward the wall centered between the furthest sink and toilet.

"I have offered you everything," he hissed through gritted teeth while advancing another step.

"I never accepted anything from you. Jason, please. Let's get back to work."

"What you accept doesn't matter. You were offered and you rudely rejected," he said.

My hands started to shake, and my legs felt weak. I had never seen him act this way. With another step, he was only a few feet from me. I had backed into the wall, my hands instinctively rising with my palms facing open to him at my stomach. *Please leave me alone*, I internally begged - my mouth not moving to form the words.

"Why couldn't you give *me* a chance? What did that poorly dressed homeless-looking loser do to earn your affection?"

I then recalled the silver Porsche with the tinted windows that passed us after our jog the day before. It finally clicked where I knew this car from. It was Jason's pleasure car, which he rarely drove. "J ... Jason. I ..."

With another step, he pressed his heavy weight against me, crushing me into the wall. Through his pants, he pressed his hardened groin into my stomach. I was frozen in shock. I felt his hand reach down my waist to slide his grip behind my left leg. He then lifted me up and thrust his pelvis into my groin.

"JASON," I screamed, prompting him to quickly cover my mouth. I screamed into his hand, which partly covered my nose. I couldn't breathe enough and began to see spots of blackness. I struggled, clawing at his grip while trying desperately to shake my face away.

He continued his assault. The more I struggled, the more aggressively he advanced until I felt my skull smack into the wall. It stunned me, causing my body to momentarily go limp. He took his hand from my mouth, allowing me to catch my breath. He backed up from pinning me, but then I felt his free hand slip into my pants. Above my underwear, he felt me. With some space now between us, I took my knee and raised it up hard and sharp to meet his groin.

"Ow, DAMMIT!" he yelped, jumping backwards. With my only chance of escape, I darted past him and swung the squeaking door open. Dashing into the hall, I raced to the elevator and pressed the button, bracing to feel his hands grab me. My heart pounded inside my chest.

I watched the floor light turn on. The doors crawled open and I raced inside. Pressing the first-floor button repetitively, I watched the doors close, and I began my descent.

When they opened, I rushed out of the building to locate my car – unable to catch my breath. Once safely locked inside, I began to hyperventilate with my head and hands on the steering wheel – too traumatized to look myself over. My brain continuously replayed what I had just endured. My heart pounded as the adrenaline still pumped. I heard a thud outside, making me jump. It was from the construction work nearby, but I almost thought Jason had hit the car.

Fighting tears while my nerves calmed, I could finally check myself. I slowly raised my hand, reached around to the back of my cranium, and gently touched the throbbing spot where my skull had impacted the wall. When I brought my hand back in front of me, I saw no blood and sighed with a bit of relief. The sight of my untucked shirt over my pants brought to mind his hand reaching to touch me against my will. I felt disgusting. I felt dirty and wrong.

What did I do to deserve this? Nothing. Absolutely nothing. How could he do this to me? How could he? I decided I shouldn't restrain the tears that wanted release; I started to cry in my shaken state. I thought about telling Ty – I couldn't keep this to myself. He should know what happened, but how would he react? I found my cellphone in my back pocket. The glass had cracked but I managed to dial Ty's number. When he didn't answer, I felt my throat tightening. Please, Ty. I *need* you.

On the second dial, he picked up on the first ring. "Hey, how's work?" he answered.

I couldn't speak with my throat continuing to tighten into a knot.

"Elizabeth? What's wrong?" I could hear the concern in his voice as he listened to my sniffles.

When I managed to loosen the knot in my throat, I struggled for words. "Jason. He att-attacked me. I was in the bathroom ..." I sighed painfully as I recalled his disgusting touch. "I was looking in the mirror and the door opened."

He said nothing as he listened. I only heard his breathing intensify.

"He pinned me against the wall with comments about my rejection. ... Ty, he knows about us. He saw us walking home yesterday. I think he's jealous. He snapped and assaulted me." I wiped my left eye. "He ..." I couldn't say the words. I didn't want to tell Ty how he touched me.

I heard something shift from Ty's movement. "Elizabeth, tell me what happened."

I took another breath. "He thrust himself into me and when I resisted, he smashed the back of my head into the wall." With my left hand, I reached to the raising bump where my skull impacted. It throbbed. "I almost lost consciousness." I heard Ty growl a deep animal snarl. I didn't want to tell him about Jason's hand down my pants or how I might be suffering from a brain injury. "I'm too shaken up to drive. I want to go home."

"I'm coming." The phone cut from the call.

He's coming? What was he going to do? I felt calling him was a mistake. With the head trauma and stress, I began to feel faint. I placed my head on the steering wheel above my hands, which gripped the leather rim. I thought about calling the police and filing a report. I thought about my job and how if I didn't say anything, we would still have to work together.

I didn't want to deal with police or people claiming I was lying – everyone knew I didn't like Jason. They'd think I was making it up to get rid of him. I would be shunned. Coworkers would turn on me. Would the police believe it? There were no witnesses. No witnesses meant it was my word against his. He'd claim my head injury wasn't caused by him; there was no proof he did it. He was going to get away with this. I was going to have to continue to work with him and I knew I couldn't.

My job meant a lot to me despite my struggles. My career was something I'd worked for with many years of schooling and training. I could work somewhere else, but would Jason follow?

After a while, I saw someone approaching my car. I was relieved to see Ty. Opening the car door, I stepped out to meet him. He was shirtless with no shoes, wearing old dark blue jeans that hid bits of loose black fur. His anger was displayed in his tensed muscles, bulging veins, and lowered eyebrows.

I closed the distance between us, wrapping my arms around him. He was so angry that he didn't hug me back. "Are you okay?" His voice was deep. Ty placed his hands at my hips and gently pulled me away from him. I released my arms and stepped back to look up at him. "Where. Is. He?" Ty practically snarled the words.

"Forget him. I'm quitting. I will be okay."

Ty repeated himself. "Where is he, Elizabeth?"

"He's somewhere in the hospital," I whispered so quietly that I barely heard myself.

CHAPTER TWENTY-FIVE

WOLF TEETH

T y turned and started walking to the building's main entrance. My eyes widened and my heart started to race as I followed him into the building. Ty might just kill him. I trailed behind Ty, trying and failing to look unaffiliated. The main floor receptionist, Debbie, didn't stop him as she watched me walk behind. Heads turned as he drew attention.

Despite Jason being potentially anywhere, Ty knew exactly where he was going. He rushed to the stairwell and jogged up the steps. I struggled to keep up, practically tripping over myself. "Ty, stop," I begged.

He pretended not to hear me. When rushing down the empty early-night hall, Ty found Jason in a patient's room checking a chart. It was a patient from this morning's car accident. The forty-year-old woman lay unconscious in the bed attached to large amounts of equipment.

Before Jason could process who rushed him, Ty grabbed him by the collar and shoved him against the wall. Jason's chart crashed to the floor in his surprise. He started to shove back until he saw Ty's teeth were no longer human – his teeth elongated and sharpened from the gums as he snarled into Jason's face. The shock of Ty's wolf teeth while human, something he never told me about, sent me into a panic. I stepped back only to accidentally shut off the room lights. In the dim room now lit only by monitors I could barely see Jason's horrified face. Ty held open his scissor bite with a powerful throat snarl. He didn't need words to get his message across.

"What - what the hell?!" Jason cried.

"I will be your worst nightmare if you EVER even think about harming Elizabeth again."

I saw Jason's hand reach for an unseen object. Before I could warn Ty, Jason took something from his lower pocket and stabbed it as hard as he could into Ty's abdomen. Ty gasped, releasing his grip from Jason. Seizing the opportunity for escape, Jason rushed past me, opening the door to reach the hall as Ty collapsed to his knees.

"Tyler!" I rushed to his side. In the darkness, I could smell the blood dripping. I turned on the lights, fetched two towels from the room's bathroom, and pressed one against the wound.

Ty winced. "Dammit," he complained.

I had to get him to my car. "Get up; we need to get you out of here. What were you thinking, revealing yourself like that? Hold this on the wound." I placed his hand over the towel and then used the other towel to clean up the floor.

Out in the hall, it was painfully quiet. I pulled Ty by the hand and led him to the stairwell, moving so quickly down the steps that it felt as if something could have been chasing us. The adrenaline made me forget about Jason's assault, the impending threat of Jason's knowledge, and Ty's teeth - now normal again. All that mattered in that moment was getting Ty home and getting us both healed. Debbie looked puzzled as she saw us speed-walk past. Ty held the towel firmly against him while he followed me through the sliding doors. Back at the car, I fumbled my keys momentarily before I got my car opened.

"Get in," I commanded. He slunk into the passenger seat, wincing at his discomfort. I reached over him to pull the seat belt and clicked it in.

Looking over at Ty during a red light, I saw him breathing more heavily than typical. He rested his head against the glass, waiting for me to tell him how stupid that was, but he didn't need to hear it. It was written on his beautiful face, apparent by his narrowed eyebrows, deep frown, and closed eyes. With every passing car's headlights, Ty's bloodied towel was highlighted. Despite his wound and our recent trauma, it was impossible not to admire him. His abs ripped up his chest to meet perfectly toned pecs. His strong arms finally began to relax.

As I pulled into the driveway, the safety of my dark house greeted us. I said nothing as I turned off the car and walked over to the other side. When I opened the door, he lifted his head with sorry eyes. "Don't look at me that way," I said while I unbuckled him. He held the cloth to his wound as he slowly got out and followed me into the house.

Once inside, I sent him to my bedroom while I headed into the upstairs hallway bath. After washing my hands and retrieving medical supplies, I joined Tyler in the bedroom. He was lying on my bed, already changed into shorts. The bloodied towel rested on my nightstand. Ty said nothing while he watched me sit beside him. Looking at the wound, I observed a deep and rounded puncture that had clotted and couldn't be stitched. I treated him with antibiotic cream and then covered it with a large bandage.

"Are you okay?" Ty finally spoke.

"I will be." My eyes lowered to the bed sheet beside him.

"I'm sorry," he said.

I looked at his face. His eyes were soft and apologetic. "It's okay. We'll be okay." I reached over and gently kissed his lips. I repeated those words in my head. We'll be okay. We'll be okay. I had to believe that – to hold onto that. He raised his hand and gently moved it to the back of my head. I felt him lightly touch the lump that had formed and still throbbed. He pulled away and frowned when I winced.

"I could kill him. I wanted to," he said.

"Scaring him halfway across the country was good enough." A sad smile formed on my face. Jason had hurt us both. I wished to never see Jason again, but if Tyler killed him, it would only make us worse off.

"Hardly."

I remembered Ty's teeth, all sharp and terrifying. I remembered the jolt of fear I felt when seeing him that way. Looking into the memory, I was scared *for* Ty and not scared of him. I was afraid of what Jason might do after discovering Ty's secret. "When were you going to show me those if not for Jason?" I pointed to his teeth.

Ty smirked. "I've been showing them to you for ages; you just never *looked*."

"What do you mean?"

"How else do you think I can eat raw meat so easily in human form? Surely my human teeth are not sharp enough."

"You're kidding," I slapped his arm. "So *that's* how you do it!"

He chuckled. "In your defense, I never really *tried* to show you."

"Hmm." I thought about how we didn't eat dinner tonight. Unless he mentioned it, I was too tired to care. "I'm going to shower. I'll be back."

I brought a clean pair of PJs and underwear to the bathroom. In the shower, I soaked in every drop of steam. Flashes of Jason's touch plagued my thoughts. His fingers down my pants, his groin pressed into me. I sat down on the floor of the shower and hugged my knees as the water flowed over my head, pressing into my bruised skull. It hurt. I wanted to bury what I'd been through. I wanted to tell Briana. She could keep a secret. Perhaps she could convince the other employees of Jason's true nature. Maybe he had done this to someone before. I wasn't sure what would happen. The day had been so overwhelming that it was difficult, actually impossible, to relax.

When I rejoined Tyler, he was resting with his eyes closed. I flicked off the lights and lay next to him. Would he stay tonight? After what Jason did, I doubted he'd leave. When I crawled over him to his far side, his doze broke.

"Hey," he said quietly.

"Are you going to leave me tonight?" I questioned.

"No. I'm staying right here." He shifted over to me and pulled me into his chest. I placed my ear in its favorite spot, right against his powerful heartbeat. Like magic, despite our pain and trauma, we slept peacefully in each other's arms.

Screaming. That's all I heard. It wasn't the quiet peace of night. It wasn't the calmness of normalcy. Someone was yelling in pain next to me. I quickly sat up when I realized it wasn't in my dreams. Ty was yelling in agony.

I reached for the night lamp and flicked it on. Looking at Ty, I saw his face was scrunched as he gasped. His one hand was holding his calf while his other held his abdomen over the bandage. "Tyler! What's wrong? What is hurting?"

"My leg. My stomach!" he cried. He cradled his pained body where the agony centered. I tried pulling his hand away from his bandage, but he only pressed harder.

"Ty, let me see – dammit!" I said while continuing to fight his hand away. Finally, he complied and allowed me to look. Dark red blood was leaking through the bandage.

Ty let his head fall back to the pillow while holding up his pained leg, still grabbing at his calf muscle. I pulled the bandage off to reveal the wound that should have been healing, only to see a clotting mess. Chunks of dark blood had oozed onto the bandage. A large dark purple ring had formed on the skin around it while blood so dark it might have been black pooled in the wound's center. I had never seen anything like it, and it terrified me. I tried to formulate possibilities. The visual didn't match serosanguineous drainage. It didn't look infectious. Tissue necrosis and gangrene, periwound dermatitis, hematoma, edema - nothing matched what I saw. But Ty was not a normal person and feasibly this wasn't a normal complication. I rushed to retrieve fresh bandages while my mind raced through more possibilities. Ty remained quiet aside from his gasps and cries, failing to give any guidance as to what this might have been in relation to his species. Was this his body's reaction to the stabbing? Perhaps a strange infection? My brain twisted, searching for an answer.

"I don't understand what's wrong with your wound. Have you seen this before?"

He continued to wince and complain of pain. Finally, he answered, "I don't ... I don't think so."

Despite Ty's complaints, I worked to clean his injury. Why wasn't it healing? He had easily dealt with wounds far worse than this. The ring around the wound was particularly scary. Based on my previous experiences, purple rings and lightning lines off wounds related to blood infections.

Blood infection! That had to be it. Ty's wound seemed to be the starting point of an aggressive blood infection. His leg pain could be related or a coincidence. Blood infections were serious, but at least it indicated a direction for treatment - a relief despite the severity. He needed heavy antibiotics. Checking the time, I saw it was two in the morning. The hospital was open through the night with very limited staff. I tried to remain collected. What would I do if Ty was any other patient? I'd rush treatment. I'd take him to the hospital and get him a whole team of doctors. But that wasn't an option, was it?

"Ty, can we get you to the hospital for treatment? I think you have a blood infection – an abnormal one that's highly aggressive," I said while applying a fresh bandage.

Ty was catching himself from the pain. "You already know my answer."

He didn't give a reason, but just as when his back was injured, keeping Ty away from the medical profession was a way to protect him and his species. I wasn't confident I could handle this new problem. "I will have to head up there to gather supplies," I said while leaving the bed and searching for clothes. I thought about how I'd need to steal what Ty required. "How is your leg pain? It's not just a charley horse?"

Ty gently turned his head to the left and back to the right. "I've never felt this before," he gasped, "it feels like something is stabbing from my ankle to the thigh with it being the worst below the back of my knee." Ty's face was bunched again. "Around the wound, it feels like a throbbed stinging." He placed his hand over the bandage.

"I'll see if I can get you pain meds."

Skipping the work clothing, I wore an all-black outfit with a hoodie for the cameras. I searched my closet for a backpack as Ty watched through his pain. While leaving the room, I heard a low growl from my bed.

Opening the front door at two-thirty in the morning, I was greeted by the wind of the night. The darkness of the cloudless sky left many stars to be wished upon. In my head, as I crawled into my car, I wished upon them all for Ty to be okay.

The engine roared to life and away I drove to the place to which I didn't know whether I'd ever return. I thought about sending Briana a picture of Ty's injury and info about his pain for her opinion, but it might have sparked too many questions. I also didn't want to risk the picture getting into public hands. I was out of my league with what I was facing.

When I got close to the building, I parked in a camera-free street near the hospital and began speed-walking. As I reached the parking lot with my hood up, what I saw sent a shock down to my pelvis. Jason's car. The silver trim, the chrome tires. His car was in my spot. So many emotions flooded me as I sat dumbfounded. So many questions came to mind as I processed the fear, sadness, then rage. Why was *he*, of all people, still here at three in the morning? Why was he in *my damn parking spot?* I dreaded running into him. He might attack me again. He might ask me about Ty's condition. Jason might stop me or worse.

I briefly considered keying his car. Instead, I readied myself for the raid. Such offenses were criminal. I thought about doing time. I thought about Mr. Rogers, the sweet and relatively old chief of police in Jacksonville, who was more than ready for retirement. Everybody loved him, unless you were a criminal, with his white hair and beard – a look comparable to ol' Saint Nick. Rogers had watched me grow up; he called me "just a good kid" and I'd always hate to disappoint him, but here in Medford, the police department would be more likely to snag me, no questions asked.

Walking through the main entrance, I saw no one at the counter. It was too easy to sneak past and rush toward the medical bank where the pharmaceuticals were stored. Opening the door to the storeroom, I searched the shelves for the antibiotics I was most familiar with: glass bottles and boxes of Doxycycline, cephalexin, and amoxicillin. I opened my pack and placed the two boxes and one bottle inside. Nearby were the painkillers. Kadian was my go-to. I also grabbed Bactroban to put around his wound. Zipping up my pack, I put it on my back and made my exit.

As I turned the corner, Jason was walking straight toward me. I gasped – an obvious and obnoxious gasp. My hands started to shake as my heart pounded.

"Nurse Elizabeth?" He raised an eyebrow, then took a moment to peer around, likely looking for Tyler.

"Back off. I'm warning you." My voice cracked mid-sentence.

"What are you wearing?" He paused. "Is your freak of nature creature here?" His face bore a creepy smile.

"Mind your business." I wanted to try rushing past him, but my legs wouldn't move.

"I have to say, Liz – I never expected you of all women to be into bestiality. What are you doing here, anyway?"

My face reddened. "Like I said ... none of your business." I tried to swallow, but my mouth had dried up. All my resources went to sweating – drowning my body from the stress.

His eyes shifted to the backpack. What do you have there?" he asked, tilting his head in curiosity.

When he stepped forward, I started to panic. "STAY BACK! I'm warning you!" I stepped back. He had caught me off-guard in his bathroom assault, but this time I was ready.

I watched him chuckle as he stepped even closer. "What's in the bag?"

This man was sick. His behavior made me feel I was in the presence of a budding murderer – a borderline psychopath. He wasn't the Jason I had worked with for some years now. He was someone else.

"Are you stealing meds?" He sighed, "I surely hope not."

A wave of anger flooded. "It's your fault. ALL OF IT."

"Hardly. That monster shouldn't have messed with me. You shouldn't be helping him. Give me the bag before the police arrive," he demanded.

"The only monster here is *you*," I huffed. "What did you stab him with?"

"Why? He's sick? Good." He stepped closer.

I had to escape. Pulling the bag from my back, I removed the bottle of amoxicillin. Readying my keys, I tossed the bottle to Jason. "Catch."

When he fumbled to catch the glass bottle, I raced past him, forcing my legs to fly. As I shot through the doors, I barely heard Jason's threat called out to me: "I WILL WIN!"

I ran so fast that I slammed into the door when I reached my car. When I hit the gas hard, the tires spun faster than the traction could catch. I could smell the burning rubber as I peeled off toward home. When I pulled into the driveway the adrenaline was still pumping, and I had to remind myself to calm down. This state of mind was dangerous for treating a patient. Before exiting the car, I performed breathing exercises. In through my nose, out through my mouth. I struggled to calm myself, especially when time was of the essence. When my heart was pounding half as hard, I opened the car door and made my way inside, careful to ensure the front door was locked behind me.

Despite my slow climb of the stairs, the anxiety over Ty's condition made my heart pound again. "Ty?" I called for him when reaching the top of the stairs. Inside my bedroom, he was still on my bed. Despite my having been gone only an hour, his condition had worsened. I rushed to his side. I placed my hand on his forehead, but he was covered in sweat. "Hey, Ty? How are you feeling?" I was panicked but did my best to keep my composure.

"Honestly, horrible," he coughed. "The pain is unbearable."

"I have some painkillers." I worked to improve his condition. I started him on a high dosage of doxycycline and cephalexin, and then provided the Kadian. Once he had swallowed the pills, I pulled his abdominal bandage off. From the sweat, it had already peeled partly away from the skin. The wound had worsened. The ring of purple now stretched further out, barely hidden by the bandage. "I'm honestly not sure what this is. I have never seen this before. It's aggressive. We might have no choice but to hospitalize you."

"No." His breathing was heavy. "I can't. You know why. And Jason might try something."

"What will we do if this doesn't work?" My eyes started to tear. I already lost him once. Losing him again was an unbearable thought.

"I have a last resort," he assured, "just trust me."

After leaving to wash my hands, I returned with cotton swabs to use with the Bactroban.

Ty tolerated me wiping the medication around the wound, but when I swabbed it into the edges of the injury, he cried out. "Ahh! Dammit!" His face was in knots as he exhaled heavily through the sting.

"That pain medication should be starting to work." I could feel my heavy frown.

"I guess it doesn't like me," he half joked.

"Something is wrong. I don't understand any of this." I was growing frustrated with myself. What was I doing wrong?

"It's not you. We don't react to regular drugs like regular people do. I'm not exactly a typical patient."

"Then what do you do for medical treatment and surgeries?"

"Our healers do their best. My father is one of them."

"Is that the *last resort* you mentioned?" I asked.

"Yeah," he said. I watched him adjust his position, propping himself up on a few high pillows.

"Then why aren't we going to them?"

"I want to see what you can do first. I'd rather not bring this to my father. They would all be beyond furious if they knew I showed my wolf teeth to a regular human, especially someone else in the medical field."

"Oh. We can leave out that detail. And what's the worst they'd do, Ty? I'm really worried whatever is going on will kill you."

"Regular human meds can sometimes work or buy time," he winced as I applied more medical cream, "but if there's not enough improvement by morning we will go to my father."

"Fine. But you better hang in there," I practically threatened him to pull through.

"I'm stronger than you think." He smiled through his discomfort.

I sighed while glancing back down at the wound. The purple ring reminded me of the jelly ring candies my dad used to buy me on his way home from work. The ring was turning darker to match the dark blood still oozing. Taking out a thermometer, I offered it to him. "Put this in your mouth under your tongue." He did as instructed without complaint. After a few minutes, the temperature read a staggering one hundred five degrees. "What is normal body temperature for you?" I questioned.

"One hundred degrees is typical."

"I see. You're at one hundred five."

"It's high but not deadly high. I had a fever higher as a kid."

"Still really concerning."

I left to get a few washcloths from the towel storage closet. Before reaching for them, I paused to breathe – allowing myself a moment of weakness. I inhaled heavily, closing my eyes as my full lungs ached at maximum capacity. With release, I allowed a single tear to escape my watering vision. How many more times would I see Tyler suffering in pain, facing a grave injury that could rip him from me? The stress had been beyond overwhelming. My knees felt weak. I wiped my eyes before taking the cloth to the hallway bathroom. I soaked one in cold tap water before returning to him. Pausing in the doorway, I watched him breathing on my bed. His eyes were closed. Blood slowly dripped to the sheets while his abs tensed from pain.

When he didn't feel me join his side, he opened his eyes to look for me. The beautiful blue eyes I adored were hazed with his discomfort. The injury seemed so minor, so minuscule compared to what he'd already been through, yet this small wound had him suffering in a way I had never seen. His heavy eyes stared up at me as I walked over and sat beside him. When I placed the wet cloth on his forehead, he raised his right arm and gently put his hand on my wrist. "What?" I asked, confused by his touch. I lowered my hand away.

He gave me a sad smile. "The meds must be starting to work. The pain isn't as bad."

I leaned down to kiss his cheek. "Try to get some rest."

Ty closed his eyes while I worked on him. The ring hadn't increased but looked no better. I could see him wince as I wiped around the wound's perimeter and then applied more Bactroban. Leaving the wound uncovered, I stayed awake by Ty's side for the rest of the early morning. As he slept, my restless mind wandered. What would tomorrow bring?

Judging from our first meeting, Tyler's family was extremely intense. I didn't know their true faces, each one a blanket of fur and fangs overwhelmed with grief. I buried Chogan's death as a tragic case of self-defense. That's what it was, but did his family now see this? I could be walking right into ruthless jaws. What about Ashton? He apparently tried to kill me before. What if Tyler was wrong about his intentions? Ashton could try again.

I wondered about their homes and if they behaved differently than regular people. Would they all have log cabins, stick homes, tree houses? Did they wear unique clothing and dance around fires? Maybe they perform ceremonies, wear large jewelry, or have unique body mods. Looking at Ty, it seemed extremely unlikely.

Unable to sit still a moment longer, I retrieved a bag from the closet and began placing items inside with only the desk lamp for light. A change of clothes and my stored hunting knives were added first. I then went downstairs and deposited my gun, a flashlight, water bottles, and bags of snacks within the bag's compartments. I didn't know how long we would be gone, and I didn't know what to expect.

Downstairs, I pulled Ty's breakfast from the freezer and placed the meat into a pot of warm water to defrost.

At six, my phone chimed. I was sitting on the bed next to Ty, watching him breathe. Carefully reaching over him to take my cell phone, I saw Briana had texted me.

Hey! There is a rumor goin around about u. Call me.

I couldn't be bothered to deal with the drama.

With the morning here and Ty still asleep, I left the bed to dress for our trip to his family. As expected, no improvement had been made through the night. I was fully prepared to take him to his father. From the top of my dresser, some fresh jeans and a T-shirt were ready for me. I slipped on fresh black underwear, my denims, and then my bra and shirt.

It was time to wake him.

I walked over to his side and gently placed my hand on his forehead. His temperature was burning by regular standards, but just warm for him. I reached down to kiss him, slowly placing my lips upon his. His pleasant mild musky smell and my gentle stroking of his beard set my heart fluttering.

I caressed my hand through his gorgeous hair, then down his chest until he finally awoke. His movement was slow. When his eyes focused on me, he gave a light smile. He must have seen the fear in my eyes. He looked down at his abdomen and sighed lightly.

"Morning," I said while partially holding back a yawn.

"I guess we are going to see my father," Ty said without looking up from his wound.

"Yes. I'm about ready to go. We need to get you ready and eat breakfast. Can you sit up?"

"I think so." Ty was weak as he started to move. I grabbed his arm and helped pull him upright. He winced with discomfort.

From the nightstand, I grabbed more meds with the glass of water half full and handed it all to him. He put both pills in his mouth and emptied the cup.

"Okay, try to stand." I stepped back to watch. He stood up with a hidden wince and then walked to the master bathroom, closing the door behind him.

After prepping Ty's breakfast, I started to cook for myself. I was half finished eating when Ty finally joined me. He slowly stepped down the stairs, still shirtless.

We ate in silence. I tried to see his wolf teeth behind the bites, but he kept them away from sight. As we finished up breakfast, Ty turned his head to the door. His eyes filled with concern. "What's wrong?" I asked.

"Shh." He continued to listen toward the door. After a few minutes I heard a knock. "Don't answer that," Ty whispered.

"Why?" I questioned quietly.

"It's a police officer. He wants to question you. I have a bad feeling."

"Shit." I held my breath.

It was five long minutes before Tyler heard him leave.

"This is about the hospital mess, isn't it?" I then remembered Briana's text. Maybe it was a warning.

He nodded. "At least we will be gone for a while."

"We will? How are you so sure?"

"I'm not. Just a hunch."

"Oh. Well, we will need to cover that." I pointed to the wound.

I made quick work of cleaning up breakfast. Ty watched pitifully – his body tired from fighting whatever plagued him. When I finished cleaning, I retrieved a bandage, the antibiotic cream, and his fresh clothes – a black T-shirt and sweatpants. Once the wound was creamed and covered, I turned around to let him dress. Hearing him struggle behind me, I wanted to turn around, but Ty still wouldn't let me see him without pants on. Respecting boundaries made us a stronger couple despite the absence of harmonious sexual bonding. Thoughts of his lower half slipped me into the gutter until he said I could turn to him. Looking at him then, his tired eyes and bluing lips were the only signs that something was wrong.

It was approaching seven-thirty when I sent Ty to my car. I made sure to pack even more clothes and food for myself in a second bag. If Ty was right, I could be away for a week – maybe longer.

I soon joined him in the car. Buckling my seatbelt, I reminded him to do the same. He complied slowly, certain movements proving painful. I turned the car on and started to back out of the driveway when I realized I had no idea where I was going. "Um. Where to? I have no clue where to go."

Ty pointed away from town and then continued to point the whole way. Either the bumps of the car were hurting him, or he was weakening further. Every time I asked for more directions, he would only point.

When he pointed to the left for his final direction, I missed the turn and had to back up the car twenty feet. With my car stopped, I peered down the narrow dirt road in the middle of a vast forest stretch. On each side of the entrance were two huge maple trees reaching to the sky with beautiful spring foliage upon their ancient branches. The street stretched so far into the woods I couldn't see its end. From the road, it seemed the forest swallowed it up.

TRESPASSERS WILL BE MAULED

I turned to look at him. "Down there?"

"Yes," he whispered.

Ty looked worse than ever. The drive had taken twenty-five minutes and it might as well have taken all day by how fast he was going downhill. I felt sweat pooling under my arms while my core jittered. It took everything in me to stay calm and keep my head.

Looking back at the road, it wasn't far from what I imagined. Of course Ty's mystical family lived down a creepy old dirt road in the middle of nowhere. I tried not to let my past haunt me now. I tried not to paint Ty's family as dangerous and excessively estranged. Cautiously, I turned my car down the narrow road. As we moved along, the woods seemed to stretch further, giving me the illusion of standing still. A mile in, I noticed a sign painted to show a white wolf skull above blood-red lettering that read "Trespassers will be mauled."

It had the intended effect.

Another few miles in, the woods started to break. I slowed my car as I approached a group of homes barely visible through the dense trees. As I pulled in, multiple people and a wolf stood waiting for us. I stopped my car at the road's limit and observed them, reading their body language.

I was mildly disappointed by their unremarkable appearance but impressed by their beauty. In the middle of the gathering stood a mature man with black hair and a light beard that grayed along his jawline. He wore a button-down black polo and dark blue jeans and was incredibly handsome. The resemblance to Ty was obvious; this man was his father. My eyes swung to the equally gorgeous, enviably slim woman next to him, Ty's mother. She had brown hair, but it wasn't as vibrant as someone younger would have. Her eyes were sad, and her frown was harsh. To her side stood a large gray and white wolf. I recognized Ashton's coat and eyes, which I could never forget after his attack; my car still bore the scars. When our eyes locked, Ashton's lips rose up to expose his teeth. He obviously still hated me, and it seemed to be a shared feeling among the group. On the other side stood two young women and a young man, all three apparently in their late teens.

I ignored the glares, turning to observe the remaining individuals. Angeni was sitting on the nearest porch. Her face sported a callous smile as she looked at Ashton and then at me. She was clearly hoping Ashton would lunge after I exited my car.

Ty's condition was failing as he began to lose consciousness. Without thinking, I opened the driver door and rushed around the front of the car. Ty's family melted away. They could have evaporated into dust in that moment. "Ty? Ty!" I implored while opening the passenger door, but he was unresponsive. I tapped his cheek, shook his shoulders. His lips were even bluer. Desperate, I turned back to his family and was startled to see they had already surrounded me except for Ashton and Angeni, who held their positions.

"Move aside," Ty's father commanded. His voice was deep and powerful. The teenage girls held their hands to their mouths, instantly worried.

His mother, Catori, gasped at his condition. "What happened?" she asked. Her tired eyes were haunting.

"He was stabbed by something. I didn't see what it was, a knife maybe. He isn't responding to antibiotics. I think it's a blood infection," I said while pointing to Ty's abdomen.

I watched Ty's father peel the bandage and inspect the wound. "We have a remedy we can try," he said.

A headache built in the back of my head as I watched Ty's father and the young man pull Ty from my car and begin carrying him toward the cabins.

"Tyler said you are a healer?" I asked Ty's father.

"Alianna, quick. Get the door," he commanded, ignoring my question.

I grabbed one of my supply bags and then followed.

Alianna, one of the teenage girls, raced ahead and opened the door of the third home to the right. As we walked, I studied the cabins. They stretched around in a narrow oval with its front open to the dirt road at the northern end. Huge trees scattered around the cabins, effectively hiding them from aerial view. They were beautiful, clearly constructed from trees of the surrounding forest. Each cabin was crafted slightly differently, yet they looked very similar. I quickly counted fifteen large cabins, surely too many for the number of people who seemed to live here.

Walking up to the cabin, I noticed meat strung up along a horizontal rope drying in a patch of sun. It was mostly red meat with a few large fish.

Ty remained unresponsive as they entered the house. Catori turned in front of me before I could enter. "You can leave now," she said sharply, crossing her arms and glaring into my face.

"I'm not going anywhere." My heart pounded.

She studied me, looking up and down. "Empty your pockets and give me your bag."

"Fine." I handed her my bag and then showed her my pockets. She put the bag over her shoulder and then opened her arm to gesture inside. With slight hesitation, I stepped in.

First, I noticed a musky smell like Ty's scent but stronger. I crinkled my nose while taking in the room, my eyes widening at the space. The living room had a subtle orange and blue color theme laced with white accents and a balanced furniture arrangement. The white brick fireplace stretched up the wall on the right. Deerskin throws draped the couches and a stuffed squirrel sat upon the mantel.

As I walked around looking for Ty, I reached the kitchen. The décor had shifted to a taste of country – white marble countertops, a stainless-steel sink, a huge freezer, but no refrigerator. I saw few cooking appliances and limited counter space. A dirtied meat processor rested inside the sink, blood trickling down its metal sides.

"Tyler?" I called for him. With no response, I followed the commotion. Through a hallway to the left, I reached a bedroom where Ty was laid out on a twin bed. I watched his father struggle to make Ty drink a strange liquid with an orange tinge. He then removed the bandage and pressed a green substance into the wound. Ty cried out, but it was muffled. After five minutes, Ty's lips were less blue, and his eyes less sunken.

With the medicine applied, Ty's father turned to me and glared. He stood up, crossed his arms, and heavily frowned. "Who did this?"

"Uhh ... someone stabbed Ty with something."

"I get that. Who?" he said sharply.

"I don't know." I convinced myself this wasn't a lie. I didn't really *know* Jason.

Ty's father sighed heavily in frustration and rushed past me, shoving me out of the way. I frowned at his back as he walked down the hall.

There wasn't much inside the room. The small bed rested against the white wall. In front of the window was a thinly built brown dresser with some items atop it. On the far side were a rocking chair and a small armchair where the young man and one of the teen girls rested. On the edge of the bed, I sat beside Ty and stared at the green substance, curious about what his father gave him.

"You're Elizabeth, right?" the young man asked. He had light freckling and red hair. His face was warm, with light eyes and smooth skin.

"Yes. You can call me Lizzy." I gave him a smile, which he returned.

"Okay, Lizzy. Nice to meet you. I'm Messer. We don't get to meet many new friends. Oh, this is Alianna. She is Tyler's sister." He tossed his thumb back toward her. I looked over at the teen girl sitting on the rocking chair.

"Hi Alianna," I greeted.

"Hello," she smiled lightly. "Are you Tyler's girlfriend?" She giggled a young laugh.

I smiled with my teeth showing. "Yes."

Alianna studied me up and down, while a photo on the dresser grabbed my eye. It was a picture of a young man with black hair and brown eyes who resembled Ty in the face but had a narrow build. On the bottom of the photo was some writing: *Chogan, 2018*. My heart sank in my chest.

"We all know what happened with Chogan. Don't blame yourself. He was a real jerk, and *nobody* liked him ... except maybe Ashton and Angeni. Even his parents didn't get along with him," Messer said as I studied the photo.

"I didn't know that," I said.

"Do you love Tyler?" Alianna asked, distracting me.

I turned to look at her. "Very much. I'd do anything for him."

"I see that ... I really do. Coming here, after everything ... it's brave."

Ty started to open his eyes, turning his head toward me.

"Ty? Are you okay?" The ring was fading, and the clotting blood looked redder behind the green medicine. "Wow, that's amazing. He already looks better. What did he give him?"

"It's a broad-use healing tonic made with ground-up wild herbs," Messer said.

"Which wild herbs?"

Messer shrugged. He turned to Alianna. "Let's give them some privacy, Ali."

"Okay." She bounced up and skipped out of the room, her dark brown hair flowing behind her. Messer followed, closing the door behind him.

As Ty came to, I sighed a heavy breath. Kissing him above his eye, I relaxed my shoulders. The strain in my neck started to release.

I watched Tyler look around the room, taking in where he was.

"Where is Ashton?" he asked, concerned.

"He's outside somewhere all wolfed up and clearly just as pissed about me being here as the rest of them. Well ... most of them."

"Stay away from him," Ty warned.

"With pleasure. Let's just focus on you. I'll get you some water from the kitchen." I left the room and bumped into Catori. She was washing her meat processor. "Can I have some water for Ty?" I asked her.

She rinsed her hands and opened a cabinet nearby, pulling out an ordinary glass cup. From a secondary waterspout on the right of the sink, she filled it with water and handed it to me. Her body language was tense, and she wouldn't make eye contact. "*May* is the proper word. Not *can*. Didn't anyone teach you how to speak?"

My eyes widened as her attitude startled me. "Uh ... thank you," I said while taking the cup before hurrying back to Ty.

For several hours, Ty slept peacefully, leaving me drained. I held his hand, played with his hair, and avoided looking at the photo. For a while, I debated leaving Ty's side. My stomach growled and the photo was glaring into my temple.

Creeping out of the room, I decided to leave the house while

I waited for Ty to recover. I sat on the front porch of the cabin and observed these rare yet somewhat ordinary people. They didn't wear unique clothing, live in trees or stick houses, have paint on their faces, or wear large jewelry. But they did live within cabins, had strung-up meat, morphed into wolves, and resided deep in the woods away from the rest of the world.

Two naked four-year-old children were running past the cabin, oblivious to my intrusion. My eyes widened at these little girls. I watched in awe as they quickly changed their form into wolf pups and began wrestling with their puppy teeth, biting into each other's thick fur hide. They were ridiculously adorable in both forms. For close to an hour they chased each other around and wrestled with high-pitched yelps of excitement. Their beautiful dark golden coats matched their dirty-blond human hair. I smiled and giggled at their mischief.

One of the girls tried to steal some of the strung-up meat next to the cabin – nipping and pawing at it as she struggled to reach.

A woman I had not previously seen came out of the cabin across the oval from me, calling, "Callie, Emma – no! Come on in for lunch." The two girls quickly changed into their human form, leaving a pile of caramel-colored fur behind them. They raced into the house, leaving me in awe of their existence. The loose fur danced in the wind and away from the center of the oval.

Ashton walked in front of the cabin only feet from me, his hackles raised. His eyes glared into me while he let out an obnoxious snarl, snapping his jaws in clear threat. I fumbled backwards in shock. Only moments later, Ty stood behind me in the cabin door frame.

I pulled myself to the side of the porch and turned to watch Ty. He was furious, baring his fangs while letting out an equally vicious snarl. Ashton snorted at Ty in reply and walked away, his tail lowered almost between his legs. When I looked back at Ty, his teeth were human again.

"Are you okay?" he asked while reaching his hand down to me.

"Yes, are you?" I took his hand and he pulled me up. Under his shirt I inspected his wound, relieved to see it was scabbing over. The purple ring was completely gone. "You look so much better."

"I'll be okay thanks to you."

Angeni walked with a laundry basket in her arms. She gave me a dark look as she passed. Moments later, the two naked children came racing back outside. With Tyler beside me, they finally acknowledged me. "Tylerrrrr!" they said almost simultaneously.

"Hey girls!" Ty rushed down to greet them. They both jumped in his arms and hugged him. "Elizabeth, this is Callie in my right arm and Emma in my left. The latest twin girls born." Ty said, proudly presenting them. Emma whispered something in Ty's ear. "Yes, that's my girlfriend," he replied, smiling. Emma giggled. Ty placed them down and they quickly morphed back into wolf pups, chasing each other down and around the cabins.

"Are you able to change into a wolf that quickly?"

"No, the younger you are the faster you can change. It's a perk of being young. Also, we tend to have twins. Not always. Chogan and I were single births but my sisters are twins. It's great when there are two."

"They really play a lot, don't they?" I said, trying to ignore the mention of Chogan. It reminded me of my true status here. Despite the reason, I killed one of their own. I didn't blame Ty's parents for turning a cold shoulder to me for that reason alone.

"Yes, it's a huge relief for the adults. Pups tire each other out."

"Who are their parents?" I asked, perplexed by their lack of supervision.

"The cabin they ran out from is used by Uki and Blaze. Both are from Messer's clan. Uki is Messer's blood aunt. Messer's planned marriage to my sister, Alianna, will be a strong union with the Hati clan. Uki and Blaze often stay here for the warmer months and typically leave when it's winter. A lot of their clan members join us in the warmer seasons. I expect most of them to head over soon."

"Ah. Well they are the most beautiful and unique children I've seen. Do they always run around naked?"

Ty chuckled. "It's typical for wolf children to stay nude. It's normal in our communities since they change form so often. Shyer young children may stay in wolf form for months at a time despite their parents' complaints. We don't encourage them to wear clothes until they are around eight years old or when puberty starts. That's when their shifting process slows, and they'll change form less often."

"Fascinating," I said.

"I'm sure it's strange to an outsider. Very few outsiders become a part of our world."

"Saying that only makes me feel as unwelcome as I actually am."

"Don't worry about it, Liz. Just lay low while they adjust." Ty smiled.

Deep down, I knew I would never truly be accepted even if I hadn't killed Chogan. I wasn't one of them. As Angeni said, I didn't belong here. Being different from Ty never bothered me before.

"Let's walk to my cabin," Ty encouraged, feeling my discomfort.

"That sounds nice." I felt overwhelmingly excited at the mention. Ty's place. Would it be like his parents' home? Ty took my hand and started his walk down the row of cabins until he reached the one at the far southern end. This cabin faced the rest and looked newer than some of the first homes. It featured a beautiful wrap-around porch, a stone chimney, and large windows. He paused, allowing me to take it in. "It's gorgeous. Did you build it?"

"Yes, a few years ago. My family helped though."

"Can we go inside?" I asked.

Ty led me up to the door and opened it. As I walked in, my jaw dropped at the beauty of the space. To the right was a large living room. On its outside wall was a large gray stone fireplace accented with an impressive buck. As I walked around, I saw on the mantel pictures of a youthful Ty with his parents. To the right of the fireplace was a medium-sized window with red curtains. Two wooden chairs with pale beige cushioning sat opposite from each other at the ends of the fireplace. A large rustic coffee table centered the room above a dark brown carpet. On the other wall was another huge buck sporting a massive set of antlers any hunter would be proud of. This buck was only slightly smaller than the one above the fireplace.

"Do you like them?" Ty questioned, following my gaze.

"They're huge. Are they of your own hunts?"

"Yes. Two of the best I've taken down. They didn't come down easy, either. Nearly lost a tooth biting that one." Ty pointed to the larger buck.

I continued to look around. Behind the living room was a large kitchen. I was surprised to see it had a refrigerator, a dishwasher, and more unusual, I surmised, for the community – a stove. "You have a stove?" I asked.

"I renovated the kitchen hoping you'd one day be here with me. I know you'll need to cook for yourself." Ty's smile beamed brighter than the sun.

"When did you do this?" I was almost speechless. It had pale green cabinets, white marble countertops, white subway tile backsplash, a stainless-steel sink, and adorable country accents of red, including a small decorative bucket of faux red apples on the counter. A beautiful free-standing white island sat in the center while a wine-rack built into the cabinets reached out above the refrigerator-freezer combo.

"Over the winter. I was bored when you were working. My work was slow."

"It's beautiful." The design looked plucked from a kitchen décor magazine.

"I'm glad you like it. Come this way." Ty gestured to the dining room.

The space had a lovely white rustic worn table that looked antique. The walls were pale green, accented by two white frames waiting for photos – one on each side of the wall. Leaving the room,

Ty led me to the left into a hallway that led to an office. Inside the room, I walked around Ty's antique wooden desk decorated with an old eagle statue. A small stack of papers rested in the center.

Across from the office, Ty showed me a beautiful half bath, its walls a royal blue to complement the white fixtures.

"Come this way." Ty excitedly pulled me toward the sunroom at the far left of the house, which I hadn't seen from outside. The room was empty but had incredible potential.

"I'm blown away by this house, Ty. It's so beautiful."

"Come upstairs."

"Oh, my goodness, there's more?" I joked, overwhelmed by everything.

I walked with him to the stairs we had passed when going to the office, which were situated between the dining room and half bath. The wooden stairs spiraled ten steps up. At the top, a hall lined with windows stretched both left and right, showing off the forest behind the house. Ty guided me to the left. The space opened into the master bedroom. The room was incredible, encompassing the entire depth of the home. From the front window you could see out to the other cabins. The window was framed with two gray fabric curtains. Ty's bed rested against the outside wall and had a beautiful gray comforter set. Behind the bed was a stunning wall-to-ceiling life-like painting of ten thin pine trees mostly clustered above the headboard. The rest of the wall was open and painted a gray-ish-yellow color. In the corner of the room near the front window were modern light fixtures that hung down each on their own separate black cord. Their clear glass and rounded shape made them resemble bubbles. More of them were on the other side above the second nightstand, both of which were large steel octagons. Under the bed was a gray carpet heavily speckled with black. The ceiling was high above – a beautiful dark wood rich with color and pattern.

Ty gave me a moment to observe before leading me to the master bath and closet. The bath was windowless against the front of the house. It was large and mostly white with a huge open rain shower dotted with gorgeous royal blue tiles.

Next, Ty showed me the master closet, which was next to the master bath. He opened the double doors to expose the walk-in that rivaled the bathroom's size. Most of the left half was filled with Ty's clothing. The other half was completely empty.

"Let's go to the other bedrooms and bath," Ty said. He took my hand and led me out of the master.

Down the hall, Ty brought me to the less impressive bedrooms. There were four of them and one full bathroom they'd share. No doubt, Ty planned to house his children here.

I felt lightheaded.

"Liz, are you okay?" Ty's face grew concerned as he saw me wobble. He held onto my arm, helping me support myself.

"I just feel a little dizzy. I think I need to sit down and maybe eat something." My stomach growled.

"I will get your bags. You'll be okay alone for a bit?" Ty guided me to sit down on a bed in one of the spare rooms.

"Yes, thank you."

"Hold on right here for me." He left the room. I heard his speeded steps down the stairs and then the front door close behind him.

Ty's home was nothing like I imagined. I always thought cozy, small, stuffy, animal skins everywhere. That's also how he had made it seem. This house was something out of a magazine. Where did he find the money to afford all of this, even with having hand built and installed it all? Admittedly, I always pictured Ty as being somewhat poor, which had never bothered me.

My thoughts shifted to Ty's spare bedrooms and the twin wolf girls. Looking at these rooms, I realized they were perfect for children to grow into. Surely Ty wanted a family. Why not with Angeni? Why me? I thought about not belonging here. Would our children be wolf children? Would Ty be disappointed if they weren't? Would they be excluded if they were not wolf? I do want children with Ty, but it all feels so real after seeing this, and we've never talked about it.

This house and community felt like a fairy tale, heaven in the wilderness – in the heart of the forest I had forgiven and longed to love, yet who never seemed to love me back.

I got up and stepped into the hallway. Looking out the windows, I watched the huge trees sway slowly in the light breeze. They surrounded the home – a mystically perfect blend of evergreens, oak, and maples. Each one was carefully trimmed so that its branches were only in the canopy, and I suspected they had stood in place for centuries. Wandering down to Ty's room, I walked around the master, exploring his space. Tyler could have made a fortune as an interior designer.

On his steel octagon nightstand, a carved frame held a cherished picture. My eyes fluttered at the photo of us together that I gave him at Christmas. Seeing where it ended up swelled my heart.

Looking at this bedroom, at this house and community, it was no wonder Ty wanted to come home to it at night. I had been here only a short while, yet I was in love. I remembered Ty telling me about how he wanted to leave. I doubted he still felt this way, with the main cause of his stress no longer around.

I heard Ty enter the house and climb the stairs. He must have gone to the spare room I had rested in. I heard him call for me.

"I'm in your bedroom!" I responded. Saying that out loud felt strange.

Moments later he entered, holding both of my packs.

"Got the one from my mother. She removed your weapons though, sorry."

From the bag I removed some of the granola bars I packed, which reminded me of Bennie. My heart still ached for him. I missed all my pets.

Ty patiently watched me eat, his beautiful blue eyes fixed on me. There was something in them I hadn't seen so strongly before. It looked like hope.

"Well. What do you think? What's on your mind?"

I swallowed a bite. "It's all very overwhelming."

"If you like it, we can stay here - together. But it won't be without challenges -" Ty trailed off.

"Would *you* like that?" I asked.

"I do love it here, for the most part. Staying here together ... it would require a fight and a lot of changes."

"What do you mean?" I questioned.

Ty raised his hand to rub the back of his neck. "We'll talk about it later. It's a lot to discuss and it's been a long day."

"You could say that again. Long week. I'm drained."

"Do you want to go home? You can stay here for the night," Ty encouraged.

"I don't know if staying is a good idea, Ty. Your family is already on edge with me being here. They probably wouldn't appreciate me spending the night in your bed only feet from their own homes."

Ty lightly shrugged and nodded. "You're probably right, but at least I'd be spending more time here with you around."

"There is one thing I've been hoping to see. I didn't want to ask you at my place, but out here ..."

"What is it?"

I briefly considered retracting my request, but I was too curious. "I'd love to see you shift. I'd love to see you standing in front of me in your alternative form."

Ty chuckled. "Is that all? I don't see why not. It's been a while since I stretched. We'd have to go outside. My nails scratch the wood floors. Are you sure you won't be afraid?"

"I won't be." I smiled. A new wave of excitement and nervousness flooded me.

"Are you sure you're feeling better?"

"Yes, come on!" I said, getting up and grabbing his arm to pull him out of the room.

"Okay, wait, wait. I need to change into special stretchy shorts. I just got these sweatpants and I'd hate to tear them up. I'll be right down. You go ahead out the back door. It's off the dining room."

I bounced out of the room and down the stairs before he could change his mind. The back door was unlocked. I looked out the glass into the wilderness and second-guessed my answer. Maybe I *would* be afraid. Opening the door, I walked out into the breeze. The wind had picked up since I had gone inside. It made the trees dance in a familiar magical-rocking motion. I watched the pine needles and leaves whip around, never tiring of the sound they made.

Minutes later, Ty arrived at the door. He wore only a pair of blue shorts that reached down to above his knee.

"I'm concerned. I don't want to scare you."

"If I'm to be in your life, I need to be open to all of you. Besides ... I've seen you before."

"I know. It's just ... the process is somewhat creepy. Seeing the kids change is so seamless, it's no big deal. But watching an adult ..."

"How long does it take you?" I questioned.

"About three minutes. Promise me, you won't freak out?"

"I'll try not to."

"That's very reassuring," he said sarcastically.

"Just start, Ty. You know I love you."

He sighed. "Well, when you put it like that."

Ty walked ten feet away and then turned to face me. Before he could start, Ty's father came rushing around the house.

"Son!" he shouted. "What do you think you're doing exactly?"

"Father. I was going to shift."

He walked to stand in front of Ty with his back to me. "No. She's not one of us. She doesn't belong here. Take her home, now."

"I will not."

"Don't make me assert," his father challenged.

Ty growled deep in his throat. "Fine, I won't shift. Come on, Liz. Let's go back inside." Ty walked around his dad and took my hand. I looked back to see the man narrowing his eyes into Ty's back. Ty closed the door and locked it. "So much for that. I probably shouldn't anyway. There may be some infection still in my system."

"I shouldn't have asked."

"It's not your fault."

"Yes ... it is. He's right, you know. I don't belong here." Ty's eyes turned from anger to sadness. He took me and hugged me. I naturally wrapped my arms around him. He was so warm.

"Please don't say that," Ty begged.

I rested my cheek against his chest and sighed. "You know it's true."

"It is for now."

I pulled away and walked slowly into the kitchen before turning to face him. "Ty, I'm scared for us. Your family is a big part of your life. What you have is amazing. I cannot give you what you want."

"What I want is you."

"Is that enough?" I looked at the bucket of faux red apples and noticed one seemed to be missing.

"Why wouldn't you be enough?" he asked.

"I can't give you wolf children. I can't ever truly belong. I'll never be able to shift like you," I snapped, now looking at him again.

"You could if you decided."

"What?"

Ty walked over to me and took my hand, placing it above his heart. "If you wanted to be like me, you could. And with wolf blood in your veins, our children would be born shifters."

My jaw dropped. "Wait. What?"

"My blood can turn you. It is something I've thought about, but it's risky. Humans don't always become shifters without complications. We don't need to risk that. You're perfect as you are."

My breath was short. "Why haven't you told me this before?" I let my hand slip from his chest while taking a step back.

"I didn't want you to feel pressured."

"Your family and our differences already put pressure on me," I confessed. Ty frowned, struggling to find words. "And you need to tell me what else you're hiding. I *need* to know. Now."

"Fine. Let me gather my words," he replied, looking down to the floor. "My father is the patriarch of our clan and my grandfather was patriarch before him. Patriarchs are usually called the chief. My grandmother, Mama Rain, was the previous matriarch before my mother took over. The leadership position is inherited in each clan, so the first-born child of the clan leaders becomes the new patriarch or matriarch when their parents decide to step down. Angeni is still pushing my parents about the arranged marriage for two reasons. First, she has feelings for me that I do not reciprocate. But second, she also wants authority. Because she has an older brother, she'll never be matriarch in her family, the Shadow clan. For years she has looked forward to improving her status by becoming the next matriarch of the Varg clan."

I thought about Angeni's wicked smile earlier today. "So as your wife, she would become matriarch when your parents step down someday?"

"Yes. Marrying me means being the matriarch – the female leader – at some time in the future."

"What is so great about being a clan leader?"

"They make the decisions, are most esteemed, and their children are most valued. My first-born would become the new clan leader one day."

"Children ... Angeni will give you better children. It makes her the superior choice for that reason alone." I had never felt inferior to Angeni until now, but a wave of jealousy flooded over me. Ty rolled his eyes, but I was serious. "Anything else you left out?"

"I don't think so. Oh wait, we go a little rabid on blood moons, but it's not that bad."

My eyes narrowed while I declined to think about what that meant. "I should be going soon. This is a lot to process."

"I understand," he said.

After gathering my bags and saying goodbye to Ty, I headed out, having told Ty to let me walk alone. The long trip to the car through the trees and cabins gave me one more moment alone to take in the magical and impossible world I had been tossed into. A large red wolf halfway down my path lay on a porch like a pet dog. He opened his eyes when I stepped past. I smiled at him and he wagged his tail; no doubt it was Messer.

Reaching my car, I saw the passenger door was still open. I closed it and opened the second door to toss my bags in. When I closed the door and walked around to the driver's side, something out of place on a nearby tree grabbed my attention – a white object with thin red rims. There were two of them side by side with a knife stabbed in each one. My knives.

I walked up to the strange scene on the tree and pulled out one of the knives. Still impaled on the blade was half of a faux red apple.

CHAPTER TWENTY-SEVEN

MESSAGE OR WARNING

That night, I lay on my couch curled up in a blanket with a pint of ice cream and watched a few new werewolf movies, completely amused by their interpretations.

I replayed the day again and again, trying to process what shouldn't be possible. It should have been fiction, a strange movie similar to what was portrayed on my screen – yet here we were. I was swept off my feet by someone with a ton of baggage I was only now fully aware of. I should be angry at Ty for never disclosing the extent of his lifestyle and therefore keeping secrets from me. His hard-to-swallow magical world unfolded in my eyes over and over. Maybe his delay was intended to keep me from being scared early on. It was all very unsettling.

The cabins in the woods were beautiful beyond comparison. Something my thoughts kept returning to, which disturbed me more with each replay of the day, was the faux red apple stabbed into the tree with my own blades. It was obviously a message, but what was it meant to imply? The fake apple may have been symbolic, implying my relationship with Ty wasn't genuine. Or maybe each half represented us, and my knives stabbing them could have represented how my love would cause our downfall. That would mean the stabbed fake apple was a warning. Perhaps the apple was only me, ripped apart. Was it a threat of vengeance or just an expression of jealousy?

Who put it there? Surely it was Ashton. He was probably threatening me to keep out. Or maybe it was Angeni since she wanted Ty for herself. Maybe it was one of Tyler's parents. Really, it could have been anyone. My final realization was most disturbing. Someone took the apple while we were upstairs. The invasion of Ty's space showed me the person's lack of respect for his home.

I considered telling Ty about the apple, but I feared no good would come of it. Ty could snap against the clan members. Telling him could cause a fight. I decided it was best not to tell him. Shifting my thoughts, I considered being a part of his world. Changing form into an animal had never been something I dreamed of, but I didn't think it would bother me. What would be the cost? There was always a price.

Ty wanted children. It was obvious. We hadn't discussed it, but we really needed to. He claimed he didn't need me to become like him, but he knew that our children wouldn't be wolf shifters unless I accepted his blood first. I also realized that as just a human I would never be accepted. I'd always be an outcast and never Ty's true companion. If I took the blood, would they accept me as one of their own? It was still doubtful, especially with what I'd done, but at least as an Amarok, I'd be able to defend myself and my place beside him. Such tension felt toxic to be around and I'd only had a small taste.

Part of me wondered about an alternative path – a path without Tyler and his world. It seemed much simpler, normal, boring. His world was exciting, exhilarating – a challenge. My feelings were conflicted.

Ty had called earlier, but I told him I needed time to process. He was obviously worried about my thoughts. In a way, his worry was justified as it was the first time that I had seriously considered everything – the good with the bad. Moving into a fantasy world would be a permanent decision. I wondered what Briana and my mother would think. Would I still be able to have them in my life? They'd both wonder why I sold my house, and of course they'd want to see my new home. There would be secrets I'd need to keep from them, and that bothered me.

I allowed myself four long days of rest, recovery, and heavy thinking. No work, no boyfriend, no mom, no friends. Just me alone in the world. This process freaked Tyler out. He showed up at my door a few times, concerned. It was difficult to dismiss him. He protested, pouted, crossed his arms, but ultimately respected my space – for the most part. I saw him watching me in my backyard last night, his black fur leaving him almost invisible. I wanted to go to him, to sit with him. But I knew I needed to separate myself from his world. He was being as patient and understanding as he could manage. I also felt he was being protective considering everything we'd been through so recently. Seeing him pacing in the yard, fully animal – I felt a youthful excitement toward him. A primal creature, yet really a compassionate being. What about me drew him in? How did I manage to capture such a being? His heart belonged to me. He made it as clear as possible, yet I still questioned it.

As I watched him from my kitchen window, I considered what would happen if we were to go through with everything and then not work out as a couple. I remembered his claim of mating for life. How true was this? Was this true even with the loss of all love? Or maybe it meant we would always be bonded.

On the fifth morning, I submitted my formal resignation. I would no longer be working at the hospital. I couldn't go back after what I had gone through. When Briana found out I had quit, she was devastated. The phone call started with confusion, then horror, then anger.

"How dare you leave your best friend!" she boomed. "This place will suck without you! Why did you quit, what happened? Does this involve Tyler?"

After a lot of pressure, I finally caved about what Jason did to me. I told her that I needed to get away. She became incredibly sympathetic, understanding, and even apologized for her reaction.

"Stay away from him, Briana. He's dangerous."

She promised she'd kick his ass for me, but my shocked panic of the visual reined her in. I was physically far stronger than Briana, yet Jason had overpowered me – even if just for the moment. She must stay far from him. I asked Briana to spread rumors of Jason's true nature. Rumors were going to spread regardless. At least coming from Briana, they'd be mostly truthful. She agreed to the request.

At noon, Ty called me. "Hey Liz, I was hoping I could see you today. Can I come by?"

I thought momentarily. "No. No you can't."

Ty started to protest. "It's been five days, please?"

"No. But I want to come to you again."

"Oh, okay, yeah sure." I could hear his smile.

"I'll be there in an hour if that's alright?" I questioned.

"Sure, but I must warn you. We have a full community right now. See you soon."

He hung up before I could question him. The rest of the Hati clan must have arrived.

I decided to prep for a stay, unsure of how long I'd be there. Without my job, there was little reason to return home, providing his family didn't protest. When I was about to leave, I heard a knock on the front door. I opened it to find Chief Rogers standing on my porch.

"So sorry to bother ya, Elizabeth. I need ta check on this residence. A silly claim by a local made ... uh ... well. They say ya have a wild animal being kept on the premises. I ignored the call until some other locals started to call in wolf sightings."

I was momentarily stunned. This must have been Jason's doing. "What? That's hilarious!" I said before fake giggling. "There are no wild animals here. Would you like to come inside?"

"Oh sure, ma'am. Thank ya so much. I felt it wuz a ridiculous call, but with nothing much eva happening, figured I might as well investigate and say hello while I wuz at it," he explained while walking inside.

"I totally understand," I said while leading him to the kitchen; "allow me to put on some coffee. Surely you could use some."

"That'd be rill nice."

I watched him out of the corner of my eye. He was observing the living room and then looked at my new back door. I became overwhelmingly concerned he knew more than he was letting on. "So, how are things in 'downtown' Jacksonville? Not much happens around here," I said.

He turned his attention back to me. "Nah, aside from the usual small things – it's quiet. Teenagers been givin' me some trouble with the spray cans. That was most of my work yesterday."

"It's a wonder where they find these cans to buy. Smithy's Hardware keeps everything under lock against the kids."

"I found it's their parents buying the stuff and their kids stealing it. I swear, nuttin' but cotton in some of their heads."

I giggled through my nerves, hoping Mr. Rogers didn't notice my tense body language. "Sounds about right for some of them." I poured the coffee into two cups. Remembering how Mr. Rogers liked it from when he dealt with my father's death, I added a tablespoon of sugar and some coffee creamer from the refrigerator.

"Thank ya, darlin'," he said, taking the cup and sipping the hot liquid between his white mustache and beard. "As much as things can quiet down in this town, it's still better than bein' retired. You rememba how my knee is goin' bad? I don't think I can handle this job much longa. Be a sad day to leave the police force, though."

"I'd be sad to see you retire, but you'll be staying here, right?"

"Oh yeah. I'm here fer life ... and death. Not goin' anywhere."

"Good. Glad to hear that. The town wouldn't be the same without you."

He smiled through his beard before his lips firmed into a line with a new thought on his mind. "So uh. I didn't want ta bring it up since there's no proof it was you. Someone stole drugs from the hospital in Medford recently. I was tipped it mighta been you."

"Is that so?" My heart dipped.

"I'm sure ya'd never do that. But I thought I'd bring it up. More likely those teenagers." I nodded, not wanting to lie. "I swear they be the death of themselves," he continued.

"I hope not. It would be a real tragedy," I added.

"Certainly would. Well, I better be goin'. Thank ya for the coffee. It was nice chattin' with ya real quick."

"You're welcome and likewise."

After seeing him out, I texted Ty I was now on my way, but it didn't say the message was delivered. As I got in my car, I thought about Jason's jealousy and how far he would go to hurt me simply for rejecting him.

As I drove closer to the mystical woods, I grew uneasy. There would be more people and more chances of confrontation. I was once again entering their home yet uninvited by nearly everyone there. I was the outsider who presented a real danger to their people. Plus, I continually interfered with their family affairs.

As I approached the wooded entrance to the community, Ty was sitting on a moss-covered rock, wearing no shirt or shoes, merely some black shorts. It was only then that I really felt how much I missed him. As I pulled up to Ty, he approached my car window.

"Hi Liz." He kissed me momentarily. I barely returned it.

"Uh ... where should I park my car?"

"Bring it down the trail. We don't need it being spotted. It would draw attention."

Ty walked alongside the car as I slowly moved down the narrow trail. Ty had to keep avoiding the trees that almost kissed my car. As I approached the cabins, I could hear unique music playing, but it stopped before I reached the source.

When I pulled my car over to the right, Ty placed his hands on my opened window's door frame. "You ready?" he asked.

My hands started to shake. I was more nervous than the first time I had been there. "Tell me everything will go well. Lie to me."

"Everything will be fine ... and that's not a lie. You'll see. The community is holding a reunion party. I won't let you crash it," he teased.

"You're not helping." I stared at his beautiful bare chest to distract myself. He gave me the moment.

"Hey Lizzy!" a familiar voice called. Ty pulled away from the car as Messer approached. "Glad to see you're back, and just in time for the start of the reunion. The clans join this time of year and we party to celebrate. I can't wait to show you around!" Messer boomed as he peeked into the car.

His friendly welcome was more comforting than Ty's. I smiled at him. "Glad to see you, too. You both got my back?"

"Of course," Ty said. Messer nodded in agreement.

I opened the car door and followed them to the center of the cabin oval. There, at least thirty people of various ages gathered around a large bonfire. It was clear I was interrupting. They all stared. Several of the members slid instruments down to their sides as they watched me approach.

Ty placed his hands on my shoulders and stood tall behind me. "Everyone, this is Elizabeth – my partner. Please make her feel welcome." Before anyone could react, Ty gestured for me to sit on a large log offset to the fire. He then sat behind me, blissfully ignoring the gawking.

Ty's father was the first to speak. "Yes, Elizabeth is a human Ty brought home recently. That's a long story but let's get back to the festivities. Cupun, Panuk, Tarkik – please continue your playing." I watched the group whisper among themselves as the three older men Ty's father addressed started playing their string instruments again. The three of them were talented musicians.

Overwhelmed, I didn't notice Ty's hand placement until his fingers trailed over the gaps between mine. I could feel Ty's eyes on me as I observed the now much larger group. There were those I'd already seen – Ty's parents, his sisters, Messer, Uki, the twin girls, Ashton, and Angeni. A few unfamiliar wolves lay between the log benches that circled the fire. Their red coats were close to Messer's color, but with a black undercoat. Between them, three women gossiped on the log directly across from me and Ty. One was Uki, but the other two were new to me. The oldest woman was farthest to the right; both appeared to be Uki's sisters.

Messer joined my side, prompting the oldest of the female trio to scowl at him. No doubt she was Messer's mother.

Uki's nude twins soon walked over to greet us. This time, they were dirty and visibly tired. "Hi Callie and Emma ... you both look tired," Ty said, seeing Emma rub her eyes.

"Hi Tylerrr," they said together in sync.

Too wrapped up in all the new faces, I didn't listen to Ty converse with them. On another log to the right there were multiple couples, including a pregnant woman and her hovering partner. She looked close to due date unless she was expecting twins. She had black hair and ivory skin. Her mate was equally beautiful, with tight curls and dark skin highlighted by his large brown eyes and beaming smile – a proud father-to-be. His hovering was something I often saw in new fathers. Next to the pregnant woman sat a slightly younger couple, likely in their early twenties. She had brown hair and a light blanket of freckles. Her partner was a brown-eyed young man with black hair and olive skin.

I then noticed a black pup rush up to Uki's sister. My jaw dropped and quickly pulled back up as I watched her expose her breast and start nursing the pup cradled on his back.

"Easy, watch those teeth!" She tapped the pup's nose. "This

wouldn't be so painful for me if you turned human for nursing," she complained. I could barely hear her through the music.

"Who are they?" I asked Ty while trying not to stare.

"Most of them are part of Messer's clan. The pup is three-year-old Yutu. Little monster baby, that one. He doesn't have anyone to play with, so when he rejoined the twin girls today, he had a blast with them. His parents are Lily and Amon. Blaze, Uki's partner, is there on the ground. And the other wolf lying there is Amon.

Lily must have seen me glance at Yutu. "What's a matter, neva seen a woman nursing a wolf pup before?" she taunted.

I just lightly shook my head side to side. I couldn't tell if her smile was friendly or sinister. Maybe both.

The younger red wolf Ty identified as Amon stood up and did a cat stretch before yawning. I was overwhelmed with the size of his off-white teeth. He snorted at Lily and the pup.

"Ew, Amon. Go away, ya nasty beast," Lily complained. All of us chuckled. It made me feel more at ease. I looked at Ty. He was so happy and at home here.

Amon walked over to Blaze and took a mouth full of his scruff. Blaze went from a mellow lap dog to a snarling beast in a half second. The sound of his snarls, his pulled-back teeth, and his wide eyes made me quiver. "Looks like they are ready to battle. Messer, get the caps," Lily commanded.

Amon released Blaze's scruff, allowing him to stand. He shook off the assault and snapped his teeth at Amon.

"Blaze wins every year. I don't know why they bother," Lily continued.

Messer hurried off into a cabin and returned with a small box, handing it to Lily. She opened it and gave four of the contents to Uki. Uki got up and stood in front of Blaze. He opened his mouth and she placed four dark blue caps on each of his four fangs. I could see Lily do the same to Amon.

"They are going to fight?" I asked Ty.

"Yes, battle. It's a new gathering and holiday thing. Just for fun. The winner and the partner only get bragging rights," Ty explained.

"Should I leave?"

"Only if you want to. I understand if you're not comfortable with seeing this. We can go to my cabin."

I wasn't sure if I wanted to see it. I thought about Ty's future and how seeing this now could prepare me. It was also part of their culture, and to be in his world, it'd have to be a part of mine, too. "I will watch. Just ... stay close to me."

I wasn't sure what to expect. Teeth snapping, fur flying, jaws snapping – surely. But this seemed like a lot of effort and discomfort just for bragging rights.

Ty stood up and reached his hand out to me. I placed my hand in his and he led me to where everyone began gathering. Four trees made a perfect square. The two wolves moved inside it while everyone else stayed along the perimeter. Messer and the pregnant woman's husband each brought out a small stand and placed it on opposite sides of the arena.

"Who determines the winner?" I questioned.

"They do. In order to win, one must pin the other down for nine seconds. Their mate acts as their coach and referee," Ty explained.

"Kick his ass, Blaze!" Messer called out.

Their hackles were raised on their backs. Amon snorted and licked his lips. The wives each stepped up on the opposing stands behind their mates. It all looked incredibly serious for something done for fun.

"Y'all know the rules. Don't forget like last year. No cheap bites in da groin, no cap removal, and avoid the eyes," Uki warned.

One of the instrument players handed both women a white flag. They soon raised them as high as they could in the air. The surrounding crowd cheered and whistled in excitement. The women counted down from three. When they reached one, they dropped their flags and Amon lunged for Blaze's neck.

Blaze snarled over the sound of the crowd.

"Get him, bite him!" Messer cheered.

Blaze showed his experience as he stepped his paw between Amon's front legs. His head quickly followed, and Amon went flying over Blaze's back as he tossed his head up. I hadn't noticed before, but Blaze was larger.

"Come on, Amon! You fell for that again!" Lily scolded.

Amon quickly jumped around to reface Blaze, but before Amon could block, Blaze grabbed him by the scruff. Using his front legs and weight, he wrapped himself onto Amon, and the younger wolf struggled downward to the ground. Amon yelped and struggled to unpin himself from Blaze's weight. The women simultaneously counted down. Before they could reach five, Amon had turned his hind legs under Blaze's weight and kicked upward, sending Blaze off his pin.

I then noticed Ty cheering next to me. "Yeah, Amon! Nice work! Don't let him get the pin!" Ty bellowed.

I smiled at the crowd's excitement, now understanding the reason they battled. It was no different than a karate or boxing match.

The wolves circled each other, their hackles standing. Blaze raised his lips, showing the thick blue caps. Amon was the first to lunge. He jumped into Blaze's side, biting into his shoulder. Blaze retaliated by grabbing the underside of Amon's belly. Amon instantly let go and released a piercing yelp. I covered my ears in reaction to the sound.

"Heck, Blaze! Don't go for the belly. That's a cheap shot," Lily objected.

Blaze snorted toward her. With Blaze's attention turned, Amon bit the side of Blaze's face. Blaze jumped back on his hind legs. Both wolves stood on their hind legs with their front legs wrapped as Blaze bared his teeth in a vicious growl. Amon didn't let go. He tried using his weight to overpower Blaze, but Blaze stood stronger and heavier – he pushed his strength down onto Amon's frame, making him buckle and tumble backwards to the ground. Blaze snatched onto Amon's throat with a powerful pin. Amon struggled to kick Blaze off again, but Blaze had shifted himself to the side. The women counted up to nine; the crowd aahed and cheered. Blaze was off Amon and as the defeated wolf, Amon bowed to the victor.

"Nice job, Amon! Maybe next year, buddy!" Ty called out.

Amon walked over to Ty with his head lowered. I was overwhelmed seeing him standing next to me so casually. Ty whispered something in Amon's ear. Within a minute, Amon tossed his head back and howled a breathtaking song. Blaze joined in, as did the wolf children. My eyes watered at their incredible, surreal raw beauty.

I watched the women remove the caps from their husband's teeth. I chuckled when Blaze licked Uki's face – her punch to his shoulder an expected reaction.

"How about you take me on next, Blaze?" Ty shouted at the couple.

"Oh, please, Tyler. Blaze wouldn't stand a chance," Uki said dryly.

Ty chuckled before turning to me. "Black wolves and white wolves are naturally the strongest," he whispered in my ear.

"You can fight me, Tyler. I'd kick your ass," Angeni challenged as she approached us. "I'd kick her ass too, back to where she belongs," she said, pointing at me.

I felt Ty's mood shift. "Piss off," he hissed at her. He took my hand and led me toward his house. I felt her eyes on my back as my heart raced.

"You KNOW she doesn't belong here!" Angeni screamed. Everyone went silent. "She's not one of us. She will never be one of us!"

I looked back to see her arms crossed, her face red with as much anger as Tyler. When Ty didn't react to her statement, she threw her arms up and rushed off. I watched her boots stride in a fit of stomps, a distinct purple A on each heel.

CHAPTER TWENTY-EIGHT

DECISIONS

Ty pulled me inside his cabin and slammed the door shut, locking it. With his hands and forehead pressed to the wood, he breathed heavily to collect his composure. The minute dragged until he turned to me. "I'm sorry about her," he said.

I rubbed my forearms, comforting myself. "You know it's not just her. She was bold enough to blurt what everyone feels. She's right; we are from two very different worlds."

Ty's blue eyes watered. He held his head low to me with his shoulders sagged – his spirit wounded. "There's something about you that feels more right than anything I've ever felt before." He stepped closer to me with his arms gently open. "Don't you feel it, too?"

I soaked in his words. He was right. Despite our differences, despite his family's rejection – we were a perfect pair with a magnetic pull I had never experienced before or since meeting him. It was there not long after I found him. Initially, it had scared me.

Even if Ty's family and friends made this difficult, even if I should become an animal – I don't think I could pull myself from Ty's magnet any longer than I had.

"Did all of that scare you?" Ty pointed his thumb back toward the community center.

"No. I thought it was incredible. I was consumed by it like everyone else. Your family and friends are beautiful, magical ... I can't imagine a world without you. And despite my fears, despite Angeni's words – I'm in love with you *and* your world. I know it will be a great challenge, but I've always been strong. If these past five days alone taught me anything, it's that the longer I'm without you, the weaker I feel. The nightmares return; the longing for you was frustratingly strong. Being by your side feels right even though everyone around us says it shouldn't."

Ty pulled me into his chest. I wrapped my arms around him, hugging him firmly. He nuzzled his face down into my hair. "You have no idea how relieved I am to hear this," he said, sighing heavily. When he released his hug, I reached up to him and kissed his bottom lip. He was borderline irresistible. I trailed my hand down his bare chest and over his abs. Goosebumps formed under my touch. With him seeming so certain of us, I wondered if he'd allow me to bed him.

Before I could attempt to seduce him, he placed both of his hands on the sides of my face and kissed me softly on my forehead. "I'm going to get your bags from the car," he said smiling while pulling away. I felt myself pouting while he exited. Surely, he did that on purpose. His chuckle as he descended the porch steps confirmed my suspicion. What a massive tease!

"I'll get ya in bed eventually," I whispered to myself, smiling at the thought as I watched him walk away.

"I'm counting on it!" he called from ten feet away.

Of course he heard that. I watched from the open door as the festivities continued. The community bustled with life and happiness. Angeni was the only one scowling at my presence – or so I thought. Ty's parents were sitting on the steps of the cabin two homes down. I could sense their tension. As Ty passed by them, they stared him down and began to say something I couldn't pick up. Ty's reaction was to toss his arm up at them, barely glancing in their direction.

I closed the door, feeling the tension creeping in. Ty's home was exactly how we had left it. The living room had no TV; there were no electronics. Their entertainment came from each other – the community. I momentarily wondered where the home's electricity was coming from.

I walked to the kitchen. Caressing my hand along the marble counter, I again admired Ty's taste and work. The faux red apples still in their decorative container, minus the one. I briefly wondered if Ty had noticed yet.

It dawned on me that Ashton was absent. Or was he? I had never seen him in human form before. He could have walked right past me and I would have been oblivious. The thought made me squirm.

"Liz?" Ty called after opening the front door.

"Kitchen." I heard him place my bag down while I walked out of the kitchen.

"There you are."

"Slow wolf, that took you forever," I teased with a side smile.

He huffed. "Slow. You'd like slow eventually," he playfully taunted.

My mouth dropped slightly when his words clicked. My brows narrowed. "You wouldn't know what I like. At this rate, it seems you never will." Ty walked over to me and grabbed my hands, pulling me harshly into his groin. I gasped before continuing. "You're just one giant tease," I playfully hissed.

"*Giant* seems fitting," he commented.

I raised an eyebrow, my smirk involuntary. "Oh really? This girl couldn't truly know." I ran my hand down his bare chest. Of course I knew. I had felt him through his clothing before.

"I look forward to showing you." His bulge grew through his shorts.

I pulled on the rim of his shorts. My desire was painful. Bolts of excitement shot down my spine and into my groin. "How about right *now*," I challenged.

I started to reach down his shorts only to be stopped by his hand. He lowered his mouth to my ear. "Not yet," he responded with a coy expression.

"Are you sure you're not broken? I'm beginning to wonder." I knew it wasn't fair to pressure him, but moments like that were starting to really get to me.

Ty laughed. "It's not the right time. Family and friends outside and all. Come on, we are having dinner soon. The children get told our story. I feel you should hear it, too."

"Sounds nice. You sure I can sit in?"

"Of course. Just let me get a T-shirt." He winked and then rushed upstairs.

When he returned, he had added a black T-shirt and black sneakers to his outfit.

Back at the log circle, the large calm fire licked toward the darkening sky. Ty sat us down on the log with Alianna and, as Ty had mentioned, Leanna -Alianna's twin. This time, I was ignored by the masses while they all chatted about the food. Lots of meat was passed around as everyone started feasting on their dinners. Whole deer and fish mostly. Some cooked, some raw. Ty got up to grab what he could.

"Do you think he'll marry her?" I heard Alianna whisper to her sister.

Ty returned with some roasted corn and meat. He handed me a bit of both.

"Corn? Where did you -?"

"Some of us eat veggies and fruit, but it's mainly a festivity thing."

I looked around and spotted the basket of corn next to the fish.

As everyone finished eating, Ty's father, whom Ty told me to call Chief, spoke to the crowd. "Our blood goes back countless generations, many years of careful pairing." Everyone quieted to listen. "The survival of our species depends on our ability to carefully coordinate each new generation. The couple feels the pairing in their blood, confirming their compatibility. I firmly believe that preventing human mutts from breeding in is important to keep our traits and lineage pure – superior."

I looked at Ty. His expression was serious, his fists balled.

"I'm proud of the newest pregnancy produced by the Varg clan. We greatly look forward to meeting the latest wolf pup, or better yet *pups*, to join our united tribes." Ty's father raised his glass to the couple. "I wish you many joyous years ahead." Everyone clapped and cheered except for Ty. I could see Angeni's sneer through the flames. "I also look forward to the completed union of Messer and my daughter Alianna, so that the Varg and the Hati clans shall be officially united by their bond." Everyone clapped again while some whistled at the young pair.

The wolf pups had shed their fur, standing into adorable children. Callie and Emma sat on Uki and Blaze's laps. Yutu rushed to Lily. She picked up the reaching naked three-year-old and kissed his neck. He was also beautiful, with curling dark brown hair, dark amber eyes, and dimples.

"There are two stories passed down to each generation. These two stories are both entwined in our blood, a sacred tie to the earth and our very existence. Tonight, I will share the story of the blue wolf goddess, Amaguq," Chief continued, "An estimated two thousand years ago, a mysterious dark gray wolf with a steel cast now referred to as blue, stalked three Inuit clans – our original ancestors."

Chief explained how the beautiful and impossible animal, with a color never seen before, was hunted by the young chief of the southern clan. During the struggle, both the chief and the wolf goddess were wounded, exchanging blood. The goddess escaped, leaving her blood inside the chief. Soon, the chief succumbed to a terrible brief sickness - something the clan's healer had never seen before. Hunters tried to find the blue wolf again, but she was untraceable. After the clan expressed their goodbyes to the chief, his body began to change. The transition scared the healers as they distantly watched him transform into a black wolf, the first shifter of our history.

"Chief Lupo's blood is said to be shared among all the tribes along with the magic of the blue wolf goddess," Ty's father finished.

Everyone clapped at the story's ending.

"Beautifully told as always," Blaze said to Ty's father, "Eh, when will the rest of your clan get back from their store?"

"Tonight. Soon," he responded.

"About time, eh?" Lily complained.

Soon after, the sound of vehicles approached from the dirt road. Six jeeps pulled in near my car. I was a bit surprised by them, having been under the impression the Amarok didn't use vehicles.

"And not a moment too soon!" Blaze called out to them.

More community members began to exit the vehicles. An elder woman stepped out of the first jeep.

"She is my grandmother on my father's side. Everyone other than me, my sisters, and my cousins calls her Mama Rain," Ty said into my ear.

She wore a black shirt with white pants and had beautiful dark gray hair. Her face was tired, yet her stride youthful as she walked over. A large purple gem on a delicate silver chain rested around her neck.

Ty told me about the newcomers, explaining their relation. The second and third cars had Ty's aunts, sisters to Ty's father, and their husbands. The rest of the cars were Ty's cousins, including Ashton, as Ty disclosed to me. Ashton glared at us when he spotted my presence.

"Just ignore him," Ty said to me, feeling my tension.

Ashton wasn't how I pictured him. He was short, my height, and seemed younger than me. He had a narrow face, black hair, and brown eyes. His muscular build was overall smaller than Ty's. He wore a black and red plaid button-down shirt with jeans a size too large for him. His skin was a bit darker and his eyes a bit narrower. His human form made him far less intimidating.

"How did the sales at the shop go?" Amon asked Mama Rain.

"Very well," she responded with a smile.

"Grandmother, I'd like you to formally meet my girlfriend, Elizabeth," Ty said.

She investigated me, prompting my face to redden. "She's lovely, I'll give you that, Junior ... why a human?" she asked as if I wasn't part of the conversation.

"It's hard to explain how I feel. There's a pull I never experienced before. You wouldn't understand," Ty said. He wrapped his arm around me. My eyes stayed soft despite my discomfort. Everyone stayed quiet as they listened in.

"A pull. I experienced this only once and it was with a human I met before settling for your grandfather. He was the match chosen for me, but this human was magnetic. If he hadn't been mysteriously killed, I would have married him instead," his grandmother explained.

Ty looked surprised. The crowd whispered among themselves.

"Mother ... you never told me that," Chief stated, confused by his mother's story.

"It was never relevant. A pull happens for a reason ... even when it's with a human. Best leave this couple to do as their hearts and blood know." Her eyes narrowed at her son. She then glanced back to me. Taking my hand from my side, her dark blue eyes bore into me like acupuncture needles as she caressed my hand's veins. "If you're to stay, you must promise. Take good care of my Tyler, be loyal to the clan, and always have your clan-mates' backs. I know you killed Chogan, but I also know that boy was disloyal to his brother and had a harsh heart. I trust you had good reason and I forgive you for it."

I nodded, tears welling in my eyes, and gave her a light smile. "Thank you."

When she dropped my hand, I felt a weight lifted. She turned to the dead-quiet crowd around us. Waving her arms and flicking her fingers, she dismissed them. "Go on y'all. Get back to it."

Ty left my side to have a private talk with his grandmother. I watched him pull her gently to the side and whisper something before hugging her. Receiving her pardon and blessing drastically lifted my discomfort within the community, and Ty surely felt the same. It was clear she was the matriarch of this clan, even though she no longer officially held the title.

As darkness overtook the shadows, Tyler led me around the festivities. Clan members lit torches and the pups chased each other endlessly. I was feeling more comfortable with the family as they started to feel more at ease around me.

"You should braid your hair! Can I do it?"

"Do you have a house in town?"

"Why do you smell like roses?"

The questions I received from the younger clan members were amusing. My hair was braided by Leanna while I was quizzed on all sorts of subjects. Undoubtedly happy I was being accepted, Tyler affectionately watched me from the opposite log bench as I braided Emma's hair.

Blaze came in from down the line of cabins and saw the commotion around me. He crossed his arms with a big smile. "That's too sweet, eh, Tyler?"

Ty chuckled at the mess I was in. "They seem to like her," he replied to Blaze.

I side-smiled at them, feeling tired from the day. "That was a lot of fun. Let's do this again soon, okay girls? I'm going to get going," I said with a shy yawn as we finished braiding. Ty watched the teens and children say their goodnights before I joined his side. Blaze walked off with the girls to rejoin Uki.

"I know this has been a long day. Do you want to stay with me for the night or head home?" Ty questioned, placing his hand over mine and gently squeezing.

"I'm going to head home. I was planning to stay, but I'm still feeling somewhat uncomfortable," I said while pulling the braiding from my hair.

"Okay, but join me inside my cabin for a bit. I have something to show you."

Ty led me into his home and up the stairs. Once in his bedroom, he pulled back the curtains to reveal the amazing night view. Stars peeped through the tree branches; the torch and bonfire lights glowed against the surrounding darkness. I rested my hands on the window frame and soaked in the raw beauty. The place was unimaginably magical.

When I turned to face Tyler, he was beside me on one knee presenting a sapphire ring.

CHAPTER TWENTY-NINE

REVELATION

My visit to my mother was interesting.

"You're engaged! Oh my God! Let me see that ring! That is happening fast. Wow, are you sure about him? This ring is amazing. What kind of gem is this? Wait ... you're not pregnant, are you?" She blurted out every question I expected.

"No! I'm not pregnant, jeez, Mom."

"Sorry, hun. This was pretty quick. Oh, how exciting. I'm gonna help you plan the wedding. Oh! You can get married at that shabby-chic place up north, eh? That would be so nice."

"Err ... his family will be planning for us. They already have most things arranged."

"Really? How did they manage that so quickly? I'd love to meet his family. Where will it be? When?"

"Um ..." I twiddled with my ring. "In the woods in front of his house."

"In the woods? With the bears?"

"Ha. Not quite."

"If that's what *you* want. Can I at least buy you a dress?"

If I was honest, the whole thing wasn't what I had pictured. I imagined my wedding in a grand chapel where I'd walk down the aisle to meet him at the altar.

"Yeah, we can do that. It's expected to be in a few weeks, so we have to look soon."

"Oh my God. A few weeks! That's so soon! Why the rush?"

"His family, well, they are unique people. That's actually something I need to talk to you about."

Back at home from my mother's house, I showered with my ring. It was a large round-cut royal blue sapphire fixed on a platinum band. On each side of the center stone was a smaller clear diamond and a swirled pattern engraved in the platinum band.

As the water trickled over the sapphire, I replayed his proposal over and over. Standing at the window, I turned to see him on one knee presenting this ring. I remember my hands coming over my mouth as I gasped.

"Elizabeth River Allard. Will you be my one and only for the rest of my days? My woman to hold, my friend to console. Will you become Elizabeth River Bardon?" His eyes were soft, full of promise. He was offering me *his world*. My heart was racing with excitement.

"Yes. Yes, I will." He then rose up, placing the ring on my finger, and hugged me with a huge smile. Tears sparked by my flooding emotions rushed into my eyes. We were both so full of joy. Some of the cousins saw his proposal through the window and the news quickly spread.

It was a beautiful moment, a beautiful night. I replayed every part of yesterday – ingraining it deeply into my memories. It was the night I became confident about our path together.

As my hair dried, I remembered Mom's excitement about my engagement. Of course, she wanted to be at our wedding. And I'd want Briana there, too. But how would Ty's clan feel about them both attending?

Flipping through the channels, I settled on an old romance movie, and started to spot clean the house. It was three in the afternoon when the doorbell rang. I bounced over to the door.

"I didn't expect you, Ty ... oh, Mr. Rogers. Sorry. I thought you were someone else."

"Hello, Elizabeth. I apologize but I need to take ya down to the station for questioning."

"Oh, is everything okay?"

"We aren't sure. There's somethin' we need to review regarding the recent hospital issue. The hospital released the tapes to the Medford police, and they asked us to work with 'em in investigatin' the recent drug theft."

"I see. I'll get my things."

The drive to the station was painfully slow. Sitting in the back of the chief's old police car, I was utterly aware that I might be in serious trouble. I tried to maintain a poker face, unsure if they had anything on me. I had been careful not to expose my face to the cameras, but maybe I slipped up.

"That's a real nice ring ya have there," Chief Rogers stated while adjusting his rear-view mirror.

"Thanks," I replied.

When we pulled into the half-circle driveway of the department, which was a gray house in the center of town, a young officer was there to greet us.

"That was fast," the man stated as we got out of the car.

"Yeah, let's get inside," Chief Rogers instructed. I followed the men through the white door. Rogers led me into an office room. There was a simple desk in the center with a few flatscreen monitors on top of it. He sat behind the desk and gestured for me to sit in front of it. "Here's the video of the hospital theft. I gathered all the video that shows the thief. Dr. Smoldred is the only witness, and he claimed the culprit was you," he said while turning one of the monitors around to face me. I watched the short video. My throat tightened at Jason's involvement. "But as ya see, it would be yer word against his since the thief's face wasn't caught on camera. It's almost as if the person knew where all the cameras were. And then I found out ya quit working at the hospital shortly after. Now, I have enough here to ask the judge for a search warrant."

"Do as you must. This wasn't me. You won't find anything," I said dryly, not looking away from the tape.

"I have to admit, I am really suspicious. But I cannot see why ya'd steal a bunch of antibiotics and pain drugs. It's the work of an addict."

"You're right to be suspicious based on what info you have to work with ... but come on, Mr. Rogers. You've known me forever. I am NOT that kind of person."

"No. Yer certainly not. I'd trust ya aren't the kind of person to maybe steal them for someone else, eh?" His eyes lowered to my ring.

"Why would I do that? I was working there at the time of this incident. I didn't quit until five days later. I could have easily treated any patient within the hospital. Surely, I would have simply admitted someone in need of help."

"I suppose. The night of the theft, the cameras caught ya abruptly leaving and then soon after, you returned following a shirtless man. This was hours before the thief arrived. Did ya know him? ... And why did ya quit?"

Based on Rogers's words, it seemed I wasn't caught on camera in the parking lot with Ty. I didn't want to lie, but there was no way around it.

My eyes lowered to my ring, replaying the awful memory I had worked to ignore beneath my recent happiness. "I was helping that man find a patient. When we couldn't find who he was looking for, I saw him out and then went home for the night. I quit because I had a bad experience there. A coworker hurt me, and I didn't report it. I just needed to get away."

Mr. Rogers's tone softened. "Oh dear, are ya alright?"

"I am, yes. I just want to move forward. I couldn't work there anymore and needed to move on. The timing was coincidence."

"It was Jason who hurt ya, wasn't it?"

I nodded. "Yes. That could be why he's trying to frame me now. If I'm in jail for a crime I didn't commit, he wouldn't have to worry about being exposed for the monster he is." Tears welled.

"I see. I'm very sorry. Are ya sure ya don't want to pursue justice against 'im?"

"I'm sure. The system would only slap him on the wrist since there's no evidence of the assault."

He didn't press further. As I waited for him to fill out forms, I watched the surveillance videos again. Jason truly was a monster. The *me* in those video frames was irrefutably scared. "Can you take me home now?" I asked him.

"Yeah, I jest need ta complete some paperwork."

His paperwork was taking forever. I fiddled with my fingers, messed with my ring, sighed, and looked around the room. The ceiling had fifteen tiles.

When Chief Rogers reached for a new pen without looking, he knocked over an empty mug, which fell onto the keyboard. A different video started playing on the screen. Losing hope of leaving anytime soon, I watched the film play out the content after Jason attacked me and hurt Tyler: Debbie at the front desk working late, a few parents with sick children, a blood bank visit.

I saw Jason in multiple frames. He behaved so casually after what he did to me and Ty. I watched him answer his phone and then head down the stairs to the main entrance. There, he met with a hooded person wearing a blue sweatshirt and skinny jeans. This person stood carefully out of camera view and took something from Jason. I noticed the distinct custom boots with a purple "A" on the heel as she walked out of the building. My heart sank when I made the connection. It was Angeni. She was meeting with Jason and took something from him. A knife? A syringe? A pen? My heart raced. I had to tell Tyler.

"Alright, we're done here. I'll take ya home now," Rogers said.

Back in my house, I paced around while processing what I had seen. Jason wasn't acting alone. Angeni was behind Ty's strange wound, which I was now convinced was actually a poisoning. I tried to put myself in her boots, feel what she felt. It wasn't hard to understand her jealousy, but I would never have hurt Tyler. *Ever.* Was she trying to kill him? Maybe she didn't expect me to bring him to his family for help. Ty would have surely died if I hadn't.

One thing I knew for certain, Angeni was dangerous. I was so focused on Jason and Ashton that I didn't see the true threat. I had to call Tyler. Rushing to his contact info, I called him. The seconds dragged with each failed ring until his voicemail answered.

My heart sank. I was sweating. I felt panicked. Did she hurt him? I called again. With the second voicemail, I grabbed my keys and hustled to the door. As I opened it, Ty was walking up my front steps.

"Tyler! Ugh, thank God," I sighed, wiping my hand across my forehead.

"What's wrong?" he questioned, concerned about my greeting.

"You were not answering your phone. I was worried."

"Oh. I must have it on silent."

"I'm glad you're here. There's something I need to talk to you about," I said, grabbing his wrist and leading him inside.

"Sure, but why do you smell like the inside of a police car?"

His comment took me by surprise. "Erm. How do you know what that smells like?"

His lips pressed into a line. "Never mind. What did you want to talk about?"

I led him to the kitchen. "Chief Rogers showed up at my door," I said while leaning on the counter. "He wanted to take me in for questioning about the hospital raid. I didn't confess, but when he was showing me surveillance footage from that day, I saw something."

Ty's demeanor changed. "Do they have anything on you? I will go crazy if they take you from me."

"No, but that's not what I'm worried about. Ty, I saw Angeni in the footage. She was in contact with Jason and retrieving whatever he stabbed you with."

Tyler was obviously taken back by my claim. "What? Angeni? No way! There's no way. She'd never. You saw her face?"

"Well no. Not exactly. The person in the video was wearing the same boots as Angeni has. Black with a custom purple A on each heel."

Ty raised his eyebrow. "She wouldn't do this to me, Liz. She wouldn't."

"But I saw the boots. It was definitely her! She's dangerous. We should expose her."

"All you have to go on are the boots this person was wearing. How do you know they were custom? How do you know someone else doesn't have those same boots? How do you know he was handing this person the thing he stabbed me with?" Ty's voice was sharp.

"I ... I don't, but –"

"You can't be sure it was her. I know Angeni. You may think she's out for you. For me. She's not. She's not like that."

"How can you be so sure?" I returned his sharp tone. "The first time I came to your community someone had left me a message. When I was leaving, two of my knives were stabbed into the tree next to my car with half of a fake apple from your kitchen pierced under each blade."

Ty's eyes widened. "What? Why didn't you tell me?"

"I didn't want to upset you, but my point is that someone in your community was sending a message. I thought it was Ashton, but the surveillance video shows Angeni has it out for *us*. Come on,

Ty. It was her. You saw how she verbally attacked me in front of your house. Have you noticed how she looks at us? At me?"

"This is ridiculous." Ty crossed his arms, his eyebrows lowered.

I was too annoyed to care that we were having our first fight. Ty didn't believe me, and my frustrations were growing.

"Oh, is it? Let's recap the fact that we ruined her life plans and defied the wishes of your parents. She has every reason to hate our guts, especially my guts. After years of waiting to be old enough for you, likely crushing on you the entire time, when she's finally old enough for wedding plans, you chose not only someone else but a human no less!"

"No. Let's recap that you kept a secret from me," Ty scolded.

"What? ... The apple? *That* is what you're focused on?"

"Angeni is innocent. I'll see you later." Ty stormed out my back door and ran into the woods before I could protest.

"Dammit!"

The rest of my night was spent fuming about his reaction. He not only didn't believe me but turned the conversation into a stab about the apple secret. He acted as if he never kept things to himself in the past. Angeni was the one who threatened me and tried to kill Tyler. I had to prove it.

CHAPTER THIRTY

TAKEN

"I can't believe you're getting married! ... I'll be honest, I really thought nobody was good enough for you," she laughed at her statement. "This ring is amazing. So gorgeous."

"Thanks, Bri. I want you to be there, but I'm not sure how private this private wedding will be."

"I hope so too. If not, I'll be bummed, but hey - it's about you and Ty and what you both want."

"How's Andrew?" I asked.

"Andrew has been the sweetest. He's taking me out for dinner again this weekend," Briana boasted.

"That's awesome, I'm really happy for you." I smiled at her.

"I wish we still worked together. The hospital hasn't been the same without you."

"I needed a new path after what happened." I looked out the window of Briana's kitchen. Her house would have been quiet if not for her pet parrot, who occasionally squawked with greeting and curse words.

I deeply wished I could tell her everything, but the fewer people who knew my new family's secret, the better.

"I miss you though. We don't see each other enough."

When I arrived home, I collected the mail. Among the few pieces of junk mail was a letter sent from Chief Rogers. Inside the house, I ripped open the letter.

Dear Elizabeth Allard,

I wanted to apologize for bringing you abruptly to the station. We agree you are innocent of any involvement with the hospital case and I thank you for your cooperation with our investigation. Unfortunately, we have not located the true culprit and with no further leads, the case has been dropped. Let us know if you hear anything. Thanks.

– Kyle Rogers

The letter should have brought me some relief, but I felt worried I'd somehow be outed later. Rogers was hard to fool, but with the case dropped I was likely in the clear. I tossed the letter with the junk mail on the counter and opened the refrigerator. My distraction with Ty had left me without much in the house. I started to clean out old carrots, rotten lettuce, and decayed apples when I heard a tap at my back door.

Momentarily startled, I jumped up from the noise. Moving to the back of the house, I saw Ty out of my kitchen window. He was waving at me with an innocent smile. I hadn't forgiven him for not believing me, but his smile was hard to resist.

When I opened the door, I saw he was wearing a white T-shirt and a pair of old black shorts.

"Hey, I thought I'd swing by. Maybe invite you back to my place?" he questioned.

"Sorry, I have to catch up on some chores."

"Oh, I thought you'd be done by now."

"I was spending time with Briana. I needed some girl time."

"Ah. No problem." His face poorly hid his agenda.

I crossed my arms. "Alright. What is it? You seem to have something more on your mind."

"I was hoping that I'd show you my transformation ... now."

My eyes widened. "Um. Yeah, sure. That would be great." An adult person's transformation was something I had wondered about for some time.

"Okay, come on," he said.

I followed Ty into the woods behind my home for several minutes before he stopped. My anticipation was growing. Out here all alone, there was nobody to intervene. Nobody to bother us. Tyler took off his shirt with a seamless flash of his arms. I momentarily admired his impressive physique.

"Okay. Give me a second," he said. I could tell he was afraid to show me. His breathing was deep and unsteady. He breathed in heavily through his nose and released it slowly through his mouth. "Here goes."

I focused on his face. In a few moments, I noticed black hairs growing on the bridge of his nose. They started slowly. One by one, black hairs grew longer and then started under his eyes. It was fascinating. His black head of hair didn't change much as the fur overtook his face and then migrated down his arms and chest. It wasn't scary until his face started to elongate toward me. His nose turned black and rounded as a snout formed. Ty opened his mouth to adjust his jaw as his teeth changed their shape. Fangs elongated while molars sharpened. I almost missed his ears growing upward into furry points. His size grew as his bones changed shape.

I stepped back when he fell forward onto all fours. Within minutes, a huge black wolf had replaced my fiancé. I was in awe, unaware my mouth gaped open at him. I closed it when he snorted. He gently shook off the stretchy shorts he was still wearing. I watched him stare at me, no doubt waiting for me to say something.

"That was amazing. I don't know what else to say. I wasn't sure what I expected, but it wasn't quite that. That doesn't hurt?" Ty shook his massive head side to side to say no. "So, the transformation takes longer as you get older?" He nodded. "Can I ... can I study you?" He nodded again, but I had already started to walk around him. He was beautiful. A gorgeous glossy black coat softer than velvet. It was longest on his shoulders. I trailed my fingers through his back fur, which was chest level to me. I wasn't going to be shy about the moment.

Ty kept his eyes on my face, shifting his head to the other side as I walked around his back end. I tried lifting his tail, but he resisted me – shy with his backside. I came around to his face. His eyes were still that gorgeous blue. Ty was bigger than any shifter I'd seen aside from his father. Feeling bold, I lifted his lip. His teeth were massive, comparable to a lion's – yet they matched his size. They were a lovely off-white color.

"You're beautiful, Ty." I could see the corner of his lip lift to a subtle smile. He was amused by my response.

Ty then bowed his head into my chest. I involuntarily reacted by hugging his head. I kissed his face while thinking about myself in this form. How powerful it must feel. How amazing it must be to run through the wilderness as a formidable animal, one with nature.

Ty abruptly tossed his head up from my arms, almost smacking my chin. "Hey!" I was startled. "What's wrong?"

His body was tense, hackles starting to rise on his shoulders. Something was *very* wrong. Tyler turned to the deeper wilderness and pricked his ears forward. He then turned his head back to me and pushed into my chest while letting out a piercing whimper.

The message was clear. Get back to the house. Panicked, I turned and raced for my back door. When I reached the forest's edge, I heard the horrible yet terrifyingly familiar sound of snapping jaws, yelps, and snarls.

"Tyler!" I cried back toward him.

Heart racing, I ran into my house. Frantically searching for my gun, I found it upstairs in my nightstand. Almost flying down the stairs, I sprinted back to the woods only to be met with silence. It was painfully quiet. What happened?

My arms held the gun stretched out in front of me. My eyes darted in every direction, expecting attack. As I made my way slowly and quietly, I reached a patch of thorn brush through which I could see Ty's wolf form lying on the forest floor. I rushed around it to reach him. He was unconscious, breathing, and bloodied. But most evident was the large needle in his back attached to a dart.

As I pulled the dart out, I felt a strong push and then a sharp heavy pain against the back of my skull. The world slipped from my consciousness.

CHAPTER THIRTY ONE

TYLER

Her face with those chocolate brown eyes and beautiful smile. I could see her, shadowed under a murky gaze. She was blurry. It was a very unpleasant blur, like trying to see through muddy water. But she was there. I tried to touch her. I reached out to her. She'd only slip from me. Every time our fingers nearly met, she would slip back. I struggled harder. I needed her next to me. She was my rock, my reason – I had to protect her. Why was she slipping away?

As my consciousness returned, so did the pain. I felt my tail first. I managed to move it. Why wouldn't my eyes open?

Pain on my left side, pain on my lower back, and a deep pain on my shoulder. It grew with intensity the more I acknowledged it.

My eyes started to open, but they were so heavy. My nose was burning; something foul was in the air.

Strange sounds filled my ears, sounds I didn't recognize. A beeping sound, like the sound a truck makes when it backs up. Dirt shifting under tires.

Then my eyes opened. I didn't know how long I had been unconscious. The room was blurred. I lifted my head with every ounce of strength I had. I couldn't help the light whimper I released from the pain. Looking around, I could see I was in a cage inside a dimly lit room with metal walls. Straw bedding lay under me. When I inhaled a large breath, it stung my lungs – but not from my wounds. There was something dangerous in the air.

I then saw the source. Wolfsbane was hanging from the corners of the cage. I could barely stand. My legs were weak. I must have been injected with a diluted form of wolfsbane as well. I tried to howl for Elizabeth, but my voice was too tired.

After what seemed like several hours, the room door opened. A familiar man walked inside. The wolfsbane masked his scent, but I soon realized how I knew this person. It was Jason.

I built a low growl in my throat, raising my lips.

"Thought you could have her, didn't you?" he said while walking around the cage. He started to fumble with something on a table. It looked like vials. I watched him adjust and mix liquids. "The thing is ... a woman like that ... nobody deserves her ... except me. But certainly not you. She's better off without you. After all, I'm the better man."

There was an off tone to his words. It was like listening to a madman. No, he *was* mad. Jason had flat out lost his mind.

"You see, when your broken-hearted actual fiancée came to me after hearing you mention me when talking on the phone to Elizabeth, she told me your little secret. Then she gave me the tool to poison you. All it took to execute my plan was a little provoking using your precious love. She put up a good fight in that bathroom," he chuckled sadistically.

I snarled viciously at his statement and he laughed harder.

"Angeni was a great distraction. I knew we'd be able to get rid of you with that dart. That's right. I'm shipping you out of the country with her. She gets you and I get to have Elizabeth. She'll forgive me someday. I'll *make* her."

I stood up and snapped my jaws at the monster before me. He couldn't do this. I wouldn't let him.

"I know what you're thinking, Tyler. You'll stop me. But look around. You're in a cage surrounded with wolfsbane." He picked up a gun beside the table and inserted the dart. "You're not going anywhere."

I backed up to the edge of the cage. Jason raised the dart gun and aimed it. I braced for a hit, but before he fired the shot, I heard someone enter the room.

"Whoa. Stop! He needs a break between doses. You'll kill him if you're not careful, and the deal was that I get him alive," Angeni said. She walked over to Jason and crossed her arms when turning to observe me. "Beautiful, isn't he? Tyler was promised to me a long time ago. I'll be damned if some human wench takes him from me. He's mine. He'll learn to love me after enough time in a cage."

"Do you think he will turn human during shipment? I don't need anyone raising an eye at us. He has to stay as a wolf," Jason said without removing his eyes from me.

"He couldn't if he tried. He needs energy to change back. Wolfsbane and sedatives are all we need to keep him weak or knocked out. Plus, I've been bribing away any questions."

I looked away from them, my head lowered. Elizabeth was right. Angeni had orchestrated everything. My heart was in my stomach. Sitting in the corner of the cage, I pretended I was back with her. The pain in my hide was easy to ignore with my breaking heart taking over. I might never see her again.

"You must be wondering how we coordinated grabbing you," Angeni said to me. "You made it too easy when you told Messer of your plans to show that wench your true form today. It was easy to overhear. You gave me just enough time to prepare with Jason."

Jason and Angeni left and returned several times over the hours. I wondered if Liz was safe. Did they hurt her? I ached to know.

From inside the shipping container, I could hear the shipping yard bustle with commotion. I wondered if howling would bring attention to the situation, but if Angeni and Jason were as crazy as it seemed, it was unlikely to help.

As my strength started to return, I was able to stand for longer and search for weaknesses in the cage when they weren't watching. For a long time, they left me alone. My stomach growled. I tried to change back to human, but each attempt was futile. I listened closely to my surroundings. The sounds were decreasing, but some sounds of night persisted. I now could hear the water splashing nearby as a boat passed. I could hear talking - muddled and distant.

The container door opened again. The outside darkness crept in.

"I don't know why you're getting so mad. I only said I felt like we are being watched. Who knows what that man-stealing wench is up to?" Angeni said while entering. "There's a storm over the water. It's delaying tonight's shipping plan."

"The shipping delay could ruin everything. If they are out there, we need to sedate him. Heck, it's midnight. I'm too tired for this garbage."

Out there? Who? Elizabeth?

"It's been enough time since we last darted him. Hit him with another dart," Angeni commanded.

Oh no. What do I do? If Elizabeth was out there, she was in so much danger. I did the only thing I could. I screamed and howled.

"Hey! Stop!" Angeni cried. "Quick! Dart him!"

I didn't watch as they fumbled with the gun. I did my best to twist and turn, hoping he'd miss. I screamed and howled as loud as my voice allowed. Inside the metal container, it was so deafening that Angeni covered her ears. I heard the click of the gun, felt the dart in my flank, and soon the ground was slipping below. I collapsed.

"You got him! Yes!"

"That's heavy wolfsbane mixed with powerful sedatives. He's going out longer than the last time."

I fought the dart for as long as I could. My brain swirled as I struggled to stay awake. As my eyes shut, I heard something alarming. Someone had opened the shipping container, and the sounds of chaos unfolded until the darkness defeated my consciousness.

CHAPTER THIRTY-TWO

UNLIKELY HELP

I could see my father's back. I saw him in the puddle of water I lay within. He was standing, surrounded by a bed of thorns. I struggled to my feet and reached out my hand, but he didn't reach back. I called for him, but the thorns grew thicker. They reached around me, trapping me. When my father turned around, I saw blue eyes - but they did not belong to my dad. It was Tyler. *Tyler!* I cried. *Ty, reach for me!* The thorns reached up my back, their sharp pricks cutting into the back of my head. They tried to enter my skull, digging deeper. The pain grew so intense I could no longer see Ty apart from my agony. He had slipped away as quickly as he appeared.

As I regained consciousness, I felt the sun peeking through the clouds and trees, beaming gently on my face, my face that lay in a shallow puddle. Thorn bushes were close by. I instinctively reached for the back of my head, gently palpating it. Pained sounds formed in my throat. I pulled my hand to my eyes to see blood at my fingertips.

My vision was spotty. I could see, but the fog and occasional black dots disclosed my concussion. Despite my condition, I quickly focused my thoughts on Tyler.

They took him. It had to be them. Angeni and Jason. Why? What did they want with him? I knew I needed help to rescue him, but who could I turn to?

I picked up my gun and struggled to my feet, wobbling from the woods to the back of my house. It was an eternity before I reached my back door. I struggled inside, fumbling to hold onto the kitchen counter. I noticed the blood smearing under my grip.

I needed to pull myself together quickly, realizing I was risking my life in an attempt to save his. I stumbled upstairs and used two mirrors to see the back of my head. There was a small gash under my hair. I worked to stop the slow bleeding. When it clotted, I carefully rinsed around it. My eyes were dilating normally, but my vision was still foggy. I staggered to my bedroom for a baseball cap and loosely fit it on. I then filled a bag with bullets, my two guns, a small flashlight, and a few throw blankets before leaving the house. I started driving, not yet sure where I was going. I couldn't go to the police. They wouldn't have been much help even if I could. I was driving toward the clan before I realized it.

I considered again who I could turn to. Who could I trust? Others within the clan might be in on Angeni's plan. I went through the familiar faces. Chief didn't trust me; neither did Catori. I thought about Lily, Amon, Uki, and Blaze, but I didn't get the right vibe from them. Blaze was strong, but would he help? Likely, he would alert everyone, and that would have been a mistake. I couldn't trust everyone. Ty's sisters Leanna and Alianna were probably good choices, but I didn't know their strength. One person's strength I knew all too well was Ashton's. I shivered at the memories he had given me. He was powerful, determined, and very loyal. I didn't like him, but he was oddly perfect.

With Angeni and Jason teamed, I was unsure Ashton and I could handle them both. I needed one more community member to pull the odds in our favor. Whoever I asked would undoubtedly be thrown into danger, risking their life. Messer came to mind. He was sweet and had taken a liking to me, but I'd hate to see him get hurt.

As I drove my car down the long dirt road, my hands trembled on the steering wheel. I parked my car in its usual spot and exited. The extended family was quiet, with only a few members outside. I worried that Ashton and Messer wouldn't be there. I got out of the car and started walking toward Messer's cabin. I knocked on the door, worried they would smell my wound.

I was relieved to see Messer answer the door.

"Hey Lizzy, what's up?"

"I need your help." I struggled to hold my tears.

"What's wrong?" His sweet face shifted to concern.

I was about to ask this young man to risk his life for us. "Can I come inside?"

"'Course, come in." He widened the door and I entered, closing the door behind me. "You smell like blood."

"Ty is in trouble. I need your help to rescue him."

"What? What happened?"

"Shhh! Are you here alone?"

"Yes, Liz – tell me what happened!"

"It's a long story, but Angeni and a man named Jason kidnapped him."

I did my best to quickly summarize the events that led to this. Messer was in disbelief. "Angeni did that? ... I can't believe it."

"Messer, you MUST believe me. I am bleeding from the back of my head, look."

"I'll definitely help you, but why can't we alarm the whole clan? Surely the entire force of us would stand a better chance than just me."

"I don't know who we can trust. Any one of them could be in on this with Angeni. But we do need more help. Ashton is scary, but he's loyal and powerful. He's perfect to ask."

"Um, are you sure? I'm pretty sure he still has a beef with you."

"He has scared me to the edge of the earth, but if he wanted to hurt me, I would be hurt by now. Come on, we need to find him." We exited the house to see Chief walking toward us.

"Hey, what are you two up to?" His eyes narrowed on me.

"Uh, I was just asking Messer to help me find Ashton. I wanted to see if I could make peace with him," I said.

"He's helping to butcher today's hunt. The smell of blood must be slipping through here. I can smell it this far away." He walked off toward his cabin, leaving my nerves shaking.

Messer led the way to Ashton. We started through the woods down a long narrow trail that led to a small clearing I hadn't seen before. Dead animals, mostly deer, were piled around the space. Ashton was alone. He had one hanging up on a tree hook, slicing it down the belly. I watched him pull out the intestines and toss them into a bin before he noticed us.

"What the hell do you want?" he turned to hiss at me.

"I need your help. Tyler is in trouble."

Like Messer, Ashton didn't take much convincing.

"I don't like you, but Tyler is family. We need to track him. You said he was taken from your backyard. That's where we need to go. There's no time to waste." Ashton cleaned himself up and then led the way to my car.

The drive back to my home was awkward. Messer and Ashton were both serious, yet Messer retained his charm. He could tell how upset I was. "It will be okay, Liz. We'll get him back," Messer assured me.

I fought the tears back. "I know you will. I don't know what I would have done without you both."

Ashton stared out the window from the backseat until we reached my driveway. They opened the doors before I had the car in park and rushed around the house. I fumbled to catch up with them.

Ashton was searching the ground, sniffing his way to where Ty had lain. "You weren't lying. I can smell everything that happened here and I see the evidence as well," Ashton said.

"It's overwhelming," Messer commented.

"Jason must have knocked you out with that branch and Angeni dragged Tyler by the scruff," Ashton explained to me.

"I can't believe she would do this," Messer's fists balled, "what a traitor!"

"Don't worry, she'll get what's coming to her once the clan has their say. That bastard Jason will, too."

I just stared at them, too upset to speak. I could see Ty's blood trail on the ground cover as Ashton and Messer led me to where Angeni and Jason had loaded him into a truck.

"I'm worried. He's lost a lot of blood just within the woods," Ashton commented. In bitterness I briefly recalled how Ty was left after Ashton's attack on him in my home, but it was irrelevant now.

"We need to shift if we are to track him by truck scent," Messer said.

"Agreed."

I looked down, guilty with the knowledge that if Ty hadn't been in the woods, showing me his shift, maybe he would be safe right now.

Messer and Ashton were not shy. They stripped down completely. I didn't notice until I turned to see Messer completely nude while tossing his underwear on the pile of clothes. I pretended I didn't notice, casting my eyes down at the blood on the leaves.

A brush of red, gray, and white walked past me before I realized they were no longer naked men. Their builds were smaller than Tyler's, but still much larger than a wild wolf.

"I'll get back to my car and follow you there."

They tracked the scent to I-5. I drove north as they tracked the truck's scent, struggling at times to see them through the brush and trees. After a couple of hours I pulled over, wondering if I had lost them. I exited my car and stood at the edge of the forest.

"Messer, Ashton!"

Within five minutes I could see them running toward me. Messer snorted.

"Sorry, I thought I maybe lost you both. We've been going for hours. You're sure you have his trail?" Ashton nodded and started off again north. "Messer, make sure you tell me when we are getting close. Signal me."

He nodded and then hurried after Ashton. I rushed back to my car. I drove more than two additional hours, reaching Portland by nightfall. Why would they take Tyler to Portland?

As we entered the city, I lost sight of them. I kept going straight, hoping they'd let me know I was going the right way. As I approached Exit 303, I heard a howl seep through my cracked window. It had to be the signal. I took the next exit bringing me west. As my headlights passed a fenced park, I spotted a naked man standing along the park outskirts, half hidden by a tree. I pulled over and Messer rushed to my car. I pulled a blanket from my backpack as he entered and handed it to him.

"Ashton tracked him to a shipping yard," he said while putting the blanket over his lower half. "Go straight, hurry."

We continued down the road, reaching the shipping yard. Ashton approached the car as I got closer. I pulled over and got out, following Messer and handing a blanket to Ashton as well.

"Tyler is close," Ashton whispered. "I think he's being kept in one of those shipping containers. I smell all three of them over there. We need to be careful. This may lead to an ugly fight. If Angeni is in human form, we might be able to grab her before she shifts. The goal is to chase them away or subdue them so we can grab Tyler." He looked at me. "Can I kill Jason?"

I was taken aback by the question, but too exhausted and desperate to care about Jason. "Do what you must to him. I just need Tyler back."

"Don't shoot Angeni," Ashton stated.

"Come on. We need to get ready," Messer said.

I prepped my guns, placing one under my clothes while the men changed back to wolves. They covered me, leading the way as we crept closer to a large red metal shipping container. They moved so silently that I could only hear the gravel shifting under their paws.

Around the maze of units, the wolves stopped and peered ahead from a corner. I peeked out from behind them. I could see Angeni and Jason having a disagreement sixty feet away. I couldn't make out what they were saying, but they soon opened the container behind them and closed the door.

"He must be in there," I whispered to the wolves. They didn't move. "What are we waiting for?"

Messer and Ashton's ears were pricked forward. Messer rubbed his nose to his front leg and then quietly snorted. Something in the air was bothering them. They listened for a while. I wished I could have heard what they were catching. I was getting ready to ask them again what the plan was when piercing howls broke the silence.

Ashton growled and nudged Messer. They started creeping forward as the howling continued. At the side of Messer's flank, I followed toward the unit with my gun pointed. As we reached the door, the howling abruptly stopped. I could hear Angeni praising Jason for a good shot. Panicked, I grabbed the door and swung it open. Both of my fiancé's kidnappers stood to the right of a large cage, a dart gun in Jason's hands.

"FREEZE OR I'll SHOOT!" I screamed at them. "Don't you freaking move." But I didn't say *freaking*. My backup positioned themselves at the door.

Despite my warning, Jason and Angeni rushed to the back of the unit while Angeni started her change. Messer pushed me aside and barreled into her. Being mid-change, she already had her teeth and bit Messer's leg. Messer yelped and grabbed her by her forming scruff, dragging her backwards out into the yard. I could see the fire in Ashton's eyes as he and Messer jumped onto her now full wolf form. She yelped, screamed, and fought their assault. In our distraction with Angeni, Jason exited the container via a back door. I could see him escaping the area as the door slowly shut. Meanwhile, Angeni ran away, followed by Messer and Ashton.

I turned my attention to Tyler. He had been darted in the flank. Wolfsbane was hanging on the corners of the cage. He had open wounds and lay lifeless aside from his shallow breathing. It was overwhelming. Tears welled as I removed the open padlock and opened the cage door. "Tyler, can you hear me?" I jumped into the cage and stroked his face over his closed eyes, devastatingly concerned I'd never see them open again. "Messer, Ashton!" I wiped my eyes.

Messer returned alone first. His ear was torn, bleeding down the side of his face. He stared at Tyler. While I waited for Ashton, I took the wolfsbane ribbons down from the cage corners and threw them as hard as I could into the yard.

When Ashton returned, without Angeni, he made a strange gesture to Messer before starting to shift back, soon leaving a pile of fur in his position.

"How is he, is he alive?" Ashton rushed to Ty's side and placed his hand on Ty's chest. "We need to get him home. Messer will carry him to your car. Help me drag him. Messer, lie on the ground to catch him. We need to balance him on your back."

Messer complied while Ashton and I struggled to pull Tyler. Messer buckled under Ty's weight, but with our help on each side, he managed to carry him to my car.

"How are we going to fit him in there?" I asked Ashton as Messer put Ty down and then shifted back to human.

"Pull your front seats up and fold down the passenger side ... quickly," Ashton commanded. They struggled to pull him inside. I did my best to assist. They laid him along the back of my folded front seat, his head touching my dashboard. I watched Messer tuck

Ty's tail in before shutting the door and sighing in exhaustion. "Now drive. Go back to Ty's cabin. We will race home after cleaning up here. And whatever you do, don't get pulled over by a cop." Ashton placed the blanket over Ty's head and neck. "We can't have the public discovering him like this."

"Right. I will meet you there." I hurried into the car and started the motor. When we started to merge onto I-5 southbound, my four-cylinder engine struggled with Ty's additional weight.

The lines on the highway blurred. It was just after two in the morning. I never drove more than ten miles over the speed limit, even though my foot wanted to crush the pedal. I was exhausted, but the adrenaline of tonight and Tyler's condition kept my heavy eyes open. The roads were mostly empty. For a stretch I removed the blanket from Ty's face and watched him breathe.

It was nearing daybreak when I pulled my car down the dirt road to his village. Since Messer and Ashton had already made it back, most of the community met my car at the end of the road. I watched them vent with anger: some cried, others blamed. Angeni's name was smeared around between them. The men pulled Ty from the car and carried him down the stretch of cabins to his home. Lily held the door open. I entered and helped clear a space on the living room floor. The teens stared as the men struggled to bring Ty through. I barely noticed Chief yell for medication and an IV. They settled Ty on the carpet.

"He's cold. Messer, grab some large blankets from my house. You remember where they are?" Blaze commanded. Messer nodded and rushed off.

I was too tired to help Ty's father. I blankly stared as he tasted Ty's blood before gathering the IV equipment. "The amount of wolfsbane and sedatives in his blood should have killed him," Chief said while inserting the needle into Ty's arm.

Uki and Lily struggled to restrain their children from getting closer. "Will he make it, Mama?" Callie asked.

"I don't know, sweetie. I hope so," Uki responded.

Messer came in with a large old blanket and laid it over Ty. Tears welled in my heavy eyes; my nerves were completely fried. Messer next went to the kitchen and brought back some towels and a pot of warm water. "Liz, do you want to wipe his wounds?" Messer asked with a softened voice.

"Yes, thank you," I said as the men finished with setting Tyler up. I dipped the towel in the water.

"He should make it. He has to," Catori said while stroking Ty's face.

Ty didn't flinch when I gently placed the warm wet cloth on his wounds. He remained as motionless as when we found him.

"Let her stay with him," Chief said. "We can all come back later to check him. There's nothing more we can do. My son's a fighter."

"You okay here alone, Liz?" Messer asked me.

"Yeah, I will just lie here with him, maybe close my eyes for a bit."

"Okay, call for us if you need anything."

CHAPTER THIRTY-THREE

RECOVERY

I wouldn't sleep. I couldn't – seeing him lie on the floor so still. Occasionally his eye would twitch, or his tail would shift. I kept pacing the room, lying next to him, checking his wounds. My eyes were heavier than iron rods, but they refused to rest.

Occasionally, community members would check in on us. I heard the door creak open. Looking up, it was Messer with two boxes in his hands. "Hey Lizzy. I brought you something. It's a box of cookies," he said while handing me the box.

"Oh, thank you, Messer. You didn't need to do that. It's me who should be giving you a thank-you gift."

"Nah, Tyler is part of this community and he's always been good to me. I had to help. The cookies are actually a pre-thank-you gift." He pointed to his ear and then opened the second box. It had medical instruments inside.

"Oh jeez, Messer – I forgot all about your ear. I can still stitch it."

"Good. I was hoping. Lily commented that it would stay this way if I didn't get it stitched back together. Mama Rain usually does this stuff, but she's not around. She's been acting kinda off lately."

"Lily is probably right. I'm tired so I'll be slow." I started to gather what was inside the box. "What about the pain?"

"Don't worry. I can handle it." I started on his ear, cutting the edges. Messer released a few pained sounds but kept his head still for me. "How is he, by the way?" Messer continued.

"He's hanging in there. Whatever they injected, it was too much for him. He's overdosed on it. I'm worried for his organs. His wounds aren't bleeding but they aren't closing either. I'm just really concerned," I said while starting the first stitch.

"Blaze thinks Tyler will shift back to human involuntarily once the wolfsbane is removed from his system. He said he's seen it before."

"I thought you have to be conscious to change like that?"

"Usually, but there are cases such as this where the body does it on its own."

"I see." We stayed quiet until I finished the last of ten stitches. "There, that should do it."

"Aw, thanks Lizzy. Already feels better."

"You're welcome," I said through a yawn.

"Hmm, you should really get some rest. I can stay with him for a while."

"That's sweet of you, but I know I couldn't sleep if I tried. I'm too stressed, too worried."

"I understand. I will leave you two alone. By the way, a bunch of the members are out hunting for Angeni and that Jason guy. It might be quiet around here for a while."

"Noted. I'll see you soon, Messer. And I know I don't need to thank you, but I'm grateful regardless. You and Ashton were an amazing team."

"You're welcome." His smile beamed. "Oh wow, it's already one in the afternoon." Messer gave a cheesy wave as he exited the house. I could hear his heavy steps off the porch.

I went to wash my hands and then sat by Ty's side with the box of cookies. I opened the box and took a nibble as my thoughts wandered. The clan was hunting for Angeni, the traitor, and Jason, the enemy. I'd love to punch them both in the gut. I imagined the oddly satisfying revenge the clan would take on them if they were caught. Torture, whippings – before this hell, such thoughts would have been disturbing.

Ty's leg shifted under the blanket. His face started to twitch, similar to how dogs do when they dream. I moved closer, eager to see more change. After a few moments, he started to whimper. "Tyler? Can you hear me? It's okay. You're safe."

I wished for some pain meds. Almost as soon as Ty started to move, he stopped. The room was quiet, and my heart sank. The medication and fluids in the bag were just about gone so I gently removed the needle from him.

It was close to three when I heard a knock on the door.

"Come in," I answered.

Ty's grandmother, Mama Rain, entered, closed the door, and approached us.

"Hey dear. How are you holdin' up?" she asked.

"It's not me I'm worried about," I said while looking back at Ty. I stroked my hand over his eyes and down his muzzle. "I miss him."

"He's made it this far. He will pull through, especially with my family's famous healing paste." She showed me a glass jar of green paste, explaining, "I spent all morning making this. It's sure to help heal those wounds. Place this paste directly on them. It's a recipe our people have used for hundreds of years, but it has to be made fresh to work to its fullest extent. Helps with pain, too. It's what my son used for Tyler on his abdomen." Her delicate voice soothed me.

"Thank you, this is wonderful. What's in it?"

"That's a secret, at least till you're officially one of us." She winked with a grin. I smiled at her charm. "Well, I'll leave you to it." She exited before I could say another word.

I opened the jar and was surprised to smell a mint-like odor mixed with an earthy aroma. It smelled more like a candle than a healing tonic. Sitting next to him, I worked the paste in and around his wounds. His ear twitched when I applied it to his back, but he was otherwise still.

I washed my hands when I was finished. Back in the living room I picked up a book and sat in the armchair. It was a chapter book left by one of the children. My eyes drifted along with the beguiling story until they grew so heavy that my body forced them closed.

I was no longer with Tyler. The space was dark. The lights shifted around, darting from one area to the next. I was then back in the woods behind my home, bleeding into the soil again. Thorns stretched around me. They tangled until the pain was unbearable. I next jumped into my car and was driving. Driving so fast, I was waiting for the police to chase me. While turning around to see behind me, I crashed, and I was snapped awake.

"Ugh ... damn," I said quietly while lifting my head from its awkward sideways position. My neck ached. I struggled to focus my eyes on Ty and was momentarily startled. Where a large wolf had lain, a man's back now rested under a blanket surrounded by tufts of black fur. I jolted down to him. "Tyler?" I gently said while wiping away the fur from his back and face. The paste was doing as promised. His wounds were healing quickly. Why was he still unconscious? I gently shook his arm. "Tyler, can you hear me? It's Elizabeth." He groaned in his throat, then moved his arm. "Yes, I am here. Open those eyes for me." Tears of relief streamed down my cheeks.

A few moments passed before he moved again. I gave him time to awaken – brushing away the fur and running my fingers through his beautiful black hair. His progress was slow, but when he finally opened his eyes, I was sobbing over him. "You're okay," I said through sniffles; "I was so scared."

"Elizabeth," he quietly called to me.

"I'm here. I'm here." He tried to lift himself, pushing his body from the ground. His arms were weak. "Slowly, go slow," I instructed.

He managed to get on his hands and knees. I helped to keep the blanket around him, and he slowly rose to a shaky stand. He looked around the room, undoubtedly processing what he last remembered. Loose fur dropped to the floor from under the blanket.

"Water. I need water," he said while refocusing his eyes with heavy blinks.

"Hold on." I gave him the blanket to hold and sped to the kitchen, collecting a glass. When he took it from me, he drank it so fast he nearly choked. "Easy. You should sit down." I helped him to the couch, and he sighed when settled. "What do you remember?"

"Everything. I think they darted me right before someone charged in. I'm gathering that was you ... alone?"

"I recruited Messer and Ashton to find you. They were the real heroes. Angeni and Jason had taken you to Portland."

"Portland ... Ashton, huh? I'll admit I'm surprised you asked him."

"I was counting on his clan loyalty despite our differences and history."

Ty gave me a soft smile. "I smell my grandmother's healing paste. I must have been out a while."

"Your father said they overdosed you with that second dart."

"Yeah they kinda commented about how they needed to knock me out for a long while."

"What were they planning?" I asked.

"Well, you were obviously right about Angeni. It was her all along. She wanted to ship me out of the country so I could be her personal love slave. Jealousy made them both lose their minds. It's definitely a problem in our species, as it obviously is in yours as well. We are easily jealous creatures. It's one of the reasons why we so carefully choose our mates."

"A bunch of community members, including your dad, have been out hunting them."

"They might catch Angeni. I'm worried Jason will get away," he said as his stomach growled.

"Let me defrost you some food." I went to the kitchen and found some venison in the freezer and placed the bag in a pot of warm water to thaw. "Venison okay?" I called to him.

"That's fine."

I rejoined him in the living room. "Those wounds are already closed. We should get you cleaned up."

Before we could go upstairs, there was a knock on the door and Chief entered. "Son! You're alright!" He rushed over and hugged Tyler.

"Yeah, I'm alright thanks to Elizabeth."

"I heard Messer and Ashton were the real heroes. They tracked you down," his father said while releasing his hug.

After more clan members greeted Tyler, we headed upstairs. I closed my eyes on Ty's bed while he showered away the paste and loose fur. I was falling asleep when he exited the bathroom, wearing a T-shirt and shorts, and then joined me in his bed.

"You look like you haven't slept since I was taken."

I yawned. "I have ... for maybe twenty minutes."

He chuckled. "You need to sleep."

"I'll sleep when I'm good and ready," I joked while pressing my hand into his chest. He stared at me for a while. I fought my heavy eyes to look back at him. "What?" I asked.

"I must have been naked for a while. Did you look?"

I raised my eyebrow at him. "Look at what?"

"Me. Down there."

"Sheesh, Ty ... I wouldn't intentionally look without your consent."

"I was just wondering."

"Hmm, would it be so bad if I looked? I'll see eventually."

"Just want the moment to be right ... and preferably with us both conscious. I know that once we see each other, things move quickly. I want you to be Mrs. Bardon first." He brushed some of my hair from my face and tucked it behind my ear. "Plus, I want to reduce the risk of pregnancy until we are ready. That's a concern, too."

"Alright, fine. But admit the other reason."

"What?"

"You're a little shy," I taunted.

"Well, yeah a little. That too."

"Ashton and Messer aren't shy, that's for sure." My face twisted. Tyler picked up on what I meant and bellowed into a loud laugh. "What?" I asked.

"Nothing, I'm just picturing them stripping in front of you and your surprise by it!" He continued to laugh.

"That's pretty accurate actually. You seem back to your old self." I pulled myself over to him and wrapped my arms around his upper body. He held me back as I nuzzled into his neck.

"Get some sleep, Liz. I'm not going anywhere."

CHAPTER THIRTY-FOUR

BLOODY MISTAKES

The thorns returned in my slumber, but they weren't visual. I felt them physically. They twiddled along my scalp through the back of my hair. I awoke from the discomfort. When my eyes managed to pull open, still heavy – I felt Ty behind me. He was messing with the hair on the back of my head.

"What are you doing?"

"I'm sorry, but you have a nasty gash under your hair. Are you okay? What happened?"

"Don't touch it." I pulled away and turned over to face him. "Jason knocked me out with a branch. It was after I ran back into the house for my gun and found you darted on the ground."

Tyler frowned. "Did you see a doctor for this?"

"Honestly, no. I was too concerned about you."

"Come on, get up. We are going to get you checked out." He sprang out of bed and started to get his shoes on.

"Now?"

"Yes. Now."

"I think I'm okay by this point."

"I need to make sure. Get up."

Pulling into the hospital parking lot felt strange. It was a step back to my old life, but I was hoping I'd see Briana. I parked in the back, displeased with the walk.

"You're sure *he* won't be here?" I asked while walking toward the building.

"He's been run out of town. But don't mention it to anyone. They likely don't know he's not returning."

As I entered the main doors I was instantly greeted by my former coworkers. In the exam room, Dr. Patricia entered in fifteen minutes. When I was working there, I had never formed a relationship with her. To my relief, she agreed I would be okay and that the gash didn't need stitches. As we were leaving into the night, I said my goodbyes to everyone. I was a bit bummed Briana wasn't there but considering the hour it wasn't surprising.

"You know, with Jason gone ... you could come back to work here," Ty suggested while we walked to the car.

"I was thinking about that. When we were in there, I felt anxious and unsafe even though I knew we were fine. I don't think I'll ever feel comfortable in that place after what you-know-who did." I sighed and got in the car, relieved to be leaving. "I will look for new employment elsewhere."

"It's up to you, but you don't have to work if you don't want to. With me, it's an option not to."

"I probably will. Nursing gives me something to do and I'm good at it."

For a while, we drove in silence. I kept looking at my engagement ring; it had never left my finger. Tyler must have noticed. "Is everything okay?"

"For the most part. Why?"

"I noticed you keep looking at it," he pointed to the ring.

I collected my thoughts. I was emotionally drained, physically tired, and mentally exhausted.

"I'm wondering if we should push the wedding back a bit. With your family hunting Angeni and Jason, I don't know if things will pull together in time. And what if she tries to crash the wedding?"

He processed what I said, looking out the window, then at his lap. "You make a good point. Delaying until they are captured is probably ideal, but I don't know how long it will take. I'll talk to my family and see what they think we should do." We didn't say anything else until I was pulling into my driveway. "I was hoping you'd spend the rest of the night with me at my place," he said.

"I was planning to. Let me take a quick shower, eat something quick, and pack some things."

It was midnight when we finally pulled down his clan's driveway. "I'm going to eat and then I'll join you upstairs," Ty said when we entered his cabin.

While he fumbled in the kitchen, I went upstairs and brought my bag to the bathroom. Taking out my toothbrush, I scrubbed my teeth clean. When we made it back into bed, we were so emotionally and physically tired that we quickly curled up in the comforters within each other's arms, both asleep in minutes.

When I awoke the next morning, I was slow to return to the light. I felt Ty's arms around my waist, his sweet breath on my head. As my eyes opened, I still felt tired, but it was no longer exhaustion. Ty's cradle around me kept the nightmares away. I started to shift, removing his arm from my waist and turning to look at him. He was peaceful, his eyes beautifully at rest. I ran my fingers through his black hair before getting up to use his bathroom.

In the mirror, my hair was a mess. My eyes were still tired. Considering recent events, though, I didn't look too bad. I brushed my hair into submission and then brushed my teeth. When finished, I walked to the front window in the master bedroom, from which I could see a peek of the horizon through the trees – a lovely shade of orange-yellow in a cloudless sky. The tree branches in the center of the community were still from the windless morning. Green as far as the eye could capture.

I then looked down toward Ty's parents' house and saw something that sent a shock wave through my core. The hair on the back of my neck stood. "Angeni!" I said loudly in my confusion.

Ty's eyes snapped open, startled. "What?"

"Angeni was caught and your dad is pissed." I crossed my arms, my eyes still on the scene outside.

Tyler jumped out of bed to the window. "Shhhhiit," he whispered as he raced for the stairs.

I struggled to keep up with him as we ran outside. I watched him slide into a crouch in front of Angeni while his father's hand rose to strike. It came down to hit Ty's raised arms. I gasped, covering my mouth in horror as Ty's skin split from the whip's crack. The awful sound sliced against the trees.

"TYLER! MOVE ASIDE!" Chief screamed into his son's agonized face.

Angeni was kneeling against a wooden pole, her wrists tied around it. Her face was soaked with tears. Her exposed back displayed five deep lashes, blood trailing from each.

"Father, stop!" Ty begged. His arms were still raised to his father.

The children's eyes were covered by their mothers' hands as everyone else watched.

"Move!" his father commanded.

"She's had enough," Tyler responded.

His father looked around at the faces of the community. Their eyes were angry but laced with pity. He cracked the bloodied whip over a close tree. "LET THIS BE A LESSON TO ALL. ANYONE WHO DARES TO PULL SOMETHING LIKE THIS AGAIN WILL FACE *MUCH* WORSE THAN THIS TRAITOROUS BITCH!" he screamed to the crowd, his face red with anger. "Lock her in our basement," he snapped to Catori.

Ty sighed to the sky as his mother cut Angeni's arms free and pulled her by the wrist to her home's door. As Ty's father stormed off, I rushed to Ty's arms. "What kind of whip splits skin like this!" I begged to understand.

"It's laced with potent wolfsbane," he gasped out as I inspected his arms.

"I hate that damn herb." Back in Tyler's cabin, I took the jar of Mama Rain's tonic and ordered Ty to his bedroom. "She deserved it," I said to him while applying the paste to his wound.

"You don't mean that, Liz."

"Yes, I do. She put us through hell. Her emotions of jealousy and anger cannot excuse her behavior. Tyler ... did you forget she enslaved and nearly killed you?" My eyebrows lowered. "How can you think she didn't deserve what she got?"

"She deserved punishment, but not that."

"I felt it appropriate. If I didn't wake you, she would have received the full course of it."

"She's an eighteen-year-old girl. Liz ... this isn't you. This is your anger talking."

"And you're just barely a man at twenty-three. I can't help how I feel."

"This shouldn't be how you feel. The Elizabeth that I know would be going to Angeni and treating her wounds despite her crimes. For your sake and hers, you need to forgive her."

"I don't think I can and maybe you haven't learned the power of my anger."

"Like my father's anger just now? Like Chogan's anger and the pain he caused me? Like Angeni's anger and what it drove her to do? Like Jason's anger at your rejection? Anger is not power. It's poor decisions, it's pain, it's hatred. Look at what anger has done to us," he snapped.

"I thought you said they acted out of jealousy, apart from your father. Besides ... not everyone deserves forgiveness. And I wasn't the one who punished her just now."

"When you were working, did you ever treat people who were bad in the eyes of society? Captured criminals? I'm sure you did. It didn't matter that they were guilty of doing something wrong. You cared for their bodies anyway, right? You need to forgive her, or this will continue to consume you both. I'm sure everyone has their backs to her and she's all alone. At least try."

I sighed, giving myself a moment to process his words. He was right. The Elizabeth before this wouldn't refuse care to someone. She was quick to forgive everyone except herself. Angeni was just another patient and I would be doing what I could to treat her, but I didn't know if forgiveness was in my heart.

"You're right. This has changed me and not for the better. I will treat her, but my feelings haven't changed. I don't think I'm ready to forgive her. At least she's been captured. That's one less worry."

"Not exactly," he said.

"What do you mean?"

"My dad just made a huge mistake in his thoughtless anger. Angeni is the only one of the Shadow clan within our community, but eventually her clan will get word of this."

"I don't like the sound of that."

"It could mean an all-out clan war." Ty sighed.

"Great. Just wonderful," I scowled while bandaging his arms.

"Let's hope it doesn't come to that, but between my refusal of the marriage and now this ... I'm really concerned."

"Was there ever a clan war before?" I naively asked.

Ty looked at the far wall and released a shaky breath, but didn't answer.

We weren't sure how it would go, but Ty wanted me to help Angeni, or at least try to. With him by my side, I knocked on Catori's door.

"She's coming," Ty whispered to me.

Moments later, Catori greeted us. "Are you okay, my son?"

"I'm fine. We are here to treat Angeni," he said.

Catori nodded and gestured for us to come inside. The home was the same as it had been the first and only day I'd been inside. I briefly replayed my first day within the community and how strange it all felt. It already seemed so long ago.

"She's down here. She won't let me help her but here," she handed me a jar, "it's the miracle tonic from Mama Rain. She knew her son would react this way and made this in the early morning. Angeni won't let me apply it though. I must caution you both, she's very distraught."

We stood in front of the basement door, the open door revealing stairs leading down from the kitchen. With the jar securely in my hands, Catori gestured us to go down. We began to descend, Ty leading the way. Each step down the creepy wooden stairs revealed more of a planked wooden wall holding open cabinets filled with terrifying devices. Things that belonged within a horror movie's torture scene. Inverted spiked collars, thick rusted chains, spiked and chained baseball bats, wooden and metal stakes, many jars of wolfsbane, and strange knives in more shapes than I could process. On the other side of the room were four large steel cages. Angeni crouched inside the far-left cage, cowering in the corner. Her quiet sobbing and our steps were the only noise. Blood stained through her shirt.

"Angeni?" Ty said softly.

"Tyler?" She sobbed. "Oh. Tyler. I'm so ... so sorry." Her sobs deepened. I watched her wipe her wrist against her nose.

"Hey, let us help you. We have some of my grandmother's tonic. Put your back to the cage and Elizabeth will apply it."

For a moment Angeni said nothing. She sobbed and kept wiping her nose. Finally, she spoke again. "You want to help me ... after what I did to you? To you both?"

"You're young. We all are. Everyone makes mistakes," Ty said.

I wanted to say *that's no excuse.*

"Your dad said you almost died. Is that true?" she questioned.

Ty sighed, crouching down in front of the cage. "Yes. That's true."

"I didn't mean that. I swear. I swear."

Ty wasn't sure what to say. I watched him struggle for words.

I spoke up. "Angeni. I admit I'm terribly angry with you, but I can also recognize your regret. I will forgive you, not for your sake but for mine. The anger you've been feeling ... the jealousy – it consumed you. I won't let my anger do that to me."

"Let us help you with the pain," Ty said to her.

She hid her face in her knees, wrapping her arms around her legs. "Just go away," she cried.

I was beginning to feel sorry for her. "Come on, Tyler. We can leave the jar with her, but I don't want to stay here any longer."

Ty nodded and stood up. His eyes were sorry. It was in that moment I understood why he wasn't angry. He felt this was all his fault.

When we left the house, Ty sat down with me on one of the fire pit logs and wrapped his arm around me.

"You blame yourself, don't you?" I asked him.

His eyes watched the trees. "Yes. I do. I don't regret choosing you, so please don't ever think that. I just wish I didn't cause Angeni so much pain and anger. I *hate* myself for it."

"Hate is a strong word, but everyone hates themselves at some point. Will she be sent back to her clan?"

"Yes, eventually. I'm worried about that." He sighed with a shaky breath. "Aren't you going to ask about the basement?"

"I was working up to it. What was all that for?"

"Do you remember when I told you about the blood moons and what they do to us?"

"Yes, you said they make your kind go a little ... rabid as you called it."

"More than a little. We lose our minds on those nights. In order to keep ourselves from killing the locals, we lock ourselves in those basement cages. Some chain themselves to large trees. Others go extremely deep into the wilderness and let themselves run wild. But those who do that live in especially remote places or travel to them."

"That makes sense. How often does it happen? Is it uncomfortable?"

"Usually every four months. I don't really know if it's uncomfortable because we barely remember it afterwards. And nobody knows why the blood moon does this to us, but it's something we must watch out for."

"Has anyone ever killed a person during the blood moon?"

"Yes, it's where the *myth* of the werewolf started. Except it's no myth of course."

A familiar red wolf rushed behind us, startling me. I gasped and grabbed my heart as Messer turned and approached. "Jeez, Messer. You made my heart jump."

I watched his body make a laughing motion with the sides of his lips curled to a smile. He lay down in front of us.

"Please, spare me the nakedness today," I joked to him.

Ty chuckled and then jumped up to grab Messer, wrapping his arm around the young wolf's neck. Messer struggled to break free as Tyler gave him a harsh head rub. "Never got a chance to thank you, ya little worm," Ty said playfully. Messer managed to escape Ty's grip. As Ty went to stand up, Messer shoved his head into Ty's backside, sending him flying over the log. I laughed heavily, harder than I had in a long time. Tyler scrambled himself into a more dignified position. "Like I said ... little worm." He chuckled while brushing off his hands.

"I see that ear healed well. Barely a scar," I commented. Messer stood up and licked me across the face. "Ew, Messer!" He then rushed off down the stretch of cabins as Tyler laughed at my disgusted face. "Who needs a dog in this family when you have him?" I chuckled with him, wiping off the saliva.

Our good mood turned sour when we spotted Ty's father. He walked quickly toward us, a remnant of anger still in his eyes. Ty lowered his head as his father reached us. "Don't you have something to do? Hunting? Splitting wood? Carving? Make yourself useful," he hissed as he passed us.

Ty's smile was replaced by a heavy frown. "Everything okay, Dad?"

Chief paused. "No. Audrie is going into labor. She's a little early. I'm concerned."

"Oh, I forgot she's expecting with everything happening. Can I help her?" I asked.

"No. We take care of our own. Elizabeth, after everything I really wish you'd choose a path that didn't involve us. You've caused enough trouble. You both have." He turned to Ty's reddening face. "Son, pull your shit together and get some damn work done around here."

"Yes, sir." As his father rushed away, Ty stood up and reached for my hands. I stood up in response. "Don't mind him ... I have an idea. It's about time I showed you my carving business. What do you say?"

"I'd love that."

His smile had returned. "Follow me." He led me around his cabin and into the woods behind it. Down a long trail, roughly a mile from his cabin was a small round clearing where several stumps and a large cut tree had been placed. A chainsaw rested under a small tarp held down by some stones. "My clan lets me take scattered forest trees from some miles out. I'm always moving my carving spot. Whatever I don't use for carving gets chopped into firewood." I watched in awe as he cut down the half-standing tree and turned all the usable pieces into various shapes. His speed was impressive, but the detail of the carvings was meticulous. In four hours, he created a three-foot bear, a two-foot fish, a two-piece six-foot eagle, and a small horse. I watched him carve the smaller details using petite knives that were hidden under the tarp.

With each piece he completed, he would ask for my opinion. I gave him the same answer each time. "Amazing." When he was finished, I helped him by carrying the horse back to his cabin. "So how much would you sell this horse for?"

"Just the horse? ... I typically get three hundred for them."

"Wow. What about the rest?"

"The eagle is sold for a thousand and the others run between two and three hundred each."

"Not bad for four hours of work."

"Ten hours total, but yeah, it's decent." We deposited the sculptures down behind his house. "Come inside. I want to shower really quick."

I followed him upstairs. While Tyler got in the shower, I took out the cell phone out of my bag. Briana had texted me. Mom had called. I felt bad for ignoring them, but things had been so hectic. When I was about to dial Mom's number, I heard a heavy and rapid knock on Ty's front door.

I raced down the stairs to greet the visitor.

"Elizabeth! We need your help. The baby is stuck and Audrie is too tired to push. Please!" Catori begged, her eyes watery with tears.

"Of course, lead the way," I said calmly.

Catori frantically led me to the cabin next door. From the entrance I could hear moans and panicked voices. Lily answered the door before Catori knocked. I was too focused to notice how this cabin looked. Too focused to address the panicked father pacing in the living room. They rushed me upstairs. On the edge of the bed,

Audrie was kneeling with her head resting on the mattress. The baby's head was mostly born with the rest still stuck inside Audrie. The infant's lips were a pale-blue color. My heart sank.

"Permission to assist?" I quickly asked the mother while Catori handed me medical gloves.

"Yes, please do something," she weakly moaned.

I reached my fingers up between the baby's head and her pelvic bone. Audrie screamed as I felt a shoulder dystocia. "Help me lay her on her back, hurry!" I commanded Catori and Lily. They rushed to lay her down on the floor. "Hold her knees up and back. It's a stuck shoulder."

Audrie cried out as I shifted my fingers inside her and popped the shoulder free. "Now, Audrie, PUSH! Push with everything you have left!" She roared as she gave everything she had. I carefully pulled and the baby was freed onto the floor. The pale newborn was lifeless.

"No, please save her!" Lily cried.

"A little girl. She can't be gone," Catori said.

"My baby. Why isn't she crying?" Audrie sobbed.

I cleared the airway of fluid and then started mouth-to-mouth on her. "She's in trouble," I said between careful breaths, "but the cord is still attached. She needs a lot of help." I turned her to the side and rubbed her vigorously, tapping her chest, rubbing her back, and pinching her feet between my assisted breaths.

"She's gone, isn't she?" Audrie sobbed.

I continued for two more minutes and then saw her arms move. Listening for her heart, I could discern a faint beat thrumming.

"She's still with us!" Lily squealed.

The women cried and sobbed with fear and hope.

After another minute of breath assists and rubs, the baby's color had returned, her arms flailed, her face tensed, and she let out a quiet cry.

Audrie sobbed with happiness as I placed the now very much alive newborn into her arms.

"You saved her! You saved her. ... I will be forever in your debt. You saved my baby girl." She sobbed as she kissed her crying baby's face.

"I'm so happy," Catori said through her now joyous tears.

As we rejoiced, Audrie started to have more contractions. "I think there's another," she announced with a wince.

With the baby girl still in her arms, I asked to check her, and she allowed me. With careful fingers, I felt a second baby starting to descend past her cervix. "Yes, there's a second," I said.

The women all rejoiced as I cut the cord of the first baby and handed her to Catori. She wrapped the crying baby girl in a blanket and took her downstairs to meet her father.

Audrie released a deep-throated growl, more animal than human, when the second baby started to crown. As the scalp appeared, the progress slowed.

"Let's get gravity to help us. Can you kneel with your arms on the bed like you were before?"

"Yeah, I think so," she said, huffing.

I helped her sit up and turn around. In Audrie's new position, the baby's head quickly came down. With the natural turn of the shoulders, I caught the newborn in my arms.

"Another girl!" Lily boasted, overjoyed.

This infant cried with life quickly. I handed her to her mother. Audrie was beyond exhausted but couldn't have been happier.

I assisted with the birth of the placentas and helped the women clean up. Audrie amazed me when she got up and carried her second baby downstairs. I followed her down and saw the father standing with Tyler and Catori while he held his first baby. Ty smiled at me as I soaked in the light of the father's eyes. Audrie brought the second baby to him and he was lost for words.

"What do you think, Marcus? Our precious little girls," Audrie said.

While the new family marveled at their newborns, the clan soon visited in groups to see the new members.

"I can't believe Elizabeth saved the first," Audrie boasted. "She was gone, and Liz brought her back! She saved all three of us."

Everyone who visited thanked me for my help. When Chief walked into the crowded cabin, the room quieted. My heart started to race as he greeted the new parents. "Wow! Two new girls! How wonderful," he cheerfully said.

"Thank you, we are so thrilled. But it wouldn't have been a happy ending if not for Elizabeth."

"What? Why?" he said, surprised.

"She saved all three of us. The first baby was stuck. I couldn't get her out after pushing for hours. Elizabeth not only got her out but brought her back to life!" Audrie explained.

Chief looked at me, unsure of his emotions. "She did?" he said.

"If she hadn't been here, I don't think my wife would have survived let alone our babies," Marcus said.

Ty watched his father cross his arms and stare at me. I was unsure if he was upset considering that he had told me not to interfere. I tensed as he closed the distance between us and wrapped his arms around me in a warm hug.

"Thank you," he said with a tone I had not heard him use before. It was soft and grateful.

My eyes widened, overwhelmed by his embrace.

I had never truly noticed how tense everyone in the clan was around me before I helped Audrie deliver her newborns, who she named Lisanna and Tessie. In hindsight, even Messer had been a bit uptight with me.

In the days following the birth, everyone including Ty's father acted differently around me. I was no longer the human stranger who killed Chogan and caused drama; I became the clan hero *doctor* who saved three community lives. Tyler basked in the attention of his heroic fiancée. Audrie and Marcus often brought the twins to me for wellness checks and they were doing so well. I swooned over their pink cheeks and rosy eyelids while they slept, longing for a newborn of my own.

When the clan had the next bonding fire with a communal dinner, Chief eagerly invited me, with open arms, "Elizabeth, come join us. Have some fresh cooked venison. I caught this one myself."

I approached the gathering with Tyler sitting down before me.

"Liz, sit beside me," Lily said while tapping the space on the log beside her.

Before I could accept, Ty stood back up and pulled me over to him. I abruptly sat down with him, allowing his arms to wrap around me. His warmth sparked my heart by an ignition only he could generate.

Lily chuckled. "Never mind."

I felt Ty kiss my forehead. Nobody seemed bothered by our affections. Ashton and Messer conversed about wolf nail length while Catori and Ty's father cuddled in the fire's warmth. The children shifted in and out of human form while rushing around us, excited to be playing in the night.

We spent hours like this around the fire. The flame – she no longer bothered my soul. I felt no fear, no discomfort, no anxiety. There was just bliss – a strange harmony around her that lifted me with comfort instead of terror. Deep in my heart, I knew that she was finally forgiven, and I had therefore forgiven myself. The pain of losing my father would always be there, shifting in and out of focus like the moonlight. No matter the distraction, my pain would always sit in the deepest parts of my heart, where no one – no matter how special – could cure it, but the pain no longer disturbed me. I embraced it, cherished it. I realized this pain was part of *my* story.

I looked at the moon – a large and bright light surrounded by stars. It displayed a subtle blue hue tonight. I saw the blue eyes of my father within this lunar blue, which wrapped my heart and soul in a blanket, surrounding me with love.

I looked at Ty, who was watching me with a soft smile.

"Am I sleeping at your cabin again tonight?" I asked him as everyone grew quiet and sleepy. Audrie, Marcus, and their newborns had already turned in for the night. The older children slept around the fire in the comfort of their extended family.

Ty's eyes narrowed. "*Our* cabin. *Ours*."

"It's not though. Not yet."

He sighed and then yawned, covering his mouth.

As midnight approached, Ty led me back to his cabin. "They are all so much more relaxed around you now," he said proudly, his glowing smile lit by the torches and blue moon.

"I've noticed. It feels strange. Wonderful, but strange." My smile returned his, but he didn't notice. His eyes fixated on his front door as he led me up the steps. Before I reached the entrance, Ty swung the door open and picked me up into his arms. I squealed with surprise as he carried me inside.

"*Our* cabin," he repeated.

He put me down and pulled me close. I felt his arms around my waist, holding me with gentle strength.

"Soon," I said with a warm smile. My heart fluttered again, an acute rhythm of happiness.

Ty took my arm and led me to the stairs, where he started up the steps. I playfully pinched his backside repeatedly.

"Hey!" he laughed as he scrambled faster to escape my assaults.

Ty used the bathroom first. When I returned from the bathroom, the sight of him lying so deliciously in his bed sent shivers up my spine. The low lighting highlighted his smile and skin, while emphasizing every curve of his bare upper body's muscles. I eyed him as I scrambled to join him.

"Like what you see?"

"I'll say it again. You're the biggest tease," I complained as I climbed onto the bedside. I sat with my legs and arms crossed.

He chuckled and shook his head. "I'll be all yours soon."

"When is soon? With Angeni caught, we have no reason to wait."

"I've been meaning to discuss that with you. I talked with my parents today and they agreed we can be wed soon. Likely in a few weeks."

My breath shortened. I thought about the timeline; I thought about what I wanted. It was time I made some demands.

"I have conditions." My smile quivered.

Ty's eyebrow raised. "You do? What conditions?"

"I want Briana and my mom at our wedding, and I want a traditional ceremony." I gulped low in my throat. "I also want my father-in-law to walk me down the aisle where my new family will be watching on each side."

Ty bit his lip, processing what I said. "You want my dad to walk you down the aisle?"

I nodded, feeling a knot form in my throat.

"As far as traditional, our weddings are close to it, so no issue there. I'll ask my dad about all of this. I am not sure how he'll feel about your friend and mom, though."

"I figured as much," I said, rubbing my arm.

Ty's eyes traced my face. "If it means that much to you, I'll be sure to convince him."

He took my arm and pulled me to him. I reached myself under the blanket and curled within his chest. "I love you," I whispered.

"And I love you."

Lying inside his warm arms, I listened to the steady rhythm of his heartbeat – my favorite sound – as it pulsed into my ear. With his heat against my body in the comfort of AC, it was the ideal balance of warmth and chill – symbolically a perfect mixture of inner pain and happiness.

CPSIA information can be obtained
at www.ICGtesting.com
Printed in the USA
BVHW071042260820
587378BV00001B/21

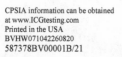